To Mary

The Battle of Ignorance

Three Voices

J. N. FOX

RAGUEL
PUBLISHING

Raguel Publishing House
Registered Office
85 Great Portland Street, First Floor
London W1W 7LT

First published in the UK in 2023 by Raguel Publishing

A CIP catalogue record for this book is available from the British Library

Hardback ISBN: 978-1-7393217-0-3

Also available as an ebook

For my muses:
My daughter, Charlotte Sunderland,
who believed wholeheartedly in The Light People.
My daughter, Tamsin Fox,
who shares my quirky sense of humour,
and is my partner in laughing crime.

In memory of my brother
Marcus Benjamin Joseph Wright.

INTRODUCTION

Elizabethan mathematician John Dee (1527–1609), alma mater St John's College Cambridge and original fellow of Trinity College Cambridge believed that numbers were the basis of all things and the key to knowledge. That through mathematics mankind had the potential to access divine powers.

By the 1580s he was attempting to communicate with angels. For him, angelic communication was a viable method of mathematics for understanding the natural world. He was convinced that angels could bring huge benefits to mankind. That they could help solve the mysteries of the heavens. He believed that they retain the knowledge of the physical world as was originally created by God. The knowledge that mankind lost through disobedience.

PART 1

Before Joshua met Jonathan

BENJAMIN

A woman stood on the riverbank. To the left and right of her the water was still, as if it held no past and had no future, yet straight ahead it was moving like the continuity of life.

On that July morning the world was floating by. The eights boats, the cyclists, the jaunty joggers, the strident strollers. She raised her hand to wave at them. They waved back, smiling, making her smile; the river brought out the best in people.

Behind her was a charming scene: a country house with newly mown lawns; her son playing Mozart on the upright piano in the hall; her daughter laughing, swinging on her swing in the rose garden. Turning, she watched a darkly handsome man walking towards her carrying a drink.

But things were not what they seemed. It was all ballast against the bigotry, which lurked at the margins of her meticulously created heaven.

It would be sunny for Lucille's sixtieth birthday party. Delsea revelled in the sunshine, acknowledging for once that luck was on their side. It had been raining earlier, a sort of steamy rain, and the thought of them all cooped up in Lucille's parlour with the children running wild and no space to play was not her idea of fun. This was to be Lucille's present – to have her children and grandchildren around her making noise. Touching Michael's hand lightly, she took her drink, fetched their daughter and followed him back to the house.

'What else?' he said once inside. She watched him closely, this man, her husband. There was a solidity about him, which she'd always loved. He was a tower of strength. What would she do without him?

'The rice,' she said.

'The rice is burnt.'

'It's only burnt on the bottom. You know how Marcus likes burnt rice.'

'Josh, will you stop that. We're going,' Michael shouted. Josh, reluctantly crashing the piano keys, insisted that he was ready. He was going just as he was. He wasn't even going to wash; what was the point? He thumped up the stairs in his boots, which he knew he wasn't supposed to wear in the house. He thought it was going to be boring. He hated going to Chippenham. He was reminded of Jonathan Ainsley, his biological father. Michael was his dad. How he hated being related to that posh git.

'How many times have I told you not to wear those boots in the house!' Michael called after Josh.

'Leave him,' Delsea said, ever ready to keep the peace between adopted father and son. Amy would not be helped into her car seat. 'My, do it?' she said. She was one determined child.

As Michael sped southwest, Delsea's mind also turned to Jonathan. Like Josh, she too could not go to Chippenham without thinking of him. She had been six years old when she met him. When she heard that the Ainsleys were back, she was consumed with curiosity about the type of people who lived in such a palatial house. Aldbourne Court, a stately home housing one of the nation's most prized art collections, was open to the public. She had long ago found ways of sneaking into the grounds. Hidden away from the public was a picturesque lake, complete with a jetty and small boat. It was there, hidden by rushes, that she liked to curl up with a book and seek refuge from the outside world. Tired of the arguments at home and the taunts of her companions, she would go down to the lake where it was so perfectly quiet that she could even hear the water ripple.

One day she was feeling incredibly sad. There was a flash of light, a draught of wind. A presence landed beside her on the water. There were beautiful colours. She sensed someone – a glimmering shape.

'Who are you?' she asked.

'An angel, with a message for you.' She thought she must have invented a companion to keep her company. Just in case she hadn't imagined it, she asked out loud, 'So what is the message?'

'Write down your feelings.'

'Do I have to?'

'Not if you don't want to. Tell no one except the golden boy.' She started to write how she felt, and it seemed to help.

She'd seen the Ainsley's at St. Bartholomew's, the parish church, which had once belonged to the Aldbourne Court estate. Watching the family as they filed into their own pew with its faded kneelers embroidered with the Ainsley coat of arms, she hadn't liked the look of them. They reminded her of the stiff figures she had seen at Madame Tussauds on a school trip.

She had heard that there was a boy, Jonathan, two years older than her, though she hadn't seen him yet. As she readied herself for church that Sunday all those years ago, she wondered whether he'd be there. The Ainsley's were several rows in front. If she remained standing, she could get a good look. She felt a sharp pinch on her meagre arm. This was Lucille's way of saying kneel down. Squeezed into the tiny space between her parents, trying to peer above the pew in front of her, she could see that the boy had blonde, honey-coloured hair. Then it clicked: he was the golden boy. A haze of late summer sun beaming through the stained-glass window heightened the effect. He was like an angel from her school play. Viciously she hoped that all angels weren't like him, if they were, she wouldn't be welcome in heaven. As they were leaving the church the vicar called to Lucille. 'Mrs Johnson, meet Lady Ainsley.' Delsea had watched this ritual the previous two Sundays. It was their turn, last and least. The golden boy smiled. At first, she thought he was looking at someone else. Tugging one of her many plaits she moved closer. He was about to say something when his mother drew him back. Then the moment was gone, and the Ainsleys moved on.

She'd had a terrible day. Her parents had fought all night. Both wounded, neither was speaking to the other. Later she was whispering in class when the teacher singled her out, stood her on her desk and slapped the back of her legs with her hand to make an example of her. There had been uproar and laughter. She'd felt humiliated. From the back of the classroom, she couldn't read the whiteboard, that was the reason she couldn't pay attention. And besides, there was nothing to interest her. If she knew the answer to a question and put her hand up, she was always ignored. The teacher looked at her superciliously as if to say: 'Don't you know you are not allowed to answer questions? You cannot be seen to be clever.'

Then at lunchtime she wasn't allowed to eat with her form. One of the dinner ladies kept sending her to the back of the queue every time she got to the front. She had to wait until every child in the school had been served before it was her turn. That was resolved by Lucille writing a letter to the unnamed dinner lady, care of the headmaster, addressed to Mrs Enoch Powell.

She did have one friendly teacher at the school who taught maths. Once when she was crying, he told her that there were more people in the world like her than like him. 'Mark my words,' he had said. 'The world is getting smaller and one day we will know what it is to be treated like the minority.' Delsea hadn't understood what he meant, but she remembered the words and felt their kindness.

In times of trouble the lake had called to Delsea in a small voice. It was as if someone very gentle and kind was saying: Peace awaits you, come. She had just settled in the boat and was about to set it adrift when the golden boy appeared. 'I say, don't you know this is private property? Didn't you see the signs?'

Of course, she'd seen the signs. She wasn't blind. She was simply fed up with other people's rules. She was tired of struggling against an enemy that was sometimes so subtle it was like fighting off feathers. Then the golden boy visibly relaxed.

'I'm Jonathan Ainsley,' he called.

'I know. Church, remember? Where have you been?'

'Africa, Nigeria.'

'Well?'

Jonathan realised he was still standing on the bank. 'Do you mind if I get in?'

'It's your boat.' The tethered boat strained gently on its rope. 'Tell me about Africa. Were the people kind to you?'

Delsea smoothed her seersucker dress. Jonathan took an instant liking to her. She had coloured ribbons dangling from the ends of her plaits. They fluttered in the breeze. 'Most of the time.' But he didn't want to talk about Africa. The thought of Nigeria made him cry. Despite the beautiful surroundings of Aldbourne Court he was lonely. The sunshine seemed to beckon from the rich upholstery, conjuring up Africa and the colourful people he'd left behind. And he was always cold. The sun in England seemed so weak.

'People here think I'm stupid,' Delsea said. It came out in a sigh, as if she was letting go of some of the pain she felt. To a small number of villagers, she was not a person. She was a novelty, an object of curiosity, an object of hatred – and even an object of art to one local artist. But equally she didn't want to dwell on Corsham. She didn't want to compound the hurt, which filled up her eyes. She found Jonathan intriguing. He was dressed like an adult. She wanted to touch him to see if he was real. He was leaning forward and she accidentally felt his hair. It felt smooth, like silk. He jerked away. People were forever feeling or patting her hair as if she were a dog. She couldn't abide people touching her hair. It would be so nice to have a friend, she thought. She didn't know that Jonathan was thinking the same thing. 'Don't you think it's strange that you lived in Africa, while I live here?'

Someone was calling him. Typical, thought Jonathan. 'I'd better go.'

'What time is it?'

He looked at his watch, 'Ten to five.'

'Raas. I've got to go to tea with the Greens.'

'Raas?'

'I know a lot of rude words in Jamaican,' Delsea said, smiling precociously.

'Who are the Greens?'

'Mom cleans for them. They are a nosy family and all the children have ginger hair. Mom thinks it's important for me to go. Their mum thinks I'm some kind of experiment. It's as though she expects me to explode or something.'

'Why do you go then?'

'Well, it isn't that bad. They've got horses. I love horses.' Animals were docile and self-contained.

'Will you come again?'

'Whenever,' Delsea said, smiling. Jonathan didn't ask stupid questions, like when would that be. Time was immaterial back home. It would be tomorrow, next week, whenever.

Delsea, Michael and the children were the first to arrive at her mom's. Lucille was still in her housecoat. The grey wig she wore to hide the scar on her head was slightly askew, showing the shiny puckered skin that had been transferred from her thigh to replace the patch where the benign tumour was removed. Sliding past Delsea she beamed at Michael.

'How you doing, Mom?' Michael said, kissing her.

'Nat so bad.'

Just then Delsea's brother Marcus arrived with Emma, his new wife – a softly spoken blonde who was proudly clutching their baby, Nico, as if to say isn't he cute. Marcus's women were always blonde and leggy. None of the family held out much hope for this new relationship, as Marcus changed women more often than he changed cars, and Emma had already committed the cardinal sin by having Nico. Marcus, the big man, was turned off by children and domesticity cramping his style. But Emma didn't know that – yet.

Lucille sighed. There were always new women to get to know. Still, she'd try for Marcus's sake – a mother's tender care towards the child she bore could never cease. She'd love Emma just a little bit; inch by inch, just like she'd taught her children, as her mother had taught her, and her mother before that. Inch by inch, then when things go wrong you still had a little love left to give.

A further two exes who still doted on Marcus dropped off grandchildren for Lucille to dote on. The women didn't stay too long, they were offended by Emma, the doer of African Caribbean things. She might just succeed where they had failed, with her provocative youth, her boldness and her as yet untapped ability to love inch by inch. Now they were making noise Lucille was happy. She made herself comfortable in her favourite chair with a glass of sweet sherry and Nico on her lap. She held him high in the air. He dribbled clear spit in her face. 'See how him fat.' She loved children to be fat. Thinness was a sign of poverty. Michael rolled a joint. Delsea wished that he wouldn't.

'Could I have a little of that for my pipe?' Lucille asked. She couldn't remember when she'd last had ganga. Not these past few years; not since Delsea and Michael's wedding, in fact. Of course, Ben had been there then. Ben, from whom she'd expected the most opposition, had bowed to the inevitable. Putting aside his old agitations Ben had taken pains to know Michael. Ben had been nervous. Lucille remembered him cramped and diminished, rolling a joint. He'd been up half the night smoking with Michael, listening to blues and drinking Jamaican overproof rum.

They were all there making noise; all except Ben. Delsea too felt his absence. 'Mom. Do you want Ben?'

'Wat I warnt wid dat man?' Delsea knew that this meant that she wanted him. 'Go get Ben, Michael.' Michael was reluctant: he was having a good time, he was winding down from the working week, easing into his stride. 'Please.' Delsea begged her husband. 'If you go, he'll come. If Marcus goes, he'll argue.' Michael couldn't argue with that. Ben lived in Corsham, the next town. Living apart from Lucille made little sense to him. But Lucille had never put his needs first. She was a woman who didn't understand that her children were not her companions.

Ben wasn't expecting anyone, least of all his son-in-law, and he was damned if he was going to be nice to anyone who was interrupting his cricket on a Sunday afternoon. Michael rocked on his heels diplomatically, trying to explain the reason for his visit. This irritated Ben. As if good old Ben didn't have anything better to do than wait to be summoned by her majesty. 'Mi to leave mi dinna fi dat badmind woman. Twenty-five years I live wid dat woman.'

Ben's nickname for Lucille was MisCam, on account of the fact that in Jamaica she had owned a dressmaking shop specialising in wedding dresses, and imported silk Cami knickers from Paris for her brides. She always wore them herself. She'd made it quite clear that he was not good enough for her or their children, or the white man who was bay-faced enough to be standing in his house, cajoling him to attend his own wife's birthday party.

On the doorstep, little by little, Ben scraped the hair from the cow foot he was preparing for his dinner. He never failed to brandish the knife in Michael's direction to ram home a point. In calmer moments Michael watched him clean it against some newspaper, on which a thick paste of hair and excrement was forming, until, naked, the cow foot lay at his feet, pink, fleshy and ready to cook. Michael was more than a little wary of Ben, with his rough ways, sudden outbursts and small kindnesses.

'Ever try cow foot. Mek yu strang like ion.' Ben was annoyed by the cowardly way in which Michael was observing him. It was as though he expected him to turn psychotic and knife him for no good reason other than he had nothing better to do. 'A weh yu a look pan? Chuh.' Ben kissed his teeth. A hissing sound came from the kitchen, the sound of water boiling over. 'Weh yu nuh turn di gas down man. Mek yuself useful.' Michael went into the dismal kitchen and turned the gas down under the pot of water, while Ben threw the stinking newspaper onto the compost heap. Michael waited for Ben to finish washing the cow foot in the Belfast sink.

'It would mean so much to her. She's sixty today.'

'I know dat, don't I. Why we nu live as man and wife? Arske yuself dat.'

It wasn't a conundrum, but Michael thought of joking to relieve the tension. But he didn't joke. He was sensible enough to restrain himself. He knew Ben would get mad. Ben didn't like people to joke at his expense.

Instead, Michael replied, 'Cos she badmind?'

'Dats right. She badmind.'

'Just this once.'

'And why she nu arske me herself. A wey she a sen yu fa? Dem tink di sun so shine out a yu dat me nu gwain refuse yu. A weh kind a pussy logic dat?' But Ben was grinning. His single gold tooth winked. Yu strike a hard bargain man. I like dat.'

In no time at all Ben came downstairs in his best church suit, a charcoal grey three piece. 'Yu nu dress man.'

Michael was wearing black jeans and a blue linen shirt, which Delsea said matched the colour of his eyes. 'No. Not today.'

'Yu nu ha no style man.' Prising open a drawer Ben pulled out a gold watch: the thick chain he fastened through a buttonhole, the watch he tucked into the waistcoat pocket. The watch was his retirement present from the rubber factory in Melksham. Thirty years he'd spent in that Godforsaken hole. Thirty years stripped raw born naked, shovelling coal, frying at the furnace. The beads of sweat were thick like grease and not one of the other men would hand him a glass of water. They called to him, usually to make him the butt of some joke. 'Hey Ben?' Then it would start. He never paid them malata backside hole, no mind. Their mouths spouted more rubbish than a sick Baccra's arse. They couldn't see the whole person. He could hardly see them, for his eyes were surrounded by rubber floaters like raining black rain. They were faceless anyway, their heads on backwards like duppy. He could still smell the stench of rubber and feel the acrid smoke clawing at the back of his throat. What for? What did he have to show for the sweat he'd poured into this country? No more than he'd had back home in Jamaica: a run-down cottage on a piece of land. Except this cottage belonged to the council. He didn't even have the sunshine. The sun was not hot enough to burn.

LUCILLE

Seeing Ben and Lucille together reminded Delsea of the old days. The cottage was always cold then, even in summer. The wind used to rattle the loose-fitting metal window frames. The lino tiles had been so clean that you could eat your dinner from them. Lucille had been proud of her home, with its sacred pictures hanging on the walls. Even back then Ben was always enraged by something. Delsea remembered him switching off the television and kissing his teeth, throwing his head back against the winged chair, cursing Enoch Powell and the government. It was Enoch Powell who, as health minister when England was desperate for nurses, begged nurses from the West Indies to come to help the mother country. Once their efforts were exhausted, he forgot their service and began to talk with a forked tongue about immigration in his "Rivers of Blood" speech a few years later. Some of the public lapped it up, with their "Don't Knock, Enoch," "White Power, Britain's Unite & Fight," "Immigration Referendum," placards.

These days Delsea was much more forgiving of Ben. She knew what had made him so mad, and why he slammed doors and swore red, blue and green. It had been nothing to do with her baby son, Josh. She could see that. In those days Ben had only been happy at weekends. He worked a tri-weekly shift, six-till-two, two-till-ten, and ten-till-six. Every Friday without fail he came home singing. There'd be a bag of sweets each for her and Marcus, two packets of cigarettes for Lucille, and a bottle of rum for him and his friends. Delsea recalled their ritual.

'Whose girl are yu?'

'Daddy's girl.' Then he'd give her the sweets.

Baba, Caleb and Aubrey Saddler – who was always referred to by his full name as he was a Bayjee (Barbados) man – would come over from Bath on the Saturday night. They were Ben's gambling and drinking buddies. The more they drank the further they stood back from the coffee table and the harder they threw down the dominoes. Thwack, 'yu raas clart tek dat.' Thwack, 'yu bumba clart yu cheat.' Thwack, 'yu blood clart a win.' Then the calypso and ska music began. The men danced. Lucille weaved between them, her tie head loose, hips jerking. She taunted Ben, driving him to insane heights of jealousy. He hated it when she showed off in front of other men.

She and Marcus would sit on top of the cooling Rayburn on cushions to protect their legs from the heat. They'd laugh themselves silly. Only Delsea knew that Lucille was wearing red knickers just to spite Ben. Red silk Cami knickers were too sexy for any man's wife to wear. Red knickers and horn-rimmed glasses. Then she and Marcus would be cajoled into dancing and everyone would laugh at her, because she couldn't dance and every Jamaican child by the age of two could wiggle and wind. The most she could do was jerk her body in time to the beat. In the end Ben would be so drunk that he couldn't raise himself to go to the toilet to pee and he'd holler for someone to bring him a milk bottle to piss in.

Unloading the food she'd cooked from the boot of their car, Delsea smiled to herself. It was a pity Ben and Lucille couldn't live together without winding each other up. She'd cooked a veritable feast: brown rice and peas, jerk chicken, yams, sweet potatoes and okras. A silence descended as they sat down to eat.

'Mek wid the dutchy.' Delsea handed Marcus the Dutch pot and with satisfaction she watched him cleave out every last ounce of burnt rice from the bottom. They all ate till they were stuffed – having too much to eat was a sign of prosperity. Lucille, bloated, burped – 'manners.' Burp – 'manners.' She always said manners. She was enjoying watching Michael eat. He had long wound his way into her affections by the sheer volume of food he could eat. There was nothing Lucille loved more than a man who could nyam him biccle! Michael was a real foodan.

After lunch the funeral talk began. Planning their funerals was Ben and Lucille's party piece. Michael had looked at Delsea as though to say do something. Delsea was unperturbed as long as the children were happy. She shrugged her shoulders. Death was not a morbid subject to them but part of life, and there was no stopping them once they got started. Their death was to be grander than life, as if only then could they be properly honoured by a Homecoming service: 'Sweet chariots, coming to carry them home.' There would be no greater glory than to die and meet Master Jesus. Marcus was to build an ornate ostentatious tabernacle. The marble would be just so. The epitaph would be just so. Lucille drunk sang.

Rock of ages, cleft for me,
let me hide myself in thee.
While I draw this fleeting breath,
when my eyelids close in death.
When I soar through tracts unknown,
see thee on thy judgment throne.
Rock of ages, cleft for me,
let me hide myself in thee.

'A buy mi plot aready,' Ben said.

'Well, a mek mi dress aready.'

Lucille, suddenly sprightly as a spring chicken, ran upstairs to fetch it. Downstairs again she slipped off her slippers, holding the dress against her. It was a shroud to be proud to be seen in, only spoilt by the arthritic toes which poked out from beneath.

'See how the silk fine.' Standing on tiptoes she did a vain twirl as if she was a girl dressing for her confirmation. Ben shook his tightly curled head and roared like a lion.

'A wey yu a go wid yu toe favour someting a crawl out a woodland.'

This was the way they dealt with each other. Insulting, crushing, teasing until one of them got hurt and the other angry, until they couldn't stand to be in the same room, until they couldn't stand to be in the same house, until they couldn't stand to be in the same town. But old habits die hard. They were casting their old spell over each other, Delsea suggested the rest of them go out.

Michael wanted to walk around Corsham. They parked in Church Square and walked a little way down Church Street, which was lined with honey-coloured terraced cottages the same as the one Ben lived in. They took in the Grade II listed Folly built in 1797 by architect John Nash. A ruin which was to the side, of the foreground of

Aldbourne Court itself. They stopped at the gate like tourists. Delsea remembered touring the house with her mother once; the state rooms with the purpose-built picture gallery by Capability Brown. Upstairs there was a collection of artifacts that had belonged to Henry Fox Talbot, the photography pioneer. Lucille couldn't hear enough about the paintings which inspired her creativity. All Delsea had cared about was Jonathan's parents. The guide found her awfully curious. It was as if she'd had a premonition that one day she'd have dealings with them, and she needed to store up as much as possible to stand her in good stead.

'Come on,' Michael said. Turning away from the black gates, passing the church to their left, they went through a turnstile and into the park. They made a picture of harmony – a pretty black woman holding the hand of a handsome white man, a tall black man and a leggy blonde, and five mixed race offspring. The men wanted to go across the top of the park to the pub. Amy spotted the swings further down. 'You go, I'll stay,' Delsea said to Michael.

'If you're sure…' he replied.

Josh went with Michael. He seemed pleased to be going to the pub with the others instead of helping her with the children. She watched them walk off, getting smaller as they left her behind. Suddenly Josh stopped and froze. The moment was timeless. She thought only time could wreck that connection between them. That symbiosis. In that instant as Josh stood still, she had a horrible feeling of dread come over her that he would die soon. He waved. She breathed easier when he walked on. The irrational fear subsided as he caught up with the others. Josh, she thought, wasn't much older than Jonathan was when he went up to Uriel University in Oxford. When he started to move away from her in exactly the same carefree way.

Delsea's mind zoomed back to the present. The children – both hers and Marcus's – were demanding her attention. Amy wanted to be pushed higher, higher and higher in competition with Addison.

'I'm higher than you!' said Kahlil.

'My higher,' said Amy. Addison was managing to jerk himself backwards and forwards all by himself.

Nico was sleeping in his pram. The sky was clouding over. Delsea hoped they wouldn't be too long at the pub; after all it was Lucille's day, and she'd only wanted to take the children out for some fresh air so that they wouldn't get too boisterous.

Josh looked scathingly around him. Even the pub was named after his biological father: The Ainsley Arms. It was built in 1608. Then it was known as Winter's Court. It had been owned by the Ainsley family since 1799. In Victorian times it was a coaching inn. It was fitting that Jonathan was the Chancellor of the Exchequer. Carved above the pub door on the Laycock Road side was a Tudor chessboard. Exchequer meant a kind of chessboard.

'Mine's a Wadsworth 6X,' he said. Marcus was buying. Flashing his money around, he wasn't playing little man to Michael's big man. Like most British born children of immigrants, Marcus rarely spoke the Jamaican language outside of their home.

'You know old Lord Ainsley owns half of Corsham and most of the land between here and Chippenham.' Marcus lived in Corsham, in one of the new houses that had been built on land Lord Ainsley had sold off.

'So what?' said Josh.

'Put it this way. He's worth megabucks. If daddio owned a fraction as much I'd stick by him.'

'Well, I don't like the way Jonathan treated my mum, your sister, you know. As soon as he got to Uriel, he cheated on her – that's all she's ever told me, left her high and dry with me. My so-called biological grandfather can stick his money. I don't care how rich he is.'

'That was yonks ago and I wouldn't be so sure about those two. They have always been very secretive. Mi nearly drap dead when I fine out dat dey were close, Lard ha mercy, one big commotion inna mi head, mi seek him out, meck him understand, to leave mi sister alone.' Turning to the barman Marcus shouted, 'Chuh, mek wid me pint man.'

'Not yonks in my mind,' Josh rebutted Marcus. Josh hated what Jonathan represented: politics. "Back to Basics." Lambasting single mothers.

'You know he's gay right. Mi si him wid dat Wright bloke.'

His uncle Marcus was not nice, always riling him about Jonathan. 'He's not gay.' It's politics with him. Charlie Wright, he understood from his mum, was an old school friend of Jonathan's. Things were improving in Jamaica. Josh understood where the intolerance of homosexuality came from. Ben had explained that slave owners and overseers raped male slaves, to ensure that they felt disgust for homosexuality. They wanted them to breed with the women in order to produce valuable enslaved children which they could own or sell at the market.

'Batty men. I can spot them a mile off.'

'Cut the crap, Marcus,' said Michael.

'I'm just putting Josh straight. His grandaddy will kick the bucket one day and the way his father carries on, eating and breathing for his party, he is not likely to have more children. That leaves liccle Josh here, if he plays his cards right.'

They changed the subject, to Josh's relief. 'Did I tell you I got that roofing contract?' Marcus was dead proud of himself.

'That's good,' replied Michael.

Everyone owed Marcus a living. He took the view that money in the family was everyone's to share and no one should be keeping scores.

The door was ajar, just as they'd left it. The house was quiet. They'd expected Ben and Lucille to be at each other's throats. Lucille had left Ben because she was fed up with his drinking and half-hearted promises to reform. But no, Lucille was sitting next to Ben on the sofa. Which was so small that it was more of a love seat.

The sight of her mother at sixty, cuddling her father, wearing horn rimmed glasses (and no doubt her famous red silk Cami knickers) was slightly shocking, and not something that Delsea wanted to think about.

Lucille got up casually, as if she'd been on her way to make a cup of tea and had somehow been hijacked by this hateful man. Deep down she loved her husband. No one could accuse her of not loving him. She defied any woman to put up with what she had from that man for so many years. She'd run from him for her own safety and she was not going to take him back unless he gave up drinking. It was the drink or her, and it was his choice.

No one was fooled by her couldn't-care-less attitude. Marcus spied her shoes. 'The shoes are wicked, Mom. Where did you get those shoes?'

'Which shoes?' said Lucille, surreptitiously throwing them into the cupboard under the stairs and reaching for her fluffy slippers.

'Yu arl warnt tea?'

Delsea remembered telling Jonathan about her dad hiding her mother's horn-rimmed glasses when any men came round. Jonathan had said that that would defeat the object of the exercise, because if she couldn't see them, she would have to feel them. They had their own way of talking. They even had a laughter scale:

1. Ha Ha
2. Amuse
3. Chuckle
4. Open laughter
5. Catatonic
6. Die laughing

Laughter was mostly what their relationship was about when they were younger. Except when they were being deadly serious, like a pendulum always swinging between those extremes. Humour in the face of adversity then deadly serious, something must be done.

DELSEA & JONATHAN

Michael thought Aldbourne Court was a fine house. He was totally unaware of the shadow it cast over Delsea and Josh. Delsea wished she could see the lake again. But that was out of the question. The black gates were locked and she couldn't take her family through the hidden ways she had got inside it as a child. Tugging the gates, she hoped they'd yield. They didn't.

The lake had been a special place. Her books were a way of escaping. In her maths books there were no shades of grey. Things were either right or wrong. But that was before Jonathan came from Nigeria. Before she had a friend. Their friendship had been just for them. Bringing others into it would have somehow destroyed it. Ben wouldn't have approved.

To Delsea, Jonathan had appeared as an intrepid explorer telling her tale after gory tale. Wide eyed, she devoured the lot. She couldn't hear enough about other countries where the people were like her. But she was sure he made half the stories up, just to amuse her, and to hear her infectious laugh. He'd loved having an audience even back then. It was no surprise to her that he'd ended up in politics. What he'd wanted then, though, was someone to listen to him. And she was content just to lie there and listen and drift with him by her side. His jacket rumpled at their feet, his hair falling into his eyes, as he squinted nonchalantly at the sun with a hand involuntarily trailing in the water. No one had troubled them then.

If Delsea had gone to the lake, she would have met Jonathan musing over his autumn budget, which meant more to him than any relationship then. He was married to his job. He had not been thinking of Delsea before this, when for some unaccountable reason he perceived her to be close by. He was sure it was the lake playing tricks on him. He must be more tired than he thought. It was when he was tired that her memory proved hardest to suppress. The loss of her was like a draught creeping under the door, which gave him a chill, a sudden coldness in his bones. His mind linked back. He could see her in that boat, with her thin legs sticking out from her plaid summer dress; her limbs glistening from the olive oil that had been rubbed into them; the five short plaits adorning her head, and her maths theory books – which she could never leave behind – face down in her lap.

He had been sad to leave Nigeria, where he was born, along with the other British children whose parents worked there. But aged eight he outgrew the expatriate school, and in the words of his mother it was time for him to be immersed in his own class and culture. The excitement of packing for England was lost on him. England sounded dull, full of dreary people. He'd met plenty of them in Lagos through his father's work. His mother, Frederica, was forever producing "nice boys" for him to play with; but he preferred the company of Mofe, his nanny's son. For years they had been inseparable, and Jonathan couldn't then imagine what life was going to be like in England without Mofe.

He found Aldbourne Court to be a grand place. It was an Elizabethan house first built in 1582 and extended by subsequent generations. At first, he was in awe. Nothing had prepared him for the splendour of it, halls of ancestors and magnificent views across a park, which had the advantage of a natural river frontage, as well as a lake which had been installed by Repton. He wished Mofe could see it. But the thought of Mofe made him cry. Then there was the whole routine in England to get accustomed to. It had taken him a good long while to get used to it. Living by the clock seemed so important; timekeeping was almost a religion. Back home in Nigeria things just happened. A time often wasn't given for the event to occur. He remembered that day by the lake when he'd first met Delsea. When he got home his mother was furious: 'Don't think you can eat when you're ready.' All she ever did was tell him off. As a child he'd never felt that she cared two figs for him. If she ever took an interest in something he'd achieved it was always to praise someone else's son for having done better.

The day he met Delsea, counting on his father's love, he'd gone straight to the library and knocked at the door. Lord Ainsley knew the knock. He smiled indulgently. Jonathan wanted to tell him about Delsea, but something stopped him. He was fast learning that what was acceptable back home in Nigeria, such as running wild with the local children, wasn't acceptable here. 'Well, Jonathan?' Richard encouraged. Jonathan had changed his mind, even though his father never stopped him from doing anything he really wanted to do. That had been the start of years of secrecy of never mentioning the person who was closest to him.

Jonathan stood up, stretching his long limbs by the lake. He looked at his watch. He should be making tracks, not dwelling on the past. What was past was past. But he couldn't help himself. She was fifteen. It was late spring. The weather had turned. It still gave Delsea a kick the way she and Jonathan pretended not to know each other. If she saw him in the village she'd pass him without a glance, though there was always that frisson of excitement. It interested her that people saw what they wanted to see. No one could conceive of a friendship between two such different people, so no one suspected there was one.

Books were no longer her only escape. She would put them aside and daydream about Jonathan. He was so caring, so unlike the boys when she was at her primary school. It wasn't just her colour that made her stand out. She was a social misfit. She couldn't do black things, like dance or sing. She recalled one end-of-year disco at senior school when she was made to stand in the middle of the floor and dance, like an ornament to add more colour to the decorations. The other girls enjoyed dancing and chatting with their friends. She wasn't a child; they treated her like an adult, but on that day, she was not even a person: she was a thing, a trinket, no more than a bauble. The music teacher in charge told her off for not dancing "properly," like Pan's People. All she could do was maths and no one cared about that then. But, worst of all, she was introverted. If she'd been cool and extrovert with a sunny smile like Marcus she would have been accepted. But she was shy and awkward. And life was not like on her British passport: "all those who may be concerned letting her pass without let or hindrance and affording her assistance and protection whenever necessary."

That's why Jonathan had been special. He was different and she was flattered that he enjoyed her company. That spring, when she was fifteen going on sixteen, she stopped being his friend and became more. They were sitting in St. Bartholomew's church drinking wine. She wondered whether God knew that the church was being used as a meeting place, and not of the spiritual kind. She hoped that they wouldn't be condemned. Sometimes they were doing their homework.

'I can't be bothered with this,' Jonathan said.

She had laughed. 'I wish I had the opportunity to be bored by exams that I had chosen to take.'

'I work when I have to.'

He hated maths, her favourite subject. 'All these proofs and theorems,' he would groan. He often overreacted, and she loved the tragedy he could bring to an everyday situation. She hated history, his favourite subject. Nothing she was taught had anything to do with her. There was no one she could relate to.

A deep sadness crept upon her; a feeling that she should not trust him. What would it be like to hate him, but she couldn't summon feelings of hatred? That confidence he had – to be always so sure of everything. To not take tentative steps, to not test the waters, to just do something you set your mind to.

Jonathan noticed the playful mood drop. She was changing the rules. Friendship wasn't enough anymore. It was as though she was building a case against him so as not to like him, as if he'd been tried and found guilty but she wasn't prepared to tell him his crime.

'What's wrong?' Jonathan made to pour her some more wine. She covered her glass.

'Too much wine…'

'I don't think it's the wine?'

'Nor the fact that I can't aspire to anything…'

Where was this coming from? She knew she was as clever as he was. Whereas he had breezed by with his Uriel offer, she was being made to climb a hill hampered by psychological torture at her girl's school, which didn't teach science. Oh God, she was able to be angry with him, if not feel full-on hatred. Matthew Arnold's poem describing Oxford as that "Sweet city of dreaming spires that needed not for beauty's heightening" certainly was not calling the likes of her.

'Why do you connect this with me?'

'Whose side are you on?'

'Why are there sides to take suddenly? If I have to pick a side, it's yours.'

'Are you though? If everything was at stake and your life depended on it, would you just walk away and leave me to drown?'

'I don't understand you sometimes, and I don't like this conversation.' He was genuinely getting fed up. 'We are not in a debating society.' This stuff was getting way too deep.

Lightly she brushed his lips with hers to soothe away any ill feeling. He had the most amazing hazel eyes.

'Look, don't,' he said.

'I'm just messing with you.'

'Messing up my head. Maybe there aren't two sides; maybe there are many sides, what do you want me to do about it? If I could, I would change the world for you, but I can't.'

That was the problem, at least between them now. She wanted him to stay – for them to stay just as they were, and never move into the big wide world.

He was aware of her slow eyes on him. He couldn't think of her that way. She was Delsea, still chewing her sleeve. There was their whole childhood at stake. There was this girl with hurt eyes and a boy who had such a grip on him that he couldn't move. The boy who was confused and hated it when he got a hard on. Just as she was building a case against him. He was trying to build a case against the boy. That it was not natural to hate the thought of having sex. There was so much pressure on him from peers. He was also leaving, going up to Uriel to read History. He was really looking forward to it. It was Wordsworth who wrote, "O ye spires of Oxford, domes, and towers! Gardens, and groves, your presence overpowers," and he couldn't wait to get there.

If he just left without another word then it would always be that he had escaped from her to Uriel. He felt he had to show her how much she meant to him. That he would go against every fibre in his body to please her. The angst of that summer...

For Delsea, it was a summer in which she did nothing except work at the local chicken factory and eat fried dumplings. She was trying to fill the hole that Jonathan would leave before he'd even left. She knew she was being pessimistic in the face of his optimism. They both wandered aimlessly about in the dark, like gormless teenagers. It was always dark. Cacca fart, if they were to meet in daylight. That would mash up everyone's head. She could see him in the dark, but he could not so easily see her and her quick changing moods. Only once had they braved an outing in the day: it was after he passed his driving test when they drove to Leigh Delamere service station on the M4, where everyone was passing through and more interested in the loos than a couple of mismatched teenagers eating fried chicken.

They sat in the porch of St Bartholomew's overlooking the graveyard – their favourite place on fine winter nights. There was an amusing inscription on a grave in the graveyard. Commemorating Sarah Jarvis, who died aged 107 in December 1753, "Sometime before her death She had Fresh Teeth." On warm summer nights they met behind the Folly.

'Why do you have to go to Uriel?'

'To get away from my parents. It's not the end of the world. I'll be back in the holidays, like now. If anything, university holidays are longer than school holidays. Don't start doubting whether I care about you or not.'

'I always thought it would be you and me against the world.'

'You could do a degree too, you know. You are clever enough to outwit the bastards of this world.'

'I'm only good at maths. I know I would be interested in science, if my school taught it.'

'Then leave and go somewhere where you can do science. You don't have to stay there for sixth form.' She had not thought of that. 'Why against the world?'

'Because the world would be against us. We can't even meet properly because of our fear. You could never meet my family, and I certainly couldn't meet yours.'

'Our families are not the test. Will you come home with me?'

'Your parents…?'

'My parents will be asleep. They just about make it to 10pm without drifting off.'

Her heart felt tight like a fist. One step. Two steps. Stop. She hadn't expected him to come out with that out of the blue. The friendly darkness closed around them.

'What's the matter?'

'My heart is beating.' Jonathan laughed. 'It's not funny.'

It had never beat like that before. Like a balled fist uncurling each finger just a little bit. Inch by inch. She couldn't breathe. Was this fear? She was with Jonathan – what was there to be afraid of? Had they not just been laughing? How she loved the dark. It was her colour. She was shining. Shining in the moonlight like a new leaf. She had wanted them to be closer for so long. She had outgrown just hanging out ages ago. It was unreal. She expected him to stop as if he had forgotten something and turn back. But he didn't.

She didn't know that he had silenced the censorious boy inside him, who tried to control his mind by whispering to him: 'You don't have to do this. You don't want to do this. You don't need to do this.'

Aldbourne was in darkness. Jonathan's parents had long gone to bed, and there were just one or two lightly stepping staff lurking about as they sneaked up to his room. She couldn't help giggling. It was so easy.

'I've always wanted to see your room.' It was a strange boy's room. A hi-fi and music. Impersonal things strung about mixed with Marlborough College gear. No photos. Posters of his causes, Anti-Apartheid and Amnesty International. Delsea – who had no cause, except to fight for those everyday rights that others took for granted – found his causes really amusing. It seemed the height of decadence to have a cause by proxy. There were history books. At school she'd refused to do the History syllabus. As far as she was concerned, British history as it was taught in schools was a white supremacist conspiracy back then. Original cartoons featuring Alexander Pope's quote; "Dunce the Second, reigns like Dunce the First." But it was the Nigerian artefacts on the surfaces that drew her attention. She had never seen anything like them. It was as though he had lived a life meant for her. She was in awe of the intricate nature of this stuff. Her English education had led her to believe that Africans were primitive people. But here they were carving the most sophisticated objets d'art.

All the giggle went out of her as she self-consciously stood by his window, her hands clenched by her side, looking out over the pitch-black park from where they'd come. A peacock called. A peculiarity of Corsham was that there were peacocks strutting purposely around. Suddenly she felt she didn't belong in his room. She was aware of her hand-knitted jumper and her homemade skirt. She was already relenting when he took her hand and led her to his bed. She sat on the edge, her nerves failing her as she chewed her sleeve. When Jonathan reached for her, she could no longer feel her heart beat. His warmth overwhelmed her. She was flushed and breathless, yet still she found time to wonder whether he loved her or not.

'Do you love me?'

'I am very fond of you.' Delsea knew that was not the same.

'We are too young for love.'

DELSEA AND TED

Delsea stirred as Michael tucked Amy up beside her. He brushed his hand against her cheek, like he stroked Cleo the cat. She was just like Cleo, purring in her sleep. 'You will be alright, I'll phone tonight.' When he bent to kiss her, she was fully awake. He looked smart as he always did when he dressed for business, his transformation from good-time man to family man to upper middle-class businessman was complete.

'Don't get up.'

'When will you be back?'

'Thursday night.'

'Give my love to Ted.'

'And me?'

'You have my special love, always.' Smiling, she kissed him back.

After he'd gone Amy wriggled closer. 'Where Daddy going?'

'To work.'

'Where Josh?'

'In his room.'

'Where Cleo?'

'Go to sleep.'

'My dummy?' Feeling under her pillow Delsea found the spare one she always kept there. Amy was getting too old for a pacifier. It would be difficult to wean her off. Amy, squashing the nipple between finger and thumb, fell fast asleep before she could even put it in her mouth, which formed a fat little circle, as if she were sighing 'oh.'

Closing her eyes, Delsea savoured their lovemaking. She could rest in the silent house. No radios talking in the background. No grand prix on the television. No classical, opera, soul, reggae, blues or jazz music blaring out. No phones constantly ringing, just blissful silence for four days – she, Amy and Josh doing their own thing in their own time, the solid house a fortress around them offering peace.

The thought of Michael doing business in Europe with Ted was amusing. Ted Earnshaw, her friend, was a nutcase. But a nutcase she was fond of. He and Delsea had worked together for a couple of years at the Water Authority. Then they'd joined Eurofone together. She had left Eurofone to join Cellstar, leaving him there, and three years ago Ted had left Eurofone to join Michael's company, Purple. The whole business of mobile telecommunications had seemed risky back then when she first got into it. She'd set out to prove that she could do it. She could take on a bigger, more prestigious role. She felt she had earned it. She had looked forward to working at Eurofone and setting new wheels in motion.

How had it come about? An opportunity for a promotion came up where she was working and she had applied for it. She knew she was capable of doing the job, but the next-in-line approach was favoured there, and she wasn't next in line. Still, she psyched herself up for the interview. She felt she stood a good chance, especially with Ted being on the panel. Ted knew better than anyone what she was capable of. She'd felt quietly confident.

She hadn't planned on Ted deliberately wrong-footing her. She was saddened by the fact that she had read their friendship wrong. At first, she couldn't figure out why he had made her look so bad. Then afterwards Ted came up to her grinning. 'Pub,' he said. It was an order. 'Darts.' They often played darts at lunchtime. She chalked his turn. He had a pint in one hand and a dart in the other. He was looking so smug she wanted to hit him.

'I'm leaving,' he said.

'So, you stuffed up my chances here?'

'I want you to come with me.'

'What makes you think I want to go with you?' He named a price that no one in their right mind would refuse. 'You what?'

'That's what says you'll come with me.'

He was right. It was double her salary. Making her an official yuppy. Yuppies earned at least double their age in years.

'What is this job?' she'd asked with suspicion.

Ted laughed. 'Whatever you make of it. You and I will work together. Define everything from scratch. It's a green field site.'

'Doing what?'

'It's a risky venture, hence the salary. Company could go belly up any time. Mobile telecommunications. The armed services have been using mobile telecommunications for their operations for a while. A company called Racal are at the forefront of supplying that. They are setting this green field company up as an offshoot to see if their mobile telecommunications have a commercial application. No one knows whether it'll take off. There are around a dozen people in the company at the moment. So, you can see we will have our work cut out building up the computer technology side of things. Are you game?'

'You bet.'

Of course, Ted didn't interview her. The parent company Human Resources wouldn't have sanctioned that. Though she wasn't aware of Eurofone before and that they were recruiting. The job offered her the chance to run her own department, and there was unparalleled experience to be gained. She was highly ambitious and she wasn't going to be put off by the way Ted had manipulated the situation. British CEOs didn't tend to scream integrity: they got themselves there by any means possible. She would do likewise. Playing it straight got you nowhere fast. Ted was always joking that he was open to bribery and corruption; that was his attitude for success. There would be extra pressure on her though to prove she had merit and had not been given the job through nepotism. She would subdue their fears by making a success of it. It was a challenge, and she was a sucker for challenges.

At the interview they asked very few questions. It was enough that Ted had vouched for her. The interviewer was a highly nervous man who was forever looking over his shoulder as though if he put her off, he would be in big trouble. He was anxious to please her. More concerned with selling her the job and garnering what package she would accept. There was no recession in the mobile telecommunications sector. The world was her oyster. He asked about her background, then declared they'd make a great team. She doubted it: he was unlikely to stun anyone with an original thought.

She had visited the company before the interview on a dummy run, as it was important to see how the current staff conducted themselves. She wanted to ensure she'd fit in. People were seconded in and out of the parent company Racal to fill whatever temporary skill gap was needed at Eurofone. But her caution wasn't necessary: it was a melting pot of race, class and religion. There were women in senior positions, no sign of misogyny, which was important to her.

On her first day at Eurofone she could still feel the excitement of that day. The green, brown and gold landscape blurring into a kaleidoscope of colour as she sped south on the A34, enjoying putting her spanking new Audi 80 sports car through its paces. She sped along the dual carriageway, weaving in and out of traffic, dancing with death.

She exchanged pleasantries with the security guard as the intercom buzzed and the barrier to the car park lifted. Excitement coursed through her, adrenaline pumping as she crossed reception. Her heels sounded hollow against the ceramic tiles of the glass building in which brightly coloured metallic tubing emphasised its construction features. On entering the lift, she checked her appearance in the mirror. She was primed for action.

Her office next to Ted's was comfortably decked out. Her name was on the door. Paintings hung on the walls. Plants burst from the confines of pots. The room was stale in the new building as no air had circulated there before. Delsea opened a window. Switching on her desktop, she browsed her online diary. Almost immediately the phone rang. 'Welcome to Eurofone, I trust everything is OK?' Ted knew her so well. He'd got everything ready. He, even had her company car delivered to her home. He'd been there a month. He hadn't taken a break between jobs as she had done. 'Everything's fine. I'll finish unpacking and be through in a moment.'

Her previous work paraphernalia was contained in a single cardboard box. She began unpacking. She opened a plastic file labelled 'working values': the things she wanted out of a job, which she'd written two years ago when she started her first job.

1. Fulfilment: job satisfaction and a sense of belonging.
2. Individuality: the right to be different, respected for who she was and the qualities she brought.

3. Trust: mutual trust between the boss and herself.
4. Flexibility: a good work-life balance.
5. Recognition: to be valued for doing good work.
6. Reward: fair and equal remuneration.

She laughed. They all still applied. She was shedding light on her working identity.

She retrieved her Mulberry organiser from her briefcase and went to see Ted, who gave her a potted history of the people involved, the situation, and what their immediate priorities were. He was Head of IT and she was his Systems Development Manager. In some ways it was wonderful working with Ted, like on their first task, when they were doing the rounds of computer manufacturers looking for hardware that could process their five-year projection of phone calls a day. Ted would lean back while smooth-talking men confused by his abstracted air tried their hardest to impress him. When they got to the crunch they'd say:

'What do you think?' to Ted, who always turned to her to ask, 'What do you think Delsea?' Then the salesmen would be embarrassed having assumed that she was his PA. They'd start all over again, by tackling her questions, trying to influence her – and she was a much tougher customer than Ted.

Ted was a family man, which made working full-time and having Josh easy. If she needed time off, they'd look at their diaries. Ted would come out with a load of dates when he'd be out of the office and needed her to cover. They'd share leave. He believed in a proper balance between work and home. There was no fuss or insinuations about letting the side down.

She kept business trips away to the essential. Most of them were pure macho posturing: having to be seen in the right place at the right time. She got by using conference calls and video links.

But Ted had his down side. He was whimsical and full of countless prejudices, which governed his life. Delsea recalled them. Asians were bloody lazy. He employed two once, but never again. The Germans were secretly conspiring to take over Europe. Americans think they own the bloody world, and Arabs were madmen. He was a nightmare to interview with, since he was impossible to please. There were equal opportunities: everyone was equally discriminated against.

At the end of an interview when she thought the candidate would fit in nicely, he'd say 'No.'

'Why ever not? He's got the right experience, fits the specification…'

'White socks. I hope you saw his socks.'

'What?'

'There's something suspicious about a man who wears white socks.'

'He may not have your impeccable taste, but he can do the job.'

'No.' And 'no' to the next one too.

'Why not?'

'Earring. I hope you saw his earring.'

'So what?'

'What will people think?'

'He's going to sit in front of a VDU, he won't be in contact with customers.'

And so it went on.

If the candidate survived his personal scrutiny and there was nothing wrong with their sartorial elegance, then there was the square regime to overcome. He would draw a square and divide it into quarters with a cross. He would shade in quarters as the interview progressed. One quarter meant suspect; two meant dodgy, and three meant highly dubious. He never got to four. This process could take anywhere between two minutes and an hour. At three quarters shaded he lost all interest and started doodling, leaving Delsea to be polite by continuing the interview, thinking it only right to give the person at least half an hour of their time.

His prejudices determined whom he spoke to and to whom he did not. Delsea never saw him so agitated as when the agency sent him a male secretary when his permanent lady was off sick. Ted couldn't get rid of him fast enough. The secretary lasted a day.

Delsea felt the urge one day to ask Ted if he realised, she was black, because he had nothing good to say about other people of colour. Ted shrugged his shoulders, showing an appropriate amount of cuff. Little things like that were important to him. She could imagine him with a tape measure in the mornings, checking that the trouser hem was one break above the shoe, and the sock reveal when he sat down. Serving nine years in the military sharpened his obsession with dress. The signet ring on his little finger had been passed down through generations, so he was ready to seal a contract in wax when required.

He'd looked at her as if she'd spoken some unspeakably vile words. 'Of course, you're black,' he said. 'But you're one of us.'

That narrowed it down. He didn't like Africans, people from the Caribbean, Asians, Arabs, and all manner of Europeans. The only people he had any respect for were the Japanese, who he proclaimed to be damned clever, and whose business practices must be emulated. Therefore, her being "one of us" required further probing.

'Who are we? Who is this "us" that I am one of?' She'd put it awkwardly but he knew what she meant.

'Don't get philosophical with me.' With that he walked off.

Delsea could answer her own question anyway; she just wanted to pull him up on his attitude. But sometimes you just have to separate the deed from the doer. She knew what he meant by "one of us": she'd worked with him long enough. "We" were people he deigned to know and "us" were people he trusted. He wasn't so bad after all; as far as prejudice went Ted was a queer card. He didn't care about the colour or the creed if a person was "one of us." She couldn't think of a more Eurosceptic person for Michael to have as his partner in Europe.

She'd loved working in mobile telecommunications; she was a pro. Her opinions were sought after. She was always one of those consulted when major decisions were being made. In short, she was valued for her abilities. She found solace in her work. It was such fun too. Each time they hit a major target they paid themselves huge bonuses and the pink champagne flowed.

DELSEA

Josh had asked Delsea to wake him up. He was meeting school friends in town. They were all back from various universities for the summer holidays. She knocked on his bedroom door.

'Josh.'

'Bugger off, Mum.'

'Josh?' No answer. 'Are you decent?' After a careful pause she went in. Her twenty-year-old son was crashed out on the bed, fully clothed except for his boots. The room stank of unwashed clothes and smelly feet.

'Josh, you need to get up, tidy all this up and have a shower. You said to wake you when I got up. Remember you wanted to be in town?'

Josh wasn't bothered anymore about meeting his friends. He was feeling awful. The relationship with his best university friend Tom Holloway had turned sour. Tom, Antonia (Toni), Tamsin and Josh had been friends since they met on their first day at Jehovah College in Cambridge. They were on the same landing in their halls of residence. They shared a kitchen, cooked meals, or ate in the dining hall or sat in the College bar together having a good time.

Then he slept with Toni after a night out. That happened a few more times. Josh thought they were having fun. Toni took it seriously. As soon as Josh was aware of that, he stopped. She was away from home for the first time, homesick. She told him that she liked waking up beside him. He backed off. She got depressed. Then Toni turned to Tom, telling him that she loved Josh. Tom tried to help her, advising her to write it down in a journal rather than expose those feelings which were not returned to Josh. Toni spent days lying in bed. For a change of scenery, she would go to Tom's room and lie on his bed instead, while he worked at his desk. Tom, like

Josh, thought that Toni would get over it. She was a looker; there'd be other boys.

Tamsin tried to help her too. She talked to her about how she read that it was common to have overwhelming feelings after the first sexual experiences, and that those feelings would pass. Toni had gone to a single sex girl's school before going to Ariel University and had never had a boyfriend before.

Toni got antidepressants from her doctor in Cambridge. They didn't seem to work. She dropped out of Ariel after the first year. Josh was then careful not to have casual sex with another college girl. He didn't want to be responsible for them missing out on the opportunities that would come their way with an Ariel degree. He had a girlfriend, Merin. He met her in town.

'I've changed my mind about going out,' Josh told Delsea. 'I'm starving. Are you making breakfast?'

'Oh My God Josh, you are not in halls now. Make your own breakfast. I don't like you lying around all day. At least open the windows to air your room.'

'It's the bumba clart holidays.'

'This is nothing to do with the holidays. Have you split up with Merin? Is that it?'

'Go away.'

'Right, I'll just take these.' Haphazardly she grabbed up a pile of dirty washing.

'Leave it. I'll do it when I'm ready.' No, he wouldn't: they'd lie around for weeks stinking up the room until she washed everything for him to take back to college for his final year.

'What time is it?'

'Eight o'clock.'

'Aw, Mum.' Josh put a pillow over his head.

'OK, I'm going.'

Delsea sat under the cherry tree. A copper-coloured Grizzled Skipper butterfly glided down to bask in the sun. Josh found her in the shade, lying on the picnic rug with a newspaper and a half-eaten slice of toast beside her on a plate. Her mug of coffee was still warm. 'Amy's crying,' he said. She had just started, the monitor burst into life.

Why did children cry upon waking? Why didn't Amy get up instead of crying and waiting to be fetched? Why didn't Josh just bring her down?

'Mum. I want to talk to you about you and Jonathan. I need to know about you and him; I've never really pressed you before.' Josh wheedled as if she were about to refuse.

'Yes. I agree we need to talk. Shall we sort Amy first? Can you deal with her while I have a shower?'

By the time she came down Josh had fixed Amy and himself breakfast. The Weetabix was creamy with Greek yoghurt, the way Amy liked it. Delsea made herself another cup of coffee and sat with them in the breakfast room while they ate their food. The French doors opened onto a small courtyard where roses climbed up the trellis on the walls.

'Where do you want to start?' About Jonathan she meant.

'I want to know how come you had me?'

'Well, I was in love with him. You know first love, where you feel it's going to last forever. Like you and Merin.'

She had an inkling that Merin was the reason Josh was so bad-tempered and rude. How she longed for him to finish with her. Merin was very alternative. She wasn't a student at the university, but someone who lived in the city. Josh had shown her photos of her: she was very pretty, with pleated curls and at twenty-two, she was two years older than Josh. Her nose was pierced. She didn't find that objectionable but the lip ring looked painfully grotesque, and if this wasn't enough to make her feel protective towards Josh, the fact that Merin acted African was. Merin was mixed-race, like Josh, though anyone would think she was just out of Africa, not Norwich. She had nothing against people exploring their roots. She'd done it herself. But Merin was persistently ramming it down Josh's throat that he wasn't black enough.

'We were talking about you and Jonathan. Don't change the subject.'

'OK, And Josh? Don't talk to me like you did this morning. I'm concerned for you. But I get the message, I'll back off.' She held up her hands in supplication.

ON REFLECTION

Delsea had been so in love with Jonathan. This was deadly serious. She and Jonathan were an inseparable pair. They completed each other. She was part moon and he was part sun.

The sun and the moon are the bedrocks of the universe. The moon is the brightest object in the night sky. It moderates earth, leading to a stablish climate, causing tides and the rhythms of life. The sun radiates light and heat, which makes it possible for life to exist on Earth. Plants need sunlight to grow. Animals, including humans, need plants for food and the oxygen they produce which is breathed.

DELSEA & JONATHAN

It was very easy on the mind to be back in Aldbourne Court in Jonathan's room. Delsea remembered him kissing her as she sat on his bed. His warmth had overwhelmed her. She was flushed and breathless yet she still found time to wonder whether he loved her. Other worrying thoughts also chased through her mind: someone might come in; her father would be angry because she'd stayed out so late.

She recollected them undressing, and how the contact of skin on skin had heightened her senses. He said kind things. He wasn't a boy talking nonsense who was only after one thing. It was all very sweet and teenage. Afterwards they lay there entwined like babes. Jonathan was smiling. He had enjoyed it. She was thinking how happy she had made him. They were both contented. All the heart-wrenching angst of the previous two months had melted away.

As she walked home her jovial mood was dimmed by the thought of her father. Ben could be fierce. How was she going to explain herself? She'd better tell the truth as far as was possible, otherwise he'd slap her. He had never hit her before, although he struck Marcus often enough. Marcus thought she was spoilt, because she was such a daddy's girl that she never got smacked. But that was because she never gave Ben any reason to be angry with her. That was not until then. His red-hot anger terrified her, even though it had never been directed at her.

She'd hoped to find the house in darkness, but to the contrary, every light in the house was burning, and Ben was waiting for her in their small chintzy sitting room. She smiled weakly at him.

'Where you been, chile?'

'Daddy.' She couldn't help her childish exclamation because he seemed more concerned than angry. He was Daddy: the father she'd known before drink, and before the obliteration of suffering. Before the years of microaggressions from workmates took their toll.

He even looked handsome in his navy pullover and blue slacks, though they were totally out of place amongst all the frilly chair backs that Lucille was forever running up on her sewing machine. She was aware that her father was good-looking. He could be suave but mostly he was self-indulgent. He did though possess something about him that made people quiet. Ignorant people might have hated him but others treated him with respect – often when they were kowtowing to his superior knowledge of cricket. There was also something about him that rendered him irreproachable no matter how badly he behaved towards Lucille.

The women of the village were fascinated by Ben. He was the first black man they'd ever seen. For most prejudice disappeared each morning along with their husbands. Feeble excuses, like having knitted him a jumper as he must find English weather cold, gained them entry to the house. Ben was often exhausted from his ten-till-six shift, and sat bleary-eyed while they simpered and talked in a breathy way, eager to engage him in mundane chitchat. Delsea had witnessed it all. They had no shame.

'A said where yu been?'

'I've been out with a friend. It won't happen again; he's leaving.'

'He?'

'Yes, he.'

'And wat yu and dis he doing till dis time a night?'

'Nothing.'

'Dis he. Him white?' That was a stupid question. She'd have to go to Bath or Bristol to meet a Jamaican boy, and then there was a good chance he'd be a relative. Ben and Lucille acted as hosts for their family and friends immigrating to Britain until they found their feet elsewhere.

'Yes.'

'Dis better be nutting yu doing wid dis boy.' Ben grunted. 'A soon kill him.'

'Nothing happened, Daddy.'

'Nuh let no white boy use yu, Delsea. Deyll be curious grant yu. Don't indulge dem.' His voice was thick with sighs.

'He's different, Daddy.'

'Dat is as lang as yu don't trus him. Get yu banty upstairs before a drop yu two bitch licks!'

When she woke up, she was still smiling, and a wood pigeon was cooing down the chimney. Skipping to her age-speckled mirror, she looked at her face. It was butterscotch brown and shiny. Her eyes were bright with very white whites – the lashes were long, black and curly. She smiled at herself. Unplaiting her hair, she lifted the thick tendrils so they stood on end. Medusa, in a pink chemise. She took an afro-comb and afroed her hair into a huge halo. Pulling the chemise over her head, she looked at her naked body. Jonathan had said she was beautiful. Her nipples were like blackberries.

She paused. Her mother had silently opened her bedroom door and was standing there watching her.

'A wey yu a do?' Lucille wasn't smiling. Her face twisted as it sneered, 'A wey yu a do?' again, louder the second time, as though she hadn't heard her the first time.

Any trace of the smile she'd had before her mom came in was gone.

'Don't tink I don't know, it's written arl over yu face.'

'Mother.'

'Don't madda me.'

'Mom. I am over the age of consent.'

'Don't tark to mi, I don't warnt know nutting. Didn't I tell yu keep yuself to yuself. Where yu meet dis boy?'

'In the park.'

'Well, yu better act like nutting happen. Yu tink Ben done wid yu and yu whiteboy? Wait till him catch yu a smile like dat. Arl hell goin break loose. Yu, tell Ben him garn.'

'Yes, he's going away…'

'And yu tink I don't ha nutting to say about dis. A weh yu mean a ha sex. Yu a Let-Go-Beast. Yu a Wanton Mare. But as him garn a let it pass. Dis once, yu hear. Yu nu mek it, happen again. Yu hear me.'

'I will see him again.'

'A weh yu a tark bout. Yu listening to me. Forget him. Yu warn't trouble. Cacca fart yu nuh see nutting yet.'

'Go away, Mom, and knock next time. This is my room. My private space.'

Water spouted from the hose pipe into the paddling pool. Delsea carted hot water from the kitchen to warm it up for Amy.

'I get in,' asked Amy.
'Yes, darling.'
'Where Daddy?'
'Work.'

'So, what happened when you found out you were pregnant?' This conversation had been going on for a whole day, with Josh following Delsea from room to room as she went about her tasks.

'Why? Why do you want to know all this? It was a long time ago.'

'I think I want to meet him. I need to meet him.'

'And what I say will make a difference to that?'

'Yes. Yes, it will.'

'Suppose you don't like what I say?'

'Just tell me. Let me decide what to do with my own life.'

She knew she was expecting when she fainted in assembly, and then her periods stopped. Somehow, she thought she wouldn't have a baby. If she ignored the situation, she thought it would go away. So, she ignored it. She starved herself so that her clothes would fit for longer. At first, she got thinner and everyone was concerned. When she started to put on weight her parents were pleased. Smocks were in fashion then and bell-bottom trousers. She fitted elastic into the fastening of her trousers, put on her smock and nobody was any the wiser.

In fairness Ben and Lucille were too busy to think. They had to juggle things between them. Apart from being a housewife Lucille had to arrange her cleaning jobs and wedding dress making work around Ben's shifts. Ben would come home and Lucille would dash off. They didn't have time to think that their daughter might be expectant. They trusted her. Then she couldn't hide it any longer. Every week before P.E. she had come up with excuses not to put on her gym skirt and navy knickers. She made up period pains, headaches and stomach aches. The games mistress informed her form teacher, who wrote to Lucille saying she should see a doctor. She didn't want to see Doctor Barlow, their family GP. He would only confirm what she already knew. Then everyone would know. Her parents. The school. The village. She couldn't avoid the shame any more. How would she face the gossip?

Her appointment became an immovable hurdle in her mind; one

she couldn't get over. Dithering she put it off. Fear hung over her like a black cloud, threatening to engulf her without warning every time she thought of it. As she walked to the surgery, she was sad. She was a sad girl on a sunny day.

Doctor Barlow was kind. He didn't lecture, except to say that she was too young to be having a child because she was merely a child herself. One hurdle straddled. How would she tell Lucille? She didn't want to trouble her. She had a lot on her mind. The police had called again about Marcus. Every time there was a crime in the neighbourhood, he was their first port of call, before they followed other leads. Marcus was never involved, but he was the only black boy for miles around. If a policeman said he had done something, his parents listened and considered it true. They weren't all bad, though, it was more that some of the detectives thought Ben got special treatment and wanted to put him in his place. The chief constable was fond of cricket and would call in to watch Test Matches with Ben when England played the West Indies.

She was supposed to be the good one. The one who did not give them trouble. She was giving trouble. Furtively she crept into the kitchen like she was about to steal something. Lucille was sulkily making dinner. The fish she was preparing had been marinated overnight in onions, tomatoes and garlic. Lucille reached into the fridge. The coconut butter shimmering in the pan made a glorious aroma fill the room.

'Wat yu skulking about for, chile?' Delsea felt underhand. She was haunted by the weeks she'd known she was expecting and covering up her bump, which had started to show, while smiling her ineffectual smile. She should have told Lucille before. Tearing at the corner of her nails with her teeth, she wanted it over. Throwing caution to the wind, she said: 'I'm pregnant.' Her voice was perilously close to trembling. Lucille stopped. Then she started peeling potatoes, fast, ripping at the skins as if nothing else in the world mattered. She kept her hands busy to prevent them from doing something outrageous, like slapping Delsea down. 'Pregnant?' Lucille repeated as if she didn't understand her. 'Yu sure?'

'Quite sure.'

'How many weeks?'

'Thirteen.' Dr Barlow had sighed at her predicament, commiserated, patted her hand and reassured her that everything would be alright.

'Lord ha mercy. And is dere a chance?' She didn't finish the sentence.

'No.' There was no chance that she was going to marry Jonathan. She'd said no with such force that her mother snapped as if she'd been hit.

'Don't flaunt yu Let-Go-Beast ways in dis house. Wey yu mean a ha sex wid man yu ha no intention a marry?'

'You don't understand. I couldn't marry him even if I wanted to. Even if he wanted to.'

'So yu nat good enough? Not good enough for him.

Well, we goin see about dat. A who him. Nobady gwain tell mi me darta nat good inough? Him force yu? Didn't a tell yu anybady trouble yu, yu fi lick dem down wid rock stone. Yu betta say dat him force yu else Ben gwain go mad.'

'He's going to go mad whatever happens and no he didn't force me and no I'm not going to say that he did.'

'Yu betta tell mi now. A who dis boy?'

'No.'

Then Lucille slapped her. 'A wrenk yu wrenk. Si how far yu feistiness get yu.' Lucille had never raised a hand to her before. Shoving past Delsea, she swayed into the sitting room where she crumpled into the nearest chair. 'A should a know something like dis would happen. A no good yu up to arl dis time. Quiet like mouse. Nu open yu mout. Not even fart pan mi.' She was talking to herself as if Delsea wasn't there. Whispering almost. Crying. Wiping her eyes with her apron that covered her housecoat.

MONTE CARLO

The European Mobile Telecommunications Conference was to be held in Monte Carlo. Michael had arranged to meet Ted at Heathrow. Ted was late. The boarding message flashed on the visual display. It was unlike Ted to cut it so fine. Michael hoped he wasn't going to miss the flight. Ted arrived out of breath, just as Michael was about to board. The air hostess smiled sweetly as they arranged themselves in the club class compartment.

For a while the sound of rustling newspapers was all that could be heard. Before long passengers dozed off over pressing reports. Not Ted though. Michael watched him scribbling away with an unsteady hand as they hit a patch of turbulence. His eyes crinkled at the corners as he narrowed his concentration, fingers flicking through the pages, searching for things that needed to be corrected.

While he was idly watching Ted, Michael was unaware that he too was being observed. 'You're under attack,' said Ted. 'To your right.' A young businesswoman looked in Michael's direction. Michael looked over his shoulder before turning uncertainly towards her. Their eyes met. He smiled, showing even white teeth in a tanned face.

'You are English. I can tell. A woman looks at you and you look behind you to see who she's looking at. I'm Bianca. Are you planning on spending some time in Nice? Perhaps we could get together for a drink?'

'I doubt it,' he replied, finding a sudden interest in an article in a newspaper. Bianca pouted, then smiled. Well, Michael was the sort of man you couldn't pass without taking the opportunity to introduce yourself.

From Nice airport they took a helicopter to Monte Carlo. Their luxurious hotel was perched on top of the Grand Prix course. Michael found his room, which was functional in a business sort of way. He was past being impressed. He'd seen the inside of so many hotel rooms and suites. They were all the same – no substitute for home comforts. He found the concierge's rude enquiry in some countries as to whether he wanted 'a warm bed' or 'a cold bed' insulting. A warm bed had a woman in it; a cold bed did not. Some of the "entertainments" he was forced to watch out of politeness beggared belief, like the club where women danced naked, stopping every now and again to pop ping pong balls out of their smooth vaginas. Business was still such a man's world.

His room, however, had one redeeming feature: a private balcony with a panoramic view of the harbour.

Later he and Ted made their way to the conference suite, where the faint smell of perfume lingered due to the extravagant flowers that decorated the room. The head of international mobile telecommunications standards made a welcoming speech.

It was sunny when Delsea woke again. Westmead, their country house in Dorchester-on-Thames, Oxfordshire, when the sun was shining was a place to behold. Drawing back the curtains she could see the river, busy as was usual at this time of year. A brightly coloured houseboat waited to enter the lock, while the swans stuck close to the bank. Amy was still fast asleep, lost in the big wide bed.

Michael's dirty clothes were scattered about the room. Delsea picked up his socks, his underpants and his shirt and placed them in the linen basket. She folded his jeans and put them in his dressing room, on the shelves where he kept his casual clothes. She seemed to spend her life picking up after him and the children. She should make some time for herself. She would take the paper and have breakfast under the cherry tree. That's if Amy would sleep late, as she sometimes did. She set the child monitor so she could hear her outside.

Most of Michael's day had been spent discussing international roaming – a concept that made making an international phone call seamless for the customer. After a shower Michael dressed for dinner, preparing himself for an evening talking shop without actually saying anything. But first he'd phone Delsea:

'How's it going?'

'Amy's not well. You know how she gets. She's thrown up again.'

'When's this appointment with the specialist, is it in my diary?'

'Yes. Next week. You are coming, aren't you?'

'What day?'

'Michael, you said you'd be there.'

'I'll be there.'

'I haven't had a moment to myself. Josh seems to need me. Sometimes he's worse than Amy. How was your day?'

'It was pretty dull really. I'm just going down to dinner.'

'We should take a break from all this. It's so long since we took a holiday. Two weeks in the sun? Just me and you…'

'It's a lovely thought. But I'm really busy right now. Perhaps later on.' He'd been working too hard. He should delegate more, and stop trying to do so much himself. He was putting his life and soul into the company, because the competition was fierce.

'Soon. OK. I promise.'

He'd said that before, but something always came up. She wanted to go away with him – no children, just the two of them, if only for a few days.

'Right. Look. I love you.'

'I love you too, darling. Goodnight.'

Delsea was thinking about Michael. When he was away, she missed his curious way of having a conversation, which centred on trying not to start one. He developed, extrapolated or offered different options to whatever she said, which was lazy. It meant he never had to think about what to say. Still, she would miss his echo.

Whenever she took it upon herself to do a bit of DIY her choice of tools was a hammer and a dinner knife. He'd interfere: 'What are you doing darling? What are you doing my love?' He'd fetch from the garage what he considered to be the correct tools. 'Look, use the spirit level, use the electric screwdriver.' She couldn't be bothered with the nonsensical way he organised things in the garage. She kept a hammer in the utility cupboard. She could accomplish everything she needed to do with the hammer and dinner knife. When he was gone though, she suffered from a perverse syndrome: a lack of mansplaining.

Josh did need his mum. Tom started bullying him after he refused to engage on the topic of Toni, regularly embarrassing him in front of other students. Tom used explicit racism ('You need a good wash, have you never heard of taking a bath, Josh?'), humiliated him ('You are the most hated student in college, you must be proud of such an achievement.'), sarcasm: 'Stop attracting attention, the world doesn't revolve around you!' and even aggressive ridicule and mockery; nudging him in the library when he was working or elbowing his head as he passed by. It was childish. The incidents themselves were petty, but it was the cumulative effect of the bullying that got to Josh. Tom seemed to think that this behaviour would somehow lead Josh to calling a truce, admitting he was wrong, and them all being together again.

Tom and Josh both had other friends on their courses, so they didn't have to rely on making those amongst the undergraduates at their college. Other students didn't seem to notice what was going on, or didn't seem to care. They were too wrapped up in themselves. Josh kept quiet, as though his concerns were not worthy of being mentioned. Although he and Tom had fallen out, he didn't want to get him into trouble by snitching. He also knew that there was no point in complaining. His college had a culture of apathy towards bullying and a way of excusing these kinds of behaviours.

Michael made his way down to dinner. Amy was not strong, but neither was she the invalid Delsea made her out to be. The visit to the ENT specialist was just for reassurance. She had a persistent runny nose and quite often vomited. Their GP had told them that there was nothing to worry about. But it had been going on for eighteen months. For Michael there was only one good thing about being away from home: it allowed him to get some decent sleep.

There was the usual crowd at the entrance sampling drinks, hesitating, waiting to see who was going to sit where, trying to avoid the bores. Just as he and Ted thought they'd been successful at seating themselves amongst an interesting set of people, Sylvie Burns joined their table. Sylvie was a red-headed French woman whose parents were Scottish.

'What an unexpected pleasure,' said Michael. He watched her cheeks blush. Sylvie was a conference groupie: conferences were good places to hunt for rich businessmen. As she peeled her king prawns next to him, the mounting pile of heads and legs reminded Michael of all the men she was known to have laid end to end. Sylvie lowered her lashes.

She could have kicked herself for being so obvious. But how else could she get close to Michael? She'd met him last year, and admired him immensely. She'd gotten the whole David and Goliath tale out of Ted. How the DTI at the last minute had decreed that by way of introducing competition, network providers couldn't sell connections direct to the customer, and had to trade through suppliers. How Eurofone had been desperate for service providers, offering to pay their advertising costs and setting up an IT bureau to provide them with computer services. For the service provider it was a licence to print money. How the twenty-year-old Michael had turned up as a hopeful. How he then built Foneland, and when the laws relaxed had sold it to Eurofone, making him millions in personal fortune. Then when the government offered two further network licences, he teamed up with a Japanese company MacroTel, forming Valentine MacroTel. Its brand name, Purple, was trying to take on both Eurofone and Cellstar.

Added to all that, Sylvie thought he was gorgeous. No doubt about it, the impact was immediate. He had serene good looks and an unassuming manner, and when he was amused, he could raise each of his eyebrows independently. Sylvie looked away. Ted found these social occasions trying. It was difficult to appear interested in people he saw infrequently. When the meal was over and they had all gone to the bar, Michael went to the gents.

'So, what's the wife like?' Sylvie asked Ted.

'Beautiful. That's why he keeps her at home,' Ted replied, not liking to be quizzed about his friend. He was still piqued that Delsea seemed to have retired so young.

'Blonde?'

'Black.'

'Brunette. Classy.'

'I mean she's black…'

'A bit exotic!'

'Exotic? She's one of us…'

'Hardly. It's hardly a meeting of equals.'

'I think you should keep your very offensive opinions to yourself.'

Ted didn't like what Sylvie was implying. Delsea had a first-class business brain. On more than one occasion she had stepped in to run Purple, after Michael had gone on hedonistic cocaine clubbing benders with Delsea's brother. A brothers' and wives' holiday staying with Michael's sister in Malta loomed large in his memory. The men had been tanked up on coke, rushing from club to club in Paceville night after night. Michael was good for nothing for a couple weeks after that. Things would have gone belly up without Delsea.

Michael didn't return to the bar. He thought he'd slip away while the going was good. He was just crossing the lobby when Harold Parker beckoned him. Fumes of whisky and beer assailed him as Harold attempted to crush his hand. 'It is good to see you, Michael. Still sticking in there?' This was a reference to their jockeying position in the marketplace. Harold's Eurofone was still number one in the UK. Cellstar was number two. But Michael's Purple's market share was fast increasing, standing around twenty percent. Both Eurofone and Cellstar had put strategies in place to see Michael off the playing field.

'If you'll excuse me, I think I'll call it a day.'

At 6:30 the next morning Michael was woken by a call from Sylvie.

'Fancy a swim?' He toyed with telling her he wasn't interested. But then again, some exercise would be good. It would make a refreshing start to the day.

'OK, see you down there.'

Sylvie was triumphant. What was it about this guy that was getting to her? The fact he wasn't interested in her at all? Or that look of permanent amusement, as if everything, especially her, was about to make him laugh out loud? Why had she invited him for a swim? She hated swimming. She grabbed a quick slurp of coffee, threw on a pair of leggings and a clean white shirt, put a comb through her long red hair, shoved her skirt into the trouser press and brushed her teeth, all at the same time. All this for a man she stood little chance with.

Sylvie couldn't imagine Michael with a black woman. His whole persona breathed intelligence. Maybe he was unable to handle a real relationship for whatever reason, she thought to herself. As the lift opened on the ground floor Harold, who was waiting to go up, gave Sylvie a lecherous look. Sylvie gave him a look of disdain of her own. Had he stayed in the bar all night? He certainly looked as though he had. 'Going for a swim…' She answered his unvoiced query.

The cool water soothed and relaxed her muscles. She was not a good swimmer. It was enough of an effort to laboriously splash up and down, avoiding Michael as he completed length after length with dedication. They had the pool to themselves. She was disappointed that nothing of substance passed between them and afterwards he didn't even show up for breakfast. No wonder he was in good shape: skipping breakfast after that late dinner the night before was wise.

The conference started before the breakfast plates had been cleared away. Michael sat next to Ted. Sylvie sat somewhere else, deciding to play it cool. Michael was proving impervious to her charms. Still, she'd love to wipe that smile off his face. She'd love to show him what a real woman was about.

Now that Delsea had finally got Amy settled in her arms, after a major crying tantrum she thought she'd catch up with Michael. 'Hello Hun. I tried to call you earlier...'

'I needed a break from the hotel. I decided to eat out for a change. I was just about to call you before going out again.'

'Who with?'

'Ted and Sylvie.'

'Sylvie? That French redhead? Ted says she's a nuisance.'

'That's her. How's Amy?'

'Better. She'd been playing in the paddling pool all morning. I couldn't get her out. She's really quite funny. She kept asking for you, so I told her you couldn't get away from work.

She said you should run very fast. Do you want to talk to her?'

'OK.

Hello, Babs, you being a good girl?'

'My good girl.'

'Tell Daddy what we did today.'

'Animals.'

'We went to the Cotswold Wildlife Park this afternoon, didn't we?'

'Animals.'

'That's good. Night-night, sleep tight, don't let the bugs bite.

I tell you what Del? I've only got a minute. I'll phone you tomorrow. Love you.'

It was Sylvie who suggested they go to a club. It was a fifties style venue she'd been to before. Sylvie followed Michael up some wooden steps to a galleried seating area, which overlooked the dancefloor. Ted watched the couples dancing while enjoying his pint. He'd much rather watch than dance. He only went along to keep an eye on Sylvie.

'Great, isn't it?' said Sylvie.

'Looks fun,' Michael replied.

'Can you jitterbug?'

'Yes, but I haven't done it for a long time.'

'Shall we dance?'

The routine came naturally to Michael, who was a good dancer. Sylvie was flirting outrageously with him. Ted, watching from the gallery, wondered what Michael was playing at with Sylvie. She was very pretty, with a creamy freckled-complexion. She was a Scottish rose. She was virtually throwing herself at him. Surely Michael wouldn't fall for that old trick? Then he lost sight of them. They seemed to have left the dancefloor. He walked round the hanging gallery to the other bar and saw them collapsed on a sofa talking. They seemed engrossed, engaging each other in a heart-to-heart. He decided to leave them to it and return to the hotel. Three was a crowd anyway. It looked to Ted like they were planning to make a night of it.

Michael saw Ted leave and didn't want to compromise himself by staying longer. 'Shall we go?' He asked Sylvie, his brow arched. They went back to the hotel. He walked Sylvie to her room, which was on the same floor as his. He held her at arms' length, as though to say this was the distance between them.

'I don't want tonight to mean anything. I needed an evening out and you kept me company. Let's leave it there,' he said, by way of goodnight. To him that was all there was to it. They'd seen Monte Carlo by night. They'd walked around while cars hooted, and bright florescent lights beckoned. He loved cities at nightfall.

Sylvie didn't want to leave it there. Maybe all she had to do was convince him that he was interested in her. What would it take? She could go to his room. What did she have to lose? He was particularly vulnerable as they had spent the evening together. Delsea didn't sound much fun. Apparently, she didn't like pubs and clubs, meaning Michael had to go out on his own. A woman like that, who wasn't prepared to bend, deserved to lose her husband. 'Michael, it's me. Can I come in?'

He opened the door in his boxer shorts, 'It's late.'

'I know. Can I stay with you? I don't feel like being on my own.' She thought she could seduce him by running her hand over his firm belly that was on show, down into his shorts.

He raised an eyebrow. 'Come in then.'

She maintained eye contact as she climbed into his bed, brazenly pulling off her dress, under which she was naked. She hoped the sight of her body would entice him.

'Does this happen to you all the time?'

'Not at all.' He was careful with what he said because she seemed needy. It wasn't his style to crush vulnerable people. 'Look, Sylvie, you can stay, but nothing is going to happen. I'm happily married.' He got the spare blanket from the wardrobe and sat in the armchair, resting his long legs on the bed. He rested his eyes without sleeping – a trick he had learnt as a new parent. He waited until Sylvie fell asleep, then went to sleep in her room.

Sylvie woke up alone and ashamed. She didn't even have being drunk as an excuse. It was a blow to her self-esteem and her womanhood: never before had she been naked in front of a man who didn't take the opportunity before him. She was offended by that on top of everything else.

MARCUS

Delsea went upstairs and locked her bedroom door. Lucille was still crying when Ben came home from his shift. She heard him return. The front door slammed. She heard him seek out Lucille, as he always did, to plant a kiss on her cheek. She could hear the love in his voice when he found her weeping.

'A wey happen MisCam, wey yu cast down?'

'Arske dat darta of yours.'

Lucille, cast down, thought of Jubilee, her home near Mandeville, in Jamaica. How the red dust gathered in corners like secrets. How lizards dropped from the rafters. She thought of her father, Joseph, on the veranda surveying his land. That was before Ben on their wedding eve sold two of his cows without even asking, to pay for his passage to England.

Ben sent for her, like a piece of luggage. Joseph ruled that she had to go; that she had to obey her husband. When she wrote to Joseph complaining about the harshness of her life in England, hoping he'd tell her to come home, he replied, 'Your duty is to your husband. Make me one promise. Bring up the children as good Christians.' Well, she'd failed. Marcus, according to the police, was a trouble-maker. Delsea was in trouble.

Delsea heard her father's heavy footsteps on the stairs, then her door handle rattle. 'Open dis door.'

'No.'

'Yu warnt mi break it down.'

'Mom slapped me. Promise you won't hit me too.'

'A nat pramising a darn ting.'

What choice did she have but to open the door? The tears were streaming down her face. What was going to happen to her?

'Dad.' She blurted out. 'I'm pregnant!'

'Pregnant? Wat yu mean pregnant? Fe who?'

'The boy I told you about.'

'No malata pickney coming in dis house, d'you hear me. When a done wid yu, I goin start on him. Arl dis time I tart yu was my lickle girl.'

She thought of that little girl. For some reason an image of Ben and her doing the washing in the bathtub came into her head. He made doing the laundry fun – letting the warm water melt the soap. She was the washing machine before they had one. Laughing together while he made up stories about Anansi the spider to tell her, as she trod the clothes up and down the bathtub with her bare feet. Lucille would get annoyed about their way of washing the clothes. Each item should be rubbed by hand, and the whites must be boiled in the boiler in the outhouse. They ignored her. It was a sort of child labour, like the young girls in the Caribbean rolling cigars against their soft, virginal inner thighs. Delsea didn't know whether that was true, or just a tale men told each other to enhance their enjoyment of smoking cigars.

Standing there in the doorway with Lucille behind him, arms akimbo as if she had him on a leash, Ben had said lots of things. Delsea couldn't remember it all. She remembered that he was too poleaxed to do anything. He was as dismayed as Lucille had been. Eventually he went away, leaving her alone, crying for what might have been.

Marcus wasn't one to be kept out of the drama. He'd been waiting in the wings. 'You've finally done it, done something which makes me look like a saint. The joy. If I had done something as bad as this Daddio would have bust my arse. Daddio is heartbroken. I got to hand it to you, Sis.'

'It's not funny.'

'Of course, it's not funny. Come on, you can tell me. Do I know him?'

'You know *of* him.'

'How mysterious! I know Kevin Darby.'

'Kevin is a weirdo.'

'He would have to be weird to be shagging you.'

'Thanks. It's nice to know I can rely on you to cheer me up.'

'Who would go for a mouse who reads maths theory books for pleasure?'

'Go away!'

'Hey, come on, Sis. Don't be sad – I'll help you. We're brother and sister. You can count on me.'

Delsea got up and closed the door. 'Lend me some money then,' she said. Marcus was an apprentice at Spencer Engineering. He earned very little; so little that he cleaned taxis on Saturdays.

'I'm broke.'

'When you get paid then?'

'What for?'

'Does it matter what for? You said you'd help me.'

'What for, Del?'

'I have to see him.' She wanted to talk to Jonathan. She couldn't meet him in Corsham: her parents would be watching like hawks, ready to tackle any boy she spoke to. 'I need to go to Oxford.'

'You are joking. Daddio would kill me.'

'I'll tell him about all the money you find cleaning taxis – in the back seats, under the seats, which you keep. Cleaning them out, more like.'

'That's my tip. Blackmail eh. Two can play at this game. If you tell me who he is I'll lend you the money.'

'And you won't tell anyone?'

'You're my baby sis. It's my job to protect you. D'you want me to sort him?'

Marcus was the same age as Jonathan, but he was broader, taller and fitter, obsessed as he was by martial arts. To prove it he did a Kung Fu kick towards her head, stopping a couple of inches away from her face. Delsea, who was used to being his target practise, didn't even flinch.

'No, I don't want you to sort him. Are you going to lend me some money or not?'

'Who?'

'If you come out of this crazy upbringing, you'll help me out. If I come out, I'll help you out.' It was their "all for one and one for all" pledge.

'OK, I come out, you come out. Now who?'

'Jonathan Ainsley.'

'What?!'

'You heard.'

'There couldn't be anyone worse. Daddio will go spare.'

'But you are not going to tell him.'

'I most certainly am not telling him that. He'd murder me just for telling him news like that, let alone what he would do to you or Jonathan fucking Ainsley. You've really done it this time, Del.'

'Stop saying that. Money. You promised.'

'Just don't say I gave it to you, right, not ever. And make sure Jonathan Ainsley gives it back to you to repay me.'

The next day the vicar came. Every time there was a crisis the vicar was summoned. Gingerly Delsea negotiated the narrow stairs down to the hall. In the kitchen the left over fish and cabbage was congealing in a pan, making her feel queasy. She could hear them talking in polite whispers. Ben was on his best behaviour. She wanted to shout that she was glad she was pregnant. Why not! Glad to be having Jonathan's child. She was fed up with them arguing about the quality of her soul.

Ben entered the kitchen. 'Reverend Toy would like to speak to you.' He spoke perfect English when they had company. Left alone with the vicar she wondered what he'd say. She wasn't prepared for his outburst.

'Ainsley, I suppose?' Delsea had heard of divine inspiration, but didn't normally associate it with Reverend Toy. The vicar went on. 'When I hear voices in the church at odd times, I investigate.' So, he was in the Vestry spying! Once or twice, they'd heard a door creak, but they had convinced themselves they were imagining it.

'Are you going to tell my parents?'

'It is for you to confide in your parents.'

But what good would it do, he thought. It would make trouble for all concerned. It was he who had christened Delsea. She'd attended his Sunday school. He'd watched her grow up. He'd thought it was good that she had a friend. There was Jonathan to consider. He had a brilliant future ahead of him. Would it not be better for both to make a fresh start?

'I would advise you to have the baby adopted.'

What could she say to Reverend Toy? Silence was her defiant reply.

It was her way of showing her independence. Her way of asserting her right to decide what would happen to the child she was carrying.

Two ladies from the church came the next day to talk to her about adoption. Interposed between them on the small sofa, Delsea was resolute. No amount of preaching convinced her that she had committed a sin by conceiving a child outside of marriage.

OXFORD GOWN

The Corsham Fete had begun, and all the villagers were involved. Books had to be collected for the second-hand stall. Tents had to be erected. Those who owned vintage cars brought them along for display – the winner of the silent auction would be able to drive one of them for a day. Bales of hay were arranged in a semicircle, forming a makeshift theatre around a stage where local bands would play well into the evening. A few charities like the Wildlife Trust set up stalls. The fire brigade brought along a sparkling engine for the curious to inspect. Food tents were serving barbeque beef burgers and German sausages. There was a Pimm's tent, a beer tent and much more. There was a Tug of War between the men, then between the women, and last, bless their cotton socks, for the children. The Women's Institute, of which Lucille was a member, created themed flower arrangements in the church for quiet contemplation, and baked cakes for afternoon tea.

As Delsea helped Lucille in the tea tent, by pouring tea for a neighbour and dishing out strawberries and cream, Lady Ainsley approached her. She was about fifteen years younger than Lord Ainsley. She was wearing a large hat, which shielded the sun from her eyes. She was beautiful though austere, with pale skin and orangey lipstick.

'Well, Delsea, how is life treating you?' She hadn't expected an answer; she was throwing out an everyday greeting because Lucille was in ear shot. 'Come this way.'

They went behind the large tent. Lady Ainsley lit a cigarette and observed Delsea through a haze of smoke.

'I saw you, you know, leave the house, that night you came home with Jonathan.' Delsea made no reply. Her mind cast back to that night. She thought: 'So what? Stop beating about the bush and say your piece.'

'Whatever spell you are casting over my son, you don't fool me. If you are setting out to snare him you won't succeed.' What the fuck was she on about?

'You can put an end to your attempts to bag him. It would be a mess.' Delsea was smiling in the face of this nonsense. 'You needn't look so pleased with yourself, though he never listens to me.'

'And this is my problem why?'

'He would be a laughing stock if he had a relationship with you.'

'I have no idea what you are on about. I'm going to help my mom.' She needed time out to examine the unsubtle dig. As far as she was concerned that was the end of their talk.

Jonathan's was the only opinion Delsea cared for. He understood why she wanted to keep their baby. He of all people knew that she felt like an outcast. How she didn't even fit into her own family. Ben was perplexed by her behaviour. Her nose was always in a book. She preferred silence to music. She was too still for Lucille; too deep. Lucille, fast and efficient, fussed around her, yelling, 'move yuself chile.' Even Marcus was embarrassed by her sometimes, because she was so unpopular.

Jonathan knew all this. This and how she felt unloved, because her parents took it for granted that she could look after herself while they concentrated all their efforts on Marcus, their eighteen-year-old son. She would have a baby: someone to love, who would love her too. She wrote to Jonathan, not to tell him about the pregnancy, but to say that she wanted to see him and that it was best for her to meet him in Oxford.

It would have to be the next Monday, as Marcus didn't get paid until Friday. She had an appointment at the hospital that day, but she would go to Oxford instead. She'd already been warned about the long wait at the hospital. She would have several hours before her parents missed her. She would get the bus to Chippenham, then the train to Oxford.

Apart from annual Sunday school trips to the seaside at Weston-Super-Mare, Weymouth and Bournemouth, she had hardly left Corsham. Going to Oxford seemed like a big adventure. That was until she arrived and remembered why she was there. She didn't expect Jonathan to be happy about her news; all she hoped for was to be understood. For someone to say you are doing the right thing by keeping the baby, if that was what she wanted to do. They had chosen to meet at the Botanic Gardens. They were the oldest physic gardens in Britain. This was across the road from his college.

Jonathan longed to see her, but her letter sounded ominous. The longer he waited the more worried he became. If Delsea was coming to Oxford then something catastrophic must be up. After pacing around, he chose a bench by the fountain pond near the Danby Gate which was built in 1632. He was pleased when she eventually came into sight. He nodded by way of a greeting. She could feel the tears come into her eyes. No, she mustn't cry. Everyone had been so horrid…

He didn't mess around. 'What's up?'

'I'm pregnant.'

'Christ!' She was going to cry. Her parents, the vicar, the ladies from church had all been awful. Was it so bad? Surely to have a child was wonderful? She had thought he would understand that. Yet he was behaving like the others. He smiled shakily.

'I don't know what to say.'

'The vicar's been spying on us.'

'The vicar?'

'He asked me just like that if you were the father.'

'And what did you say?'

'I suppose I implied that you were, by not replying.'

'God!' The vicar was as thick as thieves with his mother Frederica. Jonathan couldn't imagine that the vicar would keep this from her.

'Jonathan, don't be angry with me. He just sprung it on me. He wants me to have the baby adopted.'

Jonathan began to walk at a tremendous pace. She had to run to keep up with him. Suddenly he wavered and tore at his hair. Then he turned and said, 'What do you want me to do? What the fuck do you expect me to do?' She stood there obediently waiting for him to quieten down. 'What is this place?' She tried to change the subject, to alter his mood.

'It's owned by the university. It houses thousands of rare plants – for study purposes, I suppose. What do you want to do?'

'I want to keep our baby.'

'Oh.'

'You don't sound pleased?'

'I need to think.' Jonathan walked slowly on, and Delsea followed. They had reached the river. She may have been despairing of people, but the Botanic Gardens, in all their glory even on a cold autumn day, inspired hope.

Then Jonathan began to talk of inconsequential things. 'They had to ship tons of soil in to make this place. The land was at the same level as the river, can you believe it?' An unseasonal punter struggled to control his punt. It nearly crashed into the bridge. 'I think it might be best to have it adopted.'

'It is not *it*. This is our child. You want some nice quick solution, so you can get on with your life?' A life that seemed not to include her. 'You are the only person who's ever been kind to me.'

'That's no reason to act stupid.'

He did accept that it was his fault; but why would someone who was not interested in sex have condoms? 'I'm still at college… and what about all the things you planned to do? What about your education? You need an education, Del. You need to be twice as good as everyone else just to get by. I know, take Mofe.'

'I'd rather not.' She had yet to meet this paragon of Africa. This quintessence of man.

He ignored her. 'He is way brighter, more self-assured and outgoing than I am. He applied to Uriel. That was our long-time plan, to hook back up by going to university together here. He didn't get in. He's gone to Stanford in the States.'

'If you tell me one more thing about Mofe, particularly now, I will scream.'

'I haven't got access to my money yet. How would we bring up a child?'

Now he was the one being stupid. People who didn't have access to trust funds still had children. This was it: she was most seriously pissed off with negativity, as if she couldn't have an education and a baby! 'I don't expect you to do anything.' She knew she was being nasty.

'How would that make me feel?'

She had expected tenderness; what she got was harsh words. In some ways she knew that she was being naïve by not confronting the reality, that in five months she would have a baby – a living person. She didn't even feel that pregnant. She thought of the last time that they were together, how it had felt to be in his arms, and that made her cry all the way home.

DELSEA AND JOSHUA

Josh was feeling a little better about his falling-out with Tom. It was for the best. He chewed it over and couldn't find anything that he should have said differently. Prior to this he had avoided talking about Toni after she left.

The trouble escalated after he relented and enquired after Antonia in the second term of their second year, as he knew Tom had spent a weekend with her. He knew he wasn't responsible for her dropping out but they had been good friends in the first year and it seemed only polite to ask Tom how his weekend had gone. They were twenty; that was the most he should be held accountable for. Tom took that query to mean that Josh was interested in getting involved in Toni's welfare.

Then disaster struck: Toni began to self-harm. The whole college knew about it, though her parents tried to preserve her reputation by saying it was an accident. They said that Toni had been smoking out of her bedroom window and leaned too far out, and somehow fell. But Josh, Tamsin and Tom knew she had done it on purpose. Tom kept berating Josh about it. It wasn't that Josh didn't feel sorry for her. It was that nothing he could do would change the outcome.

'How is she?' asked Josh.

'She's in rehabilitation having physical therapy. She has paraplegia but it doesn't affect the upper body and she might regain more function still. Her parents are building an extension downstairs for her. With an ensuite bathroom.'

'Look Tom, this isn't Josh's fault. We all misjudged her; none of us realised just how fragile she was. She has built this whole fantasy around loving Josh,' said Tamsin.

'How fragile she is,' Tom replied.

'She was at home with her parents. If anyone should have been looking out for her it's them,' Josh reasoned.

'It was a cry for help,' countered Tom.

'She knew jumping out of her bedroom window onto a patio could do some damage,' said Tamsin.

Josh followed through with, 'Cut her loose, Tom, and get on with your studies. She's an intelligent woman; brilliant to get in here. She knew what she was doing. Maybe she thought she would break an ankle. Sheer bad luck that she broke her back.'

Tamsin continued: 'She did it to get Josh's attention. She's obsessed with him. What was she thinking? That Josh would change his mind and have feelings for her? How would Josh getting involved help her? Him contacting her would only encourage her. She needs time away from Josh, if anything.'

'Toni is not our problem,' Josh made clear. 'We came to Ariel to do a degree, not to deal with Antonia's mental health issues.'

'We can't just ignore her. She is one of our besties.'

'*Was,* Tom. We can all ignore her, like I do,' said Josh.

'You don't give a shit, Josh. What happened last year and this doesn't even ruffle your feathers. You really are just going to carry on this year as though nothing has happened. Toni broke her back trying to get your attention.'

'Josh is not responsible for Toni breaking her back, whether she did it because she loves him or not.'

'She's a sinkhole Tom; that will swallow you up. Whatever any of us do for her will never be enough. Recognise what she's like, Tom, and get on with your degree. Otherwise, her situation will destroy you.'

'You are as cold as ice, Josh.'

'That's harsh, Tom. Josh is talking sense.'

'We can't all desert her.'

'We can. Are you really going to devote so much time to her that it continues to affect your studies? Throw away the chance a good Ariel degree will bring you? It opens doors, Tom. That's why you came here. Not to be Antonia's Good Samaritan. Someone appropriate, in the NHS, will help her. Her parents will sort it out. You don't have to be there for her. You know what? If you are going to get so absorbed in Toni's problems, don't speak to me about it. In fact, you were my best friend here and you are continually blaming me for Toni being ill. Don't ever talk to me again. I have had enough of being judged over Toni's unrequited love.'

'So,' Josh said to Delsea. 'Jonathan never wanted me?'

'I don't know, Josh. That's something you should ask him. He didn't want the hassle – that was clear. My being pregnant was a nuisance he could have done without. I suppose he was just starting out and suddenly, I was pregnant. After that day at the Botanic Gardens, I didn't see much of him.'

She remembered the metallic sliding doors, opening to reveal pale blue linoleum. There was a smell of stale disinfectant. The delivery room was virtually empty, dominated by a high bed with oxygen cylinders and an oxygen mask dangling to one side, and stirrups with a rather intrusive angle-poise lamp, which swung back from the ceiling above. There was also a small, neat table containing paediatric resuscitation equipment. In the corner was the solitary birthing ball that she'd heard so much about in antenatal clinic. It was her link to reality, as a therapy patient clings to a cushion that reminds them of home.

Her midwife was a sour-faced professional who seemed unconcerned with the individual. Her long fingernails, even when covered by gloves, portrayed her selfish inconsiderate attitude to the unnecessary pain she caused patients by scratching at their insides. She was a glamour puss who didn't belong in a maternity ward. She treated Delsea like a production line. She assessed her stage then left, convinced by superior knowledge that there were still many hours to go, leaving Delsea alone with Lucille for what seemed like hours. Surely it wasn't right for them to be alone for so long? But then Delsea didn't know what to expect…

Lucille did know what maternity care should be like. She had given birth to Marcus and Delsea in a small cottage hospital in Chippenham, where there were few patients and the midwives had time to care properly for each woman. Though that hadn't been perfect either. Every doctor and nurse from the vicinity crowded into her delivery room when Marcus was born to witness the birth of their first black baby. She had been gaped at when she was most vulnerable like an animal in a zoo.

Delsea hadn't expected wave upon wave of overwhelming pain, which intensified when her waters broke. She recalled Lucille pressing the button to summon help. The red light went unanswered. Lucille found herself scouring the corridor for a midwife, a doctor, anybody. She found a young student midwife who was all eager compassion, who informed them that Delsea was not far off delivery so it was too late for pain relief.

At the precise moment when Delsea decided that the pain was unbearable it stopped, and the sounds of the hospital filtered through. She took stock of the surroundings, and her mother. She felt so much closer to her with this shared experience. A wan fleeting smile passed her lips, before the uncontrollable urge to push overtook her. It was a boy with long, rubbery legs. Lucille handed Delsea her son. He was perfect, his lashes transparent. Delsea looked from the child to her mother, a gesture simple in itself. But Lucille saw in her daughter's eyes gratitude and in that moment, Lucille knew that she would support Delsea if she wanted to keep her child.

Delsea stayed in hospital for five days, being mistreated. She was usually missed out when the doctor made his or her round. She wanted to ask about Josh's bloodshot eyes. When she asked a nurse instead, she casually said, 'Oh, the umbilical cord must have been around his neck when he came down the birth canal,' as though this was normal. She showed a nurse her pad, as she thought she was still losing a lot of blood. She was told it was not unusual. At three days Josh had blood in his stools, but no-one seemed to care.

She was missed out when the breakfast or morning tea caterers came round. They forgot about her when the pre-ordered lunch and dinner choices were made. She ended up having what was left over after everyone else had had their own meal from the trolley.

Five days gave her time to write to Jonathan at his college, telling him that he had a son. It didn't take long for his flowers to arrive, with their scented voices, seemingly whispering messages to her. The card read 'J.' Ben and Lucille looked the other way as Delsea arranged the flowers in a vase on her locker.

'Mrs Johnson,' the nursing sister appeared at her side the next day.

Delsea corrected her: 'Miss Johnson.'

'We would prefer you to be known as Mrs. There's a young man to see you. It's after visiting hours. He can't stay long.'

Jonathan didn't wait for the sister's permission. He was already coming towards her, 'Del.' Jonathan looked indulgently at her, 'Clever girl.'

So, all was forgiven. He was no longer angry with her. 'Look at our baby, isn't he sweet?' Wrapped in the cotton cellular hospital blanket he was a pale blue bundle with grey eyes and a tiny rooting mouth. Jonathan inspected him closely. He seemed pleased to have a son.

'Mom says all babies have grey eyes at birth. They'll apparently darken. His skin will probably darken too. You can see his true colour in his tiny cuticles.'

'Thank goodness for that. For a moment you had me worried. I thought I'd done it with someone else.' Though he joked, his eyes were full of concern. 'You're looking pale.'

'I'm fine. I have so much to tell you.'

'Me too. I'm sorry I was horrid to you when you came to Oxford. What's been decided?'

'We're all putting pressure on Daddio to let me keep him at home.'

'Has he got a name?'

'Jon's son,' Delsea joked.

'He's an Ainsley.'

'That's not very realistic.'

'I like biblical names.'

'So, do I. I thought of Josh: Joshua.'

'Who succeeded Moses. Sounds good to me. Hello, Josh Ainsley.'

'That isn't very sensible you know, Jonathan. I've kept you out of it so far.'

It was nearly ten o'clock at night; way past visiting hours. Delsea was tired. Though she was glad to see Jonathan, she wished he hadn't come so late, and that he would come back at a more reasonable time. But she knew he couldn't. He couldn't risk bumping into her family. He was no doubt going straight back to Oxford. She longed to be there with him. She would love to see him in his element.

'I'd better go and let you get some rest.'

'On your way out could you have a word with that sister? Tell her I'm worried about my blood loss and the watery blood in Josh's poo.'

'Will do. I'll write.'

'No, not to my home address.' Ben would demand to see her letters.

'Write care of Marcus at his work address. Here.' She wrote the address down. Jonathan looked at her. She nodded. 'Marcus knows. I told him. I had to confide in someone, otherwise I'd go mad.'

When the morning staff came on duty, they ordered a blood test. Her haemoglobin level was very low so she had a transfusion, and they gave Josh extra vitamin K drops. Not because she'd asked for this care, but because Jonathan had.

Ben's first reaction was that he didn't want the pickney. That was until he thought clearly about the baby's life chances. His grandchild. Who would adopt Josh? How would Josh fare? The pickney wouldn't stand a chance unless he took him in. It was his responsibility. He wasn't one to curry favour. He would bring up his grandson. Lucille could mind him. He didn't want Delsea's life ruined. With the child what chance did she stand? How would she cope alone? Life was difficult enough as it was without having one hand tied behind your back. Delsea should continue her education. Go on with her life, piece things together. Then when she could. When she was set up, she could take the boy.

'Yu can keep di baby.' Delsea threw her arms round his neck. 'Let mi finish. You can keep him on two conditions. One, yu mus finish yu education.'

'I didn't think you liked me to study?'

'Not like. Chuh. It jus a mystery to mi. Mi would like fi si yu wid some surfiticket or anadda. And secondly, yu gwain promise mi neva to si dis boy again as lang as yu unda my roof?'

'Daddy I can't promise that. I love him.'

'Dat's as maybe. Wat use dat? Love gwain provide? Mi nuh si him a provide. A mi a pick up di piece dem. Face it. Him dash yu wey. If yu nuh warnt mi put yu pan street, yu do as yu told.'

Everyone was suddenly being kind to Delsea. In spite of Daddio's initial vow that "no, malata pickney, was to set foot in his house," Ben was delighted with Josh. The house blossomed with flowers. Petals fell on polished surfaces. People they knew in the village sent their regards. But Lucille was on her guard. When she had Marcus, women knocked on her door to take the baby for a walk in his pram. She had wondered whether this was normal practice in the UK. She became suspicious when the second lot came round. She took Ben's binoculars up to their front bedroom. As soon as the women thought they were clear of the house, they stripped Marcus naked to see if he was really a monkey with a tail. She trusted no one with her children after that.

Josh miraculously slept soundly in his Moses basket through all the cooing and prodding of the constant stream of family from Bath – though he made up for it at night, when he howled to be fed every two hours. Like being tortured, Delsea was startled awake every time. Her startle reflex was very much intact.

JONATHAN

Delsea had been in the top stream in her year group at senior school, with other girls the head knew would get a clutch of 'O' Levels that the school could be proud of. By fluke she had taken hers early in the November sitting, which worked out well for her pregnancy. She was pleased with her teachers in the end. As a sort of punishment for all the academic jousting they'd suffered over the period of her education they wanted her out, but being feminists, they also wanted their top pupil to succeed. They went the extra mile, throwing every subject they were capable of teaching at their opinionated scholar to shut her up and keep her busy. Even when she became anti-establishment about the history syllabus, the teacher compromised, dispensing with the usual course to teach her two different history syllabi which she approved of instead: Roman, and Economic History.

It was enrolment day at the College of Further Education in Chippenham, and the hall was crowded with fellow students jostling to collect leaflets from departments touting courses. This was a revelation to Delsea – not at all like her school. She could choose what she wanted to do. It was her nativity play and she could choose what part she played (unlike at school, where she'd played one of the three wise men perpetually).

She took a deep breath. She might as well start with Mathematics. It was her strength after all and was independent of opinion or prejudice. She would follow her strength wherever it led her. Turn everything to her advantage. She joined a queue mainly made up of boys. When that was out of the way, she wondered what else she could do. She had long ago lost interest in the arts and humanities. All she wanted to do was Maths. Wasn't statistics similar? She would keep that on the back burner and look around.

She was stumped. She could stretch her one talent from senior school as far as it would go. Which wasn't far enough. She needed at least three 'A' Levels, Jonathan had told her, to go to university. Then she spotted the careers advice desk in the corner.

'Well,' the smiley woman encouraged her to communicate. 'Mathematics and Statistics you should broaden out. This won't add much to your appeal to employers.'

'I've never been good at anything else.' Her frustrated talents and lack of direction had often resulted in low moods.

'Delsea?' The woman said, looking at the sticky label on her chest. 'What seems to have been the problem?'

'Essays. I hate writing them.'

'What school were you at before?'

'Corsham Girls School.'

'Oh, the Girls School? They don't do science there. Maybe you are a scientist. Try Physics, or Chemistry. But if you want to go on to university...' Nobody but Jonathan had ever suggested that she might be clever enough to do a degree. 'Do you think I could go to university?'

'Of course, you have eight 'O' Levels. If you work hard enough at your 'A' Levels then why not?'

'But I don't have 'O' Levels in Physics or Chemistry.'

'Through no fault of your own. You have enthusiasm. Use that. After all, that's what men do.' Another feminist; they smiled at each other.

A rough sign hanging over his desk read PHYSICS. With her short skirt, high boots and long legs, she didn't look like the other students. As she approached the desk the boys sniggered. She fitted awkwardly into the queue. Soon it was her turn. The lecturer was a greasy-looking man with a runny nose that he kept wiping on a filthy hanky.

'With all due respect, you don't have an 'O' Level in Physics.' Delsea hated it when people started sentences like that. It meant they didn't respect you at all. She could see he was thinking she wasn't the type.

'Careers suggested I do this subject.'

'This is a practical subject,' he said, looking at her legs. He might as well have added and in his opinion women weren't practical. Something made her stand up for herself. Something always did.

'Who's taking the risk, you or me?' The lecturer was genuinely shocked by her boldness. She was fast learning how shocked men were when she behaved like them.

'There are standards I have to maintain.'

'I'm banking my future on this. Don't you think that's enough to make me succeed?'

He was about to try another rejection when the two boys behind got fed up and butted in.

'Give her a break. We are not standing here forever!'

A grubby piece of paper was pushed towards her. There were thirty or so names on the list already. She'd got her way, she wondered whether she could do it. And if she couldn't, that would mean that he might not give another girl the chance in future. That was the first time she realised that she had a dual fight on her hands, both as a woman and as a black person.

She swivelled around, taking in all the subject signs hanging above the desks. She alighted on a dejected-looking man. His sign said Computer Science. 'A' level had opened up a whole new topic that she didn't know about before. There were no crowds around the lecturer's desk. She wandered over there. He engaged her, showing enthusiasm about his subject which no one else seemed interested in. There were only two names on his list. There was no prerequisite 'O' Level required either. Delsea stopped him mid-flow. The man was rather taken aback when she demanded to know whether there was any future in computing. He'd been revelling in technology for technology's sake. How secure would she be if she did this course to keep her options open? His answer was reassuring. 'Computing is the future.'

Her name down for her three chosen 'A' Levels, she sat at a large table and started to complete her registration forms. What was her country of origin? England? She disliked the phrase 'Afro-Caribbean.' She couldn't bring herself to tick that box. Afro was a hair style. What did they do with this monitoring information anyway? It seemed like pure performative allyship. Where there was pretence that something would be done to improve the lot of ethnic minorities by gathering this data. Whereas in reality nothing was done and the forms were just filed. England was her birth right. She crossed out Afro and wrote the correct word Anglo instead to correct the record. She was Anglo-Caribbean.

Lucille had had enough of babysitting by the time Delsea got home. Josh at nearly five months manipulated every waking hour.

'Yu late.'

'I had to go to the library to get my card. I missed one bus and had to wait for another. Has he been good?'

'I never see a baby miserable so.'

'Teething I think.' Josh chose this moment to demonstrate how miserable he was by bursting into tears, as if he too were complaining about her being late. He was a grisly baby. She could only think that he was unhappy. She blamed herself. She was a bad mother. But she wasn't going to admit defeat.

'Alright, little one.' Delsea picked him up and kissed him. Then bound him to her with the long scarf Lucille used as a sling. Then it was upstairs to wash the nappies in the bathroom, which had been soaking all day. Kneeling beside the bath with her sleeves rolled up, she wondered what Jonathan was doing. She wished he were here making her laugh. He could always make her laugh. There was very little to laugh about. By the time she'd finished Josh was falling asleep. She didn't want him to sleep without his feed. She filled his bath. She placed the bowl itself inside the bath, tucking him under her arm as she washed his hair, scooping the water up and over. 'Sleepy, sleepy little man.' She soaped his fat body, rinsing him off in the clear water. All ready for bed. Then she sat down to breastfeed him while watching a soap on the television with Lucille. This was the best bit of the day. Her twenty minutes of relaxation.

Laying Josh down in his cot, which took up much of the space in her bedroom, she turned to her books and sighed. She was struggling with the pace of the Physics course. She was having to do a lot of background work which she probably would have known had she done the 'O' Level beforehand. Each set 'A' Level question presented this challenge.

At ten o'clock she went downstairs to make the bottles for Lucille for the following day. Then she thought she heard Josh cry. He was giving a whimper rather than his usual lusty wail. Back in her bedroom she smiled at the back of his head bobbing up and down. He was pushing himself up. Getting stronger. Soon he would be sitting. She picked him up and breastfed him with her second breast.

Exhausted, she undressed and got into her bed, bringing Josh in besides her so that she barely had to wake for the night feed. She could just clutch him to her.

Her life was a series of demand and supply, with no time to think and very little enjoyment. She was miserable. She felt guilty because she'd wanted this baby. She was unhappy. Well on her way to getting depressed even. The more unhappy Delsea felt, the more fractious Josh became. It was a vicious circle. As she fell asleep, she thought soon he would be awake again – 'It sounds like every night is a horror story,' Jonathan was fond of saying when she found a moment to slip out to the phone box up the road and complain to him about her lack of sleep. He had catchphrases that went in and out of favour. Too right having a baby was a horror story.

They had a family conference about money. Delsea's small educational grant and the benefit she got for Josh didn't make up for Lucille's lost cleaning wage. There was an extra mouth to feed. That was when the rubber came into the house: piece work, sacks of stinking products. All weekend Delsea cut out pressed objects between looking after Josh and her homework. Things like toilet chain handles. By the end of the weekend her fingers were red raw. Ben helped sometimes. He'd sit there watching cricket, wrestling or boxing, cutting shapes out. He never complained about the stench of rubber in the house, which they all knew he was heartily sick of.

How the time dragged without Jonathan. Writing or phoning wasn't the same as seeing him. Jonathan liked writing letters, which was more than she could say for herself. He would write down his feelings interspersed with jokes, which did make her laugh. That was something. Laughter was good for her depression.

She retrieved Jonathan's latest letter from her pigeonhole. They could correspond college to college now; no more notes behind stones in walls. Wiltshire was full of handy drystone walls from which it was easy to slip a stone out to hide a message behind. She smiled to herself at that memory. Even if intercepted no one could decipher their notes but them anyway. Smiling, she started to read his latest letter. The smile froze on her face.

September

Dear Del,

This letter is not going to be funny at all. Since we can't meet up there was not much point in my being in Corsham this summer so I decided to go backpacking in Turkey. To think really and to spend some time alone. I need to decide what I want to do. I've always been interested in politics. But I'm left of right and right of left. Stuck in the middle really. You know what I'm like. I'm exploring all avenues. I took some boring books with me, recommended by my papa, I'll see if they inspire me! He won't have it that politics has changed since his ambassadorial days in Nigeria.

As I'll be moving around, I realise that it will be impossible for you to write to me. Shame. So don't bother. I shall be back early October. Then I think we should meet. Meet me in London that weekend. My parents have a flat there. Try and come. It's been months since I've seen you.

Yours ever
Jon

Now she was pissed off. For months she had been telling him she was knackered and at the first opportunity he got to help her, he buggered off with the jet set. 'Don't mind old dowdy!' she thought. 'I'll take sole responsibility for our child.' What was with the capital anyway? Did he know how expensive it would be for her to go to London, a hundred miles away? She had wished he'd be more factual. Prior to this she was beginning to think his letters silly, lots of laughs and no meaning. She was starting to feel that they had lost touch altogether with her not understanding what was happening. What the hell was he thinking?

If there was a choice between this letter and his usual witty observations, she'd take the jokes any day of the week. Could he not even pretend for one second that he loved her by adding a kiss to his adieu?

Van
September

Dear Del,

I have still not received a letter from you – I suppose you forgot to post them! It is very difficult to write with Turkish men looking over my shoulder asking me questions in German which I don't speak.

It struck me today, as it often does, that I missed your birthday party, not that I have ever been invited. But I missed the teacakes. If I post this now, which I can't, because it's Saturday, then it should reach you in time for what, I don't know. Anyway, I hope you had a good one on your birthday. Where is your present? I'll buy it one day.

Anyway, I have booked with a mountaineering company to climb Mount Ararat, where Noah's Ark is said to have come to rest after the great flood. I now have my permit. My aspiration is to acclimatise by climbing nearby Mount Artos in preparation. I want answers. Mount Ararat where the world began again seems like a good place to get them. I will start the day before with a steep climb followed by walking on ice and snow to the top. I will stay there until sunrise to demand that the sun God, Helios that is, answers me by giving an explanation for my pitiful life.

By the way this is a romantic setting, such a pity that I am not romantic, on the balcony, overlooking lake Van. I'm watching the sunset over the mountains. Which makes me miss you. I miss you. I'm now getting ready for another night on the town. Living it up big time. First, you've got to limber up by parading up and down the main street, arm in arm with another man, all men, not a female in sight! I am certainly not linking arms with anyone. Then you have to eat noisily, and quickly. Then it's next door for a glass of tea, before parading once again up and down the main street.

All good Turks end their evening by going to the cinema. I've been twice, all sex and violence without the sex, thank God.

I've bought Mama a solid gold tray studded with diamonds,

for nothing. I must dash; I expect my friends will be giving me a going away party. Remember London. I must see you. Every night here is like a horror story!

Jon

Antalya
October

I'm staying at a home for loony Turkish sailors who strut up and down reciting 'The Rime of the Ancyent Marinere,' with no understanding at all of the subtle meaning between the lines of the "water, water everywhere" stanza. I'm by the harbour looking over what the brochures call "The Turquoise Coast." Across the harbour stretch rows of Turkish fishing boats, a few sailing yachts, a dingy and not one, not two but no ferryboats to Istanbul. I haven't the foggiest how to get home.

Well, seeing as I'm stuck here, I decided to enjoy myself by taking a rowing boat and making my escape to Cyprus. I know you have never been impressed by my oarsmanship, but come on, I was eight. After an hour the sea got up and I nearly keeled over. You would have laughed and loved it.

My plans. I shall be back in London the Friday of Freshers Week. Arrange to meet me if you can, assuming your mother will babysit. I know you must be busy with Josh, but I need you too.

Jon

PS the inmates of the lunatic asylum send their best wishes too.

She was like a wounded animal without Jonathan. Her moods got very dark. She felt useless. Josh was rejecting her. Screaming at her like a reproach, totally disdainful of her mothering skills.

Lucille kept telling her to snap out of it. She would for a day or two, by internalizing things. Her mind turned in on itself, making it tough to communicate. She stopped eating. Even when Josh didn't cry all night, she found it difficult to sleep; her Circadian Rhythm was gone. She was cracking up. She took to having a sneaky nightcap, a capful of Jamaican overproof rum, to knock Josh out and to give her some alcohol-induced relief. Her body soothed; her mind stopped racing. But then she had even less energy and self-esteem to face the next day.

Sometimes, when Josh finally slept – after screaming with grief at having such a terrible mother – she'd be so wired that she sat in a corner hugging her knees and staring into space. For a change she curled up on the floor in the foetal position. She felt so alone with her problems, there was no one to share them with, except, maybe...

'Angel, are you there? Do you even exist?'

'I have always existed.'

'Well, I can't cope with my life, never mind having time to document my emotions and feelings. I am sorry to disappoint, but I just don't have the strength anymore.'

A column of light manifested in the corner to the left of her bed where she lay weeping. Straight lines of golden light flecked with miniature stars dropped in curtains to the floor. The pillar moved towards her. Gliding slowly across her carpet. She was pinned to her bed by a heavy weight. Her torso rotated to the left, then to the right and the shadow of a dove released from her rib cage, hovered, then flew out the window, white against the night sky. The column reached her bedside, turned ninety degrees, levitated above her. Concatenated at speed into her chest, her heart absorbing it whole. Filling the cavity left by the dove.

'You called for help,' the otherworldly voice said. 'Now you have the pillar of fire and the intuition of the moon.'

There was a storm outside. The wind was blowing in many directions.

'Thanks for that hallucination,' she said, falling deeply asleep. When she woke up, she felt like an Amazon; as though she could fight an entire army.

'What am I supposed to do with all this strength, Angel?'

'Withstand prejudice and write your story!'

THEOS

The summit of Mount Ararat, Turkey

Jonathan lay fully protected from the ice, waiting for the sun to rise. At last, it began. He stood up and shouted 'Helios?' Nothing, had he really expected God to talk to him. Maybe he was not addressing God correctly? 'God?' he tried again hesitantly. A force slammed him backwards into Vitruvian Man. His limbs were moving, synchronising, turning in his outreach circle up and down again. 'Fucking hell, Leonardo da Vinci, you were right about the divine connection to the universe,' he thought. His limbs were ticking round like a clock. From above he was a human clock against the pure white snow. His neck began to move his head in a continuous flowing sideways figure of eight. His limbs synchronised with his heart-beat. You only got half of it down, da Vinci. He was certain he had this experience and for whatever reason it didn't conclude. There was no head motion in the drawing. There was nothing above the head. No, it was not the number eight. Above the head was the infinity sign representing the two chambers of the heart with direction of blood flow. Leonardo, you got this far. You put nothing there for a reason. The head and the heart synchronised to approach God, but not just physically. Because nothing else was happening to him. Body, mind and spiritually. He had to think of something. He had to feel something. "These three remain: faith, hope and love. But the greatest of these is love." Feel love, the most powerful of all human emotions. Greater people than he had no doubt used the drawing to get that far. Only to be stumped at what to think! Jonathan suspected he would time out soon if he didn't come up with what to think. He guessed the clock would set to his individual time for connection to the universe and if he wasn't thinking the right thing his time would be up. End of.

He ticked away. Was it a trap? Had people been cock-a-hoop at getting that far? Think, man! God had spoken to humanity throughout human history. But the initiation of the conversation always started with God. Therefore, think nothing. Know nothing. I am nothing. Rapid eye movements the heavens span. Then an everlasting silence descended. His time had set. 'Yes,' answered the universe.

'What is the purpose of my life?'

'To effect change towards human perfection.'

'How?'

'Only you know that. God does not intercede in human decisions.'

'You are not God?'

'Archangel Uriel, keeper of beauty and light. Regent of the sun and constellations.'

'My woman?'

'You can't have her in the sense you mean.'

'Why the fuck not?'

'Now you are angry with God? You chose your path. You are one and the same.'

'I chose to be like I am?'

'For every man or woman, there are paths taken and those not taken.'

Robert Frost: "Two roads diverged in a wood, and I took the one less travelled by, and that has made all the difference." Divine inspiration!

'You have been called, as one to do God's work. That is a great honour.'

'You are not signing off with that. Fade out, why don't you! I know I am not the only person in the universe who needs you.'

'I give way to the sun. I too can burn.'

He was being burnt alive. Such intense light coming through. Too much for his poor physical human body. He needed to cool down. Jumping up, he threw off his clothes in wild abandon. He thought he was dying. That was what people did when they were dying of hypothermia. They felt hot and stripped off only to hasten their demise. But he was conscious. He was not dying. The burning intensity stopped when he could bear no more. All was calm.

'You have the power of the sun. Use it wisely.' Humbly he climbed back down the mountain to Earth, to a new understanding of himself. Above the head of Vitruvian Man should be the infinity sign. Directly above that should be naught, a continuous circle, for nothing. He wondered briefly whether his connection time was the time of his birth. It couldn't be that simple. A man-made clock has two hands; three if you count the second hand. A human has four limbs.

LONDON

'Did you go to London to meet Jonathan?' Josh asked Delsea.

'Yes. You're enjoying this. Like when you were little and I used to make up those stories. Remember the flying bed, which took you away from danger and offered you comfort, after hard-won battles?'

'Don't embarrass me.'

Dr Barlow sat at an antique desk in his surgery, scratching his head as if he'd never heard of contraception.

'What do you suggest?' Delsea asked.

He went over to the fireplace and emptied the residue from his pipe into the grate. From a tin on the mantelpiece, he retrieved a fresh supply of tobacco to refill. What he would suggest was that she was a seventeen-year-old child, with a baby, who shouldn't be continuing a relationship outside marriage. If he provided her with contraceptives, how would he face Ben and Lucille? He would be betraying them if he let her do things they disapproved of.

'I would suggest that you concentrate on your studies. There is plenty of time for all that later.'

'I have no intention of doing all that.' She just wanted to protect herself.

'Does your mother know about you asking me for help?' There was such a thing as patient confidentiality. She was the patient, not her parents.

'I am over the age of consent. I do not need my parents' permission.'

'I don't know about that.'

'OK, thanks.' She wanted to scream, and then the so-called adults measured teenage pregnancy as a mark of delinquency in the under-class. When she, a so-called child, was trying to be responsible. She couldn't get out of there fast enough. The stupid old git. Perhaps she could ask Marcus where his girlfriend got the pill.

She told Marcus, 'I asked Dr Barlow to put me on the pill and he wouldn't. He said only if Mom agreed with it. I want to go to London to see a friend at the weekend.'

'And seeing a friend means you need to be on the pill?'

'Of course not.'

'I am not lending you money to go to London for a weekend. London raatid expensive.'

'I haven't asked you for money. I have my own savings from the chicken factory holiday jobs I did.' She had worked there from the age of fourteen. The hours she could do increased with each birthday and so did the pay. It had been hard to save anything when her parents expected her to buy her own casual clothes. They provided the basics, like school uniform. The rest was up to her. Working at the chicken factory was pure cash. The factory minibus collected her from the bus stop and took her to Sutton Benger and back. There were no transport costs involved. She packed the job in when she had Josh. She hadn't intended to spend her rainy-day Building Society savings on gallivanting about after that idiot Jonathan. Yet she did.

'Not this again, Del. He doesn't care about you!'

'That's not true. He writes to me.'

'Weh demde letter? Mi si nutting drop fi yu.'

'He writes to me at college.'

'I see him in di Ainsley Arms. I tell him look raas clart, leave mi baby sista alone.'

'Did you?'

'Bumba clart, man a tek liberty wid mi sista.'

'He is not taking liberties. Can we change the subject? Where did your girlfriend get the pill?'

'Dis outta order, a weh yu a drag mi inna dis time? Yu know Mom slap him roun di head.'

'What the fuck?'

'Inna church.'

'I say it again, what the fuck?' She knew Lucille could be unstoppable, overbearing and meddlesome.

'Him neva tell yu dat. So much fi yu "GREAT" relationship. Him family arlways thirs to leav. Him dey at di back. Congregation back turn a put way neela an hym book. A collect bag an coat. She ha wan second when nobady look. One bitch lick straight acras di face.'

'What the fuck? Did I ask any of you to interfere in my business?' She wondered why he didn't come home to Corsham for the summer holidays and had gone to Turkey instead. So, this was why they were meeting in London.

'Strange business dis.'

'Now look here Mr, you a naked man, a tell mi wat to do. When yu nu whol up dem gad dam principle yuself.'

'Hey Del. You hardly ever speak Jamaican.'

'A no wander, when di marga bitch carl mi English teacher exercise she red pen pan mi much-lavish essay. Mi essay mash up. Nu stress here. Nu strain dere, stresses and strains every dam where! Den de Coup De Grace sum. Nutting nu go so. When I heard the same words, stresses and strains go so, every day of my life. So it's the Queen's BBC English which comes to the fore.'

'Huh. Yu drive a hard bargen now. Since a Jamaican arksking mi. Mi bound by di code of bredda and sista to help yu. Gwarn a Brook clinic. Si phone book. Nu get pill. Dem ha sunting carl coil. No packet, nu nutting fi sumwan to fine. Though this is getting out of hand, Del, if he's putting pressure on you? You should finish with him. Sounds like he's only after one thing.'

'I could kiss you,' and she did.

'A weh yu a kiss me fa. Yu, know Mom rule.'

They said it together, 'Afection is nat good fi black children inna dis country. Mek dem sarft when dem need be strang.' As Mom sat eating a delicious bunch of grapes in front of them, while offering them none. 'Fruit is nat good for black children inna dis country, mek dem fresh when dem need beware. Look pan yu face in mirror. Yu beautiful, nu forget dat. When facety white folk tell yu badmind bout di colour of yu skin. Tell dem yu love being black. Dem gwarn tired insult yu, when dem si yu smile, cars dey is telling yu sumting yu love.'

'You are the best brother anyone could have.' When the road wound uphill all the way, having a bredda to lift and carry you part time made all the difference. As did having a sista to love you.

After mentioning to Ben and Lucille that she wanted to go away for the weekend she was barely tolerated. They stopped being helpful. They were determined to be cruel. Determined to make her bare the full responsibility of having a child. If Josh screamed, they ignored him where usually they would pick him up.

'It's only a weekend. I'll be back Monday morning in time for college. Surely you can manage Josh for a weekend?'

'A weh yu a go?'

'London. It is an educational visit to establish the root cause of cessation in otherwise cordial international relations.' That was the truth. She was going to see her boyfriend from Nigeria to understand WTF was going on in their relationship.

'You use big words to get away wid tings, an cloud we judgment? Weh yu a stay?'

'At a friend's. We are doing this study together.'

'Which friend dis?'

'Someone from college.' Haniel College in Oxford, not the CFE she attended, so what?

'MisCam, u know bout dis?'

'A thirs mi a hear?'

They looked at her as if she was a prostitute in Montego Bay, waiting for military service boats to come in, in order to sing her bawdy, come hither song.

'A soldier man came to mash up mi life
And I kack up mi legs
I kack up mi legs.'

'Yu nat go nowhere. A lie yu a tell. Nutting nuh go so.'

'Right don't look after Josh.' She would take him with her.

She spent time making lists of everything that she needed to take. It was an intelligence agency operation to move a five-month-old baby from A to B. She managed it. She got the coach to London, as it was much cheaper than going by train. Jonathan came by taxi to meet them at Victoria station. She immediately knew that something had changed. There was no hug or kiss – not that they hugged or kissed before the night they conceived Josh.

The connection was there; he smiled, she smiled back. But he was jumpy. Something was interfering with the natural joy one experienced from touching loved ones. He did help her to unpack and found a place for all the baby paraphernalia. But he would not hold Josh himself. He was almost finding it distressing when she tried to hand him their son.

'I'm not good with babies. I might drop him.'

'I hear my brother told you to leave me alone and that my mother slapped you.'

'That was unfortunate. They have nothing to do with us.'

'So why are you jumping like I'm scalding you every time I come near?'

'Let's not get deep and meaningful or deadly serious. Let's just enjoy a lovely weekend. It is so good to see you. I'm so very fond of you and I'm glad that you are in my life.'

'And it is good to see you too.' She had the affirmation she craved that nothing essential was wrong. 'I nearly didn't come, you know. The hassle I've had.' Jonathan nodded his appreciation of that. She didn't need an answer to it anyway. She was just getting it off her chest. She didn't feel like telling him that Ben was behaving like her gaoler.

'Well, you're here now.'

'Turkey didn't sound like much fun.'

'Put it this way: I'm glad to be back.'

'So, did Helios answer your questions? I must say though that I prefer to use Roman Gods to Greek ones, because of Emperor Lucius Septimius Severus, who was from Africa. He did great work here. Britain has a lot to thank him for. What did Sol say?'

'Sol said I should figure out my own life, as long as the aim was towards human perfection.'

'Did Sol say that?'

'An angel said it.'

'These angels. You know I have an angel too. I was told about you, when I was little. Before I even met you. I'd like to sit down, and put my feet up, if I may.' It was Friday night. She had been up at 6:30 that day to feed Josh and get him ready. To finish her packing and get herself organised for college. Seven hours of studies, then to London was pretty good going! She was still glad that Josh had not been given up for adoption. This was what was best for them both. He would not be subjected to a lifetime of wondering who his natural parents were! Thinking something was missing from his identity.

'Sit down.' Jonathan said, leading her to the drawing room. His parents' flat was like something out of a magazine. 'I've been food shopping, so I'll cook.'

'I have never thought of you doing something so mundane as cooking. Far too cerebral. The portrayal of all brains and no common sense. I thought you ate in halls?'

'Does Josh eat food?'

'He is bottle fed in the day. Is it alright if I rest while he's sleeping and you make dinner?'

'Yes, I've got this.' Delsea curled up on the sofa, promptly falling asleep. Napping was easy these days.

Over dinner she told Jonathan about leaving school. 'After we broke up,' she said.

'Did we ever break up?'

'I suppose not. Anyway, I lost all interest in school. I was so bored by the curriculum that in class I just started making witty rejoinders to anything the teachers said. Which made the whole class laugh. I would be sent to the headmistress, which in fact I loved. Because she would say, "what do you want to study today Delsea?" I would look at her bookshelves and find something that interested me. One day all the girls were twittering about the head living with the domestic science teacher and whether or not they were "lesbians," when she asked what did I want to study, I couldn't help myself. I said, you know Plato, I don't quite understand what goes on in the gymnasium? Which was a reference to homosexuality, as you know.'

'You are outrageous!' Jonathan laughed. 'Let's hope she did not know what you were referring to.'

'But she did. She said: "Delsea, let's end this charade of schooling now. Even I have had enough of this behaviour. You are too clever by half. I want you out of my school. Therefore, I am putting you in for your qualifications now." So, I took my exams in November, which suited me fine, because it got rid of something that had been playing on my mind. How could I have a baby in the spring and be there for my exams in the summer?'

'Every cloud and all that.'

She was so over her schooling. Headteachers ended up being as exasperated by her as she was by being forced to stay at each stage until a certain age. They couldn't bring themselves to expel her for being too academic, but they could put her down; to know her place in society.

Primary Head: 'Talkative and silly, foolish behaviour.' Secondary Head: 'Delsea finds work comparatively easy, but the limits set by examiners must be kept.' Teachers: 'She is capable, but not quite as good as she supposes.' 'She has undoubted ability but her approach is wild.' Delsea would love to question that teacher now. She would love to know how good the teacher thought she thought she was. Her religious education teacher at secondary school was the best. Her response to Delsea's queries always started with OMG, as in 'Oh My God we are not doing Carl Jung, we are doing the Sermon on The Mount.'

As she had read out each 'O' Level result, Marcus kept shouting 'Yes!' as he punched the air and did a Kung Fu kick. When she finished, they did a war dance right there in the sitting room.

Jonathan and Delsea were at ease. They talked about everything and anything. Nothing one said shocked the other.

When she got home from London, Marcus asked: 'Have you broken it off with him?'

'Sort of.'

'Yu luv him?'

'I do. I'm not sure he is the life I want to lead though.' Having responsibility for a baby made her take stock. She wanted someone who would hug her child. She realised that she was a sensual person and she wanted to be with someone who would hug her too.

'Why yu warnt mix up wid dem. Dat family is weird. Yu man is away wid de fairy dem.'

'Away with the fairies reminds me of primary school.' There was a lot about Corsham that was away with the fairies. 'Country dancing lessons once a week, where you had to take a boy you disliked by the hand, and dance with him like a lady.'

'It was bad for gents too. I had to dance with goggle-eyed Sue, as no one else would dance with her.'

'Like some Jane Austen ball, but with children.' The Head seemed to do nothing but wander from classroom to classroom in a daze, reading mostly Edward Lear's nonsense poetry to each class. 'Wat yu mean by Jonathan being away wid de fairies?'

'He comes into the Ainsley Arms, on a Saturday night when Wadworth Old Timer is in season. Dressed in a suit. He sits in a corner with his eyes closed most of the time, waving his hands about. The rest of us look at each other and make screw loose signs.'

She laughed. 'He wears a suit when he is above thinking about what to wear. I imagine him waving his hands about must look odd. It's his penultimate study mode. You have to understand how his mind works.'

'Do I?'

'I saw him do it a few times and asked him about it. For an assignment he has to hand in. He reads things from lots of sources and when he thinks he's done enough research he starts sorting it through in his head. He finds it easier to sort when there are no distractions, so he closes his eyes. He does all those hand gestures when he's deciding to push out or pull in an article.'

'Why him nu use pen an paypa an write it down?'

'He finds that too slow. He writes it down when it is at the editing stage.'

'A si how dis work now. Yu is as mad as each adda. Yu wid yu nose glu pan page. Him a use him han to sif tings inna him head!'

'I didn't know Wadworth Old Timer was his favourite beer.'

She was starting to see that their friendship might go nowhere beyond that. Jonathan was so impractical. They had slept in separate bedrooms in London: her with Josh, him alone. That seemed to be how it worked for him. Yet she didn't know how that could work for them. Would he visit her? Should she visit him? Neither of them visited the other, as it turned out. With him in Oxford and her in Corsham, they hardly saw each other because they were both so busy. No wonder it went wrong when each connection was so amplified. They played mental tennis well. Could she base a life on that? She was frightened of having a family anyway, never mind with someone who wouldn't help her.

Despite the growing disconnect with Jonathan, she felt liberated by the new year at the CFE. She'd proved herself once by surviving the first year, and she could do it again. In fact she was finding she was getting way ahead in the syllabuses of her subjects. Just like when she was at school. The Physics lecturer – who had given her such a hard time because she wanted to do an 'A' Level in a subject that she didn't have an 'O' Level in – was impressed. 'You hide your light under a bushel,' he'd said.

The recent attitude of boys towards her was a revelation, too. Boys who had ambushed and harangued her, asked her out. She was no longer the misfit outsider but one of them. They may have changed under the influence of testosterone when forced to admit that the person they'd taken the mickey out of had blossomed into something desirable. But her memory wasn't that short. She wasn't going to let any of them divert her from her goal of getting into university.

As for loving Jonathan, she didn't know how she really felt about him. If he were to walk through the door, she'd be confused by her feelings for him. That gave her an idea that if she took her 'A' levels in November. She could squeeze in a Gap break and spend quality time with Jonathan to try to work things out.

OXFORD TOWN

When Delsea got her grades for university, she wanted to rush outside and scream 'Yes!' into the sky! Such was her delight at her own achievement. She looked forward to meeting new and interesting people, who talked of the great things they would do, and who had the answers to all questions! But she was almost derisive of their superior worldly ambitions. Was she turning into one of these people too?

Bristol University was not far from Chippenham. It was one of the reasons why she had chosen it. She could get the train straight from Chippenham to Isambard Kingdom Brunel's Bristol Temple Meads station and still spend time with Josh in the mornings and evenings. Josh was shooting up, full of tantrums. All she could do was pull him onto her lap. His colt-like legs splayed either side of her thighs. She would rock him gently from side to side while flames danced in the open fire. He felt warm and bony like a lamb; his sweet fragrance drew from her the tenderness she felt for him. Content at last, he would fall asleep sucking his thumb. Sometimes it felt as though Josh was attached to her by a piece of elastic, which he was forever pulling on and she was forever reeling back. Perhaps he needed to be stretched. Perhaps he needed Jonathan, who had disappeared into his political calling. In a way she was sad to have finished her CFE studies and to be taking on her degree. She would be leaving behind some good friends she had made there who she doubted she would ever see again.

Ben was not impressed by her wanting to do further studies. He thought it would be more sensible for her to get a job, to help out with money. He had never heard of a degree and couldn't understand why anyone would want one. She was eighteen and felt entitled to the university education she had worked so hard for. Ben blamed white people for putting useless ideas into her head. The irony was that without Jonathan, she would never have done more than one 'A' Level. Enough to rise above the factory work she'd relied upon previously in the holidays, but not enough to be accepted on a degree course. She knew it would benefit Josh and indeed her family in the long run. She didn't know then that work would involve dealing with squabbling greedy men, and negotiating the politics of envy and malice. It hadn't occured to her that the cut and thrust of her working life would be enough to give her nightmares. When starting out she never thought that ambition would lead to a crap heap.

Ben was having a hard time at work. He was just about done with the drangcrow (John Crow –> Jim Crow) workers and the banter they thought was so funny. He would snap at them, whereas when he was younger, he'd cuss them back. Lucille was concerned by the stress she saw in him and forced him to see Dr Barlow. That was an ordeal for Lucille, as Ben did not believe in doctors or tablets. The jalopy Dr Barlow thought Ben had schizophrenia. When Delsea heard this, she thought it was rubbish. Her dad was not mad; he was as sane as she was. But she agreed that his moods were fast changing. He only had to walk down some streets for someone to insult him. Then he would start drinking. Lucille couldn't make the bowsey naked Dr Barlow understand what it was like, to listen to the radio, come across newspaper stories or television programmes that suddenly belittled your race without warning.

If her dad was mad, then it was a sort of divine madness. Socrates after all had argued that madness was divine. In the eyes of some rare ignorant medical practitioners, Caribbeans didn't suffer from stress or traumatic disorders. They always had to have the most serious of psychiatric illnesses, if they were so unfortunate as to show any outward sign of strain.

Delsea decided to take a gap after sitting her exams early. She would have six weeks off to spend quality time with Josh. Then she wanted time for herself and Jonathan. She had worked so hard for her 'A' Levels, all the while caring for Josh. She felt she needed a break. Her parents were happy to have Josh, as she had done so well, and he was at a state nursery school during the day, which meant Lucille was able to do her supplementary cleaners' jobs again.

Delsea chose to spend six months in Oxford city starting from the beginning of January, with the view of seeing more of Jonathan, who was in his final year at university there. But when she got there, he seemed to have a girlfriend. Delsea was hurt and disappointed. She had bust a gut burning the midnight oil to be there for him. She decided to get some digs and stay there anyway. Uriel University had a programme of public lectures, which anyone could attend. Rather than dwell on the torture of his betrayal she immersed herself in mathematics by attending public lectures at the Mathematical Institute as a way of distracting herself. It was her old familiar way of dealing with stress.

By the time she surfaced it was May Day in Oxford. She thought before she left, she would savour this delight. She got up at 4am. Other revellers stirred too, eager to join in the May Day festivities dating back to the fifteenth century. George Street was teeming with those who had stayed up all night spilling out of the pubs, clubs and cafés. The High was heaving with tourists. Fatigued individuals from college balls still in dinner suits shielding their bloodshot eyes from the morning sun. Lightly clad girls in evening dresses tripped over hems having freed their feet from high heels, which they carried. It was a sharp elbow fight to get to Magdalen Bridge. Despite warnings not to do so, exuberant youths stripped off and flung themselves from the bridge into the shallow depths of the River Cherwell below. People cheered. Tripping over wantonly discarded champagne bottles, she found what she thought was a good spot. When the choir began to sing in angelic voices from Magdalen Tower, she could hardly hear them. The fracas and overall excited crowds were just too loud. It was an anti-climax – just like her tumultuous six months.

The delightful encaenia procession featured the most distinguished university figures, dressed in their finery, making their way to the Sheldonian Theatre, where great and good personages from the worlds of arts and science were conferred with honorary degrees.

This was followed by students in formal gowns dashing in and out of the Examination Schools on The High. They sprayed each other with champagne. She took that as her cue to go home to Josh, whom she was missing. Her gap break was up. Drawing a veil over events she realised she was free to enjoy the rest of the summer with him. She would try not to do anything academic, and give him her full attention until she was ready to start her degree course at Bristol University in September.

Her gap break had given Delsea the notion that Oxford was just the right place for her to build a life with Josh, away from Corsham, which was too small. The place was only known for one thing. It was rumoured that Charles Dickens stayed at the Hare and Hounds in the Pickwick area of Corsham. In Corsham it was impossible to be anonymous. Oxford was cosmopolitan. It was a centre of learning where people of every nationality and walk of life congregated. She looked for suitable accommodation, and came across an advert for two large rooms on the ground floor of a family house. The area was respectable. The first thing she saw was a Labour poster from the last election faded in the porch window. The family were doing up the old farm house and needed a lodger to help fund it. She looked around. There was a pretty enclosed walled courtyard off the main room where Josh could safely play. The newly refurbished downstairs bathroom would have a dual purpose as the family's cloakroom; other than that, she would practically have it to herself. The huge family kitchen she would share was homely, and had a brickwork fireplace, inside which there was an enormous gas range. It was all lovely.

The rooms themselves needed decorating, which they agreed to her doing, if she kept it neutral. She stripped faded wallpaper and hung lining paper. She hired a sander to reveal the parquet floors, which she finished off with lacquer. Then she painted both rooms white. She raided the Habitat Outlet Centre in Wallingford and bought Laura Ashley curtains. Her hopes brightened.

Weekends meant exploring the river walks of Oxford, many of which conveniently started or ended at pubs. Down through Old Marston to the Vicky Arms. From The Perch across Port Meadow to The Trout. From The Head of the River down the tow path to The Isis. Rivers featured large in Oxford. Bells tolled, boats rowed and people passed nonchalantly by. Some engaged in fascinating conversations. It was idyllic.

THE PROFESSOR

Josh had asked the question that not even Delsea understood. Why did Jonathan and Delsea split up? She tried to dodge the bullet by saying, 'Surely, I must be telling you things you remember now. You were five…?'

'I remember living in Old Headington.'

Jonathan paid Josh's school fees; the bills went straight to him and were nothing to do with her. She didn't want him to support her, she enjoyed being independent. Since The London Episode they hardly spoke, they were down to exchanging birthday or Christmas cards. To explain her lack of contact with him, when she was eighteen, she discovered something really difficult to swallow about Jonathan, that she didn't know how to process or whether there was any point in trying to understand it.

Then Jonathan appeared back in her life for the briefest, most destructive, most confusing, most infuriating moments she had ever experienced. He was coming to Oxford for a retirement dinner with an old professor of his. And he invited her. She had known him so long that the gap in proximity was immaterial. In fact, he sent her a card invite. It was strange to see her name linked with his on that tactile stationery. It reminded her of being a girl thinking it daring in case she got caught scribbling Delsea Johnson loves Jonathan Ainsley in her exercise book, then blocking it out before discovery.

Some professor was requesting the pleasure of her company. Her one-and-only time shopping for the right dress with Jonathan. Campus on The High, with its silks and taffetas, scarves and sashes flowing from a gypsy cart at the front, was a far cry from her usual haunts. It was pure hedonism. The assistant had her work cut out. She was aware as she had ventured into this shop before, that had she not been with Jonathan the sales girl would be keeping a surreptitious eye on her, certain that she would steal something. She was all politeness. On borrowed heels Delsea tottered precariously until she had tried on every dress in the shop that suited her. In these dresses, in the mirror a tall slim elegant woman stared back at her. Jonathan shook his head. He wanted emerald green. A certain sheen of silk. It was a fantasy he couldn't convey. In the end they went to Anna Belinda's to have a dress made. The dress was so beautiful that she couldn't help opening her wardrobe a dozen times just to look at it. Just to touch it. Just to hold it against her skin.

She was Jonathan's statement, 'She's beautiful and she's mine.' He was her statement, 'She would go wherever she wanted with whoever she wanted.' They were one, they had moulded each other since childhood. They made themselves into a match, as her Indian friends would say. She went to Splinter's in Mayfair to get her hair done. It was ludicrous, like Frank Churchill in Jane Austen's book going to London for a mere haircut. It was her usual hairdresser! She had got tired of Oxford Salons who thought it courteous to say they didn't do "her type of hair." Those who did "her type of hair" were not easily found in Oxford then. Not even down trendy Little Clarendon Street. It was four hours she thoroughly enjoyed each time she went. Four hours surrounded by people her colour preening and revelling in beauty.

Getting dressed with Jonathan was the sexiest thing she ever did with him. That told a lot. Moving in harmony, dressing for action. At poignant moments their eyes met, a knowing look, a secret smile. Jonathan produced emeralds but pointedly did not clasp them around her neck. These belonged to his grandmother. Hence the certain shade of emerald green. The woman in the mirror smiled back at her.

They were gathered around a dinner table with some illustrious dons and alumni. Crystal chandeliers were winking above. Jonathan gave the semblance of listening to the professor wax lyrical about the pinnacles of his career, but all the time his eyes came back to Delsea across the table from him. He wasn't the only one. No men were paying the professor the slightest bit of attention, and his ego was such that he couldn't stand to be out of the limelight for as much as a second. It was as though she had set up a rival court at the other end of the table. The professor was unforgiving of God; after all, she did not make herself. As the plates were cleared away and the waiters were placing the puddings over their shoulders, he made his move during a lull in conversation. That brief hiatus was all he needed to raise his voice to command respect, and show his supreme disapproval of those snubbing him at his own supper.

'Delsea.' All heads turned to the professor, eager to hear what he had to say as he had identified her as the cause of his displeasure. 'Has it ever struck you that you are the lowest of the low? You are black and female.' No shit, Sherlock. A deathly silence fell; a widening, slow hush. All heads turned back to her. How would she respond? She cut him with her eyes. She didn't want to flaunt her brain cells in acknowledgment of such lowdown wit. She looked at the cerebral Jonathan, who remained silent. He would not seek to defend her when he knew that she was twice as capable of defending herself. She didn't choose to be given the stage by the professor or even want to be on his stage. She was above all that. Then she had to leave as a thought entered her head. She felt compelled to hurl the Eton Mess at him, Bullingdon style. Placing her napkin on the table, she left like a missioned spirit. Poor show that she didn't challenge the professor statistically. Who cares in these cold faithless times about a momentary unpleasantness, which vanished once she'd gone!

She set off at a cracking pace. Jonathan caught up with her and handed her coat to her.

'That was in bad taste, but why did you not answer him back with one slash of your sharp wit? I saw you cut him dead with your eyes, but not your razor-sharp tongue! We would have enjoyed that pompous man being put down. It wasn't meant personally.' No shit, Freud.

'I treated those remarks with the contempt they deserved by giving them no credence at all.'

Here's something you don't know about women, Mr Know All. Even the most dominant women in the world feel helpless sometimes. Otherwise, man-woman syndrome would reign ad infinitum, each trying to dominate the other perpetually instead of being in perfect symmetry. She didn't feel like defending herself. She wouldn't give the professor that pleasure. She performed for no one but herself. Her heels buckled as she crossed the cobbles on Brasenose Lane. Her young will so powerful that not even she had learnt how to govern it. Brasenose Lane was an appropriate place for the worst argument never had. Laterally, the brass neck, the brazenness. She rounded The Radcliffe Camera and reached The Bridge of Sighs, where she stopped and heaved a sigh. Jonathan went to get the car which was round the corner in Broad Street. She marched on in overdrive with Jonathan curb crawling her towards Long Wall Street. The best dressed woman ever wearing emeralds into the night.

She was beginning to tire herself out by her own headstrong emotions that wouldn't give so she got in the car. He wanted to help her when she didn't need his help anymore.

'Are you alright?' Of course, she was not alright, crazy man who appreciates statistics at a time like that! Here was one Mr Know All could add, to the professor's duo she was a single mum, the pit of society! Instead, she thought of Rabbie Burns, and why not? "Amid this mighty fuss let me mention. The Rights of Women merit attention." She stopped her linkage there before her brain disappeared down some unreasonable avenue. Back at Laurel Farm it was really late. Her babysitter wondered where on earth she was. The young girl had her coat on waiting in the hall to hear her key turn in the lock. She broke into an unconscious grin when she saw Delsea. Then she was curious as she opened the door wider. She'd never seen her with a man before. Delsea turned back to Jonathan. 'Would you mind giving the babysitter a lift home.' See you sometime, never!

He had gone. She calmed down. She needed to remove the turmoil from her head. She went to her dresser where she kept her kitchenware and threw the crockery at the wall, in lieu of flinging the Eton Mess at the professor. Then her life with Jonathan flashed backwards before her. Jonathan's silence. The London Episode, The Birth of Josh, The Botanic Gardens, Aldbourne Court, St Bartholomew's, The Lake, and last but not least, the Boat. Not forgetting the stupid Folly by the stables behind which they hid.

She stopped the physical destruction of inanimate objects and turned her anger outwards to thin air. Her love for Jonathan was totally unfeasible. Never mind the 'professor of ignorance.' She had Jonathan's mind and spirit. She could have taken the urge in the car to let out a torrent of emotional invective so devasting, so cruel, to hit him where it hurts like a femme fatal and then turned round and said; 'that was theoretical, why are you cast down, why are you so low, the lowest of the fucking low.' That was deadly serious. On top of what she had learnt about him three years ago, she vowed not to have anything further to do with him.

On the Monday she found a bouquet of flowers outside her door. The note said "I would like to apologise for causing offence." It was from the professor. She put them in the bin. Then took them out to the compost heap in the garden. She didn't want them in her bin. She didn't want to breathe in their perfumed air. They were foul, just like the professor. She didn't think for one moment he was sorry. This was Jonathan's doing. Did the professor think she would complain to the university? She wouldn't waste her breath on that man.

Josh was still thinking about the unhappy reality of his Ariel University experience. Tom had promulgated widely that Josh was responsible for Toni's situation. Encouraging friends that they'd made together to exclude and not talk to him. Many of those Josh was acquainted with in their wider circle of Jehovah College began avoiding him. It was horrible to be the centre of untrue gossip.

Tamsin and Josh were queuing to go into formals in their garb when Tom came up to them and told them that Toni had taken an overdose. Even though they weren't speaking to him and Josh had told him not to speak to them either.

'Not enough to kill herself though, what a surprise. I advised you to walk away; that she was a bottomless pit. She is loving the attention you are giving her. She is a drama queen, trying to get at all of us through you. You know what? I don't care. Why are you telling me and Tamsin this? She is a girl we knew for two terms. On that basis, I have to have her around my neck as a millstone for the rest of my life. Get real, Tom, sleeping around is part of the university experience. I mean, do you have something going with her that you haven't told us about?'

'She is just a friend.'

'Well, stop fussing. She isn't being friendly to you. Friends don't manipulate each other like this to keep your attention and in doing so get my attention through you acting as a go between.'

'Are you saying we can't care about people we are not in a relationship with? Because that stinks, Josh.'

'I don't give a shit; we're young. It's not our problem. Actually, I'm glad she took an overdose, maybe the hospital has referred her to mental health services. She doesn't need your sympathy, or empathy, or her parents covering up her needs and pretending that nothing is wrong with her! No doubt you told her about me and Merin and this is her response. Pathetic. I don't want to hear any more about her. I have already told you that. Drop it, drop her. She messed up our friendship and we can't come back from that, not after all the stuff said and done.'

'It is bound to be more complicated than you think, Tom. It is probably dawning on her that she's messed up her life, and it's nothing to do with her delusions about Josh, so please stop talking to him about Antonia,' placated Tamsin.

'Where do you get your morals from, Josh, some Jamaican yardie spreading his seed without any consequences, who dumped you at birth only for some millionaire to adopt you as some sort of pet project to signal to the world how magnanimous he is?'

'Fuck off, Tom,' said Tamsin. 'That was brutal and uncalled for. Where do you get your kindness from, Harrow?'

Josh was hitting his palm against his forehead in anguish. He felt trapped at Jehovah. A sitting duck for Tom's harassment. Yet he had to stick it out.

THE WALDORF HOTEL

Delsea recalled how she met Michael. She was not destined to marry her polar opposite, Jonathan. She knew someone important was coming into her life, she saw white feathers everywhere. They were a trail she followed leading her to the Waldorf Hotel. She took it as a sign from her angel. They were saying this path will take you to 'peace of mind.' That was where she first saw Michael, who was in London on business. She did occasionally foray onto Jonathan's stomping ground, but she hadn't glimpsed him there. The Parliamentary IT Select Committee PITCOM had met at the House of Commons with lunch afterwards in the House of Lords. Later she checked into the hotel. She walked into the lounge and Michael was playing the grand piano with such passion that she was immediately arrested on her way to the bar. He was playing like a man possessed. She was rooted to the spot, but then the fast flicking, action of his wrist as he turned the pages of sheet music became a distraction to the enjoyment of watching him play. So, she went up to him and found that she could read the notes on the page though she had never studied music theory, it was intuitive, like reading mathematical equations. So, she began to turn the pages for him and afterwards he took her to dinner then bed. They had lots of stamina back then. They made rapturous love and stayed in bed for three solid days with Do Not Disturb on the door, intermittently interrupted by the arrival of meals from room service.

Eurofone held an annual banquet at a hotel in Lancaster Gate, London around Christmas time. It was a huge extravagant affair. Staff were bused in from Newbury. Before dinner they stood around in their finest clothes eating an assortment of brightly coloured canapés. It was shocking how her IT lads transformed themselves into peacocks. Guys whose attempt at daily smartness involved crumpled suits worn repeatedly.

It was not unusual for her to find on entering the Systems Development department of a morning men who were so into their computer programming that they crashed right there in sleeping bags under their desks. Un-ironed shirts de rigueur, ties in drawer of your desk of course not round necks, don't be ridiculous! They were hastily put on, sort of, thrown over shoulders or knots kept loose, when the CEO walked in.

They were young, in their twenties and thirties, starving hungry all the time, which led one poor man in desperation to write 'The Dinner Lady' on a white board only for the world to join in. How many languages could they write 'The Dinner Lady' in? Every language under the sun. When the dinner lady arrived with her trolley of food, they hoovered it in one go, saying, 'Get in my belly.' Linguistic pleasures faded as Mah-jong tables formed.

She mustn't digress. The magnificent dinner was like being in a Bond movie, everyone wearing immaculate dinner suits, and evening dresses, all of them on their best behaviour. There were snake charmers, and card tricksters laid on to weave between them providing entertainment. Passing waiters distributed champagne. Everyone was in high spirits. It had been another unprecedented successful year for mobile phone telecommunications and they had all received substantial bonuses. Her surveillance of the scene came to a stop on Michael. 'Fuck Me,' unliterally she thought because they had already done that and had had three dates since, the Waldorf Hotel. It was early days in their relationship and not at all serious. She guessed that he was on the CEO's table, along with a couple of other Eurofone Service Providers who no doubt Harold Parker was trying to butter up to put more business his way.

Her feelings for Michael of late kept shifting around. He endeared himself to her in so many ways. Their relationship was at the stage where they were still discovering things about each other. Michael was gorgeous. She observed him from a distance. The jet-black hair, longish, swept back by hand with the occasional strand falling over his forehead. The chiselled features and aquiline nose. The quizzical eyebrows, the sensual lips. The intellectual dark blue eyes. The wide shoulders, the thick wrists with Rolex divers, watch. She couldn't see the make of the watch, that was from his bedside table. He was tall, dark and handsome. She needed to stop the admiration there. He knew he was being watched, their eyes met. He smiled and gave her the once over, clearly approving of her evening dress. She sent him a visual caress. She couldn't stop looking at him. It was seeing him so unexpectedly. The external environment shrank to them. All other thoughts banished until it was just the two of them.

Were her feelings for him close to love? She had vowed never to fall to bits over a man again. She had done that once and look how that had ended. Thank God the connection with Michael was broken by a Scottish pipe band piping the banquet in. Over one thousand people sat down to feast.

After dinner a big band struck up. Of course, Michael claimed her. That was quite funny. As he came towards their table where they were chilling and chatting after a heavy meal, Lisa the most beautiful blonde was ready to stand up thinking he was coming to fetch her. He grabbed Delsea's hand mid-sentence, almost dragging her onto the dancefloor to dance to, "Pennsylvania 6-5000."

'You look stunning. I have never seen you look so beautiful as with these luminous lights bouncing off you.'

'And I am not even wearing red,' she laughed. She was relaxing, enjoying herself with him. The music was slow, it didn't jar too badly with her mind, which kept musing on Fermat's Last Theorem which had just been proved. She couldn't get the solution out of her head. The dance steps seemed to be in towards Michael and out again. She followed his lead as best she could. They attracted attention when she put her arms around his neck, for a slower number, from those who thought she was getting above her station by canoodling with him on the dance floor. They were not to know she was dancing with her boyfriend.

'I've booked a suite here as a surprise.'

'I can't stay with you. I need to get home.'

'But you can stay a while. If you don't go back on the coach to Newbury and drive home from there. Get the train direct to Oxford and taxi home.' They caught the lift to his suite. She couldn't tear her eyes from his and neither could he from hers. As soon as they were inside his door, she undid his tie and unbuttoned his shirt so that she could feel the hard muscle of his chest. He put his arms around her waist while they kissed. There was no stopping even if she'd wanted to. 'Be nice to me,' he said. For her their relationship had gone way beyond being nice. His hands were wandering up her sleek stockings, where warmth awaited him. Momentarily, he scrunched her underwear, feeling the rich material. Unzipping his fly, he lifted her effortlessly. She clasped her fingers around his neck. Then he lowered her, entering cautiously at first. Then it got wild and out of control. Pressing her back into the wall. She came almost immediately, but still felt the pangs of pleasure. She clutched him till her orgasm subsided. It didn't take long for the wave of excitement to course through her again.

On the tube she was pressed against him, by the Saturday night revellers, an encounter neither of them sought to avoid. Snippets of conversation hung in the air, the thread of which could only be linked by the participants who broke off as the doors opened and closed, prolonging the pauses to allow the jostling and resettling of newcomers.

At Paddington she boarded her train and lowered the window.

'Del, I want you forever.' The train started pulling away. More urgently, 'Throw me your car keys.' She found them in time and threw them out of the window.

'Take care she shouted. See you tomorrow.' Michael had taken the train from Newbury where he lived. He would collect and return her car.

Michael thought in two short hours she'd bowled him over. He chuckled to himself, a man only needs one woman in his life, if that woman was Del. His desire for her was insatiable. Though at times her intellectual brinkmanship could be cutting. But when she looked at him in that mischievous way, he couldn't help wanting more.

Michael phoned, to invite her to sail on his company yacht to Cowes, on the Isle of Wight.

'I'm not sure.'

'Not sure about what?'

'Us.'

'You don't have to be sure, just go with the flow.'

'I am not doing that. I did that once, never again.'

'I take it you did it once and it was a disaster.'

'You could say that, it was the boy next door who I'd practically known all my life.'

'We all have the boy or girl next door relationship.' The usual sort of thing where one of you lives in a three bedroomed cottage owned by the council and the other a stately home. Where one of you gives birth to a child and the other…what…

'I have a son by him. I'm not messing around for love or money.'

'I want you.'

'I don't understand what that means? OK, Cowes it is,' she reluctantly said.

God, it seemed so long to Delsea since Michael went away to that conference. But it had only been three days.

'Hi, how's it going?' she asked Michael.

'I was up at five this morning doing prep for my presentation. Then there are breakout groups to attend, and panels that I have to participate in. I better get on with my work.'

'You love it really.'

'Like a hole in the head. For light relief I can attend a talk by an expert speaker on key strategic operational issues affecting the industry. Should I want a coffee, or God forbid some lunch, then I have to face myriad exhibition stalls trying to sell me almost everything, while avoiding other delegates who I don't want to speak to.'

'The exhibitors pay to exhibit, and it is not fair on them if the big guns don't walk round, as encouraged by the conference organisers. This is more to do with you being self-contained and not liking to be on show. Just find a corner and roll a joint.'

'I wish. So now you are encouraging me to take drugs?'

'For medicinal purposes, a bout of social arrogance, why not? Well, I'm having a wonderful time. I get pretty fed up when you aren't here, having to deal with everything by myself. I am supposed to be writing my dissertation.'

'I told you not to do that MBA.'

'That's good, you are *so* supportive of my ambitions.'

Delsea needed an MBA to help her structure her blinking notes. She had been keeping them for years. Some were as small as postage stamps. Some impossible to decipher, written when dropping off to sleep or grappling to wake. Some were written by a mad woman distressed by love, sympathy, grief, fear or anger.

'I am supportive, but you don't need an MBA. You take on study to exercise your mind where others would do a crossword or Sudoku. How's Amy?'

'She has a new phrase: "Not fair." She says it to everything I tell her to do.'

'And Josh?'

'Don't ask. He's searching for his identity. Making me drag up all this Jonathan stuff.'

'I'll be back tomorrow evening.'

'What are you doing tonight?'

'There's the farewell dinner, dinner jackets and all that...'

Delsea thought to ask about Sylvie. Having spent her career in the mobile phone sector, she knew her reputation. She knew she shouldn't go there, but she was not having it. If a man were to behave like Sylvie towards women there would be complaints galore, and he would be arrested for sexual assault or even rape. But no, what was wrong with these intelligent guys and Michael in particular? There was a time for gentlemanly behaviour, but there was also a time when you have to say 'fuck off.'

As a senior manager in the male-dominated early days of mobile telecommunications, Delsea had men complaining to her about women following them around. If they went to the coffee machine, she was there; if they went to the printer she was there, if they went to the canteen, she sat next to them. No matter where they went, even the gents, she would stalk outside the door, hoping for something more! They would come to her office and tell her they were sick of it. She would say: 'I am your female boss, not your mother, or sister, or partner, or friend who feels obliged to listen. STOP COMING TO MY OFFICE TO TELL ME STUFF THAT YOU DON'T WANT ME TO DO ANYTHING ABOUT!' At which one or two burst into tears.

'And after dinner?' Delsea asked.

'Escaping the conference by hitting the city again.'

'What, with Ted? What about Sylvie?' 'Probably gone off to pester someone else.' So, she *had* been pestering him! It wasn't just Michael who she harassed; there was a type of man she tried to hook, the millionaire sort of course, and a conference was good hunting ground. There was usually not a wife or partner around.

'I'm sick of this on your behalf.'

'You can't be sick of something on someone else's behalf!'

'I can. After all, I am in your company, in both senses of the word. I am the company secretary as far as Companies House, or signing off your accounts go. I shall use the grievance procedure to raise a formal complaint to the CEO: you. About you not telling Sylvie to fuck off, which has to be investigated and replied to within five working days.'

'You're different, but that's why I love you. Then I shall ask you to sign a Confidentiality Agreement with a gagging clause to never ask me about Sylvie again!'

'That is plain playing dirty. Look, seriously, a work conference constitutes the workplace. This is sexual harassment in the workplace. If she wants a millionaire husband, why doesn't she do the graft? Find a man with potential like the rest of us, and help him to become that millionaire.'

'Was it not you ten minutes ago who said I wasn't supporting your ambitions? What you just said undermines my business acumen.'

'You were twenty-two when we met. Just a kid.'

'A kid who had made his first millions. You were of no great age yourself, twenty-four. Technically did we not meet at the Waldorf Hotel, while on business? Was that workplace harassment?'

'If you are harassing each other, then that isn't harassment. Neither of us said no, or objected.'

'What is it then?'

'Boy meets girl.'

'You women just make up the harassment rules as you go along. I can look after myself. It is my job to look after you and the children, not the other way around. Maybe I don't make a fuss about Sylvie. Who knows what another human being will do if totally cornered? She strikes me as someone who keeps going out on the same limb. One day that limb will weaken and break and I don't want to be in her vicinity when that happens. She is not dragging me down with her. I have worked too hard to let that happen.'

'Bravo, "Speech." You can speak to me when you want to. I knew there was a reason I love and married you. You are very wise and perceptive, an old soul, my toy boy.'

CELLSTAR

'Just a quick call, Del to say I'm at Heathrow. I'll be home in about an hour. Okay. Bye.'

With Michael back, Westmead, would spring into life: music, radio, landline and mobiles would drown out the silence Delsea loved. It was like he brought the world with him. Her sojourn was over but she was glad. She hated it when he was away on business.

At Eurofone she'd had a wonderful opportunity in the competitive world of mobile telecommunications. She was good at what she did, had worked really hard and was proud of her achievements there. But she had been there quite a while. She wanted a new experience while staying within the sector. She thought of starting her own company, but that felt somehow defeatist.

She received a call from a head-hunter.

'Is that Delsea Johnson?'

'Yes, indeed,' she said tentatively.

'My name is Nicola Major from Goodman Executives. Is this a good time to talk?'

'Yes…'

'Can I sound you out about a position we're looking to fill? Head of Information Systems.' Nicola mentioned Cellstar. For a moment Delsea wondered if it were yet another headhunting agency looking to fulfil its quota of having interviewed a woman and someone from an ethnic minority. With her they could kill two birds with one stone.

She knew how the old boys network worked. Telecommunications were notoriously incestuous. Good jobs weren't advertised. People were handpicked. She had gone to the London offices of the head-hunter. The brass plaque of Goodman Executives confirmed she was at the right address. She rang the doorbell and leaned into the door-well as the rain was crashing down.

The atmosphere of the interview was relaxed. She signed the non-disclosure agreement. Then was told that Cellstar were working on a secret project called Liberty to bring mobile telecoms to the masses. The phones at this stage were basically used by business people and "loads of money" yuppies due to their enormous expense. Cellstar had teamed up with a Japanese company, who were going to make affordable handsets as fashion accessories. They also envisaged designing future technology, bringing cutting-edge products born out of the convergence of IT, telecommunication and TV to the marketplace. Delsea delivered her careful, passionate analysis of where she saw herself fitting in, and why she was the right person for the position.

She got the job on her own merits. No Ted giving her a leg up. She had put herself there. She smiled as she sat in her blue suede executive chair behind her dark oak directorial desk. She had all the outward trappings of success. This is what she could achieve. This was what she *had* achieved. She was at the peak of her IT career and had reached the height of her aspirations. Climbed the proverbial mountain. She was eager to be in action. For a few moments imposter syndrome plagued her. She had the job, could she, do it?

It was a tough challenge. Cellstar had craftily tied the Japanese handsets to their network so that no other provider could benefit from their innovation. The biggest challenge came in the form of the MD, Andrew Barrington, who had declared that a customer should be able to walk into a shop, buy the phone and walk out again with it working within seven minutes. Dare she say that was the limit of his attention span when he wanted something done. All very well Andrew Barrington, who had even pre-booked radio and TV announcement slots to launch the venture starting with the BBC Morning programme on a certain day. It was IT and Engineering who had to bust a gut to make it happen. She remembered that it was 2am the morning of the announcement that they finally got that seamless transaction through. They had an IT guy and an engineer in the retail outlet with Andrew, engineers on standby in the flash, highly technical network management centre and her exhausted

IT guys who looked like they had been to hell and back, at base in Slough all ready to demonstrate the solution. Thanks for that, Andrew. She wondered whether he ever knew how close they came to failing. Her imposter fears were groundless though, because they did it. All of them. The Liberty Champions, and she was one of them.

Men put her achievements down to being spoilt. They saw the solitaire diamond engagement ring and clocked that by the size of it, it was worth many thousands. They noticed the Cartier watch; the expensive work clothing brands – Aquascutum, Burberry – and assumed that a rich man was backing her. That must be how she got where she was.

Spoilt by being singled out, and subjected to cruel jokes, like the Post-It note stuck over her name on her office door that she removed every morning, saying TBA, To Be Appointed. Hurtful acts like putting a cross through the photo of Michael on her desk. 'We say no to mixed relationships.'

There were stereotypical assumptions. Like the finance director calling her to his office because he didn't like the hotels she stayed in for business. He said: 'Being away on business was not an opportunity to stay in accommodation better than you have at home!' He had no idea where she lived, or what her home was like! No four-star hotel even touched the luxury of her country house Westmead. After that she was only allowed to stay in three-star budget hotels.

There were slurs on her character, like 'she never says hello when she walks past my desk,' 'she doesn't care about us,' 'she snaps her fingers and expects things to be done instantly.' HR questioned her about these allegations. She couldn't imagine senior male managers being questioned as to whether they cared for their staff personally or whether they would stop to say an individual hello or goodbye to one hundred staff as they went to-and-fro in the mornings and evenings.

One of her programmers came to tell her that a colleague had said to him that, 'matters had come to a sorry end because they reported to her.' The double whammy. Without alluding to the obvious "matters." The stratified class system had been breached. The dilemma of putting her down using unbiased words. The covert acceptable face of misogynoir.

Some staff in other departments couldn't contain their resentment. IT was an expensive resource and there was jealousy about how much she must be earning as head of that department. Her racing green BMW 520i company car made them green too – with envy. They resented her lifestyle. If she was spoilt then she had spoilt herself.

Some women said she was lucky to have such a good-looking man. Picking up the photo of Michael from her desk they'd say, 'I'd shag him any day of the week.' Please put down the photo of my husband and get out of my office, you brazen hussy…

The prestige of her job was down to luck. Lucky, she thought – being brought up in almost total isolation without any other children from ethnic minorities around. No constant playmates except Marcus and of course Jonathan. If she was lucky then she'd made her own luck.

She was in the leafy atrium saying goodbye to a supplier when a gob of spit landed on her pastel green court shoe. The lovely leather tassels sullied. She glanced up to the balcony above only to see a grey suit dart backwards out of view. She continued to impress on the supplier that she was interested in the fact that they could offer the same quality office desktops and printers, but at a much lower price. Fleetingly the supplier tried to expand the brief as to whether this equipment would also be needed by the engineering department. When the supplier finally left, she went to the ladies and held the toe of her shoe under the hot tap. She was lucky that the spittle did not land on her head, at which it was undoubtedly aimed.

Things went downhill fast from there. Bob, who was responsible for service management, demanded that she swap offices with him, so he could have hers, which was next to the IT Director. He equated the position of her office to status. In his eyes he was more important than her. Though the development of systems which she oversaw was hugely important. Technical industries would get nowhere fast without their developers.

For the sake of peace and goodwill towards men, she changed workrooms with him. She knew his problem was in his head. A person of colour can make some feel belittled by their presence alone. Leaving them feeling sick and shaking with exaggerated xenophobia. She made the move but took her furniture that she had personally chosen with her. The layout of her work space therefore was still more prestigious than his. She had better taste. He was miffed even though he got what he wanted. He said he didn't expect her to take her furniture but to make do with his.

The Friday of the spit. The "Fat Boys," as they were known throughout the organisation. Two heavies with enormous beer bellies, who thought they owned the company because they played golf and were mates with the MD, appeared in her office. One was never seen without the other, like Tweedledee and Tweedledum. They had kept out of her way while her team delivered Liberty. They had needed her to manage that. She was of no further use to the company at all.

'Who employed the likes of you?' "The likes." The nimble detour enroute to avoiding offence while being offensive. Again, the covert acceptable face of misogynoir.

'We are going to put in a complaint against you. Your feet won't touch the ground, you'll be booted out of here so fast…'

The Saturday of the spit, an older woman Delsea had been friends with at the Water Authority was retiring. The woman was a long serving member of staff; she had never moved on. Her retirement party was being held at Headington Hill Hall in Oxford. Delsea accepted the invite for herself plus one. Other staff she used to work with would be there. It would be a bit of a reunion.

Michael agreed to accompany her, and to be her driver, though he didn't know anyone and disliked these sorts of gatherings, with people standing around under bright lights talking and drinking. Without music and a smattering of cocaine it wasn't a festivity as far as he was concerned. It didn't bother Delsea that within five minutes of them being there he wandered off. They often separated at parties, regaling each other afterwards with snippets of anecdotes. She guessed he would look around the premises, he loved old buildings. This one was built in 1824.

As soon as Michael vacated her side the woman's husband, seeing her standing alone, headed in her direction. He was a professor at Uriel University. She knew to be on her guard for academic trivial pursuits. Immediately he launched into the most unexpected conversation.

'My wife told me about that office fuction where you all had to dress in black.' A mock funeral. The ancient mainframe computer was being replaced with state-of-the-art equipment. 'She, said you said you would go nude as you are black! Ha ha.' Raas clart, a likely story. Where to start with this one. That his wife discussed and anticipated her as a young twentysomething woman being naked. That she involved her husband in this sexual fantasy. That he held that in his head for many years on the off chance of seeing her and telling her about it! That gave a whole other meaning to academic nudity, which was appearing in public without your cap and gown. He was a bowsey naked man.

He was an archaeologist, so was the white lecturer she had a brief relationship with back home. He kept piles of The Geographic by his bedside in order to wank off to half-naked indigenous women. She tried to draw the Professor on a subject other than her nakedness, which they both might be interested in. Cheddar Man. Britain's oldest, dating back ten thousand years, complete male skeleton found in Cheddar Gorge. Recent DNA analysis showed that he was Western European and black. Meaning black people did not arrive in Britain on "Banana Boats," they were here in the Mesolithic period.

Was it misfortune that she had come across another impertinent Uriel professor who on seeing a black woman, chose to degrade and sexually harass her? What the fuck?

It was just as well Michael wasn't near her. She had no doubt at all that he would have punched his lights out and not cared whether he got arrested defending his wife's honour. Feeling as though she were being stripped naked by the husband's eyes, she decided to move on.

'Excuse me, I see a friend I have been meaning to catch up with for some time.' Thank goodness for the small mercy of Michael's absence. She wouldn't dwell on this encounter. Life was too short to react to every fool who strayed into her path.

Every one of these people had a gate keeper, who protected them from reproach, and who they hid behind to avoid being admonished. This black friend or family member was one of them, therefore they couldn't be rebuked regarding bigotry. If they did not have an individual as their gate keeper, they supported a charity which mainly benefitted black people and hid behind giving money to that cause. If they were high profile and rich enough for the remarks to cause a stir, they could demonstrate generosity of spirit by jetting to Africa and being photographed with some black children like a saviour.

Speaking of Africa and other continents where people of colour lived, if there was strife the media had no problems filming the dead bodies of brown or black people for the world to see. Their bodies held no dignity and they afforded them none. Whatever debasement had been wrought upon those people it could be filmed in full. To show the backwardness of the situation that had brought about death and destruction. Since WWII, dead white people were rarely filmed. Those corpses were holier than thou. This falsely propagated the myth that there had been no wars in western countries since then. Emphasising how civil, safe and enlightened the West was. As though Clark's Chart of the World, was still in use.

Delsea thought a lot about mixed relationships. On the surface of it some couple's parents and family accepted their loved one's choice to enter a mixed relationship, but often they rejected the offspring. When their minds could not control their heart and withhold love from the child, they took their resentment out on others of the same nationality as the hated interloper.

All this she saw because she was one of them and increasingly people of colour were branching out in all areas of work and life. But she was heartily fed up with the encumbrance of discrimination and harassment. She wanted to be free from all that. Things for her were going way too amiss.

When Michael materialised from his unauthorised tour of the mansion, she was ready to leave.

'You know what,' she said. 'I'm ready to have these babies you so badly want.' Which meant he had to break the speed limit on the Oxford ring road, in the purple McLaren – as if the car wasn't conspicuous enough to attract police attention – in order to get home and knock her up fast, just in case she changed her mind.

'Shouldn't Michael be back by now?' Delsea thought, looking at the clock. Then she heard his car on the drive. As her mother always said if you think or speak of someone and they suddenly appear, it means they are going to live a very long life. She heard the sound of his shoes on the gravel. She was happy he was home.

They settled in for the evening. Delsea kissed Michael passionately. The house was quiet, Amy was sleeping. Amy had changed their relationship by crying at inopportune moments and wanting to be in their bed all the time. It became Amy's sleeping so that was their chance. Everything started to revolve around her and not them. They seemed to be getting back to them at long last. He led her to their bedroom. It was a delightful evening. Calm and warm outside. Standing naked in the moonlight he said she was his muse, without going any further as to what inspiration she gave him. Which was typical of his one-liners. The rest of that sentence was in his mind for his pleasure only.

Playfully she shoved him backwards onto the bed, kissing him with anxious lips. She knelt up on top of him. He reached for her breasts. In the amorous darkness she placed him inside her then interwove her fingers through his. When Michael came, she lay down, squashing herself against him. Flushed with love, they held each other tight. She looked deep into his dancing blue eyes. He looked at her with such tenderness. She knew he loved her with an all-encompassing protective attachment. She enjoyed the security he gave her.

MICHAEL

A couple of days later, just before bedtime, Josh came to Delsea and said, 'Sorry if I upset you Mum, by dragging all this up over the summer. I know you said you'd support anything I wanted to do, regarding Jonathan, but you don't always say when your feelings are trampled.'

She was worried about Josh meeting Jonathan. But she was aware that she was being over-protective. Perhaps she should leave them to it. Josh was an adult. There was a time when she looked for Jonathan's familiar gestures in Josh as he grew. 'I was hurt by your father when he seemed to concur with the ridiculous idea that it is acceptable to use the cloak of academia to insult and belittle others. Most people see straight through such artifice. Which of course I did. But we were in an academic setting. Which made it easy for this professor to cover up the jealousy that was behind his comments. He made out it was a spur of the moment clever observation.'

'What did he say?'

'That I was the lowest of the low, because I was a woman and black.'

'And Jonathan went along with that?'

'Not exactly, but he wasn't helpful.'

'Was that the last time you saw him?'

'When are you going to stop asking me questions? I've told you all there is to tell from me. I was blind then. I couldn't see beyond the fact that I loved him. It is over to Jonathan now.' She thought love could do things then, change the world for the better. She was still waiting on that.

'What is going on with you and Merin?'

'She accused me of being ignorant about my race and culture. Said I was a middle-class boy who didn't know the colour of his own skin. Because I don't read the right books, see the right films, listen to the right music.' Josh was mesmerised by Merin. There was a freshness to her. Sometimes he felt only half awake in comparison to her with all her causes and demonstrations. She made him feel lightweight, empty, as if he had swallowed a drug and she was the antidote he needed.

Delsea didn't trust herself to reply. SHE CAN FUCK OFF, she thought. Who was Merin to judge others? She wished Josh would have nothing to do with her and her projection of her low self-esteem onto him. Plenty of women would love Josh, just as he was. She may be his mother and she was aware that parents think their children are the most beauteous kids ever seen. But still Josh was tall, classic looking, male model material who could grace the cover of any magazine, with his soft brown curls and liquid brown eyes. Being half English and half Caribbean worked well for him. He was a marvellous combination in terms of beauty and temperament. Josh not sufficient for her, she was not good enough for him. Josh knew she disliked Merin. She didn't like the way she knocked the confidence out of him, and pulled him down. Anything she said would be attributed to that dislike.

They continued talking for a long time in low concerned voices, on the top step of the stairs. Michael was already snoring. Eventually Delsea said, 'It's late,' closing down further discussion. She wanted to go and be cuddled by Michael to erase Merin and her damaging opinions from her head. Why couldn't people just live and let live.

The evening with the professor was not the last time she saw Jonathan. She was going out with Michael. He was like the sea; he lured her in. She had to be careful that she didn't get out of her depth too quickly. She would wake with the creeping dawn. Thinking that she was at home in Old Headington until she noticed the unfamiliar objects surrounding her. Testifying that she was at Michael's and was increasingly spending a lot of time there. When he was out it felt strange wandering around his house seeing how a millionaire lived. Wherever she went his housekeeper followed, showering her with inane babble. In his dressing room his shirts hung stiff, professionally starched. She ran her hand along a row of suits arranged like a household paint brochure, in subtly differing shades. Right, she thought, he really needed to have so many suits, it was all just too extra.

Importantly, she didn't dream of Jonathan anymore. The nights of golden dreams had perished. Was Michael too good to be true? He continually surprised her. With him she never knew what would happen next. After a year Michael said: 'Make up your mind whether you want me or not.' So, she introduced him to Josh, and they got on like a house on fire.

She and Josh virtually lived at his house. By that time, he had moved from Newbury to North Oxford to be near her and his parents. He was that certain of their relationship lasting. She kept her rental. It created the illusion that nothing was fixed. In case she had to retreat to the periphery if their relationship soured. She kidded herself that she wasn't living with him, and that they weren't spending all their free time together.

She was to meet his parents who lived in nearby Park Town. He had told her so much about them, some of it bizarre. She wasn't sure if he was trying to reassure her or himself that she'd be accepted. She had heard tales of their hippy days. How Tony his father drove the magic bus from London to Marrakech back in the day. But of course, these upper-class hippies were just playing at being hippies. They had their castles to return to. Park Town was one of the most exclusive and expensive areas of Oxford. Where properties rarely came up for sale and when they did, you were talking many millions.

The canopied entrance was reminiscent of a church porch, except there was a warm welcoming coach light. They were ushered into the hall where the wood panelling acted like sound proofing, absorbing family secrets down the years. The décor was unimaginative. Solid oak doors. Persian rugs. Thick Liberty curtains.

Anna held out her hand to Delsea. Michael stood behind her, a hand on her shoulder, very much owning her.

'I'm so glad to meet you,' Anna said, showing them through to the garden. She was fussing, bringing out plates and drinks. Tony was the epitome of a Hollywood English gentleman. His presence reached her ahead of the man. She could see where Michael got his looks from. Tony said, 'I get the feeling I will like you, Michael always had to have the best of everything.'

The men stood around eating their sandwiches. The women sat down for their afternoon tea. His mother fidgeted, smoothed her skirt over her knees. Cupping one hand inside the other, almost wringing them. She must be a gardener, Delsea thought. Her hands were those that spent a lot of time outdoors. Involuntary, one hand strayed to her throat, where a faint flush died as she felt for the security it seemed of her double row of pearls. Anna and Delsea got on, making chit-chat about nothing. Before the afternoon was out, she realised that it was Michael who made his mother nervous, not her. It was a bonus for her that he had nice parents. Love was conspiring against her.

After another year Michael said, 'Make up your mind whether you want me or not' again. So, she took him to Chippenham to meet her mom. Lucille was delighted. She made the Jamaican ceremonial dish: curried goat and for pudding a cake called pone. She expended every effort to get along with him. So much so that she got out a bag of her medicinal/recreational drug, ganga! She made a pot of ganga tea for herself and gave Michael the means to roll a joint. It was surreal: her mother doing drugs with her boyfriend. What were the chances of that? It was like some strange peace ceremony.

Delsea stood over them with her arms disapprovingly folded watching them space out together. Annoyed, she fetched and opened a bottle of ginger wine, a favourite of Jah (Jehovah) people, Rastafari. If you said Jah, then it was often followed by Rastafari in reggae songs. She sat down on a hard dining chair, while her mom and Michael occupied the only two comfortable chairs.

'Nice,' was what Michael said time and again to each draw on the joint. Which wasn't unusual for him. He seemed to think that one sentence or one word was all he needed to convey anything.

Sometimes Delsea would get quite passionate about some topic, maybe current affairs. Go off on a fiery tirade. Michael would listen and be silent, ever so still. It didn't matter if she was eloquent or downright rude, to get a reaction. Silence, not a blank stare, she must confess. She often tried putting him on the spot by saying, 'And what is your response to that?' He would not be drawn.

She knew he wanted to move their relationship forward. She started so many conversations that went like, 'can't you understand,' then she was overcome by confusion when she saw the look on his face and would trail off. Couldn't he understand that she was terrified of taking things one step further? The very idea of all that would entail; children might make her want to run for the hills. After the trauma she had had with her teenage pregnancy that was not something she wanted to repeat.

Explaining that would entail talking about Jonathan, who she had compressed into a compartment in her brain called 'That's nonsense.' She had even put chains around the box, to ensure she never even accidentally opened it. She didn't want to go into all that nonsense which she still hadn't come to terms with. Michael was all about action. Once he had decided something he set about making it happen. She felt like saying look here, Mr Obstinate, no good will come of this. Not while 'That's nonsense' was out there.

It was easy to love two men at the same time, if the love for one was trapped in the depths of her mind and the other was very much present. She sometimes watched Michael sleep and thought why wasn't Jonathan more like him. Immediately contrary wise she thought why wasn't he more like Jonathan. She would drift half-conscious close to sleep thinking about them while snuggling up to Michael.

She thought about chickening out and introducing them to each other. Then they would both understand her predicament. They would not get on; they were chalk and cheese, as the Wiltshire saying goes. You either came from the chalk end – the White Horse and Stonehenge – or the cheese end (Cheddar Gorge). That was before county boundaries changed.

Michael became a constant. Turning up when he wasn't snowed under by business. Giving her so little notice that she gave up trying to look good for him. At first when he did that she would rush and get changed. There was no longer any point going through the rigmarole of straightening her hair with tongs, which took ages. Or putting her contact lenses in or having full facial makeup. They behaved like a married couple with separate homes, living together in either, the three of them, whichever they found themselves in.

It was all so effortless. Except every now and then Michael would say 'make up your mind whether you want me or not.' This did her head in. It wasn't that she didn't want to commit to him. She didn't want to think about it. Her life worked best when she didn't think too deeply and just got on with living. With little contemplation except for the natural topics, she chewed over in her mind.

She took him to Corsham to meet her dad. Ben, without a word, got up and went into his garden to tend to his vegetables. They could see him walking around the beds, pulling out a weed here and doing a bit of thinning there. Gardening was his passion. She watched Ben narrowly. He hadn't even dressed for the occasion. He was in his mud-caked Wellingtons and a holey brown jumper with his tam jammed firmly on his head to prevent head colds in this cold country. His eyes were screwed up against the elements as he adjusted the bamboo wigwams for his runner beans.

She stole a look at Michael to see how he was taking being ignored. He seemed to be taking it in his stride, but then he was the silent type who hated it when she resorted to 'what are you thinking?'

Then her dad came in with a box of freshly grown organic vegetables and shoved them at Michael. Ah, everything was fine. The peace offering of his lovingly grown crops was not offered to all and sundry. As it was Sunday they went to The Royal Oak on the High Street for a roast lunch.

When they came back to fetch their car which was parked at her dad's Delsea went up to her old bedroom. It was a monument to her, as if she had died. Everything was just so, just as she'd left it at age eighteen when her mom packed a few belongings for each of them. Just enough for them to carry when she left taking her and Marcus with her to live in a house, she had purchased cash with years of dressmaking savings, in Chippenham. Though Lucille had moved she retained her community duties in Corsham.

Delsea was pleased they'd accepted Michael. She must say she never understood why Ben came to a country where eighty percent of people were white, and then complained about who she met!

'Make up your mind whether you want me or not.'

She arranged a weekend with Marcus. Marcus took them to a Caribbean underground blues party in a warehouse in Bristol. Where you had to be ready for a police raid to shut it down at any moment by confiscating the booze. That didn't work because there were hidden supplies that came out as soon as the police left. There was a DJ with his enormous homemade sound system, complete with colourful flashing bulbs for atmosphere. She dressed in purple velvet trousers, silver bangles, swayed and floated to Bob Marley. Swaying didn't need much coordination. She writhed her body, twisted this way and that, jumped up and down like a puppet on a string with all the energy that youth could muster. She had afroed her hair with an afro comb, creating an enormous halo. Michael was at home with the blues experience, even though he and Marcus's ex-wife were the only white people there. She jerked around as the bass oozed like honey into the crowds. Michael loved her dimpled smiles. He laughed as she pogoed across the floor which was some achievement in the tightly packed crowd. The air was thick with ganga. The I Three wailed. He got into a rhythm, and moved beautifully. He could feel the pulse of the music which was more than she could say for herself. Then he just held her as they lovers rocked to the offbeat together. The bass so loud her eardrums vibrated, like a weird form of meditation that blocked out all stimuli. Even the contemplation in her head, which her brain rebelled against, there was no time for taking breaks. She had a lot on her mind still to process.

The next day Michael seemed to have much on his mind too. He was in the garden where he seemingly stared out to nowhere. He was back outside the patio doors smoking a joint. Why was he smoking at this time of day? In fact, he didn't smoke more than one joint a day unless it was a special occasion. Going for a stroll with his joint was usually the last thing he did before turning in at night. He ground the spent joint into the lawn. She didn't really care that he smoked marijuana. He was an interesting dichotomy; part straight and conformist, half risk taker and exciting.

When he came in it was back to 'Make up your mind whether you want me or not.' Mr Obstinate was so persistent that she could scream.

'Why are you making me think about this?'

'It's been five years, Del, I want children.' Suddenly she felt freaked out. She loved him. She gave herself permission to go there again a long time ago. They told each other that truth too. Going down the child-bearing route though was not something she wanted to do ever again.

'You experienced childbirth as a child, don't you want to experience it as a woman?' She was ready to have a full-blown panic attack. She thought, 'please stop.'

'Come here, not on your own this time, with me.' Please stop. Don't say another thing. She started hyperventilating. Reviewing traumatic instances in her head, relentless postnatal depression. She could not go through that experience again.

Then he knelt down and said, 'I have never cared for anyone but you. I love you so much. Will you marry me?' He was making it clear by putting children first that he loved her and wanted to marry her, but that meant children too. The very thing he knew she was scared of doing and the reason she had never wanted to think about where they were heading. 'Don't answer me now.'

'I want to answer, I would marry you in an instant. But children… not sure I can do that.'

'You can, it will be nothing like last time. I am not making any more personal sacrifices by giving you another five years to think about whether you want children with me. I've waited long enough. I haven't pressed you before because I know how painful it was for you last time. It is different now. Trust me.' That was the longest speech she heard him say.

Just go for it, her heart said. Her head said if she said no. Would they split up? She didn't want to lose him. To say yes felt dangerous. But who was she kidding – everything about Michael was living dangerously. She learned to parachute, jumped out of a plane at thousands of feet because he said he wanted her to experience heaven. She checked in, checked out, tumbled at one hundred and twenty miles an hour towards the ground, pulled her drogue chute, arms bent, legs bent, and flew like superwoman, pulled her main chute, linked hands with him and danced in the sky all the way to earth. That was romantic.

Michael was special to her. Jonathan was like her other half. If she was down, it brought him down. When she was cut, Michael would take over while she healed. When she was tired, she needed Michael to carry on. Why did she think she couldn't live dangerously and have another child, of course she would because Michael told her she could do it and she trusted him?

'Yes, to everything.'

They kissed and a feeling of love and wellbeing washed over her. She liked the fact that she would never have to face things alone ever again. They were engaged. But there was one immediate hitch: his fearsome red-headed sister.

'You better look after my brother. He's my only sibling. If you mess him around you will be sorry. Because you will have me to deal with.'

'I have no intention of messing him around.'

'Then I'm happy for you both.'

Her ring was stunning. To celebrate they had lunch at a renowned Michelin restaurant in Great Milton, where they had the seven-course tasting menu. There was a piano being played in the restaurant. Pianos always got Michael's attention; it was his instrument of choice after all. She however made them sit in an area where the music was not so loud. In the evening they went to a performance of Fidelio, Ludwig Van Beethoven's only opera, at the theatre in town.

Quite often she found herself reassessing Michael, and wondering, 'Who is this man?' At other times she was violently attracted to him and couldn't believe that they were together. The love between them was true. "Beauty is truth. Truth beauty. That is all ye know on earth and all ye need to know." Thank you, Keats.

PART 2

After Joshua met Jonathan

PARENTAL ALIENATION

For once Jonathan had planned a quiet evening in. As he thought how rare that was, he was interrupted by the phone ringing. He envisaged the usual scenario – finding himself dashing to Number 10 via the connecting door to face some government crisis. Things were tough then, a worldwide financial crash was taking every ounce of ingenuity he had. It was relentless.

'Hello.'

'Is that Jonathan Ainsley?' Jonathan didn't recognise the voice.

'Yes.'

'It's Joshua.'

'Josh, how thrilling.' He couldn't think what to say next. 'Great to hear from you. I hoped you would get in touch when you were ready. What are you doing these days?'

'I'm in my final year at Ariel University, doing Natural Science. I do physical NatSci, Physics, Maths, and Chemistry.'

'You take after your mother there.' Jonathan always knew that one day Josh would find him.

If Del had a hard time as a result of having Josh so young, so had he. They were teenagers. He was confused. On an emotional roller-coaster after that bombshell news. He had left home for college. It was liberating. He felt free to do what the hell he liked. Then suddenly Del turned up and said that she was expecting. He didn't want to be tied down. Who could blame him? He did what any teenager would do. He went on a bender, off the rails, getting drunk all the time, ignoring his studies. It was a horrible time.

He often thought of Joshua. Where was he? How was he? Even what he looked like; he felt deprived that he didn't even have a single photo. He had not thought that Josh being adopted would be such a closed book. That was not what the social worker said. It was meant to be an open adoption. Delsea probably resented that he had told her that he thought adoption was best. So, what right did he have to see his child? He thought he had made it perfectly clear when he visited them in hospital that he was glad she had ignored his advice.

When Josh was born, he found himself father-watching. A world of individuals, of whom he was unaware before, became the focus of his vision. Fathers in parks supervising play. Fathers pushing buggies. He imagined what Josh would be like when he grew up. That made him stop drinking, and consolidate his future. That made him return to his studies.

Even if he'd held a glimmer of hope regarding access to Joshua, once Michael came on the scene, he felt he had no rights at all to his son. He didn't think he should intrude when Delsea wouldn't even speak to him. They could have got into access rights by going to solicitors. That was too distasteful for him. They were both reasonable people, he thought, who would sort it out between themselves. He adopted a code of silence. He hardly even talked about Josh or how he felt. Only sometimes with his father who equally felt his grandson was missing out by not knowing their side of the family.

He really couldn't lay it all at Michael's door, though he'd told himself that Delsea must be completely under his control. Otherwise, what the hell was she playing at by blanking him? Cutting him out was toxic; what had he done to deserve that? It was childish: he should have called her out on it straight away. It was a major sulk, because he was not what she wanted him to be. Quite right. He was who *he* wanted to be. She didn't want to play anymore, because she couldn't have things her way. Welcome to the world of grownups, Del. Except there was a young boy, who she should have put first, caught up in it.

At times he felt like wringing her neck. That was pure fantasy. The domestic violence bill that he supported was going through. The irony was not lost on him, how someone could get that close to doing something unspeakable. It had never occurred to him that Delsea would indulge in parental alienation.

There were times when he wanted to get in touch, but he didn't want to disrupt Josh's life. Josh's parents were Michael, who had adopted him, and Delsea. He did not want to interfere. He had to respect their choices.

Jonathan knew that if they continued with these getting to know each other phone calls there would come a time when one of them suggested meeting up. As the possibility of that day approached Jonathan felt nervous. That was unlike him: he wasn't of a nervous disposition. There could be no right or wrong way to feel when meeting your grownup son for the first time. If happiness in the form of Josh was coming his way, he would greet it. If not, so be it. He was realistic.

Josh thought Jonathan sounded shocked and amazed to hear from him. Thrilled even. Talking to Jonathan on the phone became an obsession. Neither had yet suggested they meet. It was early days. Everything he'd ever wanted to know was slotting quickly into place.

Josh wanted to meet up, there was no turning back for him. He had psyched himself up to get to know Jonathan. In a way he felt happy after all the knocks from Merin. He didn't have to indulge in being Jamaican, because he was equally English. He was worried Jonathan might be disappointed in him. The phone conversations had dispelled some of that and broken the ice. Jonathan after all was someone who should be predisposed to like, if not love him. He felt no love for Jonathan. He didn't know him; inside he felt guarded. He had let that feeling be. He also felt slightly angry if it was possible to feel different emotions at the same time. How could Jonathan have a child in this world and not contact them? He would have liked to have had his father in his life. Why did his mum and dad even let him decide at the age of thirteen about being adopted by Michael? They never told him that it was either or – who had decided that? It wasn't his place to have to reject either his father or his dad. But that was what they made him do, all three of them. He was the child. He felt all this still the prospect of meeting Jonathan was exciting. What should he wear to meet his estranged father? Peeling off his white T-shirt he admired his torso in the mirror. He was neither black nor white; he was brown, a person of colour. He decided to go just as he was, with what was comfortable. It wasn't an interview.

During the long phone conversations there was bewildering detail. Like when he broached the subject of Gin Tan.

'Mum said you dumped her for Gin Tan.'

'A girl I met at university.' Jonathan thought, What has Gin Tan got to do with anything? This was beyond him. 'At no point did I ever dump your mother for Gin Tan, or any other woman, come to that. I have never met anyone else I would rather be with than your mother. Where is this stuff coming from?'

'You should ask my mum.'

'I can see that. If anyone dissed anyone it was Delsea.'

'Dissed… how Jamaican.'

'It was Del who let us fade away.'

'If you'd loved my mum so much you should have overcome whatever obstacle that was in your way. Why didn't you fight? Why did you just let things drift?'

'Your mother is happily married, is she not?'

Really, Josh thought. He wanted to say a thousand things. How his mum was transfixed the moment Jonathan appeared on television. How she went over his every word, searching for deeper meaning. How she read every article he featured in. How she stayed up on election nights anxious in case Jonathan lost his seat. How in the days before she met Michael, she cried at night into her pillow trying not to wake him. How as a small boy he had to comfort her, by saying 'I got this, Mummy. I don't want you to be upset anymore. I will look after you.' He wouldn't say this as it would be a betrayal of her.

Jonathan's first impression of Josh was physical. He seemed so familiar. There was immediately a rapport, an unusual closeness, which he had to be careful not to blow. He felt Delsea had done a good job there, Josh in person was more polite than he was on the phone. He played cricket for the university, an Ariel blue. Ben's influence, no doubt. He was self-assured, brought up like the privately educated child he was, to think the world was his oyster.

However, to Jonathan he also seemed so tenderly reared, so cosseted, that he couldn't see the reality of the situation that he found himself in as a teenager. He had wanted to keep things light; none of it was Josh's fault. He didn't want their introduction to be tainted by negativity. But that or the politeness didn't last long. Things turned on a pin suddenly: Josh wanted to fight with him. What the hell, Jonathan thought. Let's get all the emotional stuff out of the way, if they were going to continue down the getting to know each other route.

'I want to understand what was so important. More important

than me.' Jonathan thought there were elements of Delsea there: to cut the crap, be blunt and abrupt. Josh was playing cat and mouse. Psyching him out. Ready to pounce on anything he didn't like the sound of. He wasn't expecting an easy time getting to know Josh. He wasn't going to go on the defensive either.

'I wish I had been around to see you grow up. There are many ways of fighting, as you put it. Politics is one. There is no point influencing the converted. You have to come up with strategies to improve things. The judiciary, policing, prisons, drugs and immigration all touch people's lives negatively in some cases. As do other areas like, health, education, trade, industry, globalisation, free enterprise and world trade.'

'You are skilful with words. I've had it with this conversation and I haven't even got started. Let me get this straight. You ditched Mum and me because of your political ambitions. This is what it looks like from my position. Politics first, family whatever.'

'Your mother had her own things going on. She doesn't do politics, whereas I find that frenetic world invigorating. Politics wasn't something I dreamt up on the spur of the moment. Because of my father's work many people came to the house, amongst them politicians. That is where my interest stems from. I liked listening to their constructive arguments. Del and I were young teenagers. You are older now than we were back then. You're bringing more maturity to it. I hadn't resolved how to make things work between us. There were bad times. But we spent many happy years together, in laughter mostly.'

'So far so good. That was all very well, but after that where did Mum fit in? You couldn't have cared about her very much, if you let people insult her.'

'Is this what Del told you? Is this what I am accused of? Is this what I'm to be judged on, one night at a dinner party? Your mother and I are polar opposites. We see things from different angles. If she didn't want to answer and had sat there a moment longer, the conversation would have moved on elsewhere. I am not into misogyny, thinking women don't have voices and can't defend themselves.'

'It's her fault now? She didn't feel like defending herself.'

'I didn't say it was her fault. Am I supposed to defend her when she takes it into her head not to defend herself? Am I supposed to guess the moment she is relying on me to do something? That's far too complicated and esoteric for a man like me. Look you're never going to make sense of this. Other people's relationships are incomprehensible.'

'Stop hiding behind being a man. You weren't just a man. You were her partner. You should have known how she felt.'

'Telepathic communication of feelings doesn't exist, Josh. Let's not go down this rabbit hole any further.'

'Give me a straight answer. Whether she could be bothered with that particular shit of defending herself depends on how much crap she'd already fended off that day. You'd been with her long enough to know that. Did you know Mum was really upset?'

'Interesting. Are you speaking from experience? Yes, I knew she was upset. Never mind your mum and me. Let's just give us the chance to get to know each other.'

Josh, who was trying to keep his temper in check, was angered again. 'The pair of you are so selfish with your ambitions. What you wanted to do. What you wanted to achieve. Where did I fit into that?' He didn't ask to be born. He was belligerent. 'It wasn't easy for Mum you know. You sound so irresponsible, just buggering off. You couldn't have cared less. There's more to being responsible than forking out school fees. Why didn't you even send me a birthday card? Why didn't I have weekends with you?'

'I know you are angry, but it is not easy to explain. Your mother and I were childhood friends. We weren't exactly going out in the strictest sense of the word. We didn't have that sort of relationship. Sleeping together was something we did to cement our friendship.'

'This is exactly what friends do. Have sex with each other, and conceive a child to cement their friendship. I don't actually want to hear about my parents' sex life. Too much information.'

To Josh it made no sense at all. He was beginning to agree with his uncle Marcus, that Jonathan was touched in the head. But he had to hand it to him, he was being open and honest. He hadn't expected that. When you watch the Chancellor of the Exchequer on telly, you see no emotions at all. That was all he knew of Jonathan: a man on the telly.

'It's too late for me to be your dad, I missed that boat. But I am still your father. There's plenty of room in my life for you. I am glad you got in touch.'

'I need to get back to Cambridge. Woman trouble.'

'You have a girlfriend?'

'Yes, Merin. Mum doesn't like her though.'

Was complacency the reason he was denied his real father? What a fuck up. There had to be more to it than misunderstandings. There were things Josh liked about Jonathan: his self-confidence, his determination, and the fact that meeting him did give him a sense of himself and who he was. Josh was thinking if Jonathan really loved his mum, he would have given up everything for her. As his grandad Ben would say, if he met with fire, he would have ousted it. If he'd met with water, he would have crossed it.

Jonathan thought of Josh. He remembered him as a lively infant who didn't need much sleep and was full of energy. Even then according to Delsea he was self-confident. He recognised himself in him. The refusing to accept things at face value. The way he challenged anything and everything. The sensitive side he tried to hide. Jonathan had every confidence in him. Josh was keen to get on and do things. Jonathan could almost feel that need. Having a distinctive father could prove to be a hindrance and an irritant to him. It would be assumed that his achievements were not down to merit, but to who he knew.

Since Josh's visit Jonathan was restless. He wanted to take time out to get to know him. He knew that in bringing Josh into his life the media would catch on. Spinning their connection into something false and nasty. His past had been raked over and delved into before, like any politician's. His single status attracted much comment. Most of it was nonsense. But no one had connected him to Delsea or Josh for that matter. There were people in Corsham who knew about their relationship. They had been discreet over what could have been a fantastic story. Close friends and family did not indulge the press one iota. They would renew their interest. Well, let them. He was fed up with secrecy. Let the skeletons troop out of the closet. Besides, he was invincible. He wasn't just a man. He was part sun.

Jonathan reflected. After Del and Josh moved to Oxford, he still had to deal with the situation at Aldbourne. He had his own flat in London where he was doing an administrative role at the People's

Party Head Office. He preferred not to go to Corsham for weekends. On one occasion his father specifically asked him to come for a long weekend, because they wanted to sell some cottages. Such subterfuge he knew was classic Frederica. He'd been asked to get there on Friday morning. There were people invited for coffee, though his father was mysteriously absent, considering it was he who wanted him to come. There was the architect, something about doing alterations, knocking cottages together to make a decent family-sized home for sale, their estate agent, and the vicar.

While the others were talking Jonathan found himself alone with the vicar.

'I meant to say, I'm glad that business with Delsea has blown over.'

'How'd you mean blown over? What makes you think that?' The fact that he lived in London while Delsea was in Oxford seemed to have got their hopes up. Clearly his father had decided not to have anything to do with such underhand tricks.

'I can understand your affinity for her, given that your formative years were spent in Africa.' The vicar took on a conspiring tone, which infuriated him. 'It would hardly have worked, would it, when you put your mind to it.'

'Affinity has nothing to do with it.' He said it loud enough to attract his mother, who was purposely hovering nearby. Yes, there was a time when he would have traded anything to run barefoot with Mofe in the sun. But Africa was in the past.

His mother took that as her cue, as if the two-pronged attack was a mere accident. 'Are you talking about Delsea Johnson? Now there's a girl who knows when she is on to a good thing. A girl like that is bound to be crafty. Bound to be looking for a leg up in society.' Actually, at this point he tried not to laugh, with one of them getting a leg up and the other a leg over. 'What with a father who works at the rubber factory and a mother who cleans. That dreadful brother.' This was comedy gold. A two, boarding on a three on their laughter scale. Was she talking about his dreadlocks? She went on, 'Delsea knows what side her bread is buttered on. She wouldn't say no if any man was stupid enough to offer her a way out, would she darling? Let's hope that any man would have the sense to see what she was after. I mean it would be in his own interest to secure his future before entering into a permanent relationship, wouldn't you say so, Jonathan?'

She was threatening him with disinheritance. It was not in her gift, but she did have influence over his father. Was she planning to do away with Richard and change the rules?

'I think I will go now.'

'Going already? You've only just got here – your father and I were looking forward to your stay.'

'Really, mother!' was all he said.

Actually, Wadworth Old Timer was in season. He decided to walk across the park through the avenue of Broadleaf Lime trees to the pub. And who should be lurking outside St Bartholomew's church but Mrs Johnson. They were all ganging up on him.

'Jonathan,' as if she spoke to him every day! 'I'm so glad I caught you. I've just been doing the flowers for a wedding tomorrow.' She was still on the rota of women who did flower arrangements for the church. It just happened to be her turn.

Lucille was damned if she was going to let the opportunity pass without saying something. For all his prospects she didn't approve of him getting her daughter pregnant. At the sight of him there was a surge of anger, brewing in her breast.

'Don't think I approve of your relationship with my daughter.' The reply was swift, even curt.

'We don't need your approval.'

'That's as maybe. But if you think I'm going to stand by and watch you hurt my daughter, if I had my scissors on me, I would run you through.' He forgot she was a rather good dressmaker, who specialised in wedding and bridesmaid dresses. Not just a cleaner. Of course, his mother had not thought, when roping Lucille into her plot, that she might just kill him. That was not quite what Frederica had in mind. Lucille had already whacked him round the head at the first opportunity. 'I shall do everything in my power to dissuade her from having anything further to do with you.'

'Fine, you do that, excuse me.'

Continuing towards the Ainsley Arms, he knew what was waiting there. It was his mother, who was crafty. She knew he would not leave without going to the pub. Even if just for one pint of Old Timer, as he was driving. He would play along with her stupid plot. She thought showing him that both families wanted an end to this debacle that he would give up. No wonder Delsea decided to move to Oxford. Corsham was too small. So, he had just walked up to his destiny. Ben was sitting at the bar: how obvious, mother. This wasn't Ben's pub. He frequented the Duke of Cumberland.

'You don't care for my daughter. What all this secrecy about? If you cared, you would not have hidden a thing.' Ben was not just doing Frederica's bidding. He wanted answers for himself. 'It is best you stop this now. In time she will forget you.'

'Best for who?'

'Love is not afraid of anything. So let me tell you straight. You using my daughter for your own convenience. Who have to pick up the pieces – me!'

'If you really wanted the best for her, you would leave her to get on with her own life.'

'Delsea had it with you. It is you doing the chasing. I know a thing or two about my daughter. She is not afraid to open her mouth to anyone. If she loved you, she would ram it down my throat. Leave her alone.'

That told him. The jury wasn't unanimous, he noticed. His father had refused to join in with their cunning plan. But also, 'I thought this was Marcus's pub?' Two could play head fuck games, Mr Johnson. As if he should take his word that Delsea wanted them to be over. He knew Ben's daughter too. She and Marcus were close, they covered for each other.

'He's playing rugby.'

Really Mr Johnson, was that the best you could do, he thought? He would have skipped rugby, which incidentally he played on a Saturday, not a work day, to join in the dual family lynching. They were having a free for all, attacking him, instilling doubt. Yet there was a dissenter on each side. He had always had robust mental health, which was just as well with the head fuck games going on, otherwise, 'It would be in my own interest, Mother, to string myself up, wouldn't you say so darling?' He had to hand it to her, she excelled at subterfuge. It was not as though they had announced their engagement or anything.

Jonathan supposed Ben got to Del eventually. She wouldn't see him. If he phoned, she wouldn't speak to him. He hoped she'd change her mind. She didn't. For God knows how many days he churned things round in his head. This was not the end. What was happening? He decided to leave her to her own devices. Then he received a message that incensed and worried him.

> Jon
> I am marrying Michael Valentine.
> I love him. Sooner or later one of us was bound to meet someone else.
> Del xxx

Tiring of his own company, Jonathan went in search of Charlie Wright, his political ally since Marlborough College. He had never spoken to Charlie about Delsea. He was afraid Charlie would dismiss his concerns, if they weren't political. It was all sorted between them, their ambitions. He would be Prime Minister and Charlie would be Chancellor. Charlie thought they were going for a night on the town.

He shelved his plans when he saw that Jonathan was distraught. It was reassuring to Charlie that Jonathan could look haggard and suffer, beneath that steely coolness. They downed a couple of Scotches before broaching whatever subject.

'What's up?'

'There's this woman I had been seeing. I've known her for some time.' Charlie was relieved. Was this all? He had prepared himself for the worst. He looked at his watch; this shouldn't take long. 'Now you want to get out of it?'

'No. We have a child together.'

'Why am I only hearing about this now? What about our plans? This is not a good look for a potential Prime Minister. Are you sure this child is yours?'

'Of course, she's perfectly respectable.'

'Well, she can't prove anything.'

'She could. Besides which, I wouldn't deny that Josh is my son. That is not the point.'

'What is the point then?'

'She's getting married.'

'That's good, makes things tidy.'

'It's not good.'

'It would be complete idiocy to fraught her plans. This could be disastrous for your career.'

'My career. I am not interested in what this does to my career. She is not an obstacle.' Jonathan's head ached. Perhaps Charlie was right. He should forget it. Let her go. No doubt he would get over it, or used to it, one of the two. They were brave thoughts which left him feeling grim. He was a shadow of himself, he realised.

'Her father must have got to her, he's a real Jamaican macho man, her mother was terrified of his drink temper.'

'Hang on, so this woman is black?'

'She's black British, what has that got to do with it?'

'This situation gets worse by the minute.'

'This is the People's Party. We are not afraid: The creed and the colour and the name won't matter.'

'I didn't know you were religious.'

'Drummed into my head by church.'

'I think this is a blessing in disguise. She sounds like bad news. Think of your position, your status, the potential influence you will have. It's her loss.'

There was something amiss, Jonathan thought. The thing was, Delsea did not make mistakes. Precision was her thing, otherwise she would be a useless mathematician. Delsea did not forget things either. Everything she did was for a reason.

'I'm going to Aldbourne, London is getting to me. I can't think here.' He was impatient driving to Corsham, breaking the speed limit on the motorway. He was certain he could solve this mystery there. He hadn't a clue why, but get there he must.

Richard wasn't expecting his son that weekend. Jonathan followed his father to his study. Richard took in the awkwardness, the restless pacing.

'Jonathan, are you alright?' He handed him a drink.

'No thanks, I'm driving. There's something I have to tell you. I want Delsea Johnson in my life. As far as I am concerned, she has always been there and I want it to stay that way. I haven't said this before because I didn't want to hurt Mama. I know she will be disappointed in me.'

'What is this about? You said on the phone that you wanted me to meet her properly. I am struggling to understand your sudden need for me to do this.'

'I am terrified of losing her.' Jonathan was not only letting his father in on the facts but admitting them out loud for the first time to himself.

'Now you've lost me.'

'I thought she would always be there for me. Now she is getting married. Mama made it clear that if I pursued Del, then you would disinherit me.'

'Disinherit my own son? My only child? Why did you not talk to me about this?'

'When Mama sets her mind to something you usually support her.' He had made plans in case his father followed through with Frederica's threat of disinheriting him. If the worst came to the worst, then he had invested wisely.

'I give way to things of no consequence for a quiet life. I wouldn't support her in this. I've left everything to you, as it should be. It is for you to take care of your mother, if I go before her.' Jonathan was relieved to know that Frederica's threats were empty after all. There was nothing she could do to him, if he disobeyed her.

Richard sat for a long time in his study. He was sad Jonathan hadn't confided in him earlier. He had to think back to what he would have done. Maybe he would have tried to dissuade him; hoped it was a passing phase. Frederica would be horrified. What could she do? She couldn't tell her grown-up son how to behave. All he could feel was relief that he had Jonathan's confidence back. But it seemed Delsea had decided to move on. This felt a bit like shutting the stable door after the horse had bolted.

When Jonathan burst open his mother's sitting room door, she was not surprised.

'I thought you'd be back. It's all over Corsham. Mrs Johnson told Mrs Wedderburn who told Mrs Thornhill who told Mrs Barters who told me.'

'I am not interested in your gossiping flower decoration ladies.'

'Delsea Johnson has bagged herself a millionaire. I did warn you about what a little gold-digger she was. You thought she'd wait for you to declare your undying love and marry her.'

He was so frustrated by his mother's ability to misunderstand anything connected to him that no words could suffice. A Nigerian gesture palming her up and down was his response. Meaning take a look at yourself. You are such an unfeeling woman. 'You are enjoying, this aren't you? Enjoying what she's done. You are utterly ruthless. Sitting here surrounded by all the embellishments of the English establishment, plotting, scheming and judging others. What a wonderful specimen of a human being you are. I read you like a book. All it would take now that I've been stung is to drag your son, me that is, to London, hold a few dinner parties inviting some carefully vetted single ladies, and I will marry one of them.'

He snapped one hand across his body, which meant I will deal with you later. We are going to see about this. He turned his back on his mother to compose himself. A portrait hit him right between the eyes. Then it struck him: Del had not shafted him completely after all. She had sent him a sign, and he was too blind to see it until now. If they were finished, she would have given him back the emeralds taking pride of place around grandmother Gala's neck in the portrait before him. This was why he had to come back here. After weeks of indulging in a pity party the relief was enormous. All he could do was say 'six' and fall catatonically to the floor, helpless with laughter.

Now his mother was concerned. 'What's wrong with you, Jonathan? I did notice your inappropriate amusement last time we discussed Delsea Johnson. That girl has turned you silly.' Which made him laugh even more.

'He thinks he can poach my woman.'

'Who, darling?'

'Michael Valentine.'

'So, you do know more than the rest of us, what a surprise. What is this "your woman" stuff, you are not Jamaican.'

To which he laughed hysterically. His mother left the room and came back with his father.

'Your mother tells me you are having some sort of breakdown.'

'All three of us in the same room, wonders will never cease. I'm on top of the world, thanks for asking,' he said, getting up. 'They are not getting married in our church.'

'Which church?'

'St Bartholomew's.'

'It's not your church, it's the parish church,' said Mama. Even though it contained a private chapel dedicated to them and memorials to their family.

'It's our church: mine and Delsea's. That man is not setting foot in our church. You tell the vicar, that interfering busybody, that he is not to marry them in our church.'

'Jonathan, Delsea can get married in her parish church if she wants, it's customary,' said Richard.

'It's our church. It's our yaad. You tell Lucille personally that I am not having this. She threatened to run me through with scissors. You tell her, Delsea is not getting married in our church.'

Richard was looking at him as if he didn't know him. He hadn't seen that steel in him before.

'Another thing. I want that chair of the cricket club charity removed. He had the gall to say to me in the pub, "A bit exotic, what's it like? Do tell." As though Del was not a person but a walking erogenous zone, to be experimented on and sampled. Then I want you to make Ben Johnson the chairman. I hope I have made all this clear.'

'Richard,' said Frederica, 'Have you got anything to say about this?'

'He's a grown man, this has nothing to do with me. Except I will sort the cricket chair and you better do as he says regarding the vicar and Lucille. I always knew you were a born leader, Jonathan.'

A few days after her text to Jonathan, Delsea received a reply from him.

Del,
You can't just send me a text about something so monumental. We mean more to each other than that. Meet me please at Aldbourne Court. Papa wants to meet you. Mama is away visiting her sister.
Jon

What did he mean she couldn't send him a text, that was an oxymoron because she had sent him a text! Not even a single kiss at a time like this, Jonathan! Nonsense in every respect. She was not sure which was ruder, her sending him a text or him after God knows how many years inviting her to meet his father properly! Ridiculous, Jonathan. It took her getting engaged to another man for him to do that. It confirmed she had made the right decision.

But that nonsense knew exactly how to push her buttons and she was fuming. She was not having this. She would be mature about it. She would meet "he who must be obeyed" at Aldbourne Court for Josh's sake only. Josh may want to know his father one day and she didn't want to do anything to jeopardise that by creating ill feeling between them.

It wasn't their status that bothered her. She had dealt with all manner of people. But the Ainsleys had the wherewithal to make her feel small. She was the little Jamaican girl from the village. The one middle-class and upper middle-class parents had invited to tea as an educational experience for their children. She smiled. She wasn't that trembling little girl any more.

She had forgotten about the beautiful trees in the formal gardens planted by Capability Brown. Dark columns of magnolia grandiflora rose up between the windows sporting large creamy white flowers. She pulled up to the side of Aldbourne Court. No one lived in the state rooms that were open to the public. Delsea parked her car as Jonathan came out to greet her, with a non-contact, cold welcome. He was still handsome. He had improved with age.

Lord Ainsley came to the great hall to meet her. He took her hand and gave it a gentle squeeze. He'd always been this outgoing country gentleman surrounded by his black Labrador dogs striding across the countryside with his stalking stick. By then he was much older, with thin facial features. Inside, a grandfather clock made in Glasgow struck the hour, its solemn face depicting scenes from four continents, in each corner. She wondered if he would go straight to the heart of the matter, Africa. With his travels he had a much greater knowledge of the world than she did.

Her head was full of the ways educated people danced around, asking her whereabouts in Africa she came from. Her parents were Jamaican was her stock reply. However, she came from Wiltshire and salt of the earth shire people are proud to be from the shires. She could do her Wiltshire accent when called upon in some Bristol dive pub, with the best of them, because she spoke that language too. She had been immersed in it since birth.

Bigots who used to tell her to go back home to the jungle as a child were laughable. Those same families, not one generation on, boast of going to the Caribbean for their holidays. Let's not forget that everyone worshipped and must save and protect those very jungles that had filled her heart with despair.

To be fair there were also the hilarious aspects to some parental introductions. Her best friends at university were three guys. That's what happens when you read mathematics, you meet men. When she went for a home weekend with one, his father grudgingly said to him, 'You always had to have the chocolate biscuits.' Another jumped up and said, 'What d'you call this, the United Nations?' The Fuss Potential Factor, FPF as she had named it when inviting a person of colour into a white home, ran high. There were those who could not do enough to make her feel welcome too.

Lord Ainsley knew her parents and that they were from Jamaica. However, she was not expecting his opening gambit.

'Is your African heritage from the west or the east? Some families pass that information down through generations. I'm talking before the slave trade.'

That was to the heart of the matter! 'Thank you for acknowledging the slave trade and how it tore families apart. My family originates on the west coast: Nigeria and Sierra Leone.'

'Warm people Africans… generous too, even those who had little would share it with you.' For a moment Lord Ainsley reminisced. He was ashamed of how his great, great grandfather made his fortune by shipping goods like linen to the British involved in the slave trade in the West Indies and Africa. "Rule, Britannia! rule the waves: Britons never will be slaves." Though the slave trade was abhorrent and those doing business with the slavers were just as guilty, Delsea didn't think that he was really responsible for what his ancestors did. If he acknowledged it and led a life of integrity himself that was. He could only be judged on what he did.

They all had Nigeria in common, with him having been British Ambassador there, and Jonathan was born there.

Later Delsea said to Jonathan, 'Can I see your bedroom?'

'A bit of a strange request Del.'

'Not strange at all.' It was the room where she lost her virginity and where Josh was conceived.

'I work here sometimes, for my job I need a lot more space than my flat affords to lay out my papers.'

She looked out of the window at the view of the park. Peacocks were calling. It was dark when she was here last. It looked different in the daylight. Capability Brown had favoured a natural approach. Contriving vistas through clumps of trees and across the parkland. The decoration of the room had been updated. There was the same bed which she went over to and sat on.

'What are you doing?'

'I have fond memories of this room.'

'You have fond memories of my bedroom and you are marrying someone else?'

'I am thinking of Josh, not you.'

She wanted a man who gave her warmth, not someone cold, like Jonathan. He just stood there. Delsea got up and walked towards him. This was what Lucille used to do when she was angry with her, or Marcus when they were young teenagers and too big for her to slap their legs. She would back them into a corner. It's not just a saying. Being backed into a corner is physically scary. The person has three ways to escape: dart left or right or walk backwards. For some strange reason neither she or Marcus made the sideways escape. Maybe there was something genetic about maintaining eye contact with the aggressor and occasionally lowering one's eyelids in supplication. They always walked backwards.

She wondered what Jonathan would do. She suspected that most men would stand there and not move at all. Michael would. He'd just grab her when she got close enough and make a game of it by twirling her around playfully. But Jonathan stepped backwards when she got a certain distance from him. Delsea took another step forward. He took another step backwards. She knew it wasn't because he was scared of her.

'Stop this, Del.'

'Why?' She stepped forward. He stepped backward. He could only go back so far because he would be in the corner soon. She stepped forward. He stepped backward. He was in the corner.

'Now what are you going to do?' Good question. She hadn't thought this through. She could hardly deploy part two of Lucille's angry mother punishment, which was hilarious and made her laugh. She put a hand on each wall. Trapping him in the corner. He couldn't escape.

'Now what are *you* going to do?' She returned the question. Neither of them broke eye contact. He was gazing into her eyes without stopping. How far could she go before he stopped her? She undid a button on his shirt. He was taller than her. He was just looking down into her eyes, staring and smiling. She undid another button. The loving stare was arousing. She undid another button. His hand clamped hers in a stop. This was impossible. She relented and let him go. She walked very fast, almost ran out to her car. She didn't want to linger. She'd had a belly full over the years of his claptrap.

He followed her, 'Del, please stay a little longer.'

'Why?' That foxed him. 'Pray tell, why should I stay longer?' He couldn't bring himself to say it even now. Forgetting how powerful Michael's Lotus was, she almost spun it 360 degrees, reversing, turning so fast to get out of there. She almost ran him over. What a good ending that would be and satisfying too. Being Michael's car the moment she turned the ignition the radio sprang to life playing The Bangles, "Eternal Flame." How appropriate. Uncharacteristically she didn't turn the song off straight away.

She roared down the drive, past St Bartholomew's church, right down Church Street. Right past the famous Kiddie Fiddlers house. How strange that there were such normalising names for sexual deviants. Kiddie Fiddlers, Peeping Tom's, Flashers, Streakers, Knicker Thieves...

Corsham had its share of the good and the great too, including a queen. Never mind all that. He had done it again THAT NONSENSE. She had no doubt that what she felt when he looked into her eyes was love. Love was patient, love was kind. It always trusts, always hopes. She hated him. She almost stopped at the Cross Keys pub at the end of the road, for a drink to steady her nerves. But she was driving. She wanted to be at home, safe and sound with Michael. With a man that if she shoved him up against the wall would take the initiative. With Michael it didn't even need to be a wall. If she shoved him backwards anywhere, on to the sofa, on to the bed, he would get the message. Yet love supposedly never fails.

No matter, Jonathan thought. She already knew he was not demonstrative he had never pretended to be. It didn't mean he felt less. He thought she understood that, knew that. Things would come right again. They were one and the same. An angel told him that. Angels never lie.

It was a weight off Jonathan's mind – someone in the family acknowledging the most important person in his life, his favourite person. Keeping it suppressed all the time was awful. He had wanted to own his relationship with Delsea for so long. His father meeting her properly was a start. He wouldn't attempt the same with his mother. The reason she had uprooted him from Nigeria was her ghastly fear that he might run off with a native girl who would produce dozens of pickaninny who would marry natives and the whole estate would pass into black hands! The way she saw it according to her misguided standards was that he was letting the side down. Even worse, he wasn't just in a relationship with a woman of colour, they had a son, the deed was done.

BLENHEIM PALACE

Delsea couldn't insult her mom – a wedding and bridesmaid dress designer – by not allowing her to make the gowns. Lucille kept wanting to get extravagant. Delsea's had to be a showpiece; the best she had ever made. Delsea wanted something simple but elegant, in close fitting cream satin. Before it all ended in tears they compromised. Delsea would let Lucille do her very fine embroidery in the same off-white thread on the bodice. Not the bold contrasting elaboration that Lucille preferred. This greatly pleased Lucille. The gratification was further enhanced when Delsea suggested they buy a plain veil which Lucille could add lace to around the bottom and edges. Both were satisfied with the creativity involved. The embellishments gave Lucille something to get fussy about. Delsea took Lucille to have her mother of the bride outfit especially made as a treat. It didn't seem right that Lucille should make her own clothing. Delsea wanted to show thanks for the efforts her mom was making and let her know that she was appreciated.

Ted's twin girls Jane and Charlotte, Delsea's goddaughters, would carry her train. Ted was a Jane Austen fan hence he'd named his daughters after two of her popular characters. Josh would be their page boy or ring bearer, in charge of delivering the rings to them, a very responsible job indeed for a thirteen-year-old. He was chuffed to bits about it. Michael's dad Tony was his best friend. That meant of course he had to be his best man. He and Michael were having their attire made by their usual tailor in London. For Ben, Marcus and Josh, they were paying to have bespoke Ozwald Boateng suits made. Marcus was ecstatic about this and Ben declared his would be his burial ensemble, the highest compliment that could be given by a Jamaican.

A natural florist who had a flower farm in Wallingford was recommended to Delsea. They were able to peruse the growing beds for the blooms they wanted to use at the venue, for the table decorations and to assemble around their wedding cake. At the beginning of the aisle Delsea would walk through an arch of her childhood flora – meadows full of daisies from which she'd made daisy chains. They would use the larger variety, the tall Oxeyes they saw at the farm. Giant buttercups. The girls at her primary school would hold buttercups under her chin to see whether she liked butter or not. If you got a yellow reflection, you liked butter. The wild red poppies that grew in the cornfields. The abundant bluebells from the woods. She would pass on the white daffodil garlic, for obvious reasons. For her and the bridesmaid's bouquets the florist would have fresh blossoms picked very early on the morning of the wedding from Ben's front garden and transported for arrangement into floral designs. She always remembered the weather being sunny as a girl. It wasn't a feeble recollection. Wiltshire really was a warm county.

The wedding cake designer they chose had moved away from the traditional. They trusted her to pull out all the stops to get their confection right. They had been to her house for a tasting session and were very impressed with the flavours she produced. It would have three-tiers, the smooth glazing finished off in gold leaf. The bottom layer was walnut with a white silk sash and intricate brown flowers made of icing. The middle was chocolate with a brown silk ribbon and white piped flowers. The top was plain Victoria sponge for those – like Delsea – who preferred the simpler things in life. The band would again be white with tiny brown florets. The brown and white represented them. They decided not to have the traditional bride and groom on the top. They personalised their masterpiece by having an exquisite miniature grand piano as the centrepiece.

They would have a Master of Ceremonies and an event manager who would coordinate the room decoration and manage things from the Blenheim Palace end for the suppliers. He ran his thoughts past them and created a huge spreadsheet of the wedding running order. The whole thing would be videoed. Michael was responsible for selecting the videographer and the photographer. Marcus found a steel band for the drinks, reception after the ceremony. The caterer would make Jamaican canapés with cocktail sticks featuring tiny Jamaican flags. The live evening band Michael wanted was booked.

Marcus secured the DJ, so the evening would boast an eclectic mix of music.

The invitation list proved the most challenging for Delsea. Michael had so many business acquaintances, some who Delsea had never met, and she wasn't sure there was room for all of them. She was worried about inviting her best friend, Jonathan. It felt so wrong to be filled with dread about something that should be joyful. She would let him lead.

Jon, how are you? I don't know what to do about inviting you to my wedding. Xx

Don't you dare invite me to your wedding.

That's not very nice. Are you trying to ruin my special day?

Coming from the woman who less than a year ago sat on my bed and said she had fond memories of being there. You are lucky it's just a *day* that will be ruined.

Despite her in-depth experience of mobile telecommunications, she had never had a text argument before.

Coming from the man who said he was too young for love.

From the most selfish woman ever.

OMG MP for Bradford-on-Avon, Chippenham, Corsham, Melksham and the surrounding villages, if only your constituents could see you now. They would be so proud of your maturity.

I don't believe you will go through with this marriage farce.

Such arrogance. How dare you call my wedding a farce! I take it you are not coming then.

Wild horses wouldn't drag me to your sham wedding.

I can't believe you are being so awful. I am really upset.

There was a long lull in communications before a conciliary message arrived days later.

Text me where and when. No invite. End of.

The day arrived. First thing in the morning Michael and his dad checked over the venue. White printed scrolls edged in gold with black writing, stood on easels announcing welcome, and table allotment. Enormous caramel, white and black balloons of different sizes in huge bunches tumbled from each corner of the main room. A shiny square of large black tiles formed the dance floor. White linen chair covers with huge caramel sashes tied in gorgeous flat bows at the back. They would be used in the ceremony and for the wedding breakfast. Beautiful place settings, utilising the flowers they'd chosen on the farm, with fern green leaf chargers for the plate settings. A late addition was that a Gabriel College of Music friend of Michael's would play the violin to her pre-recorded backing at the wedding breakfast.

They all came. Emma was wearing a pale pink Chanel suit, which was probably original. Her mother was a sixties supermodel who had married into the aristocracy. She was looking around as though she were above the sentimentality of it all. Delsea's friends from her alma maters. Ted's wife Janice in lavender with an extravagant matching hat.

It was a lovely ceremony. The registrar had been well-briefed and Blenheim Palace did them proud. The mothers signed the register as they wanted them to have a special role like the fathers did. Michael's dad as best man and Ben had walked Delsea down the aisle. After which the reception was held on the lawn outside. While the guests were free to chat, drink champagne and eat canapés, the wedding party went off for the formal photography.

Michael said this was their moment and no one else's. He and the photographer had a plan. He didn't want the time taken up with loads of impersonal group photography – shots of them with each of their families, then with both families. That was it for the groups as far as he was concerned. He had an ulterior motive for taking so few formal shots, which he had hatched with the photographer. Delsea was glad he hadn't told her about it in advance. All she could say was that she was glad they both lost every ounce of fat before the day. They went to their bridal suite to do arty photography.

The photographer came to life. She started enjoying herself shooting tastefully playful black and white shots. They were in their prime. Delsea was twenty-nine and Michael twenty-seven. He had grown his hair longer, like it was when they first met. It made him seem younger. She loved it that way. She remembered him always sweeping it back from his eyes. They started off fully clothed in their finery, gazing into each other's eyes. Then they shared a kiss. Michael then wanted to get more creative. They were loving the fun of it. It was the most relaxed they'd been all day. She could see why he grew his hair now; it made the photographs less conventional. Some of them were with Michael in his suit without the shirt and tie. The eight pack was impressive. He took off his jacket for a few. It was calming just playing around. Not like when the adrenaline was pumping through them during the ceremony. The photographer was laughing and giving them instructions as she snapped away. By the time they finished Michael was in his suit trousers and nothing else. Delsea began to worry about the amount of time they had been missing from their own drink's reception. It was lucky that they had a female photographer to help restore her pristine bridal look.

The Master of Ceremonies called them all in for the wedding breakfast. Delsea was dreading Ben's speech. People wouldn't understand his ways. He was just as likely to curse them as praise them. She was hoping he'd get so drunk that he wouldn't be able to stand up. He didn't. He stayed just the right side of sober.

He began: 'Delsea was the sweetest thing you ever saw. Butter wouldn't melt in her mouth till she grew up. I brought her up not to trust anyone, especially not to trust men. But she didn't listen to me. Which is just as well. She bought Michael dis man into my house. He was di one she warnt. I tell her if she warnt dis man den give him nothing, dat's the only way he going to have respect fi her. Give him a little at a time. Dat's the way to keep him interested. Now she flies in the face of reason a give herself whole to dis man. Michael is the same way, both of them, own way. Deh deserve each udda. I wish dem luck.' Ben sat down, unaware of controversy. He'd said nothing out of the ordinary for him. Michael whispered to Delsea. 'Cheer up. It could have been worse. He's quite poetic when he gets going. I am glad that you flew in the face of reason.' She acknowledged that Michael was trying to make her feel better about Ben. She knew rather than felt that Ben loved her. He rarely approved of anything she did. So, what did his love mean!

Emma, who was astute, thank goodness, laughed. When the other guests saw one of the family tables laughing, they thought this was some intricate joke they hadn't understood because of cultural differences. Delsea gave Emma a secret thumbs up.

Michael had heard it all before. Delsea wasn't a good Jamaican daughter, as she didn't let Ben rule her life and gave him back-chat. Being brought up in England, she didn't share his values. Michael still didn't understand their constant reference to being naked. It was used in so many different contexts. It was important to Ben that Michael, who got to marry his daughter, wasn't a *naked* man. Naked was used in reference to hypocrisy, stupidity, lack of morals, lack of substance, lack of knowledge. For people who pretended to have these attributes, but didn't. Bowsey could precede naked. For instance, pretending to be an expert when you weren't meant you were bowsey naked. In other words, boasting when you knew nothing. Jonathan, they dissed as a fool fool: naked man. That seemed more to do with Ben and Lucille's dislike of him as far as Michael could tell. Being "jalopy," which meant broken down, worn out, useless and past the sell-by date, was worse than being naked. To be honest Michael had given up on understanding most of the Jamaican words. Just when he got the hang of it, they threw in another meaning.

After the speeches was the cake cutting, and people disappearing into silly photo booth palaver. Then all change for the evening. New guests arrived for the buffet supper and dinner dance. Delsea and Michael did their first dance to a slow number, Elvis, "Can't Help Falling in Love." She could just hold on to Michael and not worry about not being able to dance.

Things for Delsea were ruined when Jonathan turned up with Gin Tan. Gin looked at her as though she was the victor in their supposed battle for Jonathan's love and affection. While indicating that her consolation prize, Michael, was wonderful. She mouthed 'Wow, he is an Adonis' behind his back as they threw shapes on the dance floor. Yes, he was literally a beautiful object, just as Keats intended. "A thing of beauty is a joy for ever: its loveliness increases; it will never pass into nothingness." That wound Delsea up no end. She rolled her eyes at Jonathan, kissing her teeth, and gave him her drop-dead look for bringing Gin along.

As soon as she left the dance floor in disgust, a member of staff pressed a Post-It note on her. 'Rex Jones 173.' It ended in tears. She was so upset she sent a text to her brother.

Marcus I am having a crisis. Can I meet you in your room in five minutes please?

Not long after, she saw Marcus making his way towards her in his beautiful colourful Boateng waistcoat.

'What the fuck, Sis?' As soon as he opened his door, she virtually pushed him into his room. Such was her haste for privacy, as she let rip her tears. 'What is going on? I knew there would be a fucking mess when I saw Jonathan arrive bang on nine with a woman. Fair play to him, she is something else, like a higher level of beauty from another planet.'

'Yes, well, she is not my cup of tea.'

'What is this about?'

'Him of course.'

'Del's in a mess, guess what, same old, same old. Why is he here?'

'I wanted to invite him like anyone else, like a friend.' Marcus snorted in derision. She shoved her phone in his face as proof, open at the text argument.

'It is crystal clear he didn't want to be here. The guy loves you and you are forcing him to come to your wedding to someone else!'

'How do you know he loves me?'

'You whistled and he came.'

'That works both ways.'

'I better text Michael before I hear any more about this. He will be wondering where the fuck his bride is. Then you are going to tell me what has been going on from the start.'

'No. I will text him.'

'You will not. I have told you before. You mustn't text people. Phone them back instead. You are too direct and abrupt. The number of times you have pissed me off with a text message. You have clearly pissed Jonathan off.'

'You are supposed to be on my side.'

'I am on your side, clearing up your mess right now.'

'Can I see the text?'

Michael, in case you are wondering, Del is with me in my room. She is having a crisis about leaving the Johnsons behind forever and being a Valentine.

Sweet. I see Jonathan was here on the dance floor with a woman for a while. Did Del invite him?

No.

So, he decided to gate crash our wedding somehow.

Mate everyone in Corsham knew this wedding was this weekend. It's a small town. Leave him to me. I know him of old.

'You know Del, I said to Joshua that you two were the most secretive pair I have ever known and not to be too quick to judge Jonathan. Right, the last I heard you went to London to finish with him.'

'I didn't say I was going to do that.'

'I don't care, get on with all the bits I don't know about and we will see how this mess can be sorted.'

'He came to the hospital to visit me when I had Josh. He changed his mind about adoption and was willing to go along with what I wanted to do.'

'That's good. This woman who is here tonight. Is this the woman he cheated on you with at Uriel? The one that Josh goes on about?'

'Yes.'

'So, he brings this woman he knows you felt insecure about to your wedding. Nice.'

'He doesn't know that I know her.'

'So, she is not a factor in whatever happened tonight?'

'She is because I don't like her and didn't invite her to my wedding.'

'He was hardly going to come on his own! He doesn't know anyone but you. Or was that the plan?'

'I wanted the opposite. Him to be here in the day and not the evening.'

'I really am pissed off with you, Del, devoting time to your grievances with Jonathan on your wedding day. Michael is a good bloke. Why the fuck didn't you marry Jonathan, if he's this important to you?'

'He hasn't asked me and never will.'

'Why?'

'Because he would think he was being unfair to me.'

'Why?'

'I can't say.'

'He's not gay and you are trying to convert him to being straight?'

'Of course not.'

Marcus considered, 'I suppose not, otherwise Miss Universe with the diamond cut grey eyes would not still be around. Or is he already married?'

Delsea decided to let Marcus think he was married. That was easier than the truth.

'Right,' Marcus said. 'You are filling me in right up to today. Delete those text messages, while I remember.'

'You are the best brother ever.' Delsea hugged him.

'I am not! I lost track of what was happening in your life.'

'You have your own life to deal with.'

Where to start, Delsea thought. 'He invited me to this dinner in Oxford. But I am not going into that.'

'That sounds innocent enough…'

'Then he panicked when I got engaged to Michael. He demanded that I went to Aldbourne to meet his dad properly.'

'What d'you mean properly?'

'As the person in his life.'

'Don't say "person" to mislead me when I am trying to help you. You mean the woman in his life. So why did you go?'

'To give him one more chance.'

'Chance to do what?'

'Make a move and he wouldn't.'

'Is this where "coming from the woman who sat on my bed" stuff comes in?'

'Yes, but I didn't just sit on his bed. I backed him into a corner and demanded to know what he was going to do about it. I mean physically.'

'Sounds like you ran out of patience and resorted to aggression. Yes, I have been to counselling about my marriages.'

'Well done.'

'I don't want to mess this marriage to Emma up. Mom and Daddio gave us such crap role models for marriage. Being married and not being able to stand each other for long periods of time. Are there text messages about going to Aldbourne? This is where he whistles and you go running to him. Delete all the messages between you and him and stop texting him. You emotionally blackmailed him to come to your wedding. I noticed he made sure to get here when all possible wedding stuff was over. He was happy on the dance floor with Miss Universe… until you did what?'

'It was what she did that triggered me. I rolled my eyes at Jonathan and cut him dead with one look.'

'You are like Carmen and that song about love. You play with fire. The only opera I liked, by the way…'

'I have Caribbean blood. Can you get more fiery than that? I forgot we took you to see that.'

'You also both remembered exactly where you were in the argument you last had. Like true Jamaicans. Mimi-man would be proud.' Mimi-man, Ben's brother who had a stammer, was famous for continuing an argument with Lucille when she went on holiday to Jamaica and hadn't seen him for thirty years. 'Aggressive eye signals… then what happened?'

'A member of staff gave me a Post-It note.' Delsea showed it to him.

'Who the fuck is Rex Jones?'

'An alias of his.'

'Is he in the secret service, with all these clandestine goings on?'

'Don't be silly. We made up aliases in our teens, so we could leave notes for each other. This means Gin was with him when he wrote the note. When he is around me, she is no doubt watching him like a hawk. So, he used his alias.'

'You got his room number and went to his room alone on your wedding day.'

'Don't put it like that.'

'It is like that. You can't ever tell Michael that you went to Jonathan's room. Seriously Del, that's beyond the pale.

When I saw you just now in the corridor you looked distressed. That crying you do, holding a limp wrist up to your face like a wounded puppy that no one can resist.'

'OK, when he opened the door he grabbed a handful of my dress front bodice, said, "look you fucking minx, you just married Michael, what do you want with me?" Then he shoved me in a corner.'

'I said, let go of my dress. Let go of me.'

'He said, Why have you come to my room?'

'I said I wanted you at my wedding as a guest. Not to turn up when it was all over. Why bother to come at all? He seemed totally confused. I'm still hemmed in the corner. So, I punched him in the stomach.'

'That's a pretty powerful way to say let me go. So does he let you out of the corner?'

'He's still trying to make sense of why I wanted him at my wedding as a guest.'

'Do *you* even know why you wanted him there?'

'I wanted his blessing.'

'That is pretty steep! Why do you need his blessing?'

'I wanted him to be OK about my marriage.'

'I have never understood the hold you two have over each other. But this is mental. You make him come to your wedding when he doesn't want to – and by the way you want him to be OK, about you marrying Michael. You asked the impossible of him. Then what happened? I hope you left while he was still baffled by all this pussy logic, as Daddio would say.'

'He got angrier and grabbed my dress again and pushed me backwards out of the door. I nearly fell over by his forceful eviction.'

'Good man. It's half ten. Michael probably thinks he needs to stay with the guests while you are indisposed. I didn't realise how naive you were, Del, when it came to men, until now. You played a dangerous game with Jonathan. It's to his credit that no harm came to you. I'm texting Michael.

How's the fort holding up?

Ben and Lucille have gone up to their room. My mum and dad are just leaving. Us younger folk are getting ready to seriously party.

We will be down. Mrs Valentine has gone to your room to freshen up.

Thanks for this, Marcus.

A soon come you hear?

'Thanks bro,' Del said.

'Don't talk to me. My head is mash up with all dis stuff. I will ask Jonathan and Miss Universe politely to leave. I don't want any more confrontations going on. I bet she is really pissed off with you too. She no doubt has her sights set on being the next Lady Ainsley and living in a stately home. It's now pretty clear to her that you are in her way. If she wasn't aware of it before.'

PITCOM

Officially Delsea took a sabbatical following her maternity leave. She therefore kept her membership of her professional bodies. She was in London for another PITCOM (Parliamentary IT Committee) meeting. The security man reminded her as he searched her bag that the use of mobile phones was forbidden in the House of Commons. The meeting was held in an upper chamber. Delsea was amongst the early arrivals. She made her way to a far side bench near the window, which looked out on a quad where the broad sun blazed. The chamber was hot and stuffy. The minister gave his speech conveying a panoramic vision of future technology in Britain. Everyone perked up when during question time City Mobile Telecommunications wanted to know when their operating license would be granted. This wasn't the forum, but there was nothing like putting the Secretary of State for Trade & Industry, President of the Board of Trade on the spot. At a noncommittal reply people relaxed again, as there would not be a new competitor on the block just yet.

Everybody was leaving the chamber to lunch in the Lords. Because of the narrow corridors the party strung out. Delsea was dithering along, talking to the IT Director of Nine, when from behind she caught sight of Jonathan. Childishly she darted through a door so he couldn't see her, but this door turned out to lead her into a small cupboard. It was a pity that it was not the cupboard suffragette Emily Davison hid in on the night of the 1911 census to have herself numerated in Westminster. Delsea didn't want to talk to Jonathan. When she peered out of the cupboard, thankfully he had gone.

She retrieved her coat and other belongings. Clearly, she didn't look well because the security guard asked her if she was feeling OK? From sheer weakness she gripped the edge of the table for a few moments. It felt like half her strength had gone. Old memories revolved, making her head spin. 'I'm fine,' she said.

She found herself wondering why she still loved him. It was perverse hankering after something that could never be. The fact that she couldn't put her finger on it gave her a reason to continue with the folly. If she could fathom the reason for her love, logic would prevail.

Love not me for comely grace,
For my pleasing eye or face,
Nor for any outward part,
No, nor for my constant heart:
For these may fail or turn to ill,
So thou and I shall sever:
Keep therefore a true woman's eye,
And love me still, but know not why–
So hast thou the same reason still
To doat upon me ever!
JOHN WILBYE

The whole scenario was ridiculous. She was in danger of opening the 'That's nonsense' compartment in her head. She decided to think no more about it and told herself it was for the best. But she knew this much: they weren't finished. They would meet again. Such was their relationship, one eluding, the other pursuing. The pendulum swung back and forth between them. Such was the paradox of their love. All she could say was that she was happy enough just knowing the world contained him.

Michael was vetting his new advert designed to attack Eurofone and Cellstar. A woman lost in the fog stood by her car clutching her mobile for safety. 'Chauvinistic,' Delsea said as she walked into the room. Make it a man and his young daughter. The slogan 'The airwaves are purple,' couldn't be changed, it was a running theme.

'I saw Jonathan today,' Delsea said to Michael. He went very still. She knew he was thinking that she never mentioned Jonathan unless she could help it.

'And?' he muttered, his mood altering.

'I hid. I feel awful for doing that.'

Michael went back to his chilled self. Then he said, 'Seeing him wouldn't affect you, if he meant nothing to you. I can't understand what you ever saw in him, anyway.'

'I do need to see him soon. It was so unexpected bumping into him like that. It made me realise how much I miss him. We were great friends, you know.'

'Why do you need to see him? It is bloody obvious that I dislike him. I don't want you seeing him.'

'He is working on something that was started before us! I want to know how it's going. We are partners in this joint venture.'

'I'm not having this. You know how I feel about you and him.'

'You can't forbid me seeing a friend, that's very controlling.'

'But he is not a friend, is he? He is your ex, with whom you had a child. Controlling? If you value our relationship, you'll give me some space.'

Michael went into nonspeaking mode. Soon Delsea had had enough of being sent to Coventry. She bathed Amy and put her to bed. He seemed calmer, lying on the sofa watching the Grand Prix. Delsea sat in the hollow left by his legs.

'Can we talk?'

'If we must.'

'I need to do this, whether you like it or not. I am not doing it for me.'

'You have a secret project, which happens to involve your ex.'

Delsea tried playfully to lighten the atmosphere. When love goes pear-shaped, bring in Elizabeth Barret Browning. "How do I love thee? Let me count the ways. I love thee to the depth and breadth and height my soul can reach, when feeling out of sight."

'So, you say.'

'There is no ulterior motive for seeing him.'

Michael was being weird, behaving as though Delsea had cheated on him. At night it was agony, them lying there, mute. Michael thought Jonathan was coming between them. That was debatable. Jonathan would have said it was Michael who came between him and Delsea. With hindsight it was stupid bringing up needing to see Jonathan. Delsea couldn't pretend that she didn't know how Michael would react to such a suggestion.

When the shock of seeing Jonathan in the House that day wore off, it seemed possible that Delsea could be in contact with him again when she was ready. The first encounter that knocked her sideways had already happened, so, there was less to fear. She really did want to see where Jonathan had got too with his task and what his plans were. But why did she think Michael would accept it because she said so? She wasn't thinking straight. She wasn't thinking about the consequences for her marriage. She could be making it up for all he knew. He probably thought she was.

Amy was sitting in a shopping trolley in the supermarket in Headington. Delsea was amid eyeing up the vegetables, deciding what to buy when something clicked in Michael's brain. It was like the breaking of a storm, he became unhinged.

'Haven't I loved every part of you, and you want to go and be a fucking whore with him!'

'Stop this, stop swearing in front of Amy. I have done nothing wrong. I'm not going to see him. I shouldn't have said I would.'

'It can't be fixed just like that. You said you missed him. I don't know what goes on in your brain. But get this, you can't have both of us. Either me or him.'

'Oh, shut the fuck up. I chose. I married you.'

That was what was eating him alive. The fact that she missed Jonathan. Fellow shoppers slowed down, intrigued. Like viewing a car crash, they wanted to hear the gory details. Why was Michael even here? He hated supermarket shopping. Did he think she had planned a tryst with Jonathan at the vegetable stall?

The store manager approached. 'Please finish your shopping and take this argument elsewhere.' Michael left, which solved the problem.

Delsea was clouded with doubt though, the damage was already done. How would not seeing Jonathan fix that now? She may as well see him. Things couldn't get any worse. Though she was lothe to pander to Michael's control freakery she couldn't do it, because she would know that she did something in their marriage that he was dead set against. His criticism undermined her like no other. He made her feel like a traitor.

The next morning Michael was in a foul mood. He didn't even bother to say goodbye, just got in his car and drove off. When the going got tough, he hid in his office. Delsea left Amy with her grandparents in Park Town and drove to the offices of Purple. She rarely went there. Certainly not when she was working herself, her own schedules were too full. When Amy was a baby or even a toddler the thought of tackling the drive to the Winnersh Triangle business park on her own with a crying youngster was not worth the aggravation. She hated going through Reading at the best of times. There were only two roads crossing the Thames, causing notorious traffic jams. Then the hideous IDR, Inner Distribution Road. But needs must.

The offices of Purple were everything she expected, OTT. Staff in expensive Pret-a-Porter designer clothes. If she had known that that was the uniform, she would have rummaged through her dressing room for something more flattering to wear. Then she thought again. Actually, her turning up in high street fashion brands may help those struggling to afford the attire.

She knew her way to Michael's office. His secretary who she had not met was acting like his custodian. Delsea would try talking to him to resolve the situation. He was not speaking to her but she could read his body language. She could interpret his stares. He was giving her his, I don't trust myself to speak to you, stare. Which meant he was avoiding them arguing. Delsea preferred to argue, and get whatever damaging upset out of the way. Then make up.

'Mr Valentine is busy.'

'Tell him his wife is here.' There was a pregnant pause, then a smile of growing respect.

'Go in, there's no one with him at the moment.'

'What an unexpected pleasure,' Michael said. Which meant he was not pleased. He didn't invite her to take a seat accidentally on purpose. Michael's personality was what she called tricksy. She felt slightly exasperated. Let's play annoying each other, she thought.

She looked around his state-of-the-art office. Then sat in one of the two chairs by his desk, which were in the style known as Airport Chic. Not designed to be comfortable, but for the occupant to spend as little time sitting as possible, to ensure that everyone had a chance to sit at some point during the wait for a flight. In Michael's case she knew he had selected those very chairs because he didn't want anyone to talk to him at length, unless he had invited them to do so. Then they would sit at his conference table.

She took after her mom in annoying her menfolk when she was dissatisfied with them. Provoking a low-key testy discussion rather than having a full-blown row. That was the objective anyway. She decided to annoy him by addressing the airport chair directly:

'Oh, come off it, ye tangled metal excuse for a chair, you are way too hard.' She chastised the despicable chair, drawing it back and fetching another from around his conference table.

'When you have quite finished rearranging my furniture.' Meaning do not move my stuff. He disliked people shifting his things around.

This next chair gave the impression of being an ordinary club chair. As she sat on it her bottom sank in like sitting on a bean bag. It was designed for comfort, engendering free thinking and brainstorming around the conference table, which she noticed was lower than a normal table to accommodate the sinking effect of the chairs. She addressed this chair: 'Fat object, nothing can throw your shape. You are way too soft.' There was only one other chair left in the room and he was sitting in it. She went and sat on his lap. 'This chair is just right.' He was spellbound. Her idiosyncrasy disarmed him, as it always did. Under pressure he was sending her confused signals. She had achieved the desired effect. He had to move away from his tried and tested dismissive one liner's. He had to engage and speak.

'You can't come into my office and sit on my lap.'

'Why ever not? I am your wife.'

'It is not a professional look.'

'So, what. If you had said goodbye to me and Amy properly, I wouldn't need to come to your office for a speck of affection.'

He kissed her cheek. 'Now go away.'

'Whoa,' as she got up to leave, he realised he was irritated by 'speck of affection,' and drew her back by the elbow. 'I can do better than that.' They kissed properly. Mollified and having made her point, she left. It was Shelly's Love's Philosophy: "See the mountain's kiss high heaven, And the moonbeams kiss the sea – What are all these kissings worth, If thou not kisseth me?"

Lying beside Michael she was certain he was awake, feigning sleep. With the light extinguished she snuggled close to him for warmth. She listened to the beat of his heart, before reaching out for him.

He stroked her thigh. Her heart was anticipating his so she cuddled even closer. She knew every freckle, every mole on his back. She put her arm around him, reaching down. The rhythm of her movements matched his breath, slowing, accelerating, rising, falling till he couldn't stand it anymore without participating. It was an intense coming together. She, submitted to him. She, was full of him. She could feel nothing but him inside her. She prolonged her orgasm. She loved the increased sensitivity that teetering on the brink gave her. She loved that feeling of inner tension as much as she loved the release.

'I love you, Michael,' she said. 'There is no one I love as much as you.'

'I know. Sometimes I over-think things. You must know why I dislike him. He abandoned you and Josh. You have forgiven him. I can't. He doesn't deserve your friendship.'

'Sometimes I wish you would say more and think less. But then you wouldn't be you. The man I love. It wasn't that simple. I blocked him from my mind and life. We share an intellect. He made me laugh. Josh is the product of a one-night stand. We never were a couple. I could not have the happiness I have with you, with him.'

'Why have you not told me about the one-night stand before? That explains a lot.'

'Because I don't like talking about him. And you don't want me to mention him either.'

'Clearly we should talk about him.'

'No. I have said enough. Let it be.'

READING

Delsea was late for her lunch with Ted. Finding a parking spot in Jericho, Oxford was a nightmare, driving up and down cramped streets and dead ends trying to find curb parking for at least two hours. They were lunching at Brasserie Blanc in Walton Street. Raymond Blanc's first brasserie, which she often frequented. She hurried towards the restaurant knowing that Ted would be anxiously waiting. Thinking she wasn't coming.

Ted borrowed a greeting from the past. 'Hello you.' Only Ted greeted her that way. She gave him a hug. He pulled back the chair for her. Ted sparing time from his hectic schedule to lunch with a bored housewife was very kind of him except she had no time for lethargy.

She enjoyed being with Amy and had plenty to do. She would be tearing her hair out if her only outlet was the toddler group. Amy was past that age, about to start nursery school in the Autumn. Though she did miss work. She had decided to hand in her notice and not go back to Cellstar where her options were still open. Amy being a sickly child was her excuse for taking so much time off.

'What made you give up?' Ted enquired.

'Amy. I wanted more time at home with her, I missed out not having quality time with Josh when he was young. Your Janice stayed home too.'

'Janice was never a talented career woman.'

'Let's order. You are looking at this with rose coloured glasses. We often disagreed over strategy.'

The waiter approached with bread and olive oil. Then took their order.

'I'll have the cheese souffle to start and the Malabar Fish Curry. Ted, what about you?'

'For me the grilled smoked salmon to start and the lamb tagine. Wine? Delsea?'

'To start with we will have white Picpoul de Pinet,' then she looked to Ted? He was having lamb for his main.

'A glass of Beaujolais Village, with my main,' he answered.

'You always stuck to your guns though, Delsea, I liked that.'

'We did get on well in a funny sort of way.'

'Look, I wanted to see you about Michael. To check you were OK.'

'Why?'

'I just spent a week on business with him. He was sounding incredibly possessive about you. Something about some other guy you are stringing along. He said this guy had nothing to lose and he couldn't help thinking that him still being single had a lot to do with you. That he's in the wings waiting to snatch you back.'

'He's talking about Josh's father. Yes, I know he thinks that. But I am not a domestic object. I don't have Stockholm Syndrome. I would need to participate in this kidnap which I have no intention of doing. He does my head in with his morbid jealousy.'

'Look, I want to give you some advice, if I may. These alpha males you attract, this could all turn nasty.'

'That is absurd. I'm fine, I'm perfectly safe.'

'This situation sounds dangerous, Del, you are playing with fire and totally oblivious to it.' Interesting, as Jonathan would say. Marcus said the same thing about Jonathan. Neither Michael or Jonathan scared her. She couldn't see either of them hurting her. She had the intuition of the moon, which was never wrong.

'I hear you.'

'It is muggins here you turn to when it goes belly up.'

'Nothing will go wrong. I can handle myself. Has it ever occurred to you that I am an alpha female? I might let Michael lead, but here's the thing. He cannot lead me anywhere that I don't want to go. I might let him tell me what to do. But he can't make me do anything I don't want to do. Like a lot of women who want an easy life. I just let him think he is in charge.'

'What about the boyfriend who stole your company car? I had to pretend to be Fleet Management to retrieve it for you.'

'There was that,' they both laughed.

Sometimes she thought about returning to work. Michael understood her deliberations. It would have had to have been a job she really wanted to do. After being on maternity, then sabbatical, she did not feel as confident. At times she doubted her ability to ever work again. As the absence lengthened the more her doubts grew. She was aware of her privileged position. She had no financial worries and could therefore afford to stay at home as long as she wanted. Ted understood her temperament, that she relished being out there with the rampant testosterone, for her that extra challenge heightened the job satisfaction. But could she hack it after a three-year break?

Ted had made her feel nostalgic about working, the challenges, even the social life. She did try to keep abreast of things. So, she decided as a possible returnee to attend her regional Thames Valley meeting of BE (Black Executives), a working group affiliated to the People's Party that had just begun. The meeting was being held in a Reading hotel.

It was a lovely drive outside rush hour from Oxford to Reading. It was a day for smiles, and shades. Cool breezes and strong sun. White flowering nettles waved as she drove by. Glorious colours of arable farming across the Goring plains.

After the welcome coffee and social networking, it was down to business. The session got off to a bad start with everyone wanting to share their experiences of workplace harassment. Things quickly deteriorated. The social networking beforehand had allowed those discussions to begin, as small talk, which spilled uncontrollably into the meeting.

Every conceivable grievance against colleagues and employers was being aired tempered with disparaging remarks. She thought all employers couldn't be tarred with the same brush, but she kept her counsel. There were misunderstandings in the workplace, it wasn't all malice. This was hardly productive. Gathered were those strong in will seemingly made weak by fate. Middle managers trying to take their place in higher echelons.

They complained of employers being impressed when hiring. Saying they were just what the company needed only to get there and be undermined by jealous colleagues making fictional complaints to their manager who would then interfere in their jobs as though they were probationers requiring micro-management.

Complaints by other employees about their work being inadequate, shoddy, unfit for purpose. The ubiquitous complaints were unfounded. Those complained to having poor judgement. Unsound repercussions followed. Managers who had trouble discerning when they had missed or exceeded the mark. Those who couldn't tell the difference between constructive criticism being made to them or racism or sexism. In the end employing them was too much hassle for the organisation. If there was a cull, they were the first to go.

They were given the worst shifts, the least overtime and the monkey work to do. There was no chance of them being promoted to a position requiring brain power. Not even the incentives offered to others did they receive.

Their concerns were fobbed off as isolated incidents not worth making a fuss about. Passive aggressive threats were made about burning bridges. Them complaining was a clear sign they couldn't cope with what they already had. They knew they were capable of going higher. They were not being given the opportunity to shine.

Frightened Human Resources only there to protect the company failing to act, were worse than useless. It being more than their job was worth putting a stop to harassment, totally lacking in sympathy. Invoking the rules there to protect employees would be difficult without going through the mill. The company would play dirty. Was it worth it? Risking their reputation for a moral victory.

Working in these environments was wearing, like repeated shocks again and again till they were sick with fatigue. She was momentarily saddened by it all. The pathos, the banality of the wretchedness was soul destroying.

Finally, the Chair got control. 'Let's not go off at tangents, is there some good we can capture from this?' Diffusing the situation by being constructive. They ended up defining the Rules for Success.

- 🕮 They can only laugh once. After the first unsuspecting cut you are wise to it next time.

- 🕮 Use laughter, it deescalates tension. Laughter is fireproof and universal.

- 🕮 If you don't succeed aim higher. Overshooting showcases your talent useful for the next shot.

- Treat every change as an opportunity. Look for that silver lining.

- It is not always best to move straight upwards. A diagonal move up can sometimes be more effective.

- The diagonal move can conceal your advancement. You are only noticed once you've arrived.

- If you can't cope, there is always another company.

- Keep in mind who you are worth money too. Such as competitors.

- No matter how your job is curtailed, try to negotiate your way out to your advantage; compensation, placement training, laptop for applications, mobile to catch opportunities, time out for interviews, company car to get there. There is a budget for these things which is always underused.

She was glad after all that to be heading home to the seclusion of Westmead. Westmead gave her peace. She couldn't go back to living in a jumbled conurbation where everyone interfered with each other. She was sequestered in the countryside away from maliciousness. Safe from prejudice. Fewer neighbours were tucked into her small corner of the world where she only saw people she wanted to see. Though buying Westmead had been a to-do. The lady next door said to Michael accusingly that the elderly couple who sold them the house hadn't told her that his wife was black. He told Del, with no elaboration at all. He treated it as a comment that didn't need to be made. It was never mentioned again. Del sat on the village hall committee and advised on Health & Safety. She was one of them. She was sure anyway that the sellers of Westmead couldn't have cared less about the colour of her skin. Their son was married to an Indian woman. Call her paranoid but living in a cul-de-sac approachable from only one direction made her feel safer still. People were unlikely to sail up the Thames to deliver hatred.

The meeting returned her imposter syndrome. Her business path came back to her as clear as though it were yesterday. She had followed it with pride. By comparison to some of those at BE, she had had an easier time rising to the top. There weren't many women at that time earning the salaries she commanded. She had broken the mould, smashed the glass ceiling to smithereens in a field dominated by men. It was belittling though, the way some men thought it was easier for her to succeed because she was a woman. Completely dissing her efforts.

She had microaggressions in the workplace where thoughts of revenge crossed her mind with the first flush of anger. She ignored niggles designed to provoke her. Common sense always prevailed. Counterattack was futile, a waste of time. She even found catharsis counterproductive. Venting her spleen resulted in more stress than had she remained calm.

The BE group were hurt, angry and all the rest of it with good cause. She hoped they'd stay strong. She was not sure she could have withstood such battering. It had cost them so much to get that far. She hoped they wouldn't throw away years of effort because of a few bastards. It was sad to hear the struggles some had getting ahead. No amount of questionable ethnic performative allyship monitoring pretence, decreased the frustration they felt about not being able to advance using the talents God gave them.

She felt raw after attending the meeting. As though she had been exposed to poison. They were unable to recapture their careless youth where everything felt possible. They once had a spirit full of adventure, trembling with anticipation of the great things they would do. It was gone in the snap of a finger. Lost to them somehow.

She became melancholy driving home. But mostly she hoped they could put the loss of a job into perspective. In the great scheme of things, it was only a job. Being handed a wad of cash and told to piss off, laugh all the way to the bank. More lucrative work was available if searched for in the right direction.

People seemed but atoms, neatly balanced entities bouncing off one another, colliding causing instability, regaining the charge only to shoot off again.

As the brown dusk fell she was feeling more mellow. She could see moths fluttering in her headlights. She loved the way her tyres crunched on the loose gravel as she swung the car into the drive causing a flurry of wings from the Horse Chestnut tree which told her she was home.

Thanks Ted, she thought later. Nothing could persuade her to go back to that cesspit called work. She had a husband who doted on her. Too much sometimes. She only had to frown at something and he would fix it. Mr Fix-It should know, as W. H. Davies said: "What is this life if full of cares, we have no time to stand and stare." Michael wasn't the only one to stare. She liked to stand and stare too. She was scrutinising outdoor bushes from the kitchen window that were turning from flower to fruit.

She said out loud, 'I have two gorgeous children.'

'Let's make that three,' Michael chimed in from behind. That made her laugh. She turned round and hugged him good morning.

It was Friday evening. They were expecting Marcus and Emma for the weekend. The beef was cooking nicely. She made a French apple tart for afters. Ever since she learnt to bake in domestic science classes at her all-girls school, Marcus would beg her to make him apple pie. Which tasted better back then when they were young, because in Daddio's best kept garden she picked apples fresh. Daddio even managed to preserve them throughout the winter, without a freezer. He would wrap them individually in newspaper, placing them in a single layer in a wooden crate.

Their guests should arrive any moment. She hoped they hadn't had too much trouble negotiating the Friday evening traffic. The M4 could be brutal.

The formal dining room which they hardly used, preferring the breakfast room next to the kitchen, looked lovely. Lucille's hand embroidered table cloth in pastel colours was a beautiful background for the silver cutlery and crystal wine glasses. Lucille spent hours making lace, all sorts of sewing crafts. She always had a needle in her hand and the treadle sewing machine whirring away in the background of her childhood. When she was small, she used to sit on the rocking plate by Lucille's feet rocking back and forth as though it were a piece of play equipment instead of the child maiming nightmare it was with the big wheel spinning round, ready to catch her hair or fingers.

The evening was wrapped in damp. Michael helped Marcus transfer the sleeping children from the car to their beds. Marcus had all three of them some weekends, Kahlil, Addison and Nico. Marcus always bought them a bottle of red, which he handed to Delsea. Emma leaned against a kitchen base unit. She'd lost a lot of weight in the past few months since having Nico. She was feeding him herself which helped.

'Do you like the new trim me?'

'You always look great, Emma, you take after your mother.' Emma had mousy hair which she enhanced with blond highlights. Her skin was alabaster. Without foundation you could see the fine blue veins at her temple. She had a frail look about her, but actually she was really tough. She made Delsea laugh, with her combative way of folding her arms under her bosom, as if she were holding them up like a fishwife. She was a Wiltshire Sloane, into horses. When in Corsham she dressed in jodhpurs, and leather riding boots which she hardly changed out of. Her social life was full of show jumping, eventing and hunting. Delsea thought her family must have money as horses were an expensive hobby.

'You always look so elegant, Del.' Conservative but trendy when she tried she was often told.

She got out prosecco, tubs of olives marinated in garlic, cherry tomatoes, some rolled Italian ham and cocktail sticks. She placed these on a side table with some long stem crystal glasses. Each with a drink in hand. They laughed a lot their small family group. It was a scene that was played out regularly between them.

'Are people ready to eat?' Enquired Michael. Emma wanted to freshen up and change. Nico was at the stage where he still posseted on her shoulder. She showed Emma to her room which had an ensuite bathroom.

'I've put you in here. I hope it's alright.'

'That's very considerate, Del.'

'Have you got everything you need? Towels are in the drawer in the bathroom.'

She went back down to help Michael.

'What d'you think, Sis, to me educating the boys in Jamaica where they would stand a better chance.'

'I know this may sound selfish, Marcus. No. Fight for a good education here. I couldn't bear it if you moved abroad. Wat would mi do widout mi bredda?' She could hardly breathe at the thought of that loss, never mind be constructive about it. She felt panicked. No more words would come out. Then she didn't know why, be it BE or something else, tears from the depths of despair gathered in her eyes. 'Hey,' said Michael. He couldn't stand it if she cried. Without knowing why, she was crying, he couldn't fix it. The bang of the cat flap somehow stopped her from completely breaking down. Cleo, their cat, came in. She picked her up and stroked her fur tenderly. She was a good sedative. The tranquil sound of water could be heard gushing through the weir on the river. That hypnotic seranade restored her calm.

CAMBRIDGE

When Josh returned for the third year, verbal warfare broke out between Tom and him. Josh had beaten Tom academically in both the first and second year. He was the top scholar in the second year, which earned him the privilege of doing the reading in Latin at the beginning of formals.

Tom came to Josh and Tamsin as they were relaxing in the college bar.

'Can I join you?' He sat down before they could say anything.

'Toni's depression is real, you know.'

'And you are telling us this why? I specifically told you to stop harassing me about her. Under what auspices has she roped you in now?'

'She feels hopeless, disabled. That she can't control her own life, being in a wheelchair, and that her life has no meaning.'

'And this is my problem why? She did that to herself!'

'She's made another attempt on her life. She took an overdose. She wrote you a note.'

'Is she dead?'

'No.'

'Her poor parents. No doubt they rushed her to hospital in a panic. She has no compassion for them. She's just selfish. I am not interested in her suicide ideation, real or otherwise, Tom.'

'She's in hospital. She asked me to give you the note.'

'I don't want to read her note.'

'Tom, why should Josh read her note?'

'I wouldn't read her note even if she was dead. Will no one rid me of this troublesome woman.'

'You don't care if she dies! You're just a Heinz 57 mongrel who doesn't even know who your father is.'

'I know exactly who my father is. For your information he's white, not Jamaican at all.'

'Oh, is he now? Some white trash from a council estate who dumped you at birth?'

'You want to know who my father is? He's Jonathan Ainsley MP, Chancellor of the Exchequer.'

'So that's how you got in here? You didn't have to get the grades the rest of us did. No wonder you have to swot.'

'Fuck right off, Holloway.' Tom slammed Toni's note on the table between them. Josh tore it to pieces.

'Are you going to be OK for the reading tonight?' Tamsin asked.

'Word perfect, Tammie. You have no idea what you mean to me. You're always there for me. It is nice to know I'm not in this alone. You are all I have at college. I can't even put into words how I feel about you. You give me the strength to get through this. Two more terms of hell. Then we can put this behind us and get on with our lives.'

Jonathan had emailed a few times about visiting him in Cambridge. Josh could imagine Holloway's face as this was soon to happen. He felt he had the strength to take Tom Holloway on and put a stop to the harassment once and for all. He needed to be more direct, he thought.

Since he'd been back, Josh had been letting his meeting with Jonathan sink in. It had had quite an effect on him to know him again after all this time. But he felt ambivalent too about the whole thing. On the one hand he was glad he'd met him, on the other he wanted to plough his own furrow. Would Jonathan's public persona allow him to do that? It was like Jonathan was two different people. The ubiquitous one with combative tones who permeated the media, and the private person his mum had told him about. The truth was that, despite everything Jonathan had or had not done, there were things he liked about him. There was a bond between them. It was only having caught up with Jonathan that the emptiness he felt deep inside was subsiding. He felt more solid.

Yet he still resented Jonathan having had a life that didn't include him. He had felt denied, abandoned. Jonathan had walked out of his life without looking back. Josh had grieved for that loss as a young child. He hardly remembered the times when Jonathan was around. What he did recollect though was that when he was, he had to come first in Delsea's affections. There was hardly any room for him. He wanted to stay in touch with him. Though their connection was intense. Condensed as it was by the pieces coming together so quickly. It was difficult trying to form a relationship in the present, as adults. He had the power to deny him fatherhood, just as he had been deprived of him when he was little and needy. He wanted more time to understand Jonathan, who was to all intents and purposes a fairly complex character.

He recalled wanting to be adopted by Michael, only because he didn't like having a different surname to theirs. He wasn't even interested in adoption. He didn't really know what it meant. It was starting senior school, at thirteen, at Goring College, which gave them the opportunity to change his surname from Johnson to Valentine.

There was no chance of Michael's position as his dad being usurped. He had been a brilliant dad to him. He wouldn't hurt his feelings in any way, shape or form. He had been more of a dad to him than Jonathan had ever been. When Michael came into his life his mum was happy. They would include him in their hugs – family hugs, they were called. He loved that they included him in their love and affection. Michael would lift and throw him high into the air, until he giggled uncontrollably. He did ask where Jonathan had gone at first. Back to his people, Michael said dismissively. Josh thought of Jonathan crossing the sea and travelling hundreds of miles away, never to be seen again.

Josh sat looking at the only photograph of them that he had with him. Jonathan looked like he was in his early twenties. He put the framed photo of them which had been in his bedroom as a child on his desk. There was so much he could say. But he'd said enough. He was aware that any child could come up with a list of pros and cons about their parents.

Yet when he saw Jonathan at the plodge, his first reaction was 'Dad?' It sprang from nowhere, the phrase he had not used since aged nine. Why had he said it? Perhaps because he had been reminiscing. He didn't feel Jonathan was his dad. But he remembered it. Remembered he had called him that before Michael came along. He didn't know what would come out next, they were still like strangers.

For Jonathan, Cambridge conjured up memories of Oxford. Concepts he thought had vanished, came flooding back. The pace was slow compared to the frantic bursts of energy he was forced to display in the fast and furious political world. His life was out of balance with too much work. It was a pleasure just sitting on a bench by the river Cam. He looked up. The clouds were beginning to clear. It would be a fine afternoon after all. The soft lull of water was peaceful. He listened to bells ringing out in the background.

He wanted his son in his life. Though he kept putting up barriers he wasn't as tough as he made out. Jonathan felt like a fool. Josh semi-hated him and he wasn't sure if he could turn that around. It did look like neglect on his part from Josh's point of view. Sometimes Josh came across as angry on his or Delsey's behalf. Everything that was wrong in their lives was because of him. Everything that was bad was his fault. On some level he felt that Josh wanted to hurt him, like he'd made him suffer. But he could tell that he was really a sensitive person trying not to show it. He was outwardly cool but it was obvious that inside he couldn't bear any kind of bad feeling or unpleasantness between the people he loved.

They were meeting for a lunchtime organ recital at another college chapel, then following that with lunch out. Walking down King's Parade he felt more alive than he had for ages. Josh coming back into his life was the best thing that had happened to him in a long while. Josh met him at the Porter's Lodge. It was strange that Josh had called him dad. Perhaps subconsciously they were getting somewhere. They reached Josh's room, which was at the end of a corridor. As a third-year student he was in the main quad. He had a bedroom with a small sitting room attached.

Josh was making them tea, stirring sugar into his with a biro.

'Haven't you got a teaspoon?' Jonathan asked, as though they saw each other every day.

'Somewhere,' Josh said, watching the bubbles break and disperse on the surface. He was in two minds as to whether to tell Jonathan about Toni. It seemed easier than telling his mum or dad, because Jonathan was still sort of a stranger, and it would go no further.

'Have you enjoyed Ariel?'

'Sort of.' Josh was being vacant.

'What's wrong, Josh?'

The decision was made for Josh by Jonathan asking him that question.

'There's this girl I was friends with, who fell in love with me in the first year. I don't feel the same. She dropped out of college and is self-harming to get my attention. She thinks I am going to turn around and tell her that I love her after all.'

'You should speak to her. Do it now, while I'm here to support you.'

Josh picked up his mobile 'Antonia, it's me. Please stop hurting yourself. I don't love you, but there are others in your life that do: your parents, brother and sister. Your love for me is not more important than your life. I am sorry about what happened between us, as it gave you the wrong impression about my feelings for you. I haven't called before, because I thought a break from me would allow you to forget about me. Maybe one day we can be friends again. But not now, Toni. You should concentrate on yourself, not me. I hope you feel better soon.'

'I won't Josh, because I love you. I can't switch that off just like that. You have no idea what that's like.'

'Actually, I do know. I'm in love with someone who's difficult to love. I am sorry it's not you but there it is.' She put the phone down.

'Well said,' Jonathan approved. 'She'll hopefully mull that over and face the reality of the situation. Intriguing though Josh. This difficult someone is not Merin, I take it?'

'No, it's not Merin. Stop fishing.' For a moment Josh imagined that this was what it would have been like having his dad, lurking around demanding to know what he was up to or what was going on. Michael was laid back – more of a friend. Jonathan had been no more than a vague presence, somewhere in his subconscious, who breezed in and out of their lives. He never thought to go to him for help and yet without question he followed his advice. He wished he'd got to know him sooner. He had wondered what to do when he finished at Ariel. He was looking into being a Patent Attorney where he could use his degree specialism of the physical sciences. Maybe he could get a job in London, even move in with Jonathan for a while.

'How's the studying going?' Jonathan thought it best to change the subject.

'I shall get back to it once you've gone.' That sounded to Jonathan as though he wanted him gone already. But confusingly there was a photo of them on Josh's desk. In it he was relaxed, and unshaven. He was young, it reminded him that he was forced to mature too quickly. Briefly he compared himself to that photo, it was hard to reconcile who he was with that person. It was hard to reach Josh. He was glad to have shared the father son moment they'd just had. He was also perturbed by the slightly odd way that Josh kept looking at him, as if searching for similarities in their characters.

Josh was thinking that this was like his childhood dreams of his dad coming back to him, before he bonded with Michael. This was no dream though, there was no fading at the margins but distance had left his memories hazy.

'Shall we go?' Josh said, getting his things together, putting on his hoody.

Josh saw Tom Holloway scowl at him from the other side of the aisle. Then Tom childishly gave him the finger, when he saw Josh observing him, as if to say, Don't fucking look at me. Afterwards as he and Jonathan strolled into town for lunch, Jonathan enquired about that incident, which Josh had hoped had gone unnoticed.

'Do you know that boy? Why was he being rude?'

'He's at my college.'

'Who is he?'

'Tom Holloway.'

'Was he giving you or me the finger?'

'Probably both of us.'

'Is that something else that needs sorted? His behaviour seemed odd, in a public place, in a chapel!'

'I think I have it under control, Dad. There is just a term to go. It's mainly concentrating on finals now, as you know. He's not worth the hassle.'

They relaxed into the same stride. Neither of them felt the need to make further conversation. Jonathan walked Josh back to Jehovah College which was silhouetted against the warm grey sky, where they said their goodbyes. Josh had no wish to make things easy for Jonathan.

Once back in his office in the treasury, Jonathan had his secretary contact the Master of Jehovah College. He remembered Josh's comment that the ability to fight off an attack depended on how much you had already deflected that day. He was under no illusions about this boy giving Josh grief on a regular basis.

There were many distinguished parents of undergraduates at Ariel. Mr Chancellor was a call the Master felt he should accept personally.

'Good afternoon, Mr Chancellor, what can I do for you?'

'There seems to be some unpleasantness between my son Joshua Valentine and Tom Holloway.'

'This has been brought to our attention before by one of Joshua's friends who has informed us of the situation. She told us in confidence. She did say that Joshua did not want to make a formal complaint.'

'What have you done about it?'

'His tutor has enquired after his welfare. Joshua doesn't want to engage on the topic.'

'I witnessed Tom Holloway's unhealthy behaviour towards my son when I visited Joshua last week. The boy seems unstable. This needs to be dealt with. You need to be vigilant even if Joshua is prepared to tough it out.'

'We will do our best to keep them apart, but this is a small college. That may not be possible in all situations.'

'I shall hold you responsible if anything untoward happens to my son.'

'I am sure it won't come to that. Tom was his best friend in the first year. Students, young men, fall out. Often the friends they make early on are not those they end up with. They are sophisters nearing graduation. But let me assure you, if the problem escalates, we will nip it in the bud.'

'Thank you.'

Jonathan thought that if the mysterious love interest was concerned that made the situation more worrying.

EDUCATIONAL SABOTAGE

Josh was home for the Easter holidays. The household felt complete with him there. Steeped in drowsiness, Delsea looked out at the garden to see the change of season. She noticed the spring flowers blooming, from leaf to flower. Michael was being really horrible so much so that she phoned his mother Anna because he was still not his usual self and she didn't know what to do.

'When did this start?' she asked.

'Yesterday, all day he was sitting at the piano striking odd keys and scribbling on manuscript paper. He literally disappeared into creativity and I didn't think I should interrupt him. He is passionate about music as you know.'

'He has always been like that. He was a cathedral chorister at Christ Church School. A music scholar at Magdalen College School. When he used to disappear like that, we nicknamed him Michelangelo.'

'That's sweet. Anyway, then at 11pm he suddenly slammed the lid of the piano down. It was like he came down to earth and was angry that I had not reminded him of the passage of time as if it were my fault. He accused me of starving him as he hadn't eaten all day.'

'So did he eat then and did he go to bed?'

'I don't know. At some point I knew he was in bed with me. I woke up alone but I often do as he is a morning person whereas I am not. I thought it was good that he was doing something with his music.'

'It's not a good sign, dear. He's not allowed to have a piano. It drives him insane and everyone else around him. He has been warned that it was best for him not to have a piano of his own or to pursue a music career.'

'He plays beautifully.'

'If he comes across a piano, it is fine for him to play it and to enjoy going to concerts and the opera, but he is not to have a piano of his own.'

At which point Michael opened the door and shouted, 'You better not be talking to that fucking bitch Anna. She sabotaged my education and ruined my life. That fucking cunt ensured that I could never have the life I wanted.'

'Michael, stop swearing please. Yes, I am talking to your mother.'

'I can hear him, dear. He has called me worse names for looking after him. If you are going to let him keep that piano you need to be his barometer ensuring he eats regularly, sleeps intermittently, otherwise he will get really ill and need hospitalisation. When he gets like that, he can't cope with basic things like remembering he needs food, drink and sleep by himself. When we came to Josh's twenty-first and his surprise present to Josh was that extremely expensive piano, we knew that he had used the excuse of Josh's birthday to allow himself that grand piano. He probably told himself that it wasn't for him, but for Josh.' The upright piano was slow and rough.

'Well Josh does play too, he had lessons at Goring College. Michael encouraged him to get up to grade 8. What on earth are you talking about Anna? I am not following any of this.'

'I'm not sure if it is happening again. I had to nurse him through his last year at GCM, with the help of his professor. He had to produce a composition piece to graduate. It nearly killed me. What was he doing before the piano arrived?'

'He was fussing about which room it should go in, we moved everything out of the sitting room. We moved the sitting room upstairs to the front bedroom. Which I quite like because we get a clear view up and down the river, and of the lock and the canal boats passing through. Then he didn't like the sound of the piano with the carpet down. We took it up and got someone in to sand the floorboards. He said that the carpet was absorbing and dampening the sound of the piano. He has declared the room his music room. It looks fantastic I must say with the floor sanded and lacquered and nothing in it but the grand piano all opened up.'

'This does sound like a build-up to a hypomanic episode. What about Purple?'

'He is selling now it is established in the marketplace. He said he wanted to concentrate on music. I was glad when he said that, to be fair. It is not as though we need the money and it allows him to spend more time with us and not miss out on Amy's childhood. Why did no one see fit to tell me about this? I must go. He keeps coming into the hall and shouting really horrible things at me. I think I should come over to Park Town late this afternoon. You and Tony can then explain to me what you or he should have told me when we got engaged nine years ago. I need to know about what happened fifteen years ago.'

'You broke our agreement. Not to tell you this may be less stressful, but it wouldn't be true. You lied. I don't think you are taking me seriously when I mention our agreement.'

'I have no idea what you are angry about, Michael.'

'I told you not to buy those yellow towels. Yet you went behind my back and got them anyway.'

'Stop this.'

'It is not because you made a case for buying those towels to complement that bathroom. It is because you haven't acknowledged that we had an agreement. We both agreed that we should have equal choice about what went into or what was done to the house. We agreed that each could veto the other. You didn't even ask me before you bought those towels. If you had I could have considered it in light of the agreement. You dismissed my right to be there to make a choice by going shopping alone as if I am not qualified to have a view. I don't give a shit really about the towels, but I am serious about you breaking our agreement. We both agreed, no IFS or BUTS, that if one of us said no the other would accept it. You might think it effeminate that I want to be involved, you usually do. But I considered our agreement to be a contract. In the past it was sealed by a handshake and was considered to be a significant dishonour to break it either factually or in spirit. The only way to honourably break it was by mutual agreement.'

'I am not listening to this, when you are bandying around such deep meaning words as honour and trust about soft furnishing a house. You are a bully. You will say anything to get your own way. Even put the trust we have in each other, at stake because I bought some yellow towels! Honour was part of our wedding vows. If you can't truly trust me, what is the point of being together? If you can't trust me then there is no relationship. Most couples save trust issues in a relationship for extramarital affairs. Whereas after eight years of marriage to you trust is broken because I bought some yellow towels. Wow.'

'It is not because you bought the fucking towels. It is because you won't acknowledge that we had an agreement. You missed out the bit where you should have said I know we agreed that we each had a veto, but in this case can you reconsider. Do what you like, you always do, but please don't blame the breakdown in trust on you making a strong case for wanting those hideous yellow towels. As far as I am concerned you broke the agreement, and that is no trivial matter.'

'Trust and now honour in our marriage has gone. I am not staying with you if you are going to operate by coercive control. I didn't reply this morning when you saw that I was upset by what you said last night about my not feeding you and I was hurt by your behaviour. When you said: "What kind of fucking wife does not feed her husband and that you couldn't trust me to do anything right." This morning you tried to turn the tables on me by coercing me into admitting that I didn't trust you either. When I do trust you implicitly. Stop telling me what I should feel or what I should say. Your way of ending an argument by dragging me down to your level is totally unacceptable.'

'Let me try and respond to that right now. You think I am deliberately trying to coerce you into saying things you don't want to say. When have I ever been able to control you when "he" has totally spoilt you with all this answering back! Don't make me laugh. Coercing you would be a pointless exercise. You are the most headstrong, independent woman I have ever known.'

Josh came down. 'What the fuck, mum and dad? I have never heard you two argue this way before. I have been terrified to come downstairs to breakfast for at least an hour because the atmosphere in this house is toxic. Dad, I will be with you in a minute.' At which Michael yet again slammed the door of his music room.

'Mum, go away, and stop crowding him by hovering around outside his door. He doesn't like you answering him back at the best of times. Go and see Amy who has been crying for at least fifteen minutes.'

'Why shouldn't I answer him back in my own home, these are not the Victorian days!'

'Because he doesn't like arguing with you. No one can win an argument with you once you get going! You are a font of knowledge, if you sense someone is getting the better of you in an argument you start going what Dad calls lateral, using indirect creativity through reasoning to batter him down. I know Jonathan is an extrovert wordsmith and could probably handle anything you threw at him but Dad is not like that. He is an introvert, more into his thoughts. You make him anxious when you get into pulling lateral things that he doesn't understand out of the fount to hit him with.'

'He told you this?'

'Yes. You wind him up with your challenging intellect and worst of all he says sometimes you enjoy doing it. Just now you are making things worse.' There was probably some truth in that. She had a sapiosexual side to her character which got frustrated with being married to an intelligent man who wouldn't talk to her. That wasn't the whole story. She also suffered from Retired Husband Syndrome.

'So, I'm in the wrong, am I? When he's the one not making sense, going on about yellow towels.'

'This has nothing to do with the yellow towels, as I am sure you well know. By the way you must show them to me,' said Josh laughing. 'They sound incredible to have inspired such divine instability. Go away, Mum, let me deal with this. You don't understand music. It is not uncommon for musicians to descend or in this case ascend into mental illness, especially highly strung classical musicians like Dad.'

As she walked away, Delsea took a peep inside the music room. Josh was at the piano, helping Michael in any way he could. Thank God for Josh.

After supper, which Josh dominated Delsea told them both about going to Anna's with Amy.

'Gran is out of order, not letting Dad go through his creative storm and out the other end. Because she was scared, she took him to the doctors who agreed with her that he needed sedation and sleep. Leaving him in a mental hospital for a week.'

Michael remembered being in Littlemore Mental Hospital. Virtually locked in a room like a cell. Apart from his bed the room was empty, except for one picture on the wall. A flawed flower. He was so sedated that it was as much as he could do to squint at the flower, which contained the madness of a previous occupant. Like a patient who awakes during an operation, he felt mental pain but couldn't cry out. Nothing worked – not even speech. He tried to rouse his shaky mind from the depths by concentrating on the asymmetrical flower by adding the missing petals with careful mind strokes. Trying to make it whole, symmetrical once again.

An infusion of light from the door intersected his hand as he held it to that source. The light around the door grew, occupying the perimeter. Someone was talking with a hand on the outside knob. He knew that voice: Anna, his mother. She brought in a plastic chair and sat by his side. Her hair was long auburn brown, not like his, which was jet black. Her arms had splatterings of brown freckles. Behind her the possessed flower wilted. Anna was pale beneath her freckled cheeks. Her hair fell into her eyes, which she flicked away. Her eyes brimming with tears had bags underneath so it was not the first shedding of eye water. He tried to make her feel better by joining the dots of the freckles across her nose.

Hypomania – that was what the doctor told her on admission. That was why she was crying. Why had she asked if he could hear her? He could: he wasn't deaf. He just couldn't speak. Suddenly he sat up and noticed a high window with bars. He tried to intersect the light travelling between the door and window with his hand. He laid down again. He felt her leave. Felt her hand untangle from his. Felt because he couldn't wake up from the induced stupor. He felt her pick up the heart of him, his musical world. She picked it up and took it with her and never gave it back.

They decreased the sedation. He was able to get up. Anna was back. They were sitting in a circular room in an Oxford mental health facility. He knew this because those around him had issues which seemed greater. She was talking to the psychiatrist. He moved to sit between them so they couldn't ignore him. They leaned around him like water, as though he were just a giant pebble impeding the flow. He still couldn't speak. He was trying to participate in decisions being made about his future. He tried to connect with Anna heart to heart. She was not listening. She did not understand the language of love which she once knew. She listened to him as a baby when he cried, asked what the matter was and instinctively knew the right thing to do. She could not connect with him. She had forgotten how. They were treating him like a ghost who sat between them. He tried to shout through the fog of pills 'You don't fucking love me otherwise why are you discussing taking away music, the one thing I love?' It was not right that others could section his life without reference to him. He was twenty. 'Do you realise that, Mother? What has any of this got to do with you?' He looked at the psychiatrist, who he didn't know from Adam, 'or you.'

It took all his strength to say one short sentence to her. 'You don't care about me.' She was quizzical about his sudden interruption. He knew he scared her but it was his life. Then she said a platitude. 'I do love you, sit down.' Back at home Anna watched him. Watched his every movement. Just as the doctor ordered. Her love was stifling.

Then between Anna, the psychiatrist and his professor at the GCM, they agreed that he had done more than enough to graduate, and agreed a compromise reference for future use, which was not to his advantage.

'Your granny did say, Josh, that before we judge her harshly that we haven't seen anything like what was going on then. That the clinicians are aware of the link between hypomania and creativity. That they don't generally intervene unless the person is not functioning normally. Michael was awake twenty-four seven for over eight days and he wasn't functioning normally.'

'Will you all stop talking about me? It is nice that my family is concerned for me. However, I am not twenty now. I can tell if I'm getting high. Which I suppose is where the argument started last night with your mother over not making dinner.'

'Are you OK now?' He lay down next to Delsea on the sofa and cuddled her.

'I shouldn't have called you a liar.'

'No.'

'Or said all that stuff about trust and honour.'

'Actually, maybe not when your mind was ascending, but I think you meant it. I take it the agreement is our marriage vows. Explain how I have broken our agreement? That came from way down.'

'I don't like the way you are about Jonathan. The other night I was prepared to listen about you and him. After you told me about the one-night stand, you shut it down.'

'I haven't seen Jonathan properly since Josh was six years old.' The ridiculous, meet Papa, where she actually spent more time with his father than him and his coming to their wedding with Gin Tan, hardly counted as contact. 'I did have a good view of the back of his head that time at PITCOM.'

'He is often on TV. When he speaks sometimes you screw your eyes up and listen as if you don't want to miss a word of what he is saying. Sometimes you lie on your back on the sofa, close your eyes, steeple your hands under your chin when he is giving a speech and nod if he makes a point that you like. I'm not daft, Del. You scrutinise every single word he says. That means he is somehow in our house.'

'How observant of you. Now you are jealous of the television, what next, the radio? I listen to the budget and financial matters like everyone else. Just because the chancellor is someone, I used to know doesn't mean I am giving him more attention than anyone else who comes on telly.'

'Used to know. There you have it. I think you still know him. There are people you never forget. People you can pick back up with no matter the length of time since you last saw them. He is one of those people to you.'

'Still waters do run deep.'

'What is it about him?'

'You really want to know?'

'Of course.'

'When we were young, he, as you call him, promised to change the world for me.'

'You are holding him to a pledge of allegiance he made back then?'

'I am not holding him to anything, I never see him. I am just checking.'

'Checking what? I don't get you sometimes.'

'Stop being nosy. If you really must know what I am doing as he speaks, I am working out the interaction between how men will be affected by the proposals, as opposed to women, considering any other variables that come into play such as the nine protected characteristics or integrations or differentiations. Is that clear enough? dy/dx vs dx/dy. The universe demands that everything applicable to man is applicable to woman and vice versa, observing that there is a non-binary intersection between them. A little mystery about the woman you love is no bad thing.'

'Sometimes I think you are unsound.'

'As you have told me many times, that is why you love me, because I am not like any other woman you have ever known. Besides, insanity is just the things we don't understand yet – yet being the operative word.

I know, shall we play a game of Xs, where you go through your ex's and I put a cross through them one by one!' That's right, Mr, Life Gets Very Complicated Very Quickly when you date lots of women at the same time. You don't say.

Not to mention the Australian childhood sweetheart. They apparently couldn't keep their hands off each other. Even after they split up. If they found one another to be close by, they had to hook up. According to him she was always 'trying to race him off.' It was a term Delsea hadn't heard before so she asked him what it meant. Apparently, she had permission from her husband to sleep with Michael. He did not have permission from Delsea to reciprocate. Not that he had ever asked. This woman lived in Oxford. Wait till Delsea saw her. She'd race her off. Delsea wondered why they had not been introduced. Michael was so glad that she came along and rescued him from all that hedonism. Just look what those women made him do!

'A man promising to change the world for you sounds a lot like love. Well, I can't change the world for you.'

'A man saying that may be in love. But it was an eighteen-year-old boy who said it.'

'I can protect you from the world's viciousness though.'

'I know that, Archangel Michael. Protecting me is your raison d'etre,' Delsea said, smiling. 'There is no competition between you and Jonathan. I could never live with that idiot.' 'Why do you and your family insist he is a fool? He clearly isn't one.'

'You mean the man on the telly isn't one!' Idiot was a term of endearment between her and Jonathan.

Michael was deadly serious about protecting her. He tackled anyone who discriminated against her. That he should strive and agonise on her behalf was comforting. But she had known racism drive people to drink and despair, to being labelled paranoid or schizophrenic for daring to voice their true feelings and that was people who had been dealing with it all their lives. Michael would make an almighty fuss, very paternal, akin to one's dad going down to the school. Except her dad didn't have the energy to go down to the school. He was too busy drowning in his own sorrows.

Sometimes she thought Michael went too far. Whatever street they walked down, he would walk nearest the traffic. Wherever they slept he would insist on sleeping on the door side, ready to tackle any assailants coming through the door. She was not even sure he slept. He slept with her deep in his arms. She would move his arm to sneak out of bed for whatever reason. It was impossible. No matter how careful she was, he would say "Where are you going?"

Josh bounded in, having so obviously been listening.

'Stop listening to our private conversations, Josh. Haven't you got anything else to do?'

'If you are going to talk about "him," then I have as much right to hear it. After all, "he" is…'

'He is what, Josh?' they both said.

'The sperm donor. Besides, I am dying to see the yellow towels that have caused such controversy. This morning I thought you were on the verge of divorce, which scared me, and now you are cuddling on the sofa. Sound!'

'Is it safe to get the yellow towels out, Michael?' Delsea said, teasing.

'Let Josh tell you what's wrong with them. I am going to bed,' Michael said, as he kissed Delsea goodnight.

'The lemon yellow is really nice, Mum. They are nice and thick, good quality. Dad likes designer things but the grey chain pattern screams Versace. He hates labels being on show.

Mum, I have met up with Jonathan twice now. Why did you tell me that stuff about him cheating on you when it is obvious to me anyway that he adores you? He would do no such thing.'

'I don't want to talk about it. I think I should go up and be with Michael. I wasn't very nice just now, but he will keep probing me on a very difficult point. He is lucky that I don't explode with exasperation. Why can't he let it be?'

'Hang on… you are not escaping from this conversation. Dad can't let it go because he senses that there is still something between you and Jonathan and by the way he is right from what I've seen and what I am seeing before me now. Dad can't let one small vestige of love go in that direction, otherwise he thinks he will lose you.'

'I love him. What more does he want?' Michael would think her delusional if she said that she had a joint vocation with Jonathan that bound them together.

'Jehovah College Ariel. You said it yourself, he is like Archangel Michael, the avenging angel. You see: I can play your game.'

'I didn't know you wanted to play.'

'Jehovah College Ariel. My father told me how you used to play these games to entertain each other.'

'Wow, your father!'

'I know you are mentally lonely, living with someone who would rather think things than say them, except when his mind is literally in flight.' Sometimes she felt alone especially when Michael went into one of his frequent silences. It made her feel like she was living life without him.

'We do have other things in common.'

'Like the secret high life, you have with him that you don't like anyone knowing about. The holiday homes, skiing, surfing, sports parachuting, closets full of jewellery and designer clothes that you never wear or use except on holiday, where no one knows you.'

'If you've got it, don't flaunt it. We do have fun. I never had foreign holidays before I met him. So, I enjoy them now. He's made more money than a horse has hairs.'

'Jehovah College Ariel. Dr Hook. "The Millionaire."'

'Oh my god, I love playing with you! Why have we never played like this before?'

'You and Jonathan developed this language years ago. Prior to meeting him I didn't want to have anything to do with him because I thought he betrayed you and I wasn't ever going to acknowledge a father who hurt my mother.'

Her Caribbean family and loved ones would not recognise the person she was with Michael. She couldn't disco freestyle but she could dance with him. Mathematics had its own rhythm and that was the pulse of her soul any other tempo jarred her mind. She could do logical dances that had steps, like salsa, she didn't mind that music. However, she wouldn't extrapolate too far. The noise of most music to her was akin to musical dyslexia pounding her ears, creating a disjointed cacophony in her head.

He was a risk taker, Michael, which was always obvious with his entrepreneurial start-ups, consolidations and asset sales. That followed through into his love of dangerous sporting activities and the taking of recreational drugs. But she saw he was a risk taker mentally too. Not afraid to let his mind soar out of control close to the sun in order to reach the highest heights of music.

'You know, that calculation you were explaining to Dad, it sounds awesome, Mum to a NatSci like me.' Continued Josh 'I think you should write it down, prove and share it. It sounds like a step in universal theory.'

She wondered sometimes what would happen to her relationship with Michael with his film star looks and physique, if Jonathan wasn't in the background anchoring him to her? Would he stay when there was more to sample on the menu? Everywhere they went she saw women checking him out and sometimes she sensed racial jealousy from women who thought 'What on earth is he doing with her.'

GBH WITH INTENT

Delsea and Michael had watched on TV as Jonathan, surrounded by paparazzi, dealt so easily with the revelations that Josh had disclosed at Ariel: that the Chancellor of the Exchequer wasn't just a committed bachelor married to his work. Once upon a time he had a life with a woman. The fact she was a person of colour added to the speculation. The press gathered outside Downing Street were ready to harangue him as he walked home from the Treasury. They were always hoping for a scandal. They were delighted to have unearthed something against him. Though the something was never buried, if anyone had cared to look.

He had phoned his father to warn him that the press might make a scandal out of nothing. Richard couldn't have cared less about the media. 'Whatever happens we'll pull through. We always do.' Richard would stand by his son come what may. Richard informed Frederica. She thought their friends and acquaintances would know what she had always kept under wraps. She looked askance every time Josh's face appeared on television. She was calculating how many generations it would take to breed the blackness out.

Jonathan pulled his collar up to shield himself from the drizzle. He looked up: cold was in the air, he was exhausted from a long session. A woman approached him. She was obviously a hardcore reporter. Jonathan kept walking. She stalked him. 'Can I ask you about your relationship with Delsea Johnson?' Jonathan stopped, gave her a withering look of contempt, then walked on at a greater pace. Then he stopped again. 'I have this to say. Delsea is an incredible person. I'm glad to have known her. She has enriched my life and I think I have improved hers in many ways.' Bemused, he watched her brain treasuring up the whole, the numerous theories forming on her lips.

The Prime Minister was on the warpath too. The Chief Whip gave Jonathan a tongue-lashing as a result. The whip and spin doctors liked to know about skeletons in the cupboard before they exploded in the media. He was also passing on the PM's vexation. Without preliminaries, ignoring all protest from the whip, the PM had apparently let it be known in no uncertain terms that the whip was employed to know these things, and he was not interested in what he thought but in what he knew – which appeared to be very little.

The wolves were at Jonathan's door. Both those against him inside his party and the rat pack. He and the PM would dash off critics with bravado. Show their togetherness. That's how these things worked. Pose together where possible for the cameras. They made a formidable team. Even though their every action was up for scrutiny, there was no chance of Jonathan resigning. He was far too good at his job and the nation knew it. Personally, he couldn't see what all the fuss was about. Since when was it a scandal for a man to love only one woman in his lifetime?

The media had pored through relevant matriculation photographs for Uriel colleges. No girls they checked out were likely candidates. They were desperate for facts. That was to their credit, that they had no qualms about Uriel being inclusive. They had concluded that the woman was someone from his past. Jonathan actually confirmed that. He was prepared to answer the press in Downing Street. It beat being accosted in the street. They sprang into action as soon as he appeared. They vied for his attention.

'Chancellor, is it true you had an illegitimate child?' How to bring him down by revealing his hypocrisy about tax credits when he impregnated a young girl then abandoned her to the dole queue!

'As a teenager I had a son with my then girlfriend, and we agreed that adoption was the right thing to do. We had Josh's interests at heart.' Mercifully he knew Delsea thoroughly, she wouldn't say anything against him. She wouldn't interfere in his political career. 'He's making this up,' said Michael. 'You didn't agree to adoption then!'

'Actually, he's not. He never mentioned who he agreed with. He agreed with the vicar's suggestion.'

'Politicians, so slippery.'

'I think he is taking the right approach. We must think about what is best for Josh.'

Josh had gone to his pastoral care, because he was being followed by the press around Jehovah College campus, on his way to the Science block, even followed into town. People asking him how often he saw his father, trying to build a story of a mixed race abandoned child with abandonment issues. Josh did well with the single answer given to him to use: 'I was adopted and secure in a loving family.'

Then Michael looked down the drive. 'Del, we have press here too.' Fortunately, the house was set back from the road, surrounded by a moderate amount of land. On all sides there were trees. The front of Westmead faced the garden towards the river. The rooms that could be seen into from the driveway with long lenses were Josh's bedroom and the dining room. Delsea went upstairs to Josh.

'We need to close your curtains.'

'I never meant for this to happen.'

'It's fine, Josh. It couldn't be helped. Jonathan is a public figure, continually in the media eye. The three of us will deal with it, Jonathan, your dad and I.'

'Keep your curtains closed.'

They seemed to be having trouble pigeonholing Delsea. She didn't fit their stereotypical mould. So far, they had found no dirt to dig over. Their views were all conjecture. The sisterhood collective was treating her career in her chosen field as some kind of triumph. Her many talents, that was the gist of it, when they didn't even know her. She wasn't sure she wanted to be their heroine. Not many teenage mothers went on to garner success. Quite frankly she didn't care what anyone thought. She knew the truth. She went back downstairs to close the dining room curtains, but not before she was aware that a flash had gone off.

'Michael, they've just taken a photo of me at the window.'

'I'm not having this, people invading our home.'

Michael was out the front door before Delsea could stop him. It was not just the press that Michael was worried about. They lived in a quiet village on the outskirts of Oxford. He needed the press to not be a nuisance to the neighbours by blocking the street. It wasn't a nosy village; everybody was friends with everyone else; they had won community awards for initiatives including for the café created by one determined lady that was a central village hub. They saw each other at regular intervals, the Saturday organic market in the village hall, services at the Abbey, quiz nights, the annual Christmas fayre. They were into being green and had fundraised for three giant Archimedes screws to generate electricity for the grid, at the weir. Finally there was the yearly Lewis Carroll Choral Evensong incorporating the Alice Sermon. Charles Dodgson visited the village many times and preached there in the 1860s.

Michael stormed down the front steps to the road. There was always some fool who had to comment about something. It made him feel protective towards Delsea and the children. It was like Delsea had to go through life with a wasps' nest buzzing round her head, being stung from every direction. He was not having this.

'Look, you need to leave. This is private property.' He forgot that people saw him as this enigmatic, and highly private mobile phone multimillionaire. It caused more flashes to go off. The press were ecstatic: they had some news and clickbait after all. He was the CEO of a Fortune 100 company. A pillar of society when he chose to be. Their behaviour turned fawning, sycophantic, which disgusted him. He responded with unfailing good humour. It was the response of an English gentleman that had been bred into him.

'Mr Valentine, can we have a statement please?' He didn't relish losing his privacy. This development could completely change the way he had divided his life to ensure that his personal life remained sacrosanct.

'Our son Josh was adopted by me and lovingly brought up by two parents, my wife Delsea and I, with his sister Amy. Now leave, that's your lot.' He wondered how they would deal with the turn of events. He could imagine the revelation splashed across acres of newsprint. There was Josh, and Amy in the future to consider. He was a reserved individual and he wasn't going to play his emotions out in public.

The press was getting nowhere with their abandoned girl and little mixed race boy story. All they were seeing was an aristocratic family on one side of Josh's heritage and a multimillionaire on the other side. But the real person they wanted to hear from was Delsea. Her relationship with Jonathan was none of their business. If she spoke, she could see her words being misconstrued. The lies spreading like wildfire from newspaper to media and back again, deliberate disingenuous facts crystalising with each iteration. The tabloids would have a field day. There was a Jamaican saying about not telling people your business, alerting them to who you are and what your family might owe. If you did so a price for atonement would be extracted one way or another. As her mom would say, 'The higher a monkey climbs the more arse there is on show.'

The landline began to ring off the hook. Michael back in the hall yanked it from the socket.

'This is crazy,' she said. 'They are not going to stop until they hear from me.'

'Ignore them.'

'They want a scandal. Me, as the bitter wronged girl, to trash Jonathan and engage them on what a struggle it was for Josh and I before I met you. I should give them a different photo opportunity to the one of me in my jeans with my midriff showing.'

'No.' Then Michael's mobile started ringing relentlessly.

'They are working fast. It won't take them long to work out that it was just me and Josh for the years between my seventeenth year and meeting you when I was twenty-four. They will be desperately trying to research that gap. Those seven years.'

'The gap is not that great, they will discover good things, your A Level results, they won't like that for a start, as that is positive. Your first in Mathematics from Bristol University. Another thing they won't like, no negativity for them to write about there. Your education takes up five years. That just leaves your first job at the Water Authority before you started at Europhone with Ted and soon after met me. There are no skeletons to find.'

'They will go to Corsham and try to dig up dirt.' She could imagine the press traipsing up and down the quaint high street, trying for gossip in the many pubs in the village. Corsham was a close-knit community. While people might gossip amongst themselves, they weren't prepared to divulge anything to the outside world that would damage their own.

'Who from?'

'I don't know, my acquaintances from school and CFE will be supportive, I think. I've linked with some of them on social media. I don't think they would give the press the time of day. But you never know, Michael. Some people may be jealous that I have found happiness with such a distinguished man as you and for goodness' sake I also had a relationship with one of the country's supposed eligible bachelors. The knives may be out. The xenophobes will be going batshit crazy!'

'You said "supposed" about Jonathan? What does that mean? You never use words that you don't intend to use.'

'Next!'

Of course, Delsea was not on the front pages the next day. Why would anyone print a substandard photo of her through a window when they could put Michael, the most exclusive millionaire, on the front covers next to the also handsome Chancellor of the Exchequer. With tabloids, having a frenzy, headlines saying covert bigoted stuff such as What do these two men see in this woman? Sex sensation, not, well certainly not between Jonathan and her! They were making things up. Gin Tan, a nasty woman, Delsea had met for half an hour in an Oxford café describing her as needy, enforcing some weird African woman nymphomaniac theory that she had not heard about no doubt because of her "small town upbringing" to Gin's "woman of the world" view point, and her desperation to get her claws into Jonathan. She noticed Gin didn't dwell on her own desires in that direction, or give away Jonathan's secrets, the impudent cow. Women surreptitiously agreeing with Gin Tan in a round-about suggestive way that Delsea must be some sort of whore. Who gets that lucky in love twice!

Delsea took the newspaper from Michael. The tabloids carried screaming headlines speculating about the relationships between them. Anyone would think they were in a ménage à trois. It made for corrosive and compulsive reading. Why Michael insisted on tormenting himself by having all the papers delivered was a mystery to her. It was all spite that both his and Jonathan's backgrounds only inflamed. She said to Michael, 'I'm doing it, I can't stand to read any more nonsense about you, me or Jonathan. The only way this will end is if I give them Mrs Valentine, not some poor girl who couldn't defend herself from Jonathan using her for sex.'

She had had quite enough. Michael was constantly supportive and faithful. He had given her love and security that had allowed her to opt out, and bury herself at Westmead in an attempt to hide from reality. She was going to have to face the world again. Josh needed to get on with his term at Ariel. He couldn't stay at home hiding, missing tutorials.

Then Charlie Wright MP was mobbed trying to get into a chauffeur driven car. He was known to be close to Jonathan. This will be interesting, Delsea thought. She knew nothing about their friendship except he and Jonathan were at school together. One bold reporter was almost pinning him to the car door, a microphone shoved in his face. Charlie turned to face her. As if to say What d'you want to know?

Charlie was astounded by the prejudiced views being flung around. The media were sick in the head. Where was this vitriol coming from? There was as much prejudice towards Jonathan as there was about Delsea. A hornet's nest had well and truly been stamped on.

He knew that an article about the aristocracy siring mixed race children all over the world had upset Jonathan. It had concluded with why on earth were people shocked to find it was still going on. The writer had padded the article out with race, class and mixed relationships to make it seem like an authentic piece of academic research, instead of the bollocks it was. According to other articles Jonathan had taken advantage of a poor Anglo-Caribbean girl. It was inconceivable that the poor Anglo-Caribbean girl had the strongest mind of her own. There was a disturbing underlying assumption that white people were always acceptable to black people and Charlie did not suffer fools gladly.

Thrusting the microphone at him again. The woman probed. Charlie said, 'I don't recognise the portrait of the Chancellor painted by the press. This scurrilous campaign to discredit him is despicable. Jonathan is a compassionate, honest and straightforward man. This Gin Tan woman, whoever she may be, is talking nonsense. I've never heard of her! I doubt she means anything to Jonathan.'

'And Delsea Johnson, have you heard of her?'

'Yes. A fiercely independent woman, not at all vulnerable. Jonathan had affections for her a very long time ago. She moved on with her life. Did things her way. Achieved what she wanted to. That's all you need to know about that. Good day to you.'

But before she and Michael could get Purple's PR people to organise a press conference for Delsea, Ben was on telly. Delsea shouted upstairs to Michael, who was sitting in the sun on the balcony.

'They are harassing my parents.'

He shouted down, 'Your dad won't say anything negative. Him know how white people stay. Dem twiss and turn every dam ting against you.' She laughed – that was a good imitation, of Ben. 'Except he will use his best English.'

'Mr Johnson, have you got anything to say about your daughter and the Chancellor?'

'I don't hold with teenage pregnancies, but these things happen. They were two clever pickneys who sorted it out between them.' Delsea laughed: this was good.

'But surely you must have been cross?'

'Cross wid what? My daughter got every damn certificate. I am proud of her.' Good old Daddio, as Marcus would say.

'Mrs Johnson, have you anything to add?

'Both she and Jonathan Ainsley were brought up properly in the Christian faith. They are forgiven. God is kind.'

'Michael, they are talking to Marcus,' Delsea shouted.

'Relax, your family won't trash you.'

'Marcus, your sister and the Chancellor?'

'Yes, what about them?'

'Well, you must be shocked by this development.'

'I have always known about them. My sister and I are very close. We discuss everything.'

'You better not be doing drugs,' Delsea shouted, knowing full well Michael would just chill and roll a joint in a crisis. He was a man of few words, unless you pushed him to say something. Even then you might just get a stony silence.

Now they were at the gates of Aldbourne Court. The press couldn't get in but Lord Ainsley had made the long walk to the gates.

'Sir, can we have a statement?'

'I don't know what all this fuss is about. Stop harassing my family, Delsea's family and the towns-people. Haven't you got anything better to put in your poisonous papers?'

'But this is shocking and hypocritical.' Some hack shouted.

'What's shocking is your attitudes. Why shouldn't my son have a black girlfriend?' Delsea laughed, nearly falling off the arm of the sofa she was perched on. This was hilarious. They were stumped and gobsmacked! No doubt they would creep off with their tails between their legs. So much for going to her home town to dig up dirt. Delsea was first and foremost from Corsham, a Corshamite, and they didn't turn against each other. People were proud of Corsham and wouldn't let its name be besmirched. With Lord Ainsley setting the example in Corsham, the story was nearly dead in the water.

The little mixed-race kid at the centre of the storm was a posh privately educated boy who went to one of Oxfordshire's best independent schools and was reading Natural Science at Ariel!

So, they were back with a vengeance for Delsea, their last hope of a scandal. They wanted, a destitute girl left struggling by Jonathan Ainsley's negligence. They were camped on the path opposite her drive. They almost cried 'Was no one going to take down Jonathan Ainsley, MP for Bradford-on-Avon, Chippenham, Corsham, Melksham, and surrounding villages, Chancellor of the Exchequer?'

'Enough of this nonsense already,' Delsea said to Michael and Josh; they were having a family conflation throwing ideas around. 'We need to do something so Josh can go back to college.

Guys, I think I have it. I will give a press conference at the end of the drive. I am going down there in the most sophisticated and expensive designer clothing and jewellery that you have ever bought me, Michael, that I hardly wear.'

With his creative background in classical music, Michael had exquisite taste. He introduced Delsea to orchestral performance. They often went to the Sheldonian Theatre, the fine vaulting directing the eyes upwards to the famous dome and the hand painted ceiling by Robert Streater. Christopher Wren's first public building was a triumph. Delsea loved opera: Michael's favourite was La Boheme, hers was Tosca, both by Puccini. It was so dramatic when Floria Tosca evaded capture, mounted a parapet, where she flung herself off to certain death at the end.

Before her maternity break it was business clothing. At home, comfort was her master. She had never been one to flaunt it. But, that was the time to do so. What else could greedy people be distracted by, except money? They would write about her clothes, her jewellery and what a spoilt rich bitch she was. In the face of that who cared about the girl who suffered postnatal depression after the birth of her son? Delsea went into the bedroom, put on matching underwear for confidence and some flesh-coloured tights. Then she shouted 'I'm ready' and for fun clicked both fingers and thumbs, high in the air.

'Let's play,' Michael said a joint hanging from his lips while rummaging through her clothing.

'Mum, let's ramp it up by setting a scene at the end of the drive. Once you are dressed, and I've done your hair.' Josh used to help her with her hair when it was just them. He still did sometimes. Michael had no idea about combing long natural African hair. He would try and help her do the back by pulling a comb through it which would create knots and get stuck. She would say, 'take a handful near the end, tease out those tangles and work like that towards the scalp. Then you can pull a comb through it from the scalp afterwards.'

Josh said, 'Let's take the chaise lounge down for you to sit on.'

'I should go down and tell them that you will do a press conference now. That will get them excited,' said Michael.

'I love it both, any more where that came from?'

'A side table and vintage champagne possibly,' extrapolated Michael.

'You seriously are not getting out a £1,000 bottle of champagne?'

'It's a good cause. You should be the diva that you can be and control the interview.'

'Excuse me?' Delsea said, offended. 'Which diva is this?'

'Like when you are an expert speaker at conference.' She had been a speaker, the last time she tackled the juicy subject of International Compliance.

1. The Diva does not reply to questions that she does not want to answer, for her own personal reasons. She will say 'And?' when asked such questions, as in, And you think I am going to discuss that! You must be joking!
2. The Diva does not repeat herself by answering questions she has already answered earlier on in the questioning, even if put in a different format, and will encourage moving on by replying, 'Next.' From her BASIC programming days.
3. The Diva does not answer questions that the asker knows the answer to and is only asking to show off their own knowledge. 'Go figure' is the answer she will use for that. As in Go away, I'm sure you've already figured that one out, stop wasting my time. When others have genuine questions they want to ask.
4. If the Diva is most seriously displeased with the way delegates

are behaving towards her, she will bring the questioning to an abrupt close.

'I'll tell them those house rules,' said Michael.

'This is going to be sick,' said Josh.

'Let's hope so. But I don't want to come across as vacuous. So, I need a book.' One that would make Jonathan die laughing. The very book comes to mind, volume I of Marcel Proust's Remembrance of Things Past. Endless philosophising, about love and friendship, intelligent but no easy read.

'Mrs Valentine?' The interview started. Who knew that was her? She usually used her maiden surname. It afforded them the privacy Michael craved.

'How long have you known the Chancellor?'

'He moved to Corsham when I was six.'

'When did you start seeing each other?'

'I saw him most Sundays at our parish church.'

'When did your relationship start?'

'And?'

'How old were you when you had Joshua.'

'Sixteen.'

'That is young to have a child. How did you manage?'

'Like most teenagers I lived at home when I was in full time education so I had help from my family.'

'And after that?' This was hardly stretching their inquisitorial skills.

'I moved to Oxford and Jonathan paid Josh's school fees.'

'How long was your relationship with the Chancellor?'

'I didn't have a relationship with the Chancellor.'

'How long was your relationship with Jonathan Ainsley?'

'NEXT.'

'Did Jonathan Ainsley support you?'

'NEXT.'

'Surely, he was very irresponsible getting you pregnant?'

'AND.'

'Adding to the teenage pregnancy rate?'

'GO FIGURE.'

'Did you see Jonathan Ainsley after you became pregnant by him?'

'Like responsible people we discussed the best way forward?'

'When did your relationship with him end?'

'NEXT.'

'Did you feel let down by him?'

'AND.'

'Have you seen him since?'

'Since when?'

'Since you had Joshua?'

'Yes. Like a responsible father he visited me in hospital when I had Josh.' After that was the London Episode, the nutty professor, then when she got engaged to Michael and not to mention the debacle of her wedding day. 'We were together a few times after that.'

'He was irresponsible?'

'In what way?'

'Getting you pregnant?'

'That takes two. NEXT.'

'Did he support you financially?'

'NEXT.'

'Were you angry with him?'

'About what?'

'Leaving you high and dry?'

'I left him!' They hadn't thought of that, that the poor girl might be the one to tell the rich guy to piss off.

'Did you just swap one millionaire for another?'

'Millionaires are like buses, they come two at a time.'

'So, you approve of his behaviour towards you?'

'That is not a question.'

'Do you approve of his behaviour towards you?'

'He did the right thing.'

'What does that mean?'

'And.'

'Do you think he has the integrity given this background to be Chancellor of the Exchequer?'

'I think we are done here.'

'You are rich, how would a poor girl have coped with his behaviour?'

'GO FIGURE.'

They loved the newspaper stories, "Delsea Valentine is a Spoilt Rich Bitch who cannot appreciate the damage the Chancellor's behaviour would have done, to someone less fortunate. Who wore half a million pounds worth of designer clothes and jewellery to answer a few questions on their doorstep? Not even water was good enough for her: that bottle of champagne must be £1,200 at least. She clearly does not live in the same world as the rest of us!"

Morning TV, 'Delsea Valentine, what do we make of her? Control freak, or what? The way she controlled that interview. Lounging on that chaise longue sipping astronomically expensive champagne. Then that "go figure" stuff? She has these two multi-millionaire guys dancing to her tune. I for one can't see what they find lovable about her. She is obnoxious and the less we hear from her the better.'

'Jonathan, I think you owe me one. I hope you liked my hastily put together comedy play. Must have been a six at least surely!' But the euphoria of quelling the media didn't last long.

Heather, Jonathan's constituent secretary, showed the next client who had calmly walked in to his office. He was wearing a three-quarter length coat fully buttoned up. Just as she was about to close the door, she saw him pull out a handwritten statement. He began to read it as the old riot act was read, so she was already suspicious and on her guard. It was a rambling incoherent hate speech about Jonathan being a race traitor having it off with a darky.

Heather had always been good at hockey. She was so keen on the sport that when she was younger, she had risen to be an international women's hockey referee. She lived alone. She always kept a hockey stick close by in case she was unexpectedly disturbed by an intruder. One just beneath the bed on the side where she tended to sleep and another in the office coat cupboard. Because Jonathan was so busy with his day job as Chancellor that his surgeries mostly ran on into the evenings. She was often left alone afterwards tidying up and locking up.

This was her most precious hockey stick. The one she and her team won championships with. She had been managing the throughput of clients so she was behind the maniac when he suddenly pulled out a kitchen knife and began to attack Jonathan. Jonathan was tackling the man back like a wild animal. He was a public-school boy and she recognised rugby tackling when she saw it.

She was an Ashfoldian, a tomboy who flourished at that independent school where she was first introduced to hockey. She was sixty and no big girl's blouse. Just give her a hockey stick and she knew what to do with it. First, she told Jonathan's assistant who was looking for the local man's client file, to go and quickly get help. He came in so often, that his file was thick and unwieldy.

It was then all of a five-second decision to fetch her hockey stick from the cupboard. She held it with both hands for maximum impact and swung it for all she was worth. With an accurate temple blow she almost knocked the nutcase out. Momentarily the assailant became the victim. He fled past her through the open front door, shouting 'you mad old bat,' as she brandished the hockey stick at him. He staggered bloodied onto Monkton Hill. The assistant was back and told her that an armed response unit and an ambulance was on its way.

Heather rushed in to help Jonathan and was glad to see that he was still alive, though bleeding heavily. He had received serious lacerations to his arms from fending off the knife blows. She later heard the man had been apprehended in Chippenham High Street outside the furniture shop by the bridge. He was discovered to hold extreme right-wing views. At the magistrates court he gave his name as The Supreme Controller Protector of England. Protecting her from the constant shower of darkies that rained on her lands. Reminiscent of the old demonstration banners, "Britain for the British," and placards "Stop Immigration Enoch is Right."

ATTEMPTED MURDER

Delsea and Michael had watched the CCTV image on television of the man who called himself "The Supreme Controller," marching up Monkton Hill, in Chippenham towards Jonathan's weekly surgery. He wanted the races kept pure through miscegenation laws. He felt sorry for mixed race children not knowing where they belonged. His mantra was that mixing the races would end in mixed up people. As far as he was concerned Britain was mixed up enough already with boat loads of darkies constantly arriving on her shores who were entitled to everything, while the indigenous true Brits got nothing. No one was to know he was carrying a knife under that heavy coat. Like most politicians, Jonathan felt it was important to make himself accessible to his constituents. He was committed to helping those in his community.

Michael said, 'Mixing is crucial. When we are all related, we will have to stop killing each other,' through the haze of a joint. 'I have great faith in humanity. We'll get there in the end. What interests me is the convoluted loops we seem to go through on the way.'

It felt to Delsea like a crisis was brewing and all the world had achieved so far was rehearsals for the real fight. She thought calmly of God and the human race and wondered how long all this turmoil could last.

The Supreme Controller was on loop in Delsea's head, playing repeatedly. It was an epiphany moment. She realised that she could not live in this world unless Jonathan was here too, alive and making a difference. What the hell did that mean? It meant she had to get in touch with him immediately. She wanted to rush to the hospital where he had been taken, they said with serious blood loss. People would think she was mad if she did that. His security would jump to protect him from yet another crazed person. How to achieve contact when they hadn't been in touch for years and she had no personal phone number or address details. Josh knew his Downing Street flat number. That was no use. She had three options: parliamentary office, no way. She didn't want to cause a stir. His Chippenham surgery, no they would be in turmoil and surrounded by police, forensics and the press trying to keep the momentum going by interviewing anyone who was prepared to give them a take on the attempted murder of Jonathan Ainsley MP and Chancellor of the Exchequer. That was all he was to them, a story. His family home, Aldbourne Court in Corsham. Yes, but she couldn't go there. Everyone knew them both in Corsham. It was one thing people knowing that they had a child together years ago and another to make it obvious that that was not the end of it. Then she knew exactly what to do. Phone the ticket shop at Aldbourne Court and what? Threaten some poor office worker who answers the phone. Not nice, but there was no other way.

'Hello. I need to get in touch with Jonathan Ainsley.'

'We have had a lot of people phoning trying to get in touch with him personally. We have been told not to talk to anyone, but to direct you to his press secretary. You won't get through there either as they are carefully screening calls.' Oh fuck. Yes, Lord Ainsley.

'Can you put me through to Lord Ainsley?'

'No, the family are distressed, worried and concerned for their son. They are not taking calls. Jonathan has advised them not to talk to anyone.'

'You will lose your job if you don't put me through to Lord Ainsley immediately.'

'We take threats to staff seriously. We have a zero-tolerance policy in place, so I am going to cut you off now. I am only here anyway to help those who had tickets for today. We have all been affected. The rest of the staff have gone home. We are temporarily closed because of this distressing incident.'

'Wait, I *am* family.'

'What?'

'You heard.'

'If you are family, you will know their personal phone numbers.'

'It's complicated.'

'With all due respect I am shaken by this too. I don't have time for call wasters.' Delsea began to cry in wracking sobs. 'OK, tell me something that proves you are family and I will say it to Lord Ainsley.'

'Tell Lord Ainsley that Mofe asked me to call.'

'Lord Ainsley, there is a lady on the phone. I have tried to deter her. She's very upset. She says she's family but it's complicated. She told me to say that Mofe asked her to call.'

Delsea could almost feel the cogs turning in his brain telepathically. Would he remember Jonathan's best friend in Nigeria, from a long time ago? 'Or maybe the complicated means something to you,' the shop assistant said. She couldn't ask more of this lady – she'd done her best.

'OK, Put her through.' At last.

'Delsea?'

'Yes.'

All Delsea could do was cry. 'I want to see Jonathan.'

'Of course, you do. It's a terrible thing when those doing service for the good of the people can't go about their business without being struck down by lawless assailants. We have been lucky. His injuries aren't life changing. His mother is with him. He'll be a couple of days in hospital then time to recuperate at home. He has his own place now. I will give you his mobile number and Delsea, I would like to meet my grandson one day soon.'

'When did you first know about Josh?' Delsea asked.

'Since the day he was born. Jonathan came home very excited to tell me that news.'

Delsea broached the subject of visiting Jonathan when he came out of hospital, with Michael. It immediately got his back up. 'I've told you we are friends who had a one-night stand. Which was more about him getting me out of his system than anything else. Whatever he was to me once upon a time, doesn't figure now because I am committed to you. There is absolutely zero chance of anything happening between us. The man is convalescing.' She realised this was delusional nonsense. She knew she was only deceiving herself.

'If you mess me around, we are finished. I won't let you trample all over me. If you leave me, you are not having custody of Amy. I am not playing some weird game of musical chairs where Jonathan and I get to bring up each other's children.'

'I am married to you. Get over yourself and stop wallowing in selfishness. He almost lost his life and I am going to visit him whether you like it or not.'

Michael couldn't see how unfair he was being to her. He could barely contain his displeasure. Accusing Delsea of being callous. In the end, he swallowed his pride which didn't seem authentic anyway, and more to do with arrogance and ego. He agreed. Thanks for that, Michael. She really didn't need him to sanction what she could or couldn't do.

'I don't know why I am letting you do this.'

'You are not letting me do anything. I am doing it all by myself without reference to you.'

'You are uncontrollable.'

'And you have just noticed this very distinct characteristic of mine.'

'You don't do anything I tell you to do.'

'Look on the bright side. I don't do anything anyone tells me to do. I didn't promise to obey you. I do what I want to do.'

'Look who's being selfish now.'

She hadn't told him that she planned on staying the night yet! She would not drive from Oxford to Devon and back again in a day just to please him. She had packed an overnight bag so he got the gist of it. She was braced for another argument.

On cue, 'What are you doing?'

'It is too far to go and come back again today.'

'Are you going to spend the night with him? And you expect me to agree to that!'

'Not with him, at his house. There is a difference.'

'You are not going.'

'Stop telling me what I can and can't do. I am going.'

'How would you like it if I spent the night with another woman?'

'I don't know. Have you spent the night with another woman, since you mention it?'

Silence. There was something there and she was not sure she wanted to know.

'When I was in Monte Carlo, Sylvie wanted to spend the night with me.' Delsea stopped and sat on the edge of their bed to listen.

'What happened?'

'We went out to a club. We danced and chatted. That was it for me. I went to bed. She knocked on my door, woke me up wanting to stay with me. I let her in.'

'Why did you let her in? I'm not sure I like where this is going!'

'She took off her clothes and got into my bed.'

'What did you do?' She said testily.

'I sat in a chair and told her I wasn't interested. She went to sleep.'

'Seducing you was her plan, but she doesn't start as soon as you open the door. I am not sure I believe that.'

'I have already told you that there is something not quite right with her.'

'You still shouldn't have let her into your room. More so if she is not all there. She could have done anything. Accused you of anything.'

'There you go. You don't like it.'

'There is no comparison. Sylvie is not married. It is up to the married person to maintain the boundaries. You should have managed that situation better.'

'I did. I left, took her room key and slept in her room. You are like your mother. I have never noticed that before. You believe what I said and you have forgiven me.'

'My mother is not as kind as you think she is. She is fond of you and therefore she shows you that side of her character. She doesn't give you the Jamaican matriarch who is both caring and controlling at the same time. I have no other sensible choice, do I? I cannot rationally argue that that is not what happened, or jump to the conclusion that you slept with her, because I wasn't there. Only the two of you know what happened in that room. I choose to believe you over some let-go-beast woman that I have never met. Besides you told me before that Ted was there too earlier on. That strengthens the rendition in your favour. You would hardly have taken him along for the evening if you had designs on Sylvie.'

Delsea went back to her packing. She appreciated that Michael hadn't told her about what occurred in Monte Carlo, as he didn't want to worry her when nothing really happened. But to use it then. Did he think she would be jealous and angry, which would confirm that he had every right to be furious about her proposed overnight stay? Though much of her finer maths ability had disappeared with age. She could still spot a trick or two. She saw the strategy and avoided checkmate. However, she was sure he wouldn't have been averse to getting an eye full of the eye candy. She parked her feelings about that and would examine them when the time was right. The objective and what was important then was that Jonathan got her full support. Letting herself be drawn further into an argument with Michael would prevent that. He would go into fuming like an internal combustion engine. She would give in just to please him if he kept up the smouldering stares long enough.

She brought her overnight bag downstairs. Amy was watching CBeebies. She ventured into the kitchen to get a soft drink for her long journey. Michael was leaning back against the worktop with his arms folded staring into nowhere. He turned, focusing his analytical nonspeaking stare on her when she entered. She reached into the fridge for some Jamaican ginger beer. Her favourite especially the new organic brands.

'I'm sorry darling that you think I shouldn't go, but I think it important to support Jonathan, just now.' She approached him as though he were a shop manikin that needed to be rearranged. She unfolded both his arms and placed them around her waist. They slipped down and gave her bottom a squeeze, simultaneously pulling her in against his groin. He wasn't that upset with her: he still wanted her regardless of her total disobedience!

'Are you going to be alright? This will be the first time that you have looked after Amy for any length of time without me. She will get fed up of watching TV soon. You have to entertain her. She gets bored very quickly, like someone else I know. You must constantly think of things for her to do. Otherwise, she will demand that you play with her. I get the dominos out when I can't handle building blocks or Jenga anymore. She likes matching the dots. If you go out there is a bag by the door. She has wee accidents if you don't get her to the loo quickly enough. There are spare knickers and wipes in it and a change of clothes if she messes up through eating or playing outdoors. You never know when you will need them. Twenty-four hours with a three-year-old is a long time. Phone me if you get stuck about anything.'

'You realise I can't go to work?'

'That's good, isn't it? You get to look after your daughter who you so desperately wanted, to the extent that you cried after we got married because I didn't immediately want to procreate. Keep reminding yourself that I am not you. We are not joined at the hip. I am an entirely different sentient human being and we won't go far wrong.' Delsea tilted her head up for a kiss and Michael obliged. 'Right, I'm off then. Keep an even temper no matter what she does or you won't survive the tantrums.'

JONATHAN REVISITED

The country house in Devon was nowhere near as grand as Aldbourne Court, but prettily balanced with no ugly additions. It was architecturally interesting since it hadn't been tampered with. This was where Jonathan lived. The windows were shuttered giving the impression of a French chateau. The flora was very much English, a narrow flower bed running the length of the frontage was crammed with plants, with Banksia roses rambling up the wall.

They had a lot to catch up on, though it felt like just yesterday that Delsea last saw him. They had never lived in each other's pockets. They were like two pillars that stand side by side bonded by years of affection. A double helix.

Jonathan knew that in some ways he had changed over the years. No doubt Delsea had too. He hoped that neither of them had changed at heart. Had they grown apart? That was what he wanted to know. From his perspective, he'd kept her memory alive, he hadn't embellished it in any way. It was as though he'd frozen an entire episode of his life and that was the time to unfreeze it. He wanted to know whether Delsea felt the same.

Jonathan came out to meet her.

She could hardly believe they were back in touch. It was warm so they took a walk through a young maze he was creating around the back. It was shaped like a monastery. At each turn they came across sculptures of mischievous monks going about work. Delsea was glad to see that his sense of humour was intact.

They returned to the house and his library. Delsea was at home with books. She felt she had to say or do something before they lost their old closeness. Any moment civility could take over and they would be no more than old friends having a chat over a cup of earl grey tea. There were five steps and many years of uncertainty between them. She chose to act rather than rely on words. Words couldn't cross the boundaries of time, not without losing some of their meaning.

'Del…' That single utterance of her name told her everything she needed to know. She responded eagerly. It was enough for her, though she was apprehensive on one particular front. She briefly touched his arm. He made the mildest of protests. It was still a connection to the way they had always been. Coiling around each other at crucial moments.

'I did try to move on after the London Episode by dating other guys. They were a dead loss until I met Michael.'

'Yet you kept faith with me?' Yes, she did. There was a quarter of a million pounds worth of emeralds belonging to Jonathan sitting in a deposit envelope in the vault of her bank. Each year when she saw that standing order appear on her statement, she thought, 'I don't want to think about this. I don't want to do anything about this.' It was her only standing order. It predated direct debits. That's how long her inertia had been going on.

'We will come to that.' Delsea said. 'First there was this musician who thought he was a rock star.'

'Either he is or isn't a rock star. Was he famous?'

'At that time, he had cut at least one album. Later he was very famous.'

'Now my brain is really intrigued. Do you want a drink? I'm having whisky because this I have to hear, it's priceless!' He laughed.

'Go on then. He died young, in his twenties, so, I will take that name to my grave.'

'Come on! You can't just leave it there.'

'OK. Police categorisation for the black man. IC3 male. That is your lot.'

'Curiouser and curiouser, though I never imagined you as a rock chick.'

'He wanted me to go to his gigs.'

'Now I see, it is as clear as daylight.' Jonathan laughed even more.

'Stop it, I won't tell you the rest if you are going to laugh. This is deadly serious. Or have you forgotten our rules of no laughter when matters are deadly serious?'

'OK, I will be good, but can I just clarify something. Did you tell this musician at any point that you disliked rock and roll and that the sound you most revered was silence? Absolute silence except for the natural sounds of nature as you drift on a lake in a boat, a gentle hand passing through rippling water. With your other arm shading the sun from your eyes. That you would rather join the Noise Abatement Society than go to one of his gigs.'

'How well you know me. OK, you are right, I made excuses not to listen to his music and he took offence. Silence is golden.

So, then there was this Iranian guy.'

'Now you are throwing foreigners into your magnum opus on men. Who knew you were so exotic?'

'No sarcasm. Sarcasm is not allowed when being deadly serious, as you well know. He was in my Physics A Level class. He was called Assad.'

'This must have been serious. He has a name.'

'There was a lot of chemistry flying around between us.'

'I thought you were doing Physics. I need another drink if you expect me to listen, and take this seriously.'

'Then it evaporated and there was no substance to it at all.'

'I am not at all surprised. You didn't even know whether you were doing Physics or Chemistry.'

'Oh, do shut up and top up my glass. And answer your bloody mobile, it's annoying.'

'Just parliamentary colleagues thinking "There but for the grace of God, go I," or wanting to wrap me in cotton wool. Go on.'

'Then there was this lecturer…'

'How many of these guys are there? You better have a good explanation for going off on this search for perfection amongst mankind. When you see it before you! A pervy lecturer, taking advantage of his position of authority. You should have seen straight through him.'

'I can count the men I have slept with on one hand.'

'Thank God for that, as there is not much left in this bottle.'

'He compared himself to Robert Redford.'

'Criminal, absolutely criminal, especially when you adored Robert Redford as The Sundance Kid.'

'To start with he was a nice caring man. He thought I was Ella Fitzgerald, Billy Holiday, Aretha Franklin, Gladys Knight, Bessie Smith, Nina Simone, Dina Washington, Diana Ross, and Whitney Houston all rolled into one. But slowly he came to realise that actually I was none of those talented ladies but Delsea Johnson, who couldn't sing.'

'What was wrong with Gloria Gaynor, Donna Summer, Dionne Warwick and Tina Turner? They are of the same era. He sounds like a conceited twat.'

'He told me his previous girlfriend was black.'

'So, he had a penchant for black women.'

'She used to giggle with excitement at his erect penis. I didn't. I had no interest in that side of things. I was only interested because he was fun. Then he told me that this really attractive girl in his class sat with her legs open, which often caused him to drop his marker pen.'

'What a creep!'

'Then he cheated with said knicker-showing wonder while I contemplated suicide.'

'This is getting heavy, Del, and deadly serious.'

'Did I say my love life was a comedy? A Comedy of Errors more like. As Lucille would say, "We are not put on this earth to have fun." Postnatal depression, flawed men and life itself seemed not worth living. The man I really wanted didn't want me.'

'I wanted you.'

'Not in the way I wanted you.'

'Michael and I. END OF.'

'I have riled you to show some emotion at long last! So no, not end of.'

'Well? How many fingers do you have on one hand?'

'Some of them are negative.'

'Only you could count on one hand and include negatives. So, I was a negative influence on your life?'

'You are a whole book, but that's another chapter. There was a guy who was into benefits and another who took benefits.'

'So, Saint Michael is happy for his wife to go and spend a night alone in the country with another man?'

'Michael is a man of few words. He said I was not having Amy. If I thought he was going to play some weird game of musical chairs where you each get to bring up each other's children, I had better have another think.'

'Ouch. I see his point.'

'That is strange that you called him Saint Michael. Everyone seems to have a different name for him. His mother has told me more than once that when he was young, he was a virtuoso at the piano. When he was performing like that, they called him Michelangelo.'

'You really love him, don't you? I can hear it in your voice. So, what is your name for him?'

'That's private.'

'So, Michael and I aren't in your Famous Five! Which is actually The Secret Seven. Interesting.'

'He has trust issues, but only where you are concerned.'

'Hang on, I must take this call. It's the Prime Minister.'

'Where are you? People are concerned. How are you after that diabolical experience? I'm shocked and appalled, you must be completely rattled. MPs make themselves available to their constituents to help solve their issues. In the light of this the safety guidelines need to be updated. We can't let these people win. The Home Secretary wants to send extra security. I was going to say come to Chequers.'

'I am in the best possible place. I'm not alone. I am with my other half.'

'The married woman? Well, it is good that you have someone with you. You know people did wonder about your solitary life.'

'I'm good – she is taking my mind off that dreadful business by entertaining me with some very unexpected tales.'

'I will leave you to it then.'

'Wow, it sounds like he really cares. A caring Prime Minister, who'd have thought? Is that how you see me? As your other half?'

'Well, don't you see me the same way? There is no other explanation. If someone tried to kill you, I would drop absolutely everything to be by your side, as you have just done. I've made up a bedroom for you next to mine. I think I've been running on adrenaline. Suddenly I've crashed. I'm exhausted, it must be the blood loss. I'm going to bed.'

'You must be knackered, and I've kept you up.'

'We can pick up on "Tales of the Unexpected" tomorrow. If you want?'

'I need to tell you What I Did.'

'What Del Did? Quite right Susan Coolidge's What Katy Did is a natural reading progression from Enid Blyton's Secret Seven, though not date wise to be fair.'

'You are over educated you know. There is nothing anyone can say, that you don't know something about.'

'What do you expect? I am Nigerian,' Jonathan yawned. 'But the truth is I was a lonely boy at Aldbourne, with no entertainment but a vast library. I had to do something to distract myself from the boredom. You know, it's strange. No one ever thought to buy me toys.'

'That's sad. Child abuse, I'm sure. See you tomorrow.'

'Make yourself at home.'

Delsea called Michael after Jonathan went to bed. 'I arrived safely.'

'I am sorry I gave the impression that I don't care that one of our much-respected politicians has been attacked in the line of duty, as it were. It is admirable the way they make themselves equally available to everyone who turns up at their surgery. Having to put their trust in total strangers. How is he?'

'He's being over jolly. Not his usual self.'

'He was lucky to survive, survivor's euphoria. I can understand that feeling. I just wish he had someone else in his life.' She ignored the last bit of that sentence.

'Thank you for saying that. How is Amy?'

'I played Connect Four for hours.'

'She likes putting the counters into the slots in completely random order. Mind numbing. I thought you would take her to your mum to look after and go to work.'

'I knew you would think that. She is hard work. It's been good for me knowing that, seeing your life. I don't know how you do it every day. I see why you need a holiday, with just us. Some quality adult time. We need to listen to each other more.'

'This role reversal is good for her too. It will be bonding for her having concentrated daddy time.'

'You owe me an apology too, Del. We are a couple. You can't just ignore my feelings and do your own thing.'

'You were being unreasonable!'

'Forgive me for asking. Are you still in love with Jonathan? The way you steamrollered my feelings in order to go to him.'

'I am sorry I treated you like that. I am not in love with him. I am in love with you. I love him like a brother, like I love Marcus. I grew up with him as my constant playmate.

You will need to babysit for another night.' Michael took a sharp inhale of breath. 'I need to go to Cambridge from here to assure

Josh that Jonathan is alright, that I have seen him and he has not sustained any life-changing injuries.'

'That's sensible.'

'You may find it strange sleeping alone in our bed. I used to at first when you were away on business.'

She hadn't told the whole truth about her love for Jonathan. She loved him as part of herself. She loved him as she loved herself.

'Good morning. I am feeling much better, thanks for asking.'

Jonathan was wearing a T-shirt and jeans after his shower, his fair hair darker when wet. The lithe young body she had known was replaced by hardness; a solidity that wasn't there before. Delsea went over to look at his arms. He outstretched them as he saw the horror on her face. She was careful not to touch him. 'That's a lot of stitches!'

'Defence wounds,' he said. 'I am supposed to put a fresh dressing on after I shower.'

'I can do that for you. This is really healing quickly considering it happened four days ago.'

'The power of the sun. I wouldn't let them take my blood to check the haemoglobin level, or do a cross match. I was worried they might see something unusual. I insisted on fluid drips only. I knew my body would rapidly replace the blood loss. I signed some document to say I was going against medical advice. They just had to go on my blood pressure and heart rate.'

'They probably thought you were insane. When the hair grows back the scars won't even show. Can I give you a hug?'

'Go on then, since it's you. But make it a quick one.'

'Get off! You said hug, not kiss my cheek.'

'My gift from the moon is not so obvious. It is unfailing intuition. I know exactly what will happen to me next in most situations and can take measures to alleviate it if I need to. Do you remember when I found that LSD in Marcus's room and took it?'

'How could I forget!'

'The Chancellor took drugs.'

'I did not inhale.'

'You can't inhale LSD. I nearly died.'

'Don't remind me. You phoned me straight after swallowing it, absolutely panic stricken about what might happen. Mama said there is a distressed girl on the phone, who is she? I shouted at her to give me the phone. I ran all the way to the park. You were having a fit about a tree that had been hit by lightning. Thinking it was screaming in agony. The inside looked burnt out.'

'You thought you should take the other LSD tablet to accompany me on my trip to keep me safe. We were daft. You went on your own psychedelic trip instead.'

'You were so distressed about the tree that I decided to climb it to see if there was any life inside that I could see.'

'Then the LSD kicked in and you fell out of the tree. I thought you were dead so I ran away completely freaked out.'

'You waded into the river forgetting that you couldn't swim. Then you started to drown.

I ran after you, jumped in to save you, with a broken arm! Mama was furious when I got home completely out of my mind, soaking wet with a broken arm. Everyone was worried I wouldn't be able to sit my A Levels.'

'Your arm was a mess, that was before the power of the sun. But there are no marks at all from that now, the sun particles must have healed them too. It is just as well that we were secret agents and had both mastered the art of writing with either hand equally well. So, all's well that ends well. Does this hurt?'

'Ouch.'

'You're fine.' He always said ouch, when words designed to hurt or physical injuries did not cut deep.

'However, I can see that you are not. Shall we continue with "Tales of the Unexpected?" You look like you want to get deadly serious straight away. So, while I make breakfast tell me about… actually before we get to that, can I check that there isn't a Chinese man?' Jonathan looked fake puzzled.

'Stop it, otherwise I will punch you. Stop making me laugh when I am being deadly serious about men. Not in that way, but China does make an appearance.'

'You must ask me first in order to punch me… do you think I would agree to that? No. No hitting. Well, I will look forward to the Chinese contingency.

The friend who was into benefits… that is if you still want to talk about him. I distinctly felt the temperature drop when you alluded to him last night. When I say benefits, I don't mean the Department of Social Security kind.'

'He was a pedestrian black man.'

'So, what happened to him?'

'He grew up and fell in love with my benefits.'

'I see we are talking perks of the company kind.'

'As my career advanced, the more high-powered I became the greater the commensurate car package I got. First, he was in love with my black Golf GTI which had red detailing, but we were still talking. Then he fell in love with my white AUDI 80 sports car with go faster stripes; he still came round now and again. Then I got my racing green BMW 520i and I couldn't get use of my own company car.'

'Am I supposed to be interested in the GTI, 80 or 520i, or the man? I never know with you. I feel sorry for Michael for once having to put up with a lifetime of determining whether detail is significant or not.'

'Ha ha. I wouldn't say it to him. He doesn't speak our language.'

'You gave this pedestrian his Black Man's Wheels – what more could he possibly want? Then you expected him to pay attention to you. Your taste in men is diabolical, even though I say so myself. He is minus one as far as counting on one hand goes.

The friend who took benefits?'

'He was in my friendship group at university since freshers. He portrayed himself as "One of Us."'

'Being shafted by someone posing as "One of Us" is a betrayal indeed.'

'I was complicit in allowing him to take benefits. Anyway, he left me and moved to Australia. After which I cried, dug deep into my psyche, and lay in bed reading Charlotte Perkins Gilman's The Yellow Wallpaper repeatedly, while staring at patterns in the green wallpaper on the bedroom wall which gave me pareidolia.'

'Why, that is guaranteed to make anyone feel sad. Did you follow that with Sylvia Plath's The Bell Jar for good measure? Great feminist icons, I know. Actually, I don't understand the man in The Yellow Wallpaper fainting in response to his wife's mental illness seems rather feeble. Unless the author means to damn men with faint praise.'

'No Alexander Pope!'

'So, we come to the crux of the deadly serious matter. What Del Did, which by the way sounds extraordinary. What happened to us? After the London Episode as you so flippantly called it, you ignored me. When I phoned you cut the call. When I wrote, you never replied.'

'I didn't want you to distract me. I was studying really hard for my 'A' Levels to prove you and all the doubters wrong that I could have an education and a baby. Then when I let my pent-up feelings about you out after exams, I felt I needed a gap break. My parents agreed to have Josh as I had done so well academically. I had an offer from Bristol which I accepted.

My gap break was in Oxford.' Jonathan was incredulous, poleaxed. 'I wanted to spend some of your third year with you. I did read your letters, you know. I came back for my man!'

'What happened to this plan, about which I knew nothing!'

'I didn't tell you because I wanted to surprise you. Then I met Gin Tan.'

'Surprise, this sounds like a whole strategic master plan. I am not sure I want to hear more because I might just strangle you for not telling me! Not telling me caused a fundamental paradigm shift in our relationship.'

'Listen, without your mind turning to common domestic strangulation please. I figured that if I spent some time hanging around Magdalen Bridge, I would eventually see you coming out of your college.'

'This is bonkers.'

'I was eighteen, mixed-up, I know now I was being irrational. I was teetering on the edge. Mentally exhausted. I had crammed to take my exams early, on top of everything else like caring for Josh, so that I could spend quality time with you. I thought we needed time to work things out. You had mashed up my heart and you mashed down my head.'

'Are the ups and downs important? I won't pretend to know Jamaican.'

'Yes, my moods were up, down, and all over the place.'

'What about mash, it sounds like you are blaming me for being destructive. It takes two you know. This plan, dare I say it, was silly.'

GIN TAN-HUGHES

It was late January. Delsea took a break from waiting for Jonathan on Magdalen Bridge to have lunch. She went into the Nose Bag café in town. They had these big sharing dining tables there. She looked around for a place to sit and enjoy her homemade soup with roll. She saw Gin Tan. Her staring caused Gin to smile, indicating she could join her table. She went and sat opposite her. Of course, she didn't know her name until they introduced themselves to each other. She was even more beautiful close up.

Delsea said, 'I think we have someone in common, I saw you with him the other day.'

'Who is that?' Gin asked.

'Jonathan Ainsley.'

'Oh, Jonathan,' Gin said possessively. 'How come you know Jonathan?'

'We come from the same village. We grew up together.'

'Corsham, I've been. It's a really picturesque place.' Delsea was wondering whether Jonathan had taken her there. But then Corsham and the surrounding villages are tourist attractions.

Delsea said, 'I'm his girlfriend.' Gin laughed at her scornfully. 'You find that funny, do you?'

'Jonathan is Ace and, in his case, he feels repulsed by sex.'

'What do you mean, Ace?'

'Asexual. I doubt you are his girlfriend!'

'What does asexual mean?'

'I can see growing up in Corsham you are out of touch with the real world. It means he is not sexually attracted to anyone, believe me.' Delsea was angry. Gin thought her an ignorant child not wise to the ways of the world. Gin threw back her head, titillated by her superior knowledge of Jonathan. She wasn't funny. Delsea was on the verge of throwing her soup in Gin's face.

She asked Gin, 'What's so funny?'

'Poor little thing,' she condescendingly replied. 'I can see you have the hots for him. Let me advise you, he also has touch aversion.'

'What the hell is that?'

'He hates being touched by anyone.' Alarm bells rang when Gin told her those symptoms. It was all making sense now. Suddenly Delsea was overcome by insecurity. Seeing her demeanour, Gin didn't stop there. 'You've had a pity fuck, you poor thing.'

Delsea was raging inside.

'What's that?'

'Some Aces will have sex even though they have no desire, to appease someone putting pressure on them to do so.'

'You are saying if Jonathan slept with me, it was out of pity?' Gin had external beauty, but inside she was ghastly, and Delsea sensed that she was jealous of her.

'I do feel sorry for you, but there it is. He will probably form a lasting relationship with another Ace. If I were you, I wouldn't waste my time on him! There are plenty of heterosexual fish in the sea.' To which Gin laughed assertively.

Aidless, Delsea went to the ladies and cried. Alone, smitten, she cried her heart out. People can be so unfeeling. Then she washed her face, made her way back to their table carrying her pride like a full glass of water, from which it was important not to accidentally spill a drop. Grabbing her coat, she left immediately, retreating from nasty Gin back to safety. Outside, the weary rain fell ceaselessly as though to join in with her misery.

She marched up to Jonathan's Porter's Lodge. She automatically adopted Lucille's angry Caribbean woman stance, arms akimbo. To the porters she must have looked like trouble. She demanded to see Jonathan.

'I have come to see Jonathan Ainsley. He's at this college.' They thought she was out of her mind, which she was by then. She found it ever so slightly disconcerting and devastating to realise that she could never have a sexually fulfilling relationship with Jonathan.

'Is he expecting you?'

'No.'

'We can't just let you in. Can you get in touch some other way, then he can come and collect you from here.'

There were students going in and out. She was certain she could ask one of them to give Jonathan a message that she was waiting to see him. Then she changed her mind. She needed to process this stuff Gin Tan had unceremoniously dumped on her. She was indignant. She was not going to chase after Jonathan. She had had it with his nonsense. She was beyond upset, bereaved even for what might have been. She went back to her digs and cried silently to herself, which is much more painful than crying openly. She didn't want her house-mates to hear. She deliberately decided not to think any more about Jonathan.

After Delsea told Jonathan about this, he was speechless. What Del Did was indeed extraordinary.

'Are you, Ace and do you have touch aversion?'

'Yes.'

'It was your job to tell me that. I had to hear it from a stranger.'

'You chose to hear it from a stranger.'

'I couldn't handle knowing that and didn't want to think about it.'

'By the way, I was aware that you came into my bedroom last night, you were about to touch my hair, then thought better of it and left. This is why I could never ever live with you. You don't obey rules.'

'What rules, this whole touch aversion thing is just….'

'Be careful what you say next.'

'Ridiculous! Frankly ridiculous! Absolutely ridiculous!'

'Stop shouting "ridiculous" – we are not in a Harry Potter film.'

'I am sorry I checked on you in the middle of the night. On your first night out of hospital. How dare I? How stupid of me to care whether you were alright after someone tried to kill you!'

'Stop right now. This is getting out of control.'

'Ridiculous!'

'I thought we'd done shouting "ridiculous."'

'When you came out of your college, you were with Gin Tan. I followed you up The High to Carfax, along Cornmarket, along St. Giles to Browns restaurant.'

'Is the precision of the route material?'

'No.'

'You followed me to Browns restaurant is sufficient for most people. You are annoying sometimes. Go on.'

'Only sometimes. I watched you get a table. You both seemed at ease with one another and that made me sad.'

'Why sad?'

'You seemed more suited to each other than you and I, and she was the most beautiful woman I had ever seen. Half-Chinese, half-English.'

'What nonsense. So, you came to Oxford, went on the dole to follow me around?'

'Does the Chancellor of the Exchequer object to layabouts who are actually undertaking personal study and growth? Put that in your budget and smoke it! My head was mash up.'

'So, you said. Back to mashed heads again?'

'You are not taking any of this seriously.'

'I am trying to.'

'I did what I always do when I can't cope.'

'Enlighten me?'

'I drowned my troubling thoughts in mathematics, by attending public lectures at the Mathematical Institute.'

'As one does? No wonder we never bumped into each other. You should have tried the Bodleian Library where I was concentrating on my finals! But your one true love came to the rescue instead. Forgive me for saying, but does sanity prevail at any point in this sorry saga?'

'At 5:30pm that day, after I followed you to Browns, I had a lecture to go to. Then I didn't mean to, but I got side tracked, sucked into Sri Ramanujan's analysis and theories. I was totally engulfed by them. I was making relevant use of my gap towards my upcoming degree. It was so absorbing that I forgot everything, all my worries and confusion melted away. Even the passage of time was of no significance.

At weekends I studied Five Elements, Eight Principles and the Tract of The Quiet Way. By way of understanding life.'

'Sounds very intense. The Chinese have made their appearance at last. So, is that the end?'

'By no means. Are you old enough for love yet?'

'Ouch.'

'Mathematics was not my one true love, you were and you happened to have the one orientation that meant I couldn't be near you.'

'Minus one, again. For the counting on one hand.'

'This whole damned shooting racket of a world would stop and peace would reign, if everyone behaved in this ridiculous manner, where we all had to ask before touching each other.'

'Have you quite finished insulting me?'

'Yes.'

'I have been listening, though you have taken me around the world in 24 hours, I am going to treat the rockstar with no name as an anomaly, but you have told me about an Asian man, an African man, the Germans in the European car industry, the Chinese and at the very end you even squeezed in our closest allies the North American shooting racket, just so that I would understand that you loved me and you were and I'm not even sure that you are not still angry that we couldn't be together because of my orientation. As if I did not know that already. By the way you missed out the Aussies, this friend who went to Australia wasn't from there by any chance?'

'No.'

'Thank goodness, because nothing is perfect, "In My Father's House Are Many Mansions!"'

'Are we talking about Aldbourne or the one in Scotland?'

'Ha ha. "If it were not so I would have told you," you see I was listening in St Bartholomew's, whereas you were just being naughty.'

'Yes, I was naughty. When my parents fought at weekends, they couldn't go to church on a Sunday morning and face God after their unholy rows. They still sent Marcus and I though. We would skive and go for long walks instead. Collecting a leaflet from the church afterwards to give to Mom to prove we had been.'

'And Marcus?'

'St Bartholomew's, what a long time ago that was. When it rained, we had no choice but to go to church. Marcus would make us sit in the pew behind you instead of our own. There was a brass holder for name cards on each pew. He would pull your hair and knock the back of your head with his knuckles. But your mother behaved even worse. She was affronted, everyone had their place in that church and it wasn't our place to sit behind your family. When it came to turning round clasping your neighbour's hands in "Peace Be With, You," she ignored our small outstretched hands.'

'Racism in the house of God. Eternal damnation!'

'Can I say something? For an asexual person who is repulsed by sex, you were surprisingly good at it.' Then she cracked up because of all the history they had, all the things that had happened since that one sexual act and for all the things that didn't and never would happen. Jonathan said six, which made the hysteria worse. They both roared with laughter. But then neither of them could stop. He added hysterical contagion, an unexplained human phenomenon. Which made them hit themselves and laugh more. Neither of them could stop laughing because it wasn't funny.

'No seriously, you are Ace and repulsed. So how come we had sex?'

'Peer pressure. Besides, I was more malleable then, just getting to know myself.

You should leave, I'm fine. Besides, I need to work on my Mansion House speech.'

'Enough already with the mansions and houses! I will go, as I can see you are back to your usual self. Last night I thought there was a lot of false bonhomie going on for someone who had been stabbed.'

'Drunk too. Hardly surprising.'

Jonathan: 'As I was lying in the gutter
Thinking thoughts, I could not utter
I heard a passing Delsea say.'
Delsea: 'You can tell a man who boozes
By the company he chooses
And at that the pig got up and walked away.'

'For the record, Gin is not the most beautiful woman I have ever seen. She is much too superficial and self-satisfied for my liking. You know that song "The First Time Ever I Saw Your Face," that reminds me of you. I love you. I find it hard to use that word. We made out because I loved you, not out of pity.'

'Wow, revelations indeed, even back then!' No wonder he found it hard to tell Delsea how he felt when his mother was Frederica, who probably never told him she loved him in her life.

Apart from Delsea's mother no one told her as a young woman that she was beautiful. They labelled her sassy, sultry, exotic, but never beautiful.

'I know you don't think so, but it is sad for me that after all this time you have told me that you love me and I just walk out the door, without even a hug. Right, onwards, I better go see our son. He will be thinking that you being stabbed is his fault and not the perpetrator's.'

'Can I give you some advice before you go. Study the "Yin Chih Wen" some more, I don't think you have quite mastered its quiet ways.'

'When all is said and done, at the end of the day we each made the right decision for our own happiness. You could not live with me, because you would worry that I might touch you. I could not live with you as some sort of INCEL nun.'

JEHOVAH COLLEGE

There was another formal in the second term of their third year, where Tom could cause Josh maximum embarrassment. Discombobulate him before his reading of the Latin grace so that he couldn't perform the accolade awarded. All the dons were watching from their high table. Josh looked around the dining hall for Holloway; he was expecting an ambush of some sort. He smiled at Tamsin chatting to one of her girlfriends near the back of the queue.

Tom appeared, wild, drunk.

'She's dead.'

'Oh good, you are released from your strange fixation on her. Just in time for you to catch up and sit your finals, if you work hard enough, you'll still get through.'

'This is all you care about.' Tom gestured around the dining hall.

'I came here to do a degree, funnily enough.'

'She wrote you another letter.'

'Shouldn't you give that to the police or whoever?'

'She wrote three letters: a letter to her parents, one to the college and one to you.'

'The agony she has put her parents through, these last two years doesn't bear thinking about. No parents should have to go through that. They must be in bits. As for the letters, drama to the end.'

'You don't care that she's killed herself because of you. You are so nasty about her Josh, and I've had enough.'

'I was not nasty to her. I was respectful of her situation. I have rejected your obsessive interest in her problems and you continually forcing your intolerant views of my treatment of her down my throat. I am ashamed of my poor character judgement. I can't believe that I ever thought of you as my friend. How many times have I asked you to stop and leave me and Tamsin alone?'

He did care that she had ended her young life. It was a total waste. He didn't want to think about that then. He was just good for putting one foot in front of the other until the end of term. He wrapped himself in his gown for self-comfort, to prevent him completely losing it with Holloway with the entire college as witnesses. He strode purposefully towards the top end of the long refectory tables, where some students were already settling down for the evening. But then Tom, doing drunken side-jumps, accosted him again.

'You're too uppity for your own good. If she can't graduate, neither can you.' Tom punched him in the side. He felt that impact. Then an intense electric shock. He didn't realise he'd been stabbed until he saw blood oozing from his white shirt. Followed by excruciating pain. He was struggling for air. Josh just had enough strength to shout 'Tamsin,' before collapsing. He tried to say more but had no voice. He could feel his strength quickly decaying.

There was pandemonium: girls screaming, dons rushing to him. Someone attempted to stem the fast flow of blood by pressing firmly on the wound with a wad of white linen napkins. Someone else elevated his legs onto a chair to slow and restrict the flow of blood, confining it to essential organs. Tamsin ran to him, her eyes swimming with tears. He could see her face, but she was fading. She seemed to be both far away and near, her face suddenly like that of an angel. He could hear little sound. He could hear less and less. The air was quiet. Still. There was a steadfast gathering of peace. For a moment he just hung there between life and death. Slipping into unconsciousness, he passed quietly away.

The paramedics were there in no time at all. But Josh died at the scene. Holloway was apprehended by the dons, who took the murder weapon from him. The police arrived. Holloway kept saying: 'I did it, I'm compos mentis, I should have stabbed him in the heart, but he hasn't got one.'

Delsea was unaccountably worried about Josh. She had a sick feeling in the pit of her stomach. She kept phoning him, only for his mobile to go to voicemail. Her intuition was telling her that something was drastically wrong. She wanted to scream uncontrollably at her inability to contact him and set her mind at rest. But it was evening, she couldn't even phone his plodge to ask whether they'd seen him lately.

It was rare for a whole week to go by without one of them phoning the other.

Feeling useless, she ran into the garden, into the moonlight. She screamed his name to the moon. 'Joshua,' she yelled three times with the fullest blast that her lungs could manage. A pure white room opened up. There were people dressed in white inside. It was amazing to be able to make anything out with all the white on white going on. But the room was bathed in golden light and in the middle was Joshua. He was dressed in white too. He looked absolutely beautiful. She moved closer to him and stretched out her hand to touch his image, her hand passed straight through.

Then Joshua spoke strange words, 'Yes Mum. I read that I would die. It was decided. Why take me, I thought. I had nothing another could want and there was so much more for me to see here. Perhaps that was not meant to be. I have been allowed to know the true meaning of sight. We'll be together many years from now.' He pointed to a vision that appeared beside him of a very old Delsea. 'You have work to do, concentrate on that. There will be another boy who will live for the both of us.' This was Joshua's prophecy.

Michael came into the garden to find her. 'Del, there is a policeman and woman at the door. I've invited them in.' Delsea followed him back inside. Where the police told them that Josh was dead and that he had been stabbed by another boy at his college. Michael put his arms around her as sob after sob escaped her. She knew nothing about death; she hadn't experienced it before. Finally, the initial shock was over and she wept. Her eyes stung from the constant tears that pricked them.

The first person she called was Jonathan. 'The police have been. Josh is dead. A boy at his college stabbed him.'

Jonathan couldn't believe it. Stabbings were street crime. They did not occur in the safe space of Ariel University. Delsea was surprisingly coherent. It was as though the shock had produced some anaesthetic to help her cope. For Jonathan it was like a blow to the solar plexus. He stopped breathing. His arm holding his mobile felt dead, unwilling to support the conveyance of such devastating news. The phone dangled there from his unnerved arm. That short fact of Josh's death was the most he could take. The faint sound of Delsea still talking was barely audible to him. Josh, that athlete brimming with health. It didn't make sense. A cold deep pain pierced through him.

Having told Ben and Lucille, that was the most Delsea felt able to do. She put her mobile down. Her legs felt heavy, ready to collapse under her. It was very early morning. She was tired. Yet the idea of sleep was impossible. She was insensible to relief. Each moment she expected Josh to walk through the door even though it was term time, and put an end to the lie.

Michael and Delsea went to Addenbrooke's Hospital to see Josh. He looked peaceful, with no trace of his violent death on his face. The silence was deafening; they had a quiet moment with Josh before they took him away for post-mortem. They needed that time to themselves before others came to support them at home.

Lucille and Ben were the first to arrive. Ben proved to be hopeless in the crisis. He looked on like a spectator at a horror show. Lucille saw and understood what Ben was going through. She could do nothing to ease his pain. Her thoughts and prayers were for Josh. Her duty was to Michael and Delsea. Her Caribbean values underpinned all that she did. Delsea looked utterly helpless with her face full of grief. Death was so close that they were all humbly aware of their own mortality. They were four bewildered individuals forced together by horrendous circumstances. Moving smoothly around each other like cogs in a clock.

Michael carried on with the phoning. His parents and sister, Marcus and Emma. Soon friends and family arrived, going in and out of the house. Delsea thought that it shouldn't be happening. They were eating, drinking and making merry. She wanted to be alone. She ran upstairs past all the people who just seemed to be standing around. She didn't want their sympathy. She couldn't be bothered with the mild concerns of life. But the usual acts of everyday living still intruded. She thought only of Josh. How nothing could bring him back. At least he was far away where nothing else could hurt him. Thank God he was free. She would always remember him in his various stages of life. She could never forget him. He'd left an indelible mark on her existence. Nothing had prepared her for this devastation.

She and Michael were moulded together in their torment yet somehow, they remained disjointed from each other. Enough for him to take the brunt of the blow and carry on. Looking after Amy fell to him. Delsea was incapable. In the family changing room at their private gym, Michael helped Amy slip into her bathing costume.

'One step, two step, slip it on daddy.'

'Yes, that is right.' He twisted the elasticated bobble that secured her hair tighter. It had a habit of coming loose when her hair was wet. By the end of the session, it was a tangled mess, which took him forever to comb out. Amy splashed around in her arm bands. She'd soon be swimming on her own, Michael thought, as he treaded water besides her. She was laughing into his eyes. She was like her mother. He wondered whether they would ever go back to a normal life.

When Michael got home, he found Delsea still curled up on the sofa. He knelt down beside her and held her close. It was an old reaction of his to any sorrow of hers. She said to him that she felt alone though he surrounded her with love. Her thoughts were scattered all over the place: she couldn't think clearly about anything. Her usual decisiveness had leeched away. She was staring at her hands as she spoke to him through choked and faltering tears which slid down her cheeks. She had no wish to live. She wanted to end it – to be with Josh, wherever he was. Michael tried to anchor her. 'You have to go on for Amy,' he said. She knew she would eventually manage that. Learn how to juggle life and grief. Compartmentalise things the way she always did. Create a box in her head called 'beloved son,' which she could leaf through whenever she felt sad about Josh. But at the same time, keeping things simple and joyful for Amy. Prioritising her welfare above all else. There was comfort in the strength of Michael's love. She had little reserves left in herself. Michael would eventually help her to heal her sorrow. But that felt like years away. Misery was her life for the foreseeable future. They were both silent then, as if they had waited for this single moment to mingle their grief.

Lucille wanted to look at photographs of Josh. Josh when he was five, when they lived in Old Headington. They were surrounded by photos of Josh at every period of his life. There were lots of photos of Michael and Josh doing things together. Few of Jonathan and Josh. Those were the photographs Delsea couldn't look at anyway.

They were wretched that night and all subsequent nights. The days barely divided the nights. They dozed in chairs. In bed she tossed and turned. She didn't know whether she was asleep or awake half the time. She'd stand at their bedroom window, draw back the curtains to watch the stars in the night sky. They didn't have the practicality of a funeral to arrange because the coroner hadn't released the body. Consequently, it was as though Josh had disappeared from the face of the earth without a trace.

There were dozens of sympathy cards and flowers on every surface downstairs. The house was chock-full of people all the time. Lucille took over the cooking, cajoling visitors to eat. For those of them who were closely involved every proof that they were alive and Josh was dead was torture. Delsea felt angry that no matter how hard she tried there was always another trial, another mountain, another battle to fight. This final assault felt like her life's struggles had reached their term. Because nothing could ever be of greater consequence than losing her son. It was made even sadder because it seemed so stupid. Some boy, according to Jehovah College, suffering from toxic co-dependency and guilt, in mental free fall that no one seemed to notice until he attacked Josh.

Occasionally she checked how Michael was doing. The dark shadows beneath his eyes were the only outward sign of turmoil. He still had that touch of audacity she had always loved. There was a notable kindness of heart to him. He was ever so gentle with everyone telling him about how they would miss Josh. She felt his goodness in taking that weight off her. Warmth filled her whenever she looked his way. Joshua's death was a wrong which crushed him like it did her. Josh was dear to him too. But he had to be strong for Delsea. He reacted with tenacity, remaining stoic in the face of death, his stiff upper lip never quite unstiffening.

Jonathan decided to go home to impenetrable Aldbourne where he need only take media interviews that he was prepared to do. He cried the whole of that journey. When he got there, he didn't know what to do. He sat in his bathroom crying hysterically, with Mama banging on the door trying to get in to comfort him. Feelings, and thoughts that he couldn't deal with triggered off confused emotions. He felt hopelessly dejected. There was no mistaking the sorrow he felt for his lost son. The tide of grief was flowing freely all he could feel was a silent pain.

He had to put on a bold face for the media. His job persona took over. His first concern was to shield Delsea from the tabloids. It wasn't easy for him feeling so painfully close to her again. But he knew Delsea would be at rock bottom and wouldn't want to talk to the media. She would expect him to do that. He spoke to reporters. His face wrinkled by worry lines. His anger at the way Josh died spilling out. He spoke really well, the consummate performer. He was disparaging about the cruel and callous way in which Josh had been killed. He had no time for the impotence of grief. His son an innocent Ariel undergraduate murdered. It was a senseless waste of a promising life.

Life was full of unexpected twists, he observed. Josh's death had knocked him sideways. He was pained that he'd missed out on so much of his life. He and Josh would never be reconciled. Throughout Josh's life they'd spent only a few weekends together, that was all. Something that had started out good had gone spectacularly wrong. Living alone he'd lost sight of what was important. Josh had needed him. The way Josh turned to him for advice confirmed that. He could fall back on the resources within himself. He garnered his strength. He would leave no stone unturned until he had justice for Josh.

Newsextra gave Jonathan an easy ride. The presenter who was renowned for devouring her prey whole and spitting them out was being cautious. Delsea had never seen her so caring. Youth stabbings were an everyday occurrence. Joshua being killed at the height of his educational achievement was indicative of all the teenagers and young people who never reached their potential because their lives were cut short by knife crime. But Josh was the Chancellor's son. People took notice and felt empathy for him.

Watching, Michael was a little irritated, as it was, he who had raised Josh. But he took that back – it was unworthy of him. He had to put up with Jonathan because he knew that Delsea needed them both. To take over from Jonathan and become the media face of Josh's death would drag a lot of unwanted attention into their lives. There was no getting away from the fact that Delsea and Jonathan shared a deep connection. Nothing then was deeper than Josh's killing. Of course, Jonathan had paternal feelings for his son. But every black pressure group in the country would plan leverage out of this, Michael thought.

JOSHUA

It was three weeks before the coroner released Josh's body. The undertakers brought him to Westmead in the evening for his funeral the next day. Michael showed them to the dining room where his open coffin would rest, pertaining to Jamaican custom. Delsea had given the undertakers the clothes to dress him in. New black evening attire. She bought a new college gown too. The police, she was glad to know, kept the actual suit and gown he was wearing when killed, for forensic purposes. One last time he would be part of their family.

Merin couldn't get a direct train to Oxford from Norwich. She had to go via London. Most of that journey she was weeping openly as she hurried along. People kept staring at her; she must have looked suspicious in her distressed state. She wasn't even dressed for the season in her big winter coat. Grief made her feel cold. Her mind was preoccupied. She was stumbling over simple tasks like finding her train ticket, when the guard demanded to see it.

Half way through the evening their doorbell went. Michael and Delsea weren't expecting anyone. There would be time for others, the day of Josh's funeral.

Delsea went to the door. A mesmerising woman stood there. Long soft auburn natural corkscrew curls fell down to her waist. Caramel skin, bright green eyes: a Botticelli Venus. She was tiny, five foot two. Her Doc Martens defied anyone to take her for the weaker sex.

'Merin,' she said. 'I've come to sit with Josh.' Delsea threw her arms round her and burst into tears.

'I am so glad Josh knew love before he died.' Merin no doubt thought her hypocritical because Josh must have told her she was indifferent towards her. Being half-Jamaican like Josh, she knew he would be there that night, if not for the Nine Night. The Dead Yard, which they weren't observing. It can take up to nine nights after death for the soul to depart. Josh passed over ages ago. Delsea made Merin welcome with supper and afterwards they went to Josh's room, sat on his bed and played his music. Michael joined them up there as they went through his favourite bands. Delsea heard The Doors. The mention of love and funeral pyres made her weep. Then Merin came down, sat in a comfortable armchair for her last night with Josh. Her wanting to sit in the dining room with him some of the time in a way let Michael and Delsea off the hook. There was no way they could do that without having some sort of psychosis.

None of them slept that night of the vigil, only Amy. Michael and Delsea lay on sofas ninety degrees apart. Delsea took sips of brandy from her side table. Somehow Josh's murder was more shocking with him lying dead at home. She waved to Michael on his sofa; he waved back as though they were miles apart. They were still hanging in there. Lying silent while the trembling night winds whistled. Josh had not been waving, but drowning. Eventually the long night waned.

The next morning close family joined them at Westmead for coffee. The adults respectfully saw Josh if the mood took them. Lucille, Ben, Marcus, Emma, and Michael's parents. Michael's sister Rose was freaked out by a body being in the house. She sat in the garden most of the time.

Dorchester Abbey was packed. Michael, Marcus, Ben and Tony helped carry the coffin from the dining room to the hearse.

Jonathan and Lord Ainsley were waiting by the Abbey gate for the hearse to arrive. Sadly, Delsea never got round to introducing Josh to his grandfather, Lord Ainsley, like he'd asked her to do. The six men to carry Josh's coffin, in pairs, were Michael and Jonathan, the older men – Lord Ainsley and Ben – in the middle, then Marcus and Tony at the rear.

Some of the mourners Delsea hadn't seen for ages. Josh's Moulsford Prep school friends, and the parents she bonded with chatting at the school gate and birthday parties. Josh's Goring College school friends, and more parents she knew from sleepovers. Josh's university friends wore their gowns because Josh had died attending a formal. Delsea had met some of them when they had stayed with him for weekends. His tutor and the Master of Jehovah college. It was hell, going through the funeral rituals, harrowing, because Josh was so young.

The women of the family went ahead, taking seats in the front pews.

Delsea thought of the good things Josh would never get to do now. First and foremost, he had told Jonathan that he wanted to live with him and get a job in London after graduation. They would never have that father-son time now. Delsea read a poem by Christina Rossetti.

Remember me when I am gone away,
  Gone far away into the silent land;
  When you can no more, hold me by the hand,
Nor I half turn to go yet turning stay.
Remember me when no more day by day
  You tell me of our future that you planned:
  Only remember me; you understand
It will be late to counsel then or pray.
Yet if you should forget me for a while
  And afterwards remember, do not grieve:
  For if the darkness and corruption leave
  A vestige of the thoughts that once I had,
Better by far you should forget and smile
  Than that you should remember and be sad.

Michael gave the eulogy. While he was doing so Lucille started doing her pursed lip, pointing in Michael's direction then over her shoulder to Jonathan behind Delsea. The trouble was that that sort of pointing was common among people from different countries. Jonathan knew what she was doing. Delsea turned round to him – he was watching Michael and doing his aggressive eye-rolling down rejection. What the fuck? This situation was a tinderbox waiting to explode. Delsea willed the people to behave. It was her son's funeral.

It was difficult to keep things private with Jonathan there, even though Delsea had stipulated only family at the graveside. The Abbey graveyard was in open view, with trees in the distance like clouds on the horizon. A wind fluttered Delsea's coat. The coffin lowered. The family members each threw in an innocent white rose. After prayers and song, the Rector in his abundant vestments, Michael, Ben, Lucille, Marcus, Emma, Merin and Delsea closed ranks tightly around Jonathan to stop there being a photo of him on front pages with a shovel of earth in his hand, at his son's funeral, no matter how poignant. It would tug at heartstrings and turn political. It was important to Caribbeans to bury their dead themselves and not leave the grave open. They had three shovels. As a mark of respect, to counteract the eye rolling there had been during the service, Delsea gave the first shovel to Jonathan to calm things down. Then she took a turn. After that it was up to Michael, Marcus, Tony and Ben to fill the hole in. Lord Ainsley had left straight after the service. Jonathan didn't want to help with the filling in of the grave. He told Delsea that in Nigeria parents don't go to their children's funerals to spare them immeasurable heartache. In a way she could see why.

Flowers that had gone to the undertaker were displayed nearby, to be laid on top of the grave once filled. Jonathan and Delsea stepped away to view them. She saw a name that stopped her heart still. Jonathan, so in tune with her feelings, reacted immediately. They were alike that way. He bled if she bled. It was as if they had never parted. He could read her signals so quickly.

'No, Jonathan,' she took his hand, guiding him away, conscious that they were probably being watched. He didn't wince, grief seemed to have overcome his touch aversion. She called to Michael, who grabbed the offensive wreath, hurling it discus like clear out of the graveyard. Holloway murdered their son and sent a wreath! No, he could not be so cruel. Anyone could have sent it to the undertakers to make mischief. Michael dusted his palms as though they were contaminated. Delsea took his hand. For an instant she was holding both men, and didn't know whose hand to let go of. Jonathan gently prised his hand from hers, solving the dilemma.

Michael and Delsea took a detour to the Nature Reserve for some quiet reflection. They walked on a solitary path which led through a wood. The wood was old and magical. The ground soft and peaty. The only sound was the crunch of twigs underfoot. They admired some Purple Emperor butterflies high up in a tree blossom. Leaving the intimacy of the small wood behind, they took a boardwalk towards the river. They talked about Josh and how he hadn't told them about this vile boy at college. They might have been able to put a stop to the bullying if they had known. There was a large log by the river, which a tree surgeon had left. Delsea sat down and thought about the guests waiting for them to join them. Michael came and squatted besides her. Beneath his calm façade every sinew and brain cell strained as he stared at her with those intense analytical blue eyes.

'I didn't do a good job of protecting Josh.'

'Don't start down that road. You are not to blame yourself. It's not your fault. We all feel like that, guilty, like there were things we could have done to prevent it.' Delsea thought of how they had Amy not long before Josh started at Ariel. Had she taken her eyes off him? She put a lot of his moody behaviour down to Merin, which seemed unfair, having been informed of the bullying. Thinking of Merin, she thought they should get back. She didn't know anyone and Delsea wanted to thank her for coming and spending the night with Josh. But then a text from Merin: she was already gone, and wouldn't stay for the funeral tea.

'Merin's gone home.' Michael leant in; their foreheads touched as though he could transmit his feelings to Delsea that way. His reaction to their anguish. Delsea leaned in and sank into him. It was Michael by her side for most of the wake, as it should be. Jonathan wouldn't intrude by staying much longer either.

At the hotel Delsea chatted to Jonathan, who was about to depart. He would not stay for food and drink. He spotted surreptitious behaviour at the corner of his eye.

'There are press snooping around. We shouldn't stick together.'

'At our son's funeral?'

'We should go over to Michael. You know you never talk to me about him.'

'Why would I talk to you about him?' Another time she would have been heartened by them conversing.

'Do you talk to anyone about him; I am curious…'

'Of course not, I talk an awful lot about him to him.'

'I see you are a loyal wife. Not far now, introduce me properly to him and Amy, after all I am not Josh's father, and this is his funeral, I am just the sperm donor.'

'Don't say that.'

'I didn't say it, Josh told me about that the first time we met.' She was ready to keel over with grief for Jonathan being subjected to that and for Josh telling him. 'Come take my arm for support if you like?'

'I see I have permission to touch you when we are on display. Us as man and wife would never have worked even if you'd told me about…'

'Move faster, I want us over to your husband quickly, as you say you behave differently with him. I can't think why, but I have an awful feeling that with me here, if we don't cross this room soon, you might start shouting ridiculous.'

He almost propelled her across the floor. 'Look, I shouldn't have behaved like that. That was bad of me, but I waited nearly twenty years to have that argument with you. The rushed encounters we had after the London Episode weren't the right time to embark upon the subject.'

'I see, a patient woman too.'

'I was incandescent with rage.'

'I noticed.'

'I wasn't going to say ridiculous – I was going to apologise and say if you had told me about how you were, I would have appreciated your right to be different.'

'That is good to know.'

'Sometimes I can't get my head around the sexual; heterosexual, homosexual, bisexual, pansexual, asexual and the genders; male, female, transgender male, transgender female and non-binary. My mind just wants to multiply them together and come up with 101 permutations.'

'Don't do it…'

'Do what?'

'Correct the figurative speech.'

'I mean combinations, neither the order of the sexuality or gender matters.'

'Introduce me before you feel the need to tell me more about this riveting multiplication! You are not the only one with a mashed head. I am furious that I have to give way to another man at my son's funeral. He virtually threatened you with divorce by saying you couldn't have Amy if you went to see a friend you've known all your life, who had been stabbed. His generosity knows no bounds.' Michael's antagonism towards him astounded Jonathan.

'Mr Chancellor,' Michael knew the correct way to address the Chancellor: sometimes she wondered where all the people of his class learned these things. She wouldn't have had a clue about this informal address.

'Nice to meet you Michael, on such a sad day, this is absolutely dreadful. I will ensure the Justice Secretary gets justice for Josh and for you and your family. Josh was loved by all who knew him, including me. I can't think why we haven't met before. Mrs Valentine has been very remiss. Sorry, did I stand on your foot, Delsea I can be clumsy sometimes. Amy, nice to meet you at last!'

'Why at last? Can I ask you a question?' Amy was nearly four and asked more questions each day.

'Go on.'

'Do you do counting every day?'

'Yes, but sometimes, it's a little more complicated than that. It is called economics, both micro and macro.'

'What is micro and macro?'

'Small and big numbers.'

'Mummy, I told you he did more counting than you?'

'I am not so sure about that. You see, your mother can count the whole world on one hand. Well, I better be going. Come and see me, Delsea, at my surgery in Chippenham. There is a lot I can do to help you and your family get through this. You might as well make use of our connection.' After that for Delsea the day ended in pointless babble and wine.

The shot that made the front page of the tabloids was of Delsea holding on to both men. Fortunately, it was an action shot, not posed. *The Trilateral.* All three of them had to survive this together. Jonathan and Delsea still had much to accomplish.

Delsea visited Josh's grave every day. She stood there and despaired. She could pretend that he was sleeping in that earthy bed in the shadow of the yew. She could even place a plaque to that effect. But Josh wasn't sleeping. He didn't die peacefully. He was violently dead. Murdered. Dead before his proper time. Taken from them by force.

Endless graves stretched out in perfect lines. The grass neatly cut around each. Much of the grass was dry – a dusty yellow. It had been hot. She thought of the cornfields in Wiltshire where sometimes she lay, tasting the sun on her skin, relaxing, doing Maths, alone. She needed tranquillity. Jonathan would talk when she tried to think. He never understood her passion for Maths. He would stare blankly at her sheets of calculations as if they were hieroglyphics. She would shake her head, meaning don't say a thing, because inspiration was dawning. The solution in the end was so elegant and simple it had to be right. Occam's razor. The clarity of an abstract mathematical intellect was totally lost on Jonathan. Only mathematicians really understood each other. Delsea liked the jokes they told. How do you know if a mathematician is an extrovert as opposed to an introvert? They look at your shoes when talking instead of their own. Jonathan and her shared so much. How had things gone so wrong engendering all this hurt. Well, no one wanted to be in her shoes now.

She felt separated from the world by a wall of grief. She looked on like an outsider. She went for long walks with Amy in her pushchair. On her own she was afraid of the house, especially the block of knives in the kitchen in case she seized one and slashed her wrists. There were so many ways to die indoors, knives, pills and stairs where there was a nice drop, from the bannisters to hang herself. She kept trying to calculate what went wrong, what ifs, which inhibited her ability to talk to Michael. She never could do Maths and hold a conversation at the same time. They shared a companionable silence. Yet outside the May sunshine raged on, soft and hazy. Inside her heart was full of love for her dead son. A love that didn't blossom one drop at a time like the love for a man. Love for a child was so unlimited it was itself a sacrifice. Yet her heart could always squeeze out one drop more of maternal love when needed. Her life had been so bound up with Josh's.

Extended family and friends moved on after Josh's funeral. Delsea was bereft. Nothing seemed important with the cloak of death on her. She felt small. She was nothing in this vast universe. Though her Rector didn't fail in his duty of care towards a much-loved parishioner, and often came to pray with her. She felt in need of kindred spirits.

Delsea wandered down the Cowley Road in search of Jamaicans. They said 'arlright Sista a wey happen,' before she even spoke to them. They were not afraid of dying, and had time for a Sista and to listen to how Josh who was so full of promise was stabbed to death. Some called death going home and had a homecoming service. At the correct interval, which only someone brought up in that tradition knew, they'd say 'Lord Have Mercy.' Except it was more 'Lard a Massy,' which was way more comforting.

Michael became quieter. If that was possible. But maybe it was because Delsea didn't talk to him either. She usually loved the night. Sometimes she got out of bed when everyone was sleeping, just to feel that total peace and look longingly at her spiritual home, the moon. She felt like ET, 'Delsea go home, home,' she pointed at the moon. She was a lunatic. Sometimes she didn't go back to bed but slept on a sofa till dawn.

Michael wanted her back. She would brush him aside. He had become bossy. He tried to join her on the sofa, but she wouldn't budge. She clutched her wine bottle tight, in case he tried to wrestle it from her and pour it down the sink, like he did once. She screamed at him when he did that. He shouted back, 'There is no reasoning with you.' She ignored him. Then when she got angry enough, she would jump up and exaggeratedly, do household chores in a frenzy, and shout 'Is this what you want, I am not your skivvy.' Which was extra because they had a domestic services company that came and did all that. To these verbal attacks he made no reply. These eruptions startled him though.

Delsea would wander around in a T-shirt and pyjama bottoms, with her dressing gown slung on top. Her hair became as wild as long African hair gets if you don't look after it. By way of forcing her to wash and get dressed Michael would suggest they go out somewhere. This made her behave extra. She would annoy him by saying 'Don't mind old dowdy, don't mind old shabbily dressed, I'll just follow you shall I. Lead on MacDuff.' So out of character. The Shakespeare, quote? Brain, welcome back. How she missed thinking about things other than death. She tried to explain to Michael slowly as though he was the one who was mentally challenged, how she wanted to go home to the moon, enough was enough. Life on earth was pure hell.

DEVON

'Come in,' Jonathan stood back to let Delsea in.

'I take it you didn't really want me to go to your surgery in Chippenham, but to come down to Devon?'

'Of course.'

'Why did you stand on my foot?'

'Michael was narrowing his eyes at me. I stood on your foot to stop you putting your foot in it, Mrs Valentine coming from me annoyed you and I could sense that you were about to say, 'who the hell are you calling Mrs Valentine,' which would have been a very curious thing to say tantamount to blowing a whistle, giving us the instruction to start hitting each other.'

'You would have got into a fight over me?'

'No, over our son. Michael stole my son from me. There has already been enough drama with the tabloids reducing the death of our precious boy to an Agatha Christie story, Murder in the Dining Hall. I didn't want to add any more sensation. What's Michael's Alma Mater?'

'Gabriel College of Music.'

'Crickey, out of my league, that. So, your dead rock star with no name was not an anomaly after all, he somehow reincarnated himself into a genre that you found acceptable. Interesting.'

'Classical music is close to mathematics.'

'So, they say. He's an educated man who should know better. He has acted with jealousy and spite and you didn't even notice.'

'He loved Josh and Josh loved him. In many ways they were quite similar. Nurture over nature and all that.'

'I am sure he did. Biological father would be acceptable. But he didn't stop there, Michael reduced me to being a sperm donor.'

'Stop it, I don't think I can cope with this right now on top of losing Josh.'

'He gave the game away by saying he wasn't going to play musical chairs with me. He took everything he could.'

'I fail to see where I am in this scenario, of you two playing musical chairs, that reduces me to being a household object – the chair.'

'You had better ask him about that. Because I didn't say it. He did. You know very well I am an ardent feminist. This whole cycle of violence started with Michael.'

'The social worker who took us through the adoption process said she had spoken to you, and you agreed that if Josh at thirteen wanted to be adopted by Michael, then you were happy for it to take place.'

'That's right. But if Josh had grown up with me being his father and Michael his dad, happy days. We would have been connected from the start. People would have got used to the connection long before I entered parliament.'

'Ridiculous.'

'Don't you dare say ridiculous. You have apologised and I have accepted it, so you will have to find some other word.'

'Preposterous, what about your mother? Lady Ainsley, the racist, who has a wide range of gestures and subterfuge to show her superior disapproval without saying anything. You said that, not me. Would she have welcomed me with open arms?'

'She knew about you. Our vicar, is her confidant.'

'I know, she did. She saw me leave Aldbourne Court that night and had words with me at the summer fete. She thinks I set out to trap you. She thinks I wanted to ruin you. So, I doubt she cared about what would become of me!'

'At first, she did care in the wrong way. It didn't matter that I had knocked up some black girl from the village.'

'She is horrible, I can't think why you have anything to do with her. However, you are too kind and have no doubt watered the vitriol down. Tell me the actual words she used. Though I trust your judgement on whether someone is racist or not, I think I should hear an example before I condemn her outright.'

'She always knew that my running around with a lot of black articles would give me a penchant for black women and once you have tasted black you never go back.'

'She is an ignorant, nasty woman. The slave owners and overseers regularly tasted and went back. She is the one who developed the penchant from living amongst native people. A penchant for hatred, which no doubt sprang from loneliness, due to her inability in her eyes alone, to lower herself enough to make friends and companions from those around her. Loneliness creates bitterness, sometimes jealousy, which feeds anger and hatred. Does she know that you are touched in the head by touch aversion and have a penchant for nobody?'

'Of course not. That was not all dear Mama had to say. We would have a lot of pickaninny and the pure white line would come to an end. When I turned forty last year, she changed her tune. She invited me to her sitting room.'

'Preposterous… everyone having their own bedrooms and sitting rooms in the same house. When do you get to talk to each other?'

'In my father's house there are many rooms for different types of people.'

'I thought it was mansions inside houses, which I don't understand. How can mansions fit inside a house?'

'Stop being logical, it is esoteric, the texts vary between houses and mansions and houses and rooms. It's academic, anyway. My mother said from inside her room in my father's house…'

'I appreciate you trying to make me laugh at this sad time. What did the great Lady say, inside her lonely sitting room?'

'She said I can see you are still in love with that girl. You better marry her then.'

'She didn't change her tune. She knew I was safely married to someone else. She congratulated my mother on it, at the time. She was only thinking of legitimising Josh as your heir. You are the last Ainsley: she is getting worried.'

'That may be so, but it was a start. Can we get off the topic of my mother, stop interrupting me. I listened patiently to Twenty-Four Hours Around the World.'

'As if. I'm leaving if you are going to be like this. I think I had a part to play in Josh being judgemental by telling him you replaced me with Gin Tan.'

'Shut up. Leave Gin out of this. I corrected him about her. You take too much blame on that score. Josh was nervous about calling me his father in front of Michael. When we were alone, he called me Dad, did you know that?'

'He started to call you father to me. He talked about you with affection for the first time.'

'My heart is breaking, my darling boy owned me and his reward was death.'

'But there was another reason I didn't encourage interaction between Josh and your family: your mother's racism. Why would I put our son in harm's way?'

'That's beside the point, I wouldn't have introduced him to my mother either.

Can we now finally remove Gin as the cause of all this turbulence? Do you want to know why I was with Gin? You should have spent less time hanging around Magdalen Bridge and used your logic. You should have taken a detour half-way up The High down Logic Lane to think.'

'What would I be thinking in Logic Lane of all places. Do tell?'

'You should have thought about before we conceived Josh, how I would duck and swerve if you tried to touch me.'

'How would that lead me to think you were Ace? Why would I link touch aversion and Ace together? People who are not Ace can have touch aversion and not all people who are Ace are against touching.'

'Good point. Anyway, Gin is Ace. I had never met another Ace before.'

'There are at least four of you.'

'How do you make that out?'

'In a pack of cards.'

'There are indeed,' Jonathan laughed at her attempt to lighten the mood. 'Four.'

'Which Ace would you be?'

'You have to ask, the Ace of Spades – the highest card in the pack.'

'Such ego. Ergo, Michael is definitely the Ace of Diamonds, the equivalent of having the Midas Touch, any business he touches turns to gold. Anyway, I wasn't just hanging around while I waited for you. I was trying to get to grips with your hero, Alexander Pope.'

'Well bless you for that. But exactly, the little knowledge you had about Gin turned into a dangerous thing.'

'What about my father. Would he have taken to you?'

'He loves me because I made him chair of the cricket club. You see, happy days all round until our friend came along.'

'I want to go. He is not my friend; he is my husband.'

'Your husband is not your friend. Interesting.'

'My husband is much more than a friend. He is my romantic lover, something which you could never understand.' They had wonderful rich sex that fulfilled them. Lust like a dream that vanishes in the morning.

'You can't go. I didn't want to listen about you and other men, but I did because you are my friend. People like me may still want children. A percentage of us will have sex for that reason… You think I don't know that you are doing sums in your head to leave mentally, because I won't let you go physically. I know you. You are wondering about percentages.'

'I'm not actually. I'm edging towards simultaneous equations. Having sex with a man who doesn't find me sexually attractive is not sexually attractive to me. Having sex with a man who finds me sexually attractive is sexually attractive to me. There's a sort of cancellation going on. You playing Ace makes me play Ace back. It's some sort of mirror scenario.'

'Stop doing maths in your head when I am talking to you.'

'Oh my God. I have never seen you like this and I don't like it. Keep the noise down, what will your staff think?'

'What staff? There is no one here but us. I have day staff. I like being alone when I am sleeping.'

'Preposterous, living in an six bedroom whatever on your own. I am not going to mention house, mansion, or room, in that sentence, as we have been around the houses enough already today. You said that we needed to have a deadly serious talk. I am listening, talk.'

'You just did mention room, but I will let it pass.'

'Just a minute. Deviation. Bedroom is not the same as room.'

'What was I saying then?'

'Cold clinical sex, which sounds awful.'

'Not necessarily. Not being hungry does not stop you eating food if it is put before you. The asexual body acts the same as anyone else's.'

'Are you saying that not finding someone sexually attractive would not stop you enjoying sex with them? In your case that doesn't make sense because you have previously told me that you find touching distressing. In order to have children how would you get to the act itself without touching? Is there no warm up for this poor woman? Are you going to lay a sheet on top of her with an opening so that you can dive onto her in a hole in one? I beg to differ on the food allegory too. I won't eat if I am not hungry. If food is put before me when I am not hungry or the portion of food is too large for my appetite I find that to be an ordeal, not an enticing meal and I won't eat it at all.'

'I have never known anyone who has as many conditions under which they will not eat food. You are a chef's nightmare. If it's too complicated. If it doesn't look attractive. Too rich. Too seasoned. Too spicy. Not tasty. Just eat it, that is what most people do.'

'By most people you mean those who boarded at independent schools. Where meals are supervised by teachers and you learn to eat things you don't want to eat. Only you and Michael know I have issues around food. The chef never knows that I don't like the food. Michael with all his sporting activities is always on a seafood diet: he sees food and he eats it. He will eat my meal as well as his own. We then swap plates.' So much so that Amy used to run to the front door as soon as she heard her daddy's key turn in the lock and say, "Are you starving?" Because that was usually the first thing he said whenever he came home.

'Let's try having sex and see what happens.'

'No. Tell me about this whole cycle of violence which started with Michael first.'

'First. So, you are not saying no?'

'Have you tried it with anyone else?'

'No.'

'Then I am prepared to indulge you in trying it, because I know you. Within five minutes of me touching you, no, five minutes is an extremely long time for you, so within one minute you will shove me away in your oh-so charming way. But I am hoping that before that you are going to take your clothes off; that would be rather, as you would say, interesting. And dare I say entertaining!' She had not forgotten about Michael getting an eyeful of the eye candy Sylvie. What was good for the goose was good for the gander. 'Don't say the obvious, otherwise I will hit you up side your head.'

'Come on, I have to say it after what you just said. I will take off mine, if you take off yours.'

'No way. Look, just get on with it.'

'Where were we? Yes, the cycle of violence that started with Michael which you keep deflecting me from and seem reluctant to hear. Even though you don't like me leaving a hanging thread that upsets your love of balance.'

'I don't like it because you are saying my husband ultimately killed our son and his son. No, I don't like the hanging loop thingy either to be fair.'

'How old was Josh when you and Michael started living together?'

'Ten.'

'Michael rushed in like a fool where angels feared to tread.'

'No more Alexander Pope, please. Hold on, can I take issue with the great man's witticism?'

'The audacity of you, woman, go on.'

'He should have said where ordinary angels feared to tread. Archangels do not fear to tread, especially when you have used that quote in reference to Michael. Archangel Michael is invulnerable.'

'He trained Josh's mind into thinking that I was of no consequence. "Who breaks a butterfly on a wheel?" If he hadn't done that Josh would have been up there with me. Some stupid boy, who couldn't understand that while he was a genius at his school, that there would be those more capable than him at top universities. He would not have been able to describe our son in the last moments of his life as too uppity for his own good, because Josh was always higher up the ladder than he was, higher up the food chain than that stupid boy who murdered my son for no other reason than to appease his own vanity, and Michael, who knew absolutely nothing about being black. That was the catalyst.'

'Slow down, calm down… the last thing I need is for you to have a heart attack. We don't know why he killed Josh. He has been charged with murder and remanded into custody. I don't know any more than that.'

'Josh was having trouble with a girl called Antonia.'

'How do you know this?'

'Josh told me when I visited him in Cambridge. He phoned her while I was there. She was in love with him, and he didn't feel the same way about her. During that phone call he told Antonia that he was in love with another girl.'

'Merin?'

'No, not Merin.'

'Have you told the police this?'

'I gave a statement.'

'I am getting a headache with all this. My mind boggles as to why he told you about these problems and not Michael or I. But I am glad he felt able to confide in you. Please stop shouting. We are not in the Houses of Parliament, talking of houses.'

'I am allowed to let my anger out when I am grieving. I hope this headache has nothing to do with my proposal.'

'I am getting a headache simply because you are shouting.'

'I didn't stop you shouting at me the last time we met alone.'

'Get on with it. Do you know about being black?'

'Of course, I was eight when I came to England. "Give me a child until he is seven and I will show you the man." '

'Aristotle. You may know what it is like for black people in Nigeria where they are the majority. But I doubt you know about being black in this country.'

'What are we doing? Grief is confusing me.'

'I think we are about half way through the cycle of violence that Michael unwittingly started.'

'It was worth getting stabbed by some lunatic in my constituency, because it was preceded by Josh shouting from the rooftops that I was his father to all and sundry. I needed to hear that out loud. But those who did not need to hear it heard too and they didn't like what they were hearing. Leaving the Holloway boy, who is as thick as two short planks when it comes to emotional intelligence, with no other alternative but to lash out. I will never forgive that boy.'

'It is too early for forgiveness, but I am trying. I turned to Mother Teresa's version of The Paradoxical Commandments for comfort.'

'Yes, that poem is beautiful, she had it on the wall of her children's home. Don't make me cry.'

'I drove all the way from Oxford to Devon and I don't think it was to hear your speech on cycles of violence, that was spontaneous.'

'I am leaving everything to Amy. I need you to look over my will and papers, just in case some other nutcase comes crawling out from under their Neolithic stone to murder me again.'

'Is this some revenge plan against Michael?'

'Not at all. Amy is adorable, she is the image of you, the daughter we would have had had things been different. So, make haste. Let us pursue each other to my room.'

'Oh my God, you remember how you talked when you first moved from Nigeria.'

'Yes, and I remember your response.'

'I said it's called chase, you idiot. We were cute.' They tore up the stairs and along the landing. Jonathan said, 'Idiot begat ridiculous who begat preposterous.' This made Delsea laugh. 'Can I tell you something? You asked me if the man who took from me was Australian and I said no. He was a best friend, and he is from New Zealand.'

'Counting five of the continents on one hand after all.'

Delsea still had a hole in her heart for Jonathan, as he had for her. But if he thought she was going to tumble around committing adultery he was wrong. She wasn't going to squander those once in a lifetime-seconds that he had afforded her in fornication. She measured every precious second in her head. She put her arms around his neck and into that golden hair that she first saw in St Bartholomew's church, and took the kiss that she should have had when he declared his love for her. If he held her back, all well and good she thought.

He didn't. The kiss lasted nine seconds before he said, 'Get off, gross.' Jonathan knew exactly how to make a woman feel good about herself.

ANGEL

It was time for Delsea to speak with her angel. With Josh dead she didn't know, what the purpose of her life was. The most precious human being had been forcibly taken from her. She phoned Jonathan, so that they could do this together on his lake in Corsham, where they began. To her it was the most serene place. The most glorious lake imaginable. With its tall purple rushes, magnificent trees and Constable sky.

'Jonathan… I want to come to Aldbourne to speak to my angel. I know I can do that anywhere, but I want you to be there. Us to be there, on the lake.'

'Interview with the Angel. Let's hope it doesn't turn into a gothic horror story.'

'Don't joke, this is deadly serious. So that's yes then? Have you still got our boat?'

'I have the boat; she is in beautiful condition. I had it restored for posterity. The boat is tiny though. I doubt we would fit in it as adults.'

'I didn't think it was that small. I set my mind on us being in that boat. Oh, I see what you mean. We don't fit in the boat severally, only jointly. Fashion a divider of sorts, if you must.'

'We can't have a divider, that would be wholly inappropriate. There can be no antagonism when approaching good.'

'I can't believe we are having this conversation about a matter so serious. There must be treatments for your condition.'

'My haphephobia is serious. Treatment goes something like this; imagine a loved one touching your arm. Instant distress, and I am out of there. There is nothing worse than being touched by a loved one when you don't want to be touched. Loved ones do not do what they say they are going to do. They rarely let you know what that is in advance. Now imagine a stranger touching you. A stranger may say to you, you have a hair on your lapel. They carefully, without invading your person, pluck the hair away. A loved one will pluck the hair, then tell you about it afterwards. You had a hair on your lapel, but for some unknown reason they follow the removal of the hair by touching your face. It was loved ones who without warning as a child tickled me, threw me up in the air, swung me by my arms or legs all without my say so. Imagine being a very blond child in Africa with people invariably ruffling your hair wherever you go. OK, we can go in the boat if you don't try any funny business.'

This was the first time Jonathan had ever spoken to Delsea in more than two syllables about his phobia. She wondered, had they discussed this many years ago, would they have found a way to make their relationship work?

'I know exactly what you mean about loved ones wanting to touch you when you don't want to be touched. I can relate that directly to my experience. When Amy was younger, she was always attached to me. Feeding off me, splatting me in the face with tiny hands. Shoving her small fingers up my nose, putting her hand in my mouth. Needing to be picked up and cuddled throughout the day. Needing to be petted for her early morning sleep and again after lunch for her day sleep. I would be completely touched out. Then Michael comes home between six and seven. We'd bathe Amy and put her to bed, then he would make a bee-line for me, wanting to kiss and cuddle me.' Wanting to make love to her. Delsea would be screaming inside – 'Leave me alone, is my body not my own?' She would disappear to another room. She liked being in their bedroom, best of all it was a happy space. She would fiddle around straightening the bed cover, plumping cushions. Putting things away. Straightening objects on surfaces. Then there would be an almighty cry, 'Del, bring your body.' Which made her laugh.

Michael was subconsciously attuned to her feelings. She had the affirmation she needed, that her body was her own and she could 'Bring It' if she wanted to. She was going to put those three short sentences that summed up their entire relationship on his headstone. 'I want you. Make up your mind. Bring your body.'

Delsea could see that Jonathan had a freedom in a way that others didn't. He could be incredibly blunt, with no consideration for anyone else's feelings.

'Funny business like what?'

'Kissing me.'

'After that kiss we shared, I wouldn't kiss you again, if you were the last man on earth.'

'Charming.'

The boat was tiny. Jonathan was right. They sat at each end like Buddhas.

'Angel,' Delsea said quietly.

'I didn't know you could just say angel. I climbed Mount Ararat!'

'To speak to God!'

'True.'

There was a shimmering on the water, iridescence, as though oil had been poured on the surface. Delsea saw the bright colours, the radiance. Then there was a gentle breeze and Delsea tingled all over. Jonathan's hair blew: her hair didn't do that, so that added something new to the experience for her. The angel landed. Delsea felt a veiled cobweb pass over her face: the angel's wings. Then she saw a barely-visible outline beside her and was reassured.

'Angel, why did you let Josh die?'

'Man did that, not I.'

'You have always protected me from harm, why didn't that extend to Josh?'

'Death is a new beginning.'

'You expect me to go on with my life without Josh?'

'Your son was borrowed from God.'

'What am I to do now?'

'Finish your book.'

'At one stage I thought I had. Since you suggested I write I thought it was of special significance. That I needed to take the finished article to the authorities. I was holding an A4 file. A good Samaritan black man stopped me as I left my home and said, "Let me see that?" He read a few lines then said, "I know what this is." He nodded his respects then left. I was confused. I thought I needed to take the manuscript to the Houses of Parliament. I got on a coach to London. Suddenly it felt wrong to be going there. We were stopped at a traffic light. I asked the driver to let me off the coach. It wasn't a stop but he let me get off anyway. The driver helped intercept that unnecessary journey. I started walking towards Acton tube station. There were many birds circling in the sky above my head. They heralded your arrival. You landed on the pavement in front of me, I saw your shimmer. I saw you though you were invisible. You sparkled. Your wings brushed over me as soft as velvet. Then thoughts began to bombard my head. Things that were missing from the plot of my book. The heat of the incidents and crises to include in my story were flying at me with great speed. It was too much for me. My brain started frying. I was hardly able to capture it all. It was like I had brain fever. I felt faint and staggered. You steadied me and enclosed me in love.'

Knowing she was restored, Delsea carried on. Her angel accompanied her. She leant on their presence as though it were a staff that brought comfort to her. It was Friday evening. She and Michael had both taken the day off for an excursion. They hadn't decided where to go yet. She had set out early that morning before even he was awake. She wanted to go home, back to Oxford and her bed. She got the tube to Marble Arch where she got the bus home.

After that brainstorm; Delsea felt unwell. She went to see an acupuncturist. A woman who to Delsea was the most powerful woman in the world, with ancient knowledge of the universe at her fingertips.

'We come now to the purpose of your life, moon woman.'

'Ugh,' Jonathan said. 'Let me get this straight. Del has never known what the purpose of her life is? Archangel Uriel told me mine years ago!'

'This is not about you, sun man. Moon woman, deduce the failings of mortals from your life lessons.'

'What?'

'I have had you keep notes on your feelings since the age of six. I chose the right person. You have done this without once asking me why. Appraise their treatment of each other.'

'Is this the Last Judgement? Incredible?' Jonathan laughed with derision.

'It is not the Last Judgement. Only God can judge mankind. This is preparation.'

'I don't think I know enough to deduce anything,' Delsea said.

'There is your answer, sun man.'

'If I don't think I am capable now, does it matter when I do it? Is there a deadline?'

'Your book was not finished. That was why I intercepted you before. You need to write the second part. You will know when the time is right to bring out the books that hold up the mirror to mankind so they can see themselves. So, they can know themselves.'

Know thyself, Jonathan thought, first written on the Temple of Apollo 326 BC, at Delphi in Greece. 'That sounds like a very tall order for Del to deliver on. Angel, I am not going to stand around while you drive Del mad by making her deliver the unfeasible.'

'Moon woman can write the book with love, that is why I chose her.'

'I've had enough of this. Who do you think you are?' said Jonathan.

She couldn't help herself, Delsea laughed out loud. 'Jonathan, you can't say to an angel, "Who do you think you are?"'

'Four,' said Jonathan.

'Stick to your realm, sun man. God has given you the power to do your job.'

'Moon woman, do not encourage him in folly – he has serious work to do. You must work towards ending the unequal treatment created by man amongst humans. That is your realm, sun man.'

'And me,' Delsea asked again.

'Give them the books moon woman. Then give yourself peace.'

'I have new knowledge too,' said Jonathan. 'The missing information above Vitruvian Man's head. Should I give it to the Royal Society?'

'I did not give you that knowledge. You divined it directly from God. I am only concerned with knowledge I seed. The knowledge you divined for yourself, is yours alone, to do what you please with. You are clever, sun man.'

Who are you? was a good question; Delsea repeated more respectfully this time: 'Who are you?'

'Archangel Raphael, "God Heals."'

'Why are you helping humankind to develop, through these arrangements?'

'I am the herald of Judgement Day. God is a loving God. Before the last day, God wanted to experience the life of humans, to see if it was worth saving.'

'God was using the moon particles in Delsea and the sun particles in me to experience human life. Why then did Del need to write anything down?'

'For mankind. God saw that humans did not believe unless given stories. They call these examples. I represent healing on earth. God sent me to see whether humankind can heal itself, before calling the Last Day.'

'And Michael?' Delsea asked.

'I wondered how long it would take you to bring him up. What has he got to do with anything?' Jonathan virtually attacked Delsea.

'You have made me smile many times, sun man.'

'I am so glad you found me funny.'

'Michael is not your realm.'

'Is he an angel?'

'He is not an angel. Angels cannot have carnal knowledge of humans. He carries an essence of Archangel Michael.'

'Is he the only one with this imprint?'

'Many humans have that essence. Michael is of the tribe of Michael. Others have the essence of other Archangels. They are the tribe of their Archangel. Foot soldiers on earth for their respective Archangel who can communicate and act through them without their knowledge. Humans cannot win in battle, without the help of the Archangels. We help fight battles against reprobates and ignorance.'

Her angel gone, Delsea noticed the sadness in Jonathan. 'What is it?'

'Angels are about love, yet I feel sad after Raphael's visit. Humour is my way of entertaining myself.'

'I know that, Jonathan. I do "encourage you in folly" though. You have a serious job as an MP, which I am sure you take seriously.'

'Thank you for that.'

'Battles against ignorance! We can't lose if the angels are fighting with us.'

'We have been fighting that battle for a very long time. Angels are immortal, a year is just a moment to them. We may not live to see the end of the battle against ignorance in our lifetime.'

'Could you see, and feel Raphael's presence?'

'No, I heard the spoken words of the conversation in my mind. Can you see angels?'

'Yes, feel, touch and hear them.'

Delsea didn't want to see Jonathan again after this day. There was no connection between them anymore. No Josh. As far as she was concerned, they were finished.

'A deadly serious question, Jonathan, don't get angry. Should I give you your emeralds back?'

'Keep them, wear them.'

'I can't.'

'Because of Michael. They belong to Amy anyway. We don't need Michael, you've got Amy, what else do you need him for?'

'I can't believe you said that. I don't want to blow your ego. I'm not with Michael because I can't be with you.'

'From the woman who brought me the first-class production of "You Rang Sir," on her wedding day.'

'Coming from the man who took twenty-two years to work up the courage to tell me he loved me.'

'I didn't want to get your hopes up.'

'I don't know how many tears I shed about you not telling me how you felt about me.'

'You don't have the monopoly on tears about us.'

Jonathan was still her other half. Nothing could change that. Then he did something to prevent her cutting ties with him altogether. He had deliberately held this back for the moment when she would try to do so. Jonathan said, 'When I approached God on the summit of Mount Ararat part of the key was, I had to feel love. I thought of you. My love for you is so strong it allowed me to reach God.'

Absolutely astonishing. So mind-blowing that Delsea backed away. He knew she would because that was what she always did when something was too overwhelming to fathom. Immediately for her own sanity she created a compartment in her head under lock and key. A new one, not 'That's Nonsense,' which she was over. She couldn't put God in a box called 'That's Nonsense' anyway. She called it The Unfathomable. What person could deal with the unfathomable? She would never, ever go near that box.

Jonathan had made a two-pronged attack on Michael. He made Delsea think differently about him for a short while. She doubted their relationship for the first time. If Michael's jealousy had really resulted in Josh's death, she couldn't live with him or indeed herself for missing the signs. The phone rang.

'Hello?'

'I'm Tamsin – Josh's best friend from Ariel.' Delsea had never heard of her. It was like Josh, up there wherever he was, contacting her out of the blue when she needed him the most. Michael appeared. She grabbed him to herself, holding him tight for dear life. She put her mobile on speaker so he could hear the conversation.

'Were you at the funeral?'

'No. I decided not to get involved then. You see, of the four friends that started out at Ariel together I am the only one to graduate. I concentrated on my finals, that's what Josh would have wanted me to do. I felt it was important that I did it, for all four of us.'

'All four of you?'

'Josh, me, Toni and Tom Holloway.'

'Tom Holloway? Josh was friends with Tom Holloway?'

'The best of friends in the first year. In the second year he found a new set of friends from his course, that is apart from me.'

'I don't have my results yet, but we celebrated Suicide Sunday yesterday. So, I'm free to leave and go home. Which to be honest I've been wanting to do ever since Josh died. I would like to visit his grave. Really I'm phoning because I want to meet you, if that's alright? I want you to know the whole truth of what happened. I was at Josh's side when he died. I saw the life pass from his eyes. I was holding his hand.'

'Did he say anything?' Delsea hoped it wasn't 'Mum;' that would haunt her for the rest of her life.

'He shouted "Tamsin," and I ran to him. Only to see him die. That was his last word.'

'Did you comfort him?'

'I said, you are loved, Josh. I love you.'

'Thank you. But why did he call out your name? I don't understand. Why did he say Tamsin?'

'Because we were sort of engaged. We had a pact: to marry when we were twenty-five. There would have been no Toni or Merin, if I hadn't been doing the Silver Ring Thing.'

'Let me guess, you have blonde hair and hazel eyes and you were born in Africa.'

'Blue eyes, and Botswana.'

Tamsin had chased away the gloom. She would stay with Michael. It wasn't he who killed Josh.

DEADLY SERIOUS EPILOGUE

Jonathan and I are an inseparable pair. We complete each other, part moon and part sun that we are. Night and day, dark and light. I was a black girl born in England, surrounded by white people. He was white boy born in Nigeria surrounded by black people. We are a representation of harmony the Yin Yang sign.

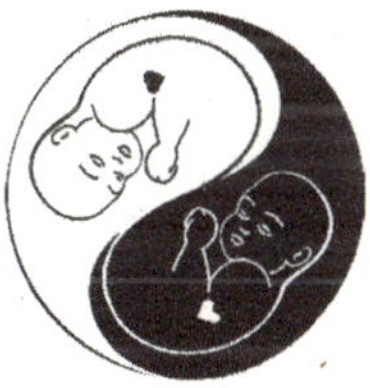

God is a loving God. There is not just Judgement Day. I was called to inspect humanity. It has been a great honour to be called, but I railed against it sometimes, as it meant making sacrifices in my personal life. I have carried out this task to the best of my ability. It has taken tens of years for me to understand the chaos amongst humanity which threatens to destabilise our universe.

There was only so much I could do in the time allotted, a half-life, but it is enough to demonstrate that the way has been completely lost. I hope my findings will be taken seriously. It is high time that the man-made issues are resolved. To make what I have witnessed palatable, I did it with love, as advised. I mention love over two hundred times.

The Unexamined Life is Not Worth Living
SOCRATES

I make no apology

ACKNOWLEDGEMENTS

Thanks to my first readers Matthew and Julie Wilkinson for their enthusiasm. To Louise Quested for a magical moment. To Allegra Wint for keeping me sane and believing in me. Most importantly thanks to my husband Thomas Fox and our daughters Carlie, Charlotte & Tamsin for accompanying me on this incredible journey. Thanks to the professional publishing team; Jonathan Campion copy editor, Euan Monaghan interior designer and Tom Feltham proof reader. Finally, thanks to Mark Radley at CPI Printers and Tom Smith from Vincent's Club for facilitating my launch party.

The Battle of Ignorance

Nine Night

J. N. FOX

RAGUEL
PUBLISHING

MURDER

For Delsea the drive to Cambridge was solemn. She, and Michael hardly spoke. It was a familiar journey, one done regularly for the last three years. Previously she had always been excited at the prospect of seeing her son at the end of it.

She recognised certain sights as progress towards their eventual destination. The blue bridge. Which she did not know exactly where it started, or where it went to. The American Cemetery, installed following World War I to honour the expeditionary forces, was another reminder. They were just familiar markers that had brought her closer to Joshua.

These were to be the most challenging days of her life. It seemed that everyone bent over backwards to help the boy who killed, Joshua at Ariel University. She was the last to find out that he had been allowed to graduate. She had left communication regarding the murder to Joshua's biological father, Jonathan. Hoping to spare herself unnecessary pain. Somehow it softened the investigation, to hear it from him, and not the harsh details conveyed by the specialist liaison officer. Jonathan had relayed most things, except that nugget of information.

Technically, Tom Holloway receiving support from Jehovah College was nothing to do with the incident. But morally it was everything, as the boys had argued about Josh focussing solely on his studies immediately before the occurrence. Yet Tom Holloway was allowed his course books in prison, and his tutors supervised by sending material back and forth. He was on remand, and not convicted of the crime. He was innocent until proven guilty.

At the arraignment hearing he pleaded not guilty even though it was premeditated. He bought a knife to stab Josh, and did so in the dining hall before the entire college. He claimed he did not intend to use the weapon unless provoked. It took very little to urge him to the deed. Just one sentence from her extraordinary son. "I came here to do a degree funnily enough."

It was the first day of the inquest. Delsea, and her husband Michael arrived at an oldish red brick building with sash windows, and an abundance of honeysuckle adhering to its walls. It seemed like an ordinary country house with its gabled porch. The only outward sign alerting to its grim purpose was to the side, where a metal infilled entrance was present, presumably for the dead.

They got there early for a premeeting with Jonathan. That was when he told them. Johnathan said 'Tom had little else to do other than revise.' He got a 2:1. They, Joshua's parents learnt that then. Delsea was angry with Jonathan for keeping it from her.

'You agreed with this. With that boy getting to sit his exams, and doing so well, while our son rots in his grave because of him.'

'I could do nothing to prevent it. Holloway's parents pushed for his continuance. There were just two months left of his third year. I could hardly argue that he should not be allowed to take his finals because Josh could not do his. That would be irrational.'

Delsea then lost it completely, and started pushing Jonathan in frustration as she made each of her upsetting points.

Michael walked away. Shutting the door, leaving them alone. He was upset too. But these next two weeks where horrendous details about Josh's injuries would be shared were hard enough, without entering a grudge about Holloway graduating.

Both Tamsin, Josh's fiancée, and Merin his girlfriend were at the inquest. Michael sat down beside them to offer support throughout the day. They both loved Joshua too. Though Michael doubted that Josh would have kept his promise to marry Tamsin.

Delsea, and Jonathan joined them just as the coroner came in, for which they were required to stand. Delsea plonked herself down irritably next to Michael with Jonathan the other side of her. They were still quarrelling in harsh whispered voices. It only stopped when Delsea said, 'Shut the fuck up Jonathan. You, posh people always stick together.'

Michael apprised her, that her comment was unfair. He could see why their relationship was untenable. He whispered to Delsea in case she had forgotten, 'There are reporters in court.' Fortunately, they were unable to access the side room where they had openly disagreed. Michael was reminding Delsea that as Chancellor of the Exchequer, Jonathan was a public person of interest.

Michael thought that Jehovah College had a reputation to maintain. It was better for them that Tom Holloway was a good student who had been driven to a moment of madness by his friend Antonia. Rather than Tom being a rotten egg with questions asked as to why they accepted him in the first place. Their poor vetting procedure, and lackadaisical attitude to bullying could put future students off. As a precursor to allowing Tom to sit his finals Jehovah probably encouraged him to plead not guilty.

It was easier for everyone except Josh's family who wanted truth and justice, to blame Antonia who had taken her own life, and therefore could not contradict whatever spin was being put on the killing. A complex decision was made regarding whose inquest should be held first, Antonia's suicide, or Joshua's killing; as the cases were interdependent, and further complicated by involving two coroners in unrelated counties.

Delsea knew she had gone over the top with Jonathan. She was not normally easy to vex. His presence exasperated her sometimes. But she had to focus. The inquest was important. It was about Joshua, not Tom Holloway. Jonathan's hands were on his lap as he sat quietly beside her. She covered one of his with hers in the briefest sorry. Michael saw, and thought there was still deep affection there. Maybe he was one step removed from the pain and emotion, being the adoptive parent.

Delsea remembered when Josh went up for his Ariel interview. She decided not to go with him as she knew she would find it stressful. Michael went instead. Joshua was not usually nervous. But his way of coping with exam stress on the day was more than enough for her. While others might get butterflies, he literally threw up. She tried to support him but he often rejected her help as fussing. It was, as though he chucked the stress down the pan, and was then as right as rain. Ready to tackle anything.

His school had not selected him as having potential to get into Ariel, or Uriel, and therefore he did not receive their targeted coaching. Josh was an introvert. They selected boys who were extrovert, sporty, and academic. She tried not to think that Josh being bi-racial had contributed to his ability being overlooked.

She was lucky. She had a friend at the Oxford Science Park. 'The Fat Man,' that was what his friends called him, and what he preferred to answer too. It allowed him to be "fat" through choice. He was a dapper dresser, which dispelled the idea of laziness, or dullness with which overweight people sometimes were labelled. He had the sharpest wit of anyone she knew. The Fat Man was a bit of a mouthful, so Delsea called him Fats. Like Fats Domino, whose music her father Ben listened too.

There was little residential accommodation on the Science Park. Fats ran a Biotech company there. He often asked her to put up his visiting academics from all over the world. That was how she got to know him. It was a win for both. She loved having a house full of people engaged in scintillating conversations, and his guests got an attentive host.

Fats had postgraduate researchers. He found her a few PHD students to mock interview Josh. That was all the preparation he got, three mock interviews.

Josh passed the Ariel assessment and interview. With throwing up in between. She hoped that Michael was exaggerating. She was so glad not to have been there to cope with that. Michael took it in his stride. He was into Formula One, and by all accounts James Hunt threw up before every race.

Josh did not get his first choice of college, it was oversubscribed. He was put in the pool where Jehovah, that had places for Natural Science picked him out. It meant going up for a second interview.

He came home from that interview and locked himself in his bedroom. Michael who had accompanied him did not know why. Delsea begged him to go over the day in detail, so that she could help Josh. Who seemingly had not spoken on the way home. In the car he had pulled up his hoody, and shrunk into himself. When Delsea knocked on his door. He told her in no uncertain words to go away.

They thought the interview had gone terribly wrong. It was not until the next morning that they learnt the cause of his unhappiness. It seemed that the crunch question was, "did he play tiddlywinks?" The chap interviewing him was a serious player. Josh did not know how to answer that non-academic question. Should he say he was interested in playing, or not. The game can be used to demonstrate strategy, and was played at club level in some universities. Josh need not have worried. He got an offer anyway.

A couple of the boys who had been prepared by his school Goring College, did not end up getting places at either Ariel, or Uriel. When Prize Day loomed the following Autumn term. Josh did not want to go back to his school, and walk on stage to his credentials in order to collect his certificates. Which as in previous years would go; "Joshua Valentine, Maths, Physics, and Chemistry, all at grade A. Joshua is reading Natural Science at Ariel," to great applause. He felt that Goring College had done nothing to help him realise his dream of reading science at Ariel. So, why should they have the glory.

As well as Prize Day, and its leaflet, the school listed their university successes in their magazine for posterity, and it was sent out to prospective parents by admissions. They cited sixth form leaver destinations on their website to encourage more applications, and boasted about the number of pupils they got into Ariel, and Uriel at sixth form Open Days. Josh was refusing to let them apply his name in any of these circumstances. He clearly felt that they had discriminated against him.

Delsea got a phone call from the Deputy Head. It had never happened before. A pupil forbidding them to broadcast his name. On top of that Josh, was refusing to go to Prize Day at all, though it was not compulsory as he had already left school in the summer. Belatedly, given his solo Ariel success they wanted to recognise his achievement by awarding him the top science prize.

She was not sure what they expected her to do. Josh had turned eighteen back in the Spring. He was a man. She saw the resemblance between him, and his father Jonathan. He displayed a lot of the laser sharp determination that Jonathan had at the same age.

Recognising that Joshua was furious with them. The Deputy Head made a kind of regretful apology to Delsea. He said that, "Ariel clearly saw something in Joshua that the school had missed. Could she see her way to getting Joshua to comply with the Prize Day celebrations?" She promised to speak to Michael who was worldly wise, and good at talking sense into Joshua.

Delsea had no trouble discerning what Ariel saw in him. She knew exactly what it was. Entitlement inherited from his father. It was in his blood. They saw that he belonged there. That he was one of them. In the end Michael persuaded Josh that it was never a good idea to burn bridges when leaving an institution. To the great relief of the school. It could now patch up their mistake, and pretend that Joshua's success was theirs.

For the inquest Antonia's letters were included in the pack of correspondence given to them. It started with their family statement which Jonathan had written. The idea of pinning the instigation of Josh's killing on her, was well and truly kyboshed. Plus, her parents were there to commiserate with Delsea, Jonathan and Michael. More importantly to keep their brilliant daughter's memory sacrosanct. Joshua had not read Antonia's letters, fearing they were reproachful.

Delsea did not know what to make of them. They were disturbing. Was Antonia sane, or insane. She could not hazard a guess. She was not a psychiatrist. She wished Josh had read them though. All she knew was that Josh's first-year friends were poisonous. Josh seemed to have been the only regular person within that set. Maybe they were too intelligent. It took a certain amount of stupidity to not dwell on damaging thoughts, and enjoy the absurdity of life.

Even Tamsin was odd. If she had been into having a full relationship with Josh, would he be alive? It was not fair to think like that. But Delsea could not help watching with dismay as Tamsin twisted her purity Silver Ring Thing around on her engagement finger. She had proudly shown it to Delsea with their pledge to each other engraved inside.

Tamsin had stayed on at Jehovah College after graduation, transferring from Natural Science to medicine. Josh dying virtually in her arms clearly had an impact on her. She must have wished that she could have done more to save his life.

The verdict of the inquest was unlawful killing. They were all pleased with that outcome. Though it was only a stepping stone towards the trial.

Delsea was dreading the trial. She did not want to look at that awful boy, or hear his twisted reasons for taking Josh's life, while purporting to be his friend. Or, how the friendship had soured leading to the killing. Somethings were better not heard. There was no justification for killing someone unless it was in self-defence.

They were psyching themselves up for a lengthy trial. When on the first day, there was a kerfuffle in court. Barristers whispering to each other, and in turn to the judge. Tom Holloway changed his mind, and wanted to plead guilty. No doubt for himself, for a lighter sentence.

He looked pointedly at Delsea as they took him away. He gave her the ever so slight Jamaican nod of the head. Which meant respect. He was not going to put her through the wringer out of regard. He would have learnt through Josh, that thoughtfulness was paramount to Jamaicans.

It was too late for respect. She would not accept such a gesture from someone who thought her son was too grand for his skin tone. He should have appreciated Josh's right to life. She hoped he got a long sentence to dwell on that. He had ruined her life. Josh was her pride, and joy.

With the inquest, and trial over, she visited Joshua's grave. Josh was still alive, within her. "Do not stand at my grave, and cry; I am not there. I did not die."